The publisher gratefully acknowledges the generous support of Jeanne and Michael Adams as members of the Publisher's Circle of the University of California Press Foundation.

THE RADICAL JACK LONDON

THE RADICAL
JACK LONDON

WRITINGS ON WAR
AND REVOLUTION

Edited and with an Introduction by
JONAH RASKIN

UNIVERSITY OF CALIFORNIA PRESS
BERKELEY   LOS ANGELES   LONDON

Jack London's "The Salt of the Earth" (JL 1143 – 1144) and
his introduction to Alexander Berkman's *Prison Memoirs
of an Anarchist* (JL 803) are reproduced by permission of
The Huntington Library, San Marino, California.

University of California Press, one of the most distinguished
university presses in the United States, enriches lives around the
world by advancing scholarship in the humanities, social sciences,
and natural sciences. Its activities are supported by the UC Press
Foundation and by philanthropic contributions from individuals
and institutions. For more information, visit www.ucpress.edu.

University of California Press
Berkeley and Los Angeles, California

University of California Press, Ltd.
London, England

Library of Congress Cataloging-in-Publication Data

London, Jack, 1876 – 1916.
   [Selections. 2008]
   The radical Jack London : writings on war and revolution /
edited, with an introduction and notes, by Jonah Raskin.
      p.   cm.
   Includes bibliographical references (p.   ) and index.
   ISBN: 978 – 0-520 – 25545 – 6 (cloth : alk. paper)
   ISBN: 978 – 0-520 – 25546 – 3 (pbk. : alk. paper)
   I. Raskin, Jonah, 1942 –   II. Title.
PS3523.O46A6   2007
813'.52 — dc22   2007023289

Manufactured in the United States of America

17   16   15   14   13   12   11   10   09   08
10   9   8   7   6   5   4   3   2   1

This book is printed on New Leaf EcoBook 50, a 100% recycled
fiber of which 50% is de-inked post-consumer waste, processed
chlorine-free. EcoBook 50 is acid-free and meets the minimum
requirements of ANSI/ASTM D5634 – 01 (*Permanence of Paper*).

For Liza, Tommy, Jack, Phil, and Eric

CONTENTS

ILLUSTRATIONS

JACK LONDON

THE ORPHAN AT THE ABYSS

WAR AND REVOLUTION

He was the Norman Mailer of his day, and the Ernest Hemingway too. How ironical that London has come to be remembered as the author of dog stories. At the peak of his notorious career as a radical, American newspaper editors called for his arrest and deportation. In a short, volatile life of four decades, Jack London (1876–1916) explored and mapped the territory of war and revolution in fiction and nonfiction alike. More accurately than any other American writer of his day, he also predicted the shape of political power—from dictatorship to terrorism—that would emerge in the twentieth century, and his work is as timely today as when it was first written. "Big things are happening secretly all around," London's prescient, radical hero Ernest Everhard says in *The Iron Heel* (1908), the novel that conjures up a society in which news and information are controlled by the government, and an oligarchy rules behind a mask of democracy. In London's future world, American citizens are robbed of their "remaining liberties," "global markets are glutted," "violence and blood" stain the society, and, although the master class brings about war, lies, deceit, and the massacre of citizens, it professes to believe in goodness, truth, and its own righteousness. After a century London would hardly have to change any of these prophecies to update his portrait. The atrocities of the war in Iraq would not surprise him, nor the machinations of the George W. Bush administration and the unrelenting propaganda of the mass media.

In the essays he collected in *War of the Classes* (1905) and *Revolution and Other Essays* (1910), he traced the global reach of capitalism, the power of the American dollar, and the technological revolutions that collapsed frontiers and brought instantaneous news from distant outposts of empire to the capitals of the world. As a participant in, as well as an observer of, the social upheavals in the world in which he lived, London himself went through an unending series of personal revolutions and wars in his own soul. Humble yet arrogant, pitiful yet threatening, he elicited complex responses from friends, family, and fellow socialists—as well as from readers.

In a blaze of creativity that might have consumed a dozen men, he burned himself up as a journalist, war correspondent, orator, playwright, memoirist, novelist, and poet. If he had been born in a future century, he probably would have become an astronaut. He boasted that he would rather burn up like a meteor in the sky than fester on earth. On the stage of his life, as in the pages of his books, he took on myriad identities— from waif to sailor to hobo to socialist to businessman to farmer to Nietzschean, Marxist, Darwinian, Freudian, and, at the end of his life, Jungian—and sometimes he played a half-dozen different roles all at the same time.

Still, at heart he identified as the orphan. In *Cherry,* his last novel, unfinished at his death, he wrote about an orphan and the condition of orphanhood that gave him a distinct perspective on the world. He felt, too, that he stood at the edge of an abyss, both interior and exterior, and he explored with passion and compassion the lives of the people in the abyss. As the nineteenth century ended, he took it upon himself to calculate the cost of "social progress" and the terrible devastation wrought by industrialism. At the beginning of the twentieth century, he became an avatar of the twentieth century, carving out whole literary and political territories that would be mapped, conquered, and lost.

A host of writers, including Sinclair Lewis (1885–1951), Ernest Hemingway (1899–1961), and Norman Mailer (1923–2007), gathered up many of the literary threads he left behind and wove them into their own literary fictions and their own identities. A writing machine that never stopped, he often turned out at least a thousand words a day, weeks on end, as though words alone might change the world and provide a kind of salvation. He funneled his own experiences into his characters— male, female, and animal. He wrote his own fictionalized autobiography again and again—in *The Call of the Wild* (1903), in which he appeared as an underdog who masters the world; in *Martin Eden* (1909), in which he presented a self-portrait of the artist as bourgeois success and depressed suicide victim; and in *John Barleycorn* (1913), a fictionalized memoir about his alcoholism. Again and again, he insisted that he did not and could not tell the whole truth. It's no wonder that biographers and critics have found him to be an elusive author and have often confused his real life with his legend. He was a master at self-creation.

As loudly and clearly as anyone in his generation, he heard and responded to the call of socialism that was echoing around the world. In the mid-1890s, before he had made a name for himself as a writer—before he owned anything of value, save for a bicycle, a typewriter, and one good suit of clothes—he joined the Socialist Labor Party. (The Socialist Party, which came to dominate the radical left after 1900, did not yet exist.) He wrote steadily for socialist newspapers and magazines, ran as a socialist for public office in Oakland, and identified with the cause so thoroughly that the man and the movement appeared to be one and the same. To his contemporaries in the radical movement, he seemed like a god on earth—Lord Byron (1788–1824) and Karl Marx (1818–1883) rolled up into one. Indeed, he behaved like a dashing, romantic hero made for the barricades and for eternity, and so they forgave his indiscretions, foibles, and flaws, of which there were many.

To the generations of radicals who followed him and to left-wing writers like Tillie Olsen (1912–2007) and Doris Lessing (1919–), he seemed like an icon of the American working class—a hero who climbed out of poverty, made himself into a dedicated proletarian writer, stormed the citadels of publishing, and gave voice to the voiceless men, women, and children outside the American dream. To the readers of left-wing literature, he came to represent the downtrodden, the outcast, and the disinherited; these readers loved him because he made socialism seem natural, inevitable, clean, and new. It was as though he had given birth to it himself out of his own shadowy past, taught it to speak the vernacular, dressed it in the garb of quotidian life, and endowed it with eloquence and majesty.

His own journey toward socialism he never entirely revealed. He promised to write his socialist autobiography and confess everything, from his initial sense of joy and hope to the sadness and disillusionment at the end of his life—much as he promised to reveal every aspect of his personality, including intimate details, in a book he wanted to call *Jane Barleycorn,* which would presumably confess his addiction to sex. Now, nearly one hundred years after his death, mystery still surrounds his evolution as a political radical, though it is clear that his passionate engagement with socialism had its roots in personal experience.

In his writings on politics, he often emphasized how he felt and what drove him, invoking "I," "me," and "my" and merging autobiography with myth and history. In "How I Became a Socialist" (1903), he described his enthusiastic allegiance to the capitalist system as a young man. "I read the bourgeois papers, listened to the bourgeois preachers, and shouted at the sonorous platitudes of the bourgeois politicians," he proclaimed. In "What Life Means to Me" (1906), he looked back at his existence in spiritual and economic poverty, about which he felt somewhat ashamed. "I was down in the cellar of society, down in the subterranean depths of misery about which it is neither nice nor proper to speak," he wrote. "I was in the pit, the abyss, the human cesspool, the shambles and the charnel-house of our civilization." In a public letter addressed to the "Comrades of the Mexican Revolution," he aimed to speak for all "socialists, anarchists, hobos, chicken thieves, outlaws and undesirable citizens of the United States." To the world he proclaimed, "I subscribe myself a chicken thief and a revolutionary." No other socialist in that era had as big and booming a voice as he—and no one seemed to have as inflated a sense of himself as a global revolutionary. "I was born into the working class," he insisted, as though he spoke for all oppressed workers and as though his radicalism was innate rather than acquired. "I am a socialist, first, because I was born a proletarian."

Born, in fact, a Californian in the shadow of the Civil War and steeped in the history and the culture of his native land, he Americanized socialism and thereby helped to popularize it. In books like *The Iron Heel* (1908), he expanded the genre of overtly political literature written by Laurence Gronlund in *The Cooperative Commonwealth* (1884) and Edward Bellamy in *Looking Backward* (1888), both of which he read and took to heart. His looks did not hurt, especially when he wore his black leather jacket, his hair ruffled by the wind; he might have been the father of the Beats or Marlon Brando's older brother. Like a socialist matinee idol, he radiated charisma and sex appeal, and from Hollywood's earliest days he recognized film as a vehicle for his talent and a way to popularize radical ideas. Women flocked around him—working-class women, socialist women, and the young daughters of the bourgeoisie in Oakland and San Francisco whose fathers were alarmed by the seductive socialist firebrand at their doorsteps.

Had London not died at the age of forty—in bad health and possibly suicidal—the world at large might not have judged him as harshly as it did. Soon after his body was cremated and his ashes buried on his vast California estate—where he had raised pigs, grown grapes, and marketed his own band of grape juice with his picture on the label—America's leading literary and cultural critics began to ridicule his idiosyncratic politics and his quirky personal life.

The Russians, of course, adored him. V. I. Lenin (1870–1924) found his stories inspiring; Leon Trotsky (1879–1940) praised him to the skies for his prescience; and

Emma Goldman (1869–1940), the Russian-born anarchist who agitated and organized in the United States, called him the "only revolutionary author in America."

Writers in other countries found his work inspiring, too. Anatole France (1844–1924), the French Nobel Prize–winning author, acknowledged his literary debt to London. Even Jorge Luis Borges, a writer of another type, called him "a skillful journalist who has mastered his trade." B. Traven (?–1969), a mysterious and enigmatic twentieth-century author, characterized himself explicitly as London's literary descendant. Traven's *The Death Ship* (1926)—a riveting novel about the inhuman conditions suffered by undocumented sailors at sea—carried on a tradition that London inaugurated in books like *The People of the Abyss* (1903), a stunning first-person narrative and a forerunner of the "new journalism" of the 1960s. George Orwell (1903–1950) borrowed from London's books, too, to write *Down and Out in Paris and London* (1933) and *Nineteen Eighty-Four* (1949). In 1928, at the start of the Depression, *The New Masses* called London "a real proletarian writer—the first and so far the only proletarian writer of genius in America."

American critics were not so appreciative. H. L. Mencken began the serious bashing of London's politics by calling him a "jejune socialist." In *The Golden Day: A Study in American Literature and Culture* (1926), Lewis Mumford noted that London "clung to socialism . . . chiefly to give an added luster of braggadocio and romanticism to his career" and that he "betrayed his socialism in all his ingrained beliefs, particularly, his belief in success and in his conception of the Superman." That same year, Leonard D. Abbott—the editor of *London's Essays of Revolt* (1926), the first posthumously published anthology of his radical writings—noted that London wrote too much too quickly, an observation that would be repeated for decades. In *On Native Grounds* (1941), Alfred Kazin depicted London as a fascist wolf disguised as a socialist lamb. "A leading hero of the movement, he signed his letters with a dashing 'Yours for the revolution,' but he was a prototype of the violence-worshiping Fascist intellectual if ever there was one in America," Kazin wrote.

Throughout much of the second half of the twentieth century, London's American biographers and critics belittled or ignored his radicalism. Viking's *The Portable Jack London* (1994) completely ignores *The Iron Heel*—a significant American political novel and a predecessor to Sinclair Lewis's *It Can't Happen Here* (1938) and Philip Roth's *The Plot to Destroy America* (2004). The Viking edition also omits a great many of his writings about race war, class war, and revolution. The two-volume Library of America (1982) edition of London's work includes only four essays by London, hardly a reflection of his thinking on the political and economic issues of his day. Moreover, neither anthology says much if anything about London as an American radical.

Then, too, scholarly books—Joan Hedrick's *Solitary Comrade* (1982) and Carolyn Johnston's *Jack London: An American Radical?* (1984)—raised serious doubts about the authenticity of his political affiliations. Not surprisingly, perhaps, overtly socialist scholars accepted London's flaws more readily than writers elsewhere on the political spectrum, as though they knew not to hold a socialist to god-like standards. Marxist historian Philip Foner, who edited the anthology *Jack London: American Rebel* (1947), noted how easy it was to find fault with London, but he went on to pay tribute to London's role as a liberator in American literature. "It was Jack London more than any other writer of his day, who broke the ice that was congealing American letters and brought life and literature into a meaningful relation to each other," Foner wrote. His anthology appeared as McCarthyism spread through academia and as radical writers like London were omitted from the canon.

All through the Cold War of the 1950s, Russians read far more London than Americans. Then, in the 1960s, when American literature and politics fused again, London's work made a comeback in the United States. H. Bruce Franklin, one of the leading radical critics of American literature, touted London's political novel *The Iron Heel* for its acumen and praised his incisive writings about the American prison system in his 1978 book, *The Victim as Criminal and Artist*. Still, academia refused to make a niche for Jack London. Granted, Modern Library reissued some of his best work, including *Martin Eden,* at the start of the twenty-first century, but no major publisher has seen fit to resurrect *War of the Classes* (1905) and *Revolution and Other Essays* (1910), in which he collected his political writing.

What purpose, then, might be served by a new anthology of London's century-old work about capitalism, terrorism, socialist revolution, and war? Traditional socialist parties in the United States and the West more generally are now largely defunct, though socialism seems to have revived in Latin America. So-called socialist regimes have fallen in the Soviet Union and Eastern Europe, perhaps never to rise again. Socialism appears to be a movement of the past, though as an ideal, it continues to appeal to the imagination. Jack London's brand of socialism, with its emphasis on brotherhood, comradeship, and feelings of class solidarity, did not directly address the practicalities of running a socialist economy or the dangers of tyrannical socialist regimes. But it contains the kind of optimism that any resurgent socialism movement would have to borrow and recycle.

This anthology provides an essential piece in the enigmatic Jack London jigsaw puzzle. Socialism may have largely vanished as a viable political solution to the problems of the world, but war, revolution, and terrorism are as alive as ever, and London illuminated those topics with brilliance. Previous anthologies, by Leonard Abbott and Philip Foner, are out of print. In their own day, they were limited in that they focused almost exclusively on the subject of work and the working class and neglected to explore London's ideas about culture, race, and art. They failed to see that London's politics derived from his own inner self and that his radicalism took him in contrary directions all at once. The personal was political for London, just as the political was profoundly personal, and in ways that radicals who lived through the 1960s would grasp, but that did not figure largely for earlier American radicals. For London, the revolution raged within as much as without, and he saw eye to eye with Daniel De Leon (1852–1914), the dynamic leader of the Socialist Labor Party, who wrote, "Reform means a change of externals. Revolution means a change from within." Neither the Viking nor the Library of America's collection of London's work—the most accessible popular editions of his writing—provides representative samples of his writing about colonialism, empire, and race. Nor do they show the evolution of his socialist writing, as this volume does. Seventeen of the twenty-four individual pieces collected here are not included in the Viking or Library of America volumes. Moreover, each piece has an introductory essay, a feature no other anthology provides.

The Radical Jack London recovers the lost dimensions of a writer who carved out an identity for himself as America's leading revolutionary writer at the start of the twentieth century. It shows how he helped create the foundations for contemporary prison literature, twentieth-century dystopian fiction, and modern-day narratives about down-and-out wanderers on the road, popularized by Kerouac and the Beat Generation writers in the 1950s. Over the course of his writing career, London wrestled with the issues of war, race, and class, and though his views often reflected uncritically the received notions of his time, his failures can be as instructive as his successes. I have included well-known essays and chapters from his best-selling books, but I have also gathered work never previously anthologized and unavailable to the general public. The material is arranged chronologically, not thematically or by genre, thus showing the evolution of his thinking as a radical from 1895 to 1916—his consistencies as well as his ongoing evolution and transformation.

In his own lifetime, London anthologized himself repeatedly; if the anthology as a literary form had not existed he would have had to invent it, if only because it enabled him to bring his fugitive work and his orphaned essays together between the covers of a book. He became a master of the anthology—that Jack of all books—and appreciated its eclecticism. When his friend and fellow socialist Upton Sinclair invited him to provide an introduction for his *The Cry for Justice: An Anthology of the Literature of Social Protest,* London rose to the occasion. In 1915, in Hawaii—a place that always inspired him—he crafted an essay that was a model of generosity in which he called *The Cry for Justice* a "Holy Book." "To see gathered here together this great body of human beauty and fineness and nobility is to realize what glorious humans have already existed, do exist," London wrote. "We know how gods are made. Comes now the time to make a world." I have aimed to follow his spirit of generosity in making this book.

Now, nearly a century after London's death, his radicalism invites understanding and compassion. In that spirit, one might point out that his membership in the Socialist Labor Party, and the Socialist Party, too, lasted longer than his two marriages combined. London found in the socialist movement an abiding feeling of belonging that rivaled the sense of home and place he enjoyed in Oakland and Glen Ellen. Socialism was a family, a location, and a destination, as much as an idea, for London, and it helped him to escape his own deep-seated loneliness. In the exhilaration of the cause, he discovered the hope and happiness that often eluded him in a lifetime afflicted with "the blues" and "morbid anxiety"—to borrow his own phrases. Wary of making attachments to people, places, and ideas—even as he craved them and found it difficult to let them go—he developed a deep attachment to the theory and practice of socialism. Once he had grasped Marx's labor theory of value, for example, he never turned away from it. He also maintained an abiding interest in the role of radicals and in the history of revolution and counterrevolution in French society in the eighteenth and nineteenth centuries.

Nearly everyone who knew him recognized what the Russian-born socialist Anna Strunsky (1878–1964)—perhaps *the* love of his life, as well as one of his most astute critics—described as the "extremes of his personality." Upton Sinclair—who engaged in furious arguments with Jack about sex and alcohol, the life of restraint versus the life of uninhibited self-expression—poured out his turbulent feelings in an essay that appeared in *The Masses,* the leading left-wing magazine of the day. Jack "fought tremendous battles in his own soul," Sinclair wrote in 1917. He saw "many sides of life at once" and felt pulled in different directions.

Georgia Loring Bamford, a longtime friend from Oakland and the author of *The Mystery of Jack London,* noted that Jack "was a deep, dark mystery, full of contradictions" and "did not know himself." (She might have said that he *continually sought* his genuine self in his writings, political activities, and adventurous life.) Edward Payne, a longtime neighbor in Glen Ellen and editor of the *Overland Monthly,* wrote in *The Soul of Jack London* (1933) that he was a man at odds with himself. "A real war was going on in Jack London's nature . . . a war in the field of his consciousness," Payne wrote. Jack's second wife, Charmian Kittredge (1871–1955)—who was with him nearly every day of his life from 1906 to 1916—observed in *The Book of Jack London* (1921) that his life was "a constant battlefield." With so many internal fires ravaging his soul, it's no wonder that he burned himself out at the age of forty and never had the opportunity to become an elder sage of revolution. Of course, he preferred to go out like a house ablaze, becoming ashes, not dust; and though he sometimes aimed for moderation, he always moved toward the extremes of human experience and the edges of human consciousness. Radicalism seeped into everything he did, said, and wrote. "I am afraid I always was an extremist," he noted near the end of his life, when it was too late to change. His best-known novels—*The Call of the Wild, The Sea-Wolf,* and *White Fang*—reveal an author deeply divided emotionally, politically, and spiritually. The longer one explores his work—fifty books poured out in about seventeen years—the more one appreciates the complexities, contradictions, and knots at the core of his identity.

His commitment to socialism was enduring. In socialism he found something far more significant than a party. He found a constellation of feelings, dreams, and desires that answered primary human needs deriving from his lost childhood, from the boyhood he never had, and from the primal hurt he carried to the end of his days. Sever London from socialism, and you sever Jack London irrevocably. So it seems inevitable that he died within a year after resigning from the Socialist Party. Socialism gave him life, infused him with passion, and he poured all his passion into socialism, too, until nothing remained.

ORIGINS OF A SOCIALIST

Individual human beings become socialists, of course, for all sorts of reasons and in all sorts of ways, and not always for the most obvious of motives and in the most direct fashion, as London himself understood. An exploration of his life suggests a multiplicity of reasons for his radicalization. At his birth in San Francisco on January 12, 1876—the year of the bicentennial and the publication of *Tom Sawyer*—his mother, Flora Wellman Chaney (1843–1921), a sort of flower child before the arrival of the flower children, registered his arrival in the world. The *San Francisco Chronicle* published the news on January 13, under "Births." "In this city, January 12, the wife of W.H. Chaney, of a son," the announcement read. Flora called the child, born out of wedlock, John Griffith Chaney, borrowing the last name of her common-law husband, William Henry Chaney (1821–1902), though he had abused her and then abandoned her early in her pregnancy.

Soon after Flora married John London (1828–1897)—a widower with several children and no career, occupation, or money in the bank—in September 1876, she changed the baby's name to John Griffith London, and all through the 1880s and 1890s, his name was officially John London, Jr., which is how his name appeared in directories for the city of Oakland, where he lived. The change from John to Jack, which he engineered on his own, may not have meant much to anyone else, but it felt monumental to him, he insisted, signaling, as it did, his declaration of independence from his peculiar parents and their odd ways. In fact, he had two fathers and two mothers, as we shall see: his distant biological parents and the emotionally and physically proximate parents (a stepfather and a nanny) who were responsible for raising him day in and day out—a complex nexus of relationships that seems to have contributed greatly to his contradictions, his dividedness, and his habit of what psychologists called "splitting."

Flora apparently wanted to forget, and to conceal, her own family secrets, including her flight from her well-to-do parents in Ohio and the existence of her common-law husband, William Henry Chaney. All through her son's boyhood, she lived in a state of denial, never uttering a word about Chaney, the leader of what seems to have been a religious cult to which she briefly belonged. (It was a cult in the sense that it was a small group bound together by the same intensely held ideas, existing on the fringes of society; Chaney was the acknowledged leader and held sway over his followers.) An itinerant astrologer and the author of two hefty tomes prized by late nineteenth-century spiritualists—*American Urania* and *Primer of Astrology*—Chaney had been married several times before he and Flora began to cohabit in the 1870s.

More than twenty years older than Flora, he was known as "The Professor"; he wrote and lectured widely, adopting one cause after another: eugenics, birth control, and the anti-Catholic, anti-immigrant Know-Nothing Party. Whether or not Jack London read Chaney's work isn't clear. He did, however, read widely in the spiritual literature of his day: Mary Baker Eddy's *Science and Health* (1875), a primary text of Christian Science; and British author Sir William Crookes's *Psychic Force and Modern Spiritualism* (1871) and *Researches in the Phenomena of Spiritualism* (1874), which persuaded London to take telepathy and clairvoyance seriously.

Chaney was a dedicated student of the Bible; he also practiced law and believed in astrology, which he called a "celestial art" and "sublime science"—according to London's older daughter Joan, who unearthed the long-buried facts of his life and who regarded him as her grandfather. Chaney coined several catchy slogans, including "The Stars incline, but do not compel," and argued that parents might produce superior offspring only if they engaged in sexual intercourse under the proper astrological conditions. When Flora informed him of her pregnancy in June 1875, he must have thought that the alignment of the stars did not incline toward a healthy child, because he demanded that she abort the fetus. Of course, he also may have believed he wasn't the father.

Flora refused point-blank and then attempted suicide: she took an overdose of laudanum, and when that failed she shot herself in the head with a pistol. In a "half-insane" condition, she was taken by her neighbors to a doctor on Mission Street. This incident made the pages of the *San Francisco Chronicle* in a lurid article that turned the quarrels between Flora and Chaney into Victorian melodrama—with Flora as the proverbial damsel in distress and Chaney as the archetypal villain. Almost everyone in the city who could read knew about their private lives. "A Discarded Wife," the headline blared, followed by a subhead that proclaimed, "Why Mrs. Chaney Twice Attempted Suicide Driven from Home for Refusing to Destroy her Unborn Infant—a Chapter of Heartless and Domestic Misery." Flora survived. She and Chaney separated, and when John Griffith Chaney was eight months old, she married John London.

By the age of six or seven, the young boy discovered that John London wasn't his real father and that his mother had deceived him. Hiding at the back of the grocery store they owned and operated, he overheard a quarrel between his parents, and, like a character in a Henry James novel that might have been called *What Jack Knew*, he experienced an epiphany. Years later, in the notes for an autobiography that he entitled *Jack Liverpool* and that he never wrote, he scrawled, "Learn my father not my father."

He discussed the taboo facts of his birth and the existence of Chaney with his first wife, Bessie May Maddern (1876–1942), on the eve of their marriage, and later with his daughters, which strongly suggests that he believed that Chaney was, in fact, his father. He never publicly acknowledged his illegitimacy, perhaps out of a sense of shame or perhaps because the secret gave him a sense of power.

He said nothing about Chaney to Mabel Maude Applegarth (1873–1915), his first confidante and one of his earliest girlfriends, though he did pour out his memories of his childhood. "When I was seven years old, at the country school of San Pedro, this happened. Meat, I was that hungry for it I once opened a girl's basket and stole a piece of meat," he wrote Mabel. "In those days, like Esau, I would have literally sold my birthright for a mess of pottage, a piece of meat." He seemed to know that he had insatiable emotional hungers, as well as a need to fill his belly with food. He also seemed to understand that he ultimately derived strength from the dislocations and the deprivations of his earliest years. "How loneliness made him observant and perceptive," he wrote of himself in the third person. In his own view, he was "plastic, fluid, flowed into any environment," and thus, in his estimation, he could triumph over any adversity.

His first biographer, Rose Wilder Lane (1886–1968)—the daughter of Laura Ingalls Wilder, of *Little House on the Prairie* fame—suggested in 1917 that an understanding of prenatal influences and psychoanalysis, especially the theories of Freud and Jung, might help to solve the mystery of Jack London as a "Boy Socialist" and as an adult revolutionary. Of course, London himself read and appreciated Freud and Jung. He understood the importance of dreams, the unconscious, the shadow side, and archetypes, too, and he psychoanalyzed himself in both his fiction and nonfiction. "I was a solitary and a lonely child," he wrote not long before his death. "I lived a dual life. My outward life was that of the everyday poor man's son . . . happy-go-lucky . . . within myself I was reflective, contemplative, apart from the kinetic forces around me."

As an adult, he would insist repeatedly that he had been born "normal and healthy," though there was nothing normal or healthy about his birth and his early years. He nearly died of diphtheria and experienced ongoing illness and infirmity. His early bouts with illness and his continuing poor health—few American writers have had as many ailments—led him to boast how strong and resilient he could be. At 5 feet 8 inches and 180 pounds—his taut body all "silk," as he called it—he aimed for physical fitness and boasted that he was "a physical culturalist," too. He rode horseback, swam, and boxed to stay fit and to show that the fittest really did survive. Still, his low, sickly origins haunted him for much of his life. No family member or close friend of his mother—only an anonymous Irish midwife—helped at his arrival in the world. Unable to breast-feed her baby, Flora entrusted him to an African American ex-slave named Virginia Prentiss to be nursed and nurtured. In later years, Jack would look back at babyhood and reduce Prentiss to her "black breast" and call her "Mammy," though she pleaded with him not to use that term.

Racism permeates much of London's fiction, as if through writing he tried to distance himself from anyone nonwhite. In *The Call of the Wild,* the canine protagonist Buck defends his white master, kills Indians, and proves his valor over lesser dogs like the German shepherd he defeats in battle.

At his most generous moments, Jack described Prentiss as his "foster mother" and acknowledged that he loved her far more than his mother and that Prentiss loved him, too, which she did. Nearly everyone, even his stepfather—whom he remembered as a kindly figure—seemed more loving and lovable than Flora. Ninetta Eames (1852–1942)—one of Jack's earliest advocates and his editor at the *Overland Monthly*—described Flora as "a horror in flesh and blood" and "unforgivably vile." The money that Prentiss lent Jack so that he could buy the *Razzle Dazzle*—the boat that he used during his days as an outlaw and a thief—showed, if nothing else, how deeply she loved him; but he gave few if any overt signs that he appreciated her generosity. Of all the adult parental figures he knew intimately as a child and as a boy, only Prentiss, the ex-slave, had money at her disposal, and that seemed to irk him, since his own biological parents were often destitute. That people of color should enjoy financial success while white people failed seemed unfair to him, a betrayal of the white man's birthright.

As a child, John—or rather, Johnny, as his mother called him—grew up, at least part of the time, in Prentiss's home and in the African American community in the San Francisco Bay Area. At an early age he learned some of the history of slavery in America, and he also learned to look down on African Americans as lazy and shiftless—passive victims of a system, not active resisters and rebels. (Later, as a young man, he mistakenly assumed that African Americans allowed Jim Crow laws to take effect in the South in the late-nineteenth century without protest, and that they did nothing to improve their lives.) His mother, Flora, disliked anyone who was not white, and if she taught her son one lesson—aside from lying and keeping secrets—it was to disdain Italians and the Irish. As though to make up for her own shameful status at the bottom of the abyss, she told her son that his ancestors belonged to pure American stock, a story he adopted as the truth.

As an adult, he would boast that his ancestors came to the New World before the American Revolution and that his family tree was strictly Northern European—Welsh, English, Dutch, German, and Swiss. Any thought of racial impurity, or blood mixing, he found repulsive, and he looked forward to the day when people who were not pure-blooded would become extinct and socialism would exist only for white people—a view not entirely unique in the American socialist movement of the early twentieth century. London's socialist friend Austin Lewis dismissed the contributions of immigrants, writing that "the United States derives no apparent aesthetic advantage from the admixture" and that "the song is choked in the throat of the Italian; the taste of the Frenchman does not improve the taste of his adopted country." Daniel De Leon, the leader of the Socialist Labor Party, insisted that the party would not and could not countenance "a Louisiana Negro breakdown" or an "orthodox Jewish synagogue where every man sings in whatever key he likes." Unity and uniformity added to the power of the socialist movement, its leaders proclaimed; ethnic groups would have to sacrifice traditions, language, and culture for the revolution.

Jack's experiences with his two antithetical mothers — one black, the other white, one loving and generous, the other secretive and withholding — sowed the seeds for his unrelenting pursuit of answers to questions about identity and the influence of the environment on the individual. He wondered about the fate of twins separated at birth, and about boys, not unlike himself, lifted at random from the abyss of poverty and transported to paradise, or, alternatively, taken from a safe haven and thrown into a hell ship. He grew up, of course, to write obsessively about orphaned boys and fatherless, motherless men, dislocated dogs and wolves, and occasionally vagabond and orphaned women, kidnapped from their homes and hurled into strange surroundings where they fought for survival, as though in a gigantic social laboratory. In the pages of his fiction, like a scientist experimenting with breeding and genetics, he observed his heroes in stressful situations: the domesticated dog, Buck, who becomes a Ghost Dog in the Yukon; the sissy bookworm Humphrey Van Weyden, who proves his potent manhood aboard *The Ghost;* and the ferocious wolf-dog White Fang, who finds happiness in a California Garden of Eden with a kind, loving master.

"They were his environment, these men, and they were molding the clay of him into a more ferocious thing than had been intended by Nature," London wrote of White Fang, another animal character that enabled him to escape from his own inhibitions and write freely about himself. "Nature had given him plasticity," he added, admiringly. Above all other traits, human or animal, he valued "plasticity" — the ability to adapt, to adjust, and not to break — and he continually touted his own plastic nature and the virtues of plasticity for all sentient beings. (The concept of "plasticity" he borrowed from Nietzsche.) "Every atom of organic life is plastic," London observed. "The finest specimens now in existence were once all pulpy infants capable of being molded this way or that." Of White Fang, he noted, as though writing about himself, "Where many another animal would have died or had its spirit broken, he adjusted himself and lived, and at no expense of the spirit."

Sociology helped him make sense of his own life, and sociologists — like the Social Darwinist Herbert Spencer (1820–1903) — provided paradigms that explained the workings of society and enabled him to understand what otherwise looked like chaos. Literature also offered a handle for him to chart and comprehend what struck him as the constant flux of experience, showing him that environments existed inside — in the heart and the head—as well as outside. Books taught him, too, that human beings could be prisoners of their own minds, and that books themselves might provide a way to escape. So, he made himself into an escape artist, finding in literature idealized worlds and selves. Not surprisingly, he admired Houdini, the great American magician—and escape artist—and enjoyed watching him perform his feats on stage.

As a socialist visionary, he sought to change the internal environment that human beings carried with them, and he knew that as a writer he had to get inside their heads in order to bring about a revolution in thinking. In this, he differed from radicals who appealed only to economic issues—wages and hours—ignoring the human need for beauty and serenity. Like Mother Jones (1837–1930)—the labor organizer known in her time as "the most dangerous woman in America"—and others, he wanted "bread and roses." But he remained skeptical about whether or not bread and roses would ever be achieved and whether the revolution might actually be won. Barbarism seemed as likely a future for humanity as socialism. At the end of the day, he did not know for certain whether the world really could be changed, and, as a revolutionary, nothing could have been more difficult to accept than that deep-seated feeling. "We are blind puppets at the play of great, unreasoning forces," he noted pessimistically. "Man is not a free agent." Even when he described how he became a socialist, he emphasized his own passivity, making it seem that he had not consciously chosen the path of revolution. Socialism had been pounded into him, he insisted. He resisted it until it was almost too late. Then, suddenly, he woke one day and found he had become his own exact opposite: London, the young bourgeois individualist, emerged from his shell, kicking and screaming, as a socialist revolutionary.

At the same time he insisted calmly and confidently that nothing was impossible, given human will power. "The world can be fashioned a fair world indeed by the humans who inhabit it," he noted optimistically. On an equally upbeat note, he explained, "I am an evolutionist therefore a broad optimist, hence my love for the human (in the slime though he be)." Socialism appealed to him in large part because it posited society as a living laboratory in which the weak, the infirm, and the impoverished might be transformed, via the revolution, into strong, healthy, well-adjusted human beings. Take humanity out of the abyss, add sun and light, roses and love, and the lowliest brutes might be transformed beyond recognition. The meek might inherit the earth, as Christ said. Apes might become angels. And yet it also seemed to him that the species always ran the risk of falling back into the deepest abyss and that humanity's primitive, savage nature would reassert itself in the most civilized conditions. Angels might also devolve into apes.

RAZZLING AND DAZZLING

At the age of two, he had been lifted willy-nilly out of his own little world in San Francisco and taken to Oakland by his hapless mother, Flora, and by his equally hapless stepfather, John London, who might have been used as the subject for a Jack London novel about an ordinary American citizen traumatized by war and revolution. A wounded Civil War veteran unsuited to a rapidly mechanizing workforce, he never kept a job for long. John London failed at everything he tried to do: managing a grocery, tilling the land, and raising vegetables for sale. A soldier, a farmer, and a shopkeeper, he never worked in a factory and didn't belong to the industrial proletariat, despite London's assertion that he came from a proletarian family. (American radicals have often gilded their roots as proletarian.) Finally, a railroad accident turned John London into a cripple and made him permanently unemployable. In hindsight, he seems emblematic of everything that went wrong with nineteenth-century American society in the rush to industrialize.

To add insult to injury, Flora took what little money he earned and invested it in wild get-rich schemes that never materialized. Jack desperately wanted to love his stepfather, to have a real father, like other boys. He steadfastly idealized his lowly stepfather, transforming him into a heroic American frontiersman—a mix of Daniel Boone (1734–1820) and Kit Carson (1809–1868)—to match his own dazzling deeds. "My father was Pennsylvania-born, a soldier, scout, backwoodsman, trapper, and wanderer," he bragged. About himself, he offered a long list of achievements to demonstrate his versatility and plasticity. "I was a salmon fisher, an oyster pirate, a schooner sailor, a fish patrolman, a longshoreman, and a general sort of bay-faring adventurer," he proclaimed.

The elder John London had few moral scruples about employment; he could not afford them. During the historic 1893 railroad strike, which tied up transportation and shipping for the whole nation, he found a job as a scab for the railroad; he also worked as a constable, arresting unemployed hobos and tramps. Jack's decision to become a hobo and a tramp might be taken as a direct challenge to his stepfather's authority—an incitement to be arrested and jailed with all the other hobos that John London incarcerated. (Predictably, Jack rebelled against his mother in the same way she had rebelled against her parents—by running away.) John London wasn't a good provider or an understanding stepfather, and John London, Jr., rebelled against him. He grumbled about the chores he had to perform at home and was angered, too, when his stepfather arrived at Oakland High School to beg for a dollar or two. His rebellion against society had its roots, in part, in his rebellion against his parents; in this regard, he shared experiences with the rebels of the 1960s, who found themselves on the youthful side of the generation gap, in confrontation with their elders.

The mismatched Londons were dysfunctional and unhappy, though Flora refused to acknowledge this. A psychic who believed in "occult divination," she held séances, communicated with the dead, read horoscopes, and plotted the transit of the planets to help her decide where to invest her money. Jack London was steeped in a spiritualism that he scorned as nonsense; yet this early exposure to the world beyond would infuse both his thought and his work, especially later in life. The art of mind reading and fortune telling offered intriguing modes of communication; science alone didn't satisfy his curiosity about the universe. He accepted things on faith, and came to believe he, like his mother, could see into the future. In fact, the older he grew, the more he seemed to return to his mother's ideas about astral projection, and, in *The Star Rover*, a novel published in 1915, the year before he died, he gave credence to her beliefs, creating a character who travels across time and space, inhabits different historical eras, and takes on the identities of historical characters through the ages.

Newspaper stories chronicling the young London's activities both reflected and contributed to his meteoric rise to fame as a radical orator on the streets of Oakland. In February 1896, just a month after his twentieth birthday, the *San Francisco Chronicle* reported that "the Boy Socialist" Jack London was "holding forth nightly to crowds" and that "while a broad socialist in every way, he is not an anarchist." "The Boy Socialist" moniker stuck, turning him into a mythical, larger-than-life figure. In the 1890s, his friends in the Ruskin Club and the Henry Clay Club—who helped to shape his political ideas and his personal style—looked to him to lead the way, and in this giddy time, he felt his power as a local legend. Arrested and incarcerated in 1897 for speaking in public without a license from the mayor, he became identified with freedom of speech and attracted even more of a following as a legendary radical.

The facts didn't always matter in matters of politics and personality, he realized. One might amend them or erase them entirely, without sin or guilt, he argued; in this sense, he followed the eighteenth-century French philosopher Jean-Jacques Rousseau (1712–1778), who noted in *The Confessions* (1782), "I may omit or transpose facts, or make mistakes in dates. But I cannot go wrong about what I felt or about what my feelings have led me to do."

Omitting and transposing facts in the manner of Rousseau was a lesson London learned from his 1894 cross-continental journey. As a "stranger in a strange land," he saw the country from the ground up as well as from the outside looking in. The

American dream had turned into the American nightmare, he concluded. After all, he experienced it firsthand. On the road, he told stories about himself, making himself up as he went from place to place and turning himself in the archetype of the American hobo. He learned to bend the truth in order to eat. "I have often thought that to this training of my tramp days is due much of my success as a writer," he wrote in *The Road,* his lyrical account — in the tradition of Rousseau's *The Confessions* — of his epic journey. "In order to get the food whereby I lived, I was compelled to tell tales that rang true," he explained in the chapter entitled "Confession." "At the backdoor, out of inexorable necessity is developed the convincingness and sincerity laid down by all authorities on the art of the short story."

In January 1900, when his Boston editors at Houghton Mifflin asked him to provide an account of his life that they might use to publicize his first book, *The Son of the Wolf* (1900) — an anthology of short stories set in the Yukon — he offered an elaborate fiction. "My literary life is just thirteen months old," he wrote, though he had been published seven years earlier, in 1893. What's more, he explained, his "revolutionaire period" had expired. In fact, his revolutionary period had just begun. Curiously, or perhaps predictably, the wealthier and the more famous he became after 1900, the more extreme his politics became. He seems to have felt that he had to reassure himself and his followers that he had not abandoned his love for the working class and his hatred of the bourgeoisie — though his life was obviously bourgeois, with servants to cook, clean, and perform all sorts of domestic chores. He wrote about this lifestyle in "The House Beautiful," anticipating the bohemian/bourgeois experience of a century later. He even defended his wealthy lifestyle as an act of defiance; he took from the rich and the powerful, subverted it, and shared it with his comrades. No American socialist ever gave a more spirited recitation of the necessity for — and proper treatment of — servants.

To his editors at Houghton Mifflin, he noted in 1900, "During my revolutionaire period I perpetrated my opinions upon the public through the medium of the local papers, gratis." He added, "But that was years ago when I went to high school and was more notorious than esteemed." In the fall and winter of 1895, he had, indeed, been a notorious, rambunctious high school student. Georgia Loring Bamford, who met him then, noted that "he was ready to destroy society and civilization" and that "he wanted nothing to do with people who, he thought, robbed the workingman in order to gain refinements for themselves." In the only essay he published in the *Aegis,* the Oakland High School literary magazine, he waved the red flag of revolution. "Arise, ye Americans, patriots and optimists!" he proclaimed. "Awake! Seize the reins of a corrupted government and educate your masses."

Had he remained a student, he might have continued to write radical essays, but he withdrew from school after a semester, and then, after passing the entrance exams, he withdrew dejectedly from the University of California, Berkeley, the following year. He had to work. Education was a luxury only the upper classes could afford, he insisted. Still, he put a positive spin on his short-lived academic experience, much as he put a positive spin on nearly everything that happened to him. "In the main I am self-educated," he told the Houghton Mifflin editors in 1900. "Have had no mentor but myself." Of course, he did have mentors, including Frederick Bamford—a former professor of English and an Oakland librarian—but he liked to cast himself as an autodidact. Only life itself could instruct Jack London.

At fourteen, he ran away from home—albeit briefly—to join "the pirates," as he called them. Casting himself as a character in Twain's *The Prince and the Pauper* (1882), London, the pauper, borrowed an aristocratic title and dubbed himself the "Prince of the Oyster Pirates," becoming the lover of "the Queen of the Oyster Pirates." In fact, he stole oysters and dubbed himself the "captain" of the *Razzle Dazzle,* which he bought with money Virginia Prentiss lent him. Moreover, he defined himself as a capitalist in pursuit of riches. Joining the upper classes seemed more appealing than overthrowing them, and as a young man he would elevate himself above the riffraff, the masses, and the mob he disdained. Better to be a Nietzschean overlord than a Marxian lumpen proletarian.

All through his teens, and with all the sincerity that each role demanded, he played "Sailor Jack," "Sailor Kid," "Jack Drake," and "the 'Frisco Kid," to name a few of the monikers he used. As schoolmates like Frank Atherton noted, it wasn't easy to determine when he was making things up and when he was telling the truth. Jack London—his pals observed—had a gift for inflating everyday exploits and for borrowing the deeds of other boys and men and incorporating them into his own life. Razzling and dazzling an audience, even of one, came to him naturally, and in his guise as "the Boy Socialist," he razzled and dazzled, too.

Facts intrigued him: facts about factories, exploitation, the financial workings of the magazine industry, and the elusive facts about his own birth as an illegitimate child. These facts he pursued and at the same concealed, turning instead to the abstract, the ideological, and the philosophical to explain himself. Still, the circumstances of his birth and his upbringing led him toward socialism—toward a sense of family he felt he never had and to a sense of belonging that was absent from the very beginning. He had been divided from himself—separated from that other self he had lost at birth and had to find or perish—and socialism healed fissures and alleviated his sense of alienation.

"A socialist is of necessity social—hence his name," he wrote in what was perhaps the most revealing remark in his pivotal 1895 essay, "What Socialism Is." He added, as though speaking of himself, albeit in the third person, "He wishes to be social—that is, to live in a society formed of social beings like himself." London, the street urchin and waif, craved socialism the way exiles crave their own country, or the way a child without parents craves a mother and a father. Socialism gave him companions, took away loneliness, and provided therapy; in the Socialist Labor Party and then in the Socialist Party of America he found not only a disciplined organization for workers but also a tribe for all the lost boys of the world.

The story of his unusual birth—which he learned in bits and pieces, fits and starts—gave him poetic license to fib, fabricate, embellish, and even lie. In 1913, the reporter, photographer, and American Indian ethnographer George Wharton James asked him two very sensible questions, "Where do you come from?" and "What are you the product of?" London replied enigmatically—and as though to honor the mysterious workings of the universe itself—"Have you ever thought, that in ten generations of my ancestors, 1,022 people happened to concentrate in some fashion on the small piece of protoplasm that was to eventuate in me." He would not furnish James with facts about where he came from and what family of origin shaped him.

He quickly gathered a lexicon of words for not telling the truth: "lie," of course, but also "untruth," "unveracity," and "mendacity," as though to differentiate each kind of inability, or failure, to tell the truth. He learned to lie and to fictionalize—and to blur the difference between the two, much like his childhood hero, Baron Munchausen (1720–1797), the legendary eighteenth-century writer and traveler who erased the boundaries between the real and the legendary. Like many boys his age, Jack also admired the enigmatic and elusive Huck Finn. If Huck could say of his famous creator Samuel Clemens that he "stretched" the truth, then surely, Jack thought, he too might be free to stretch the truth.

About orphanhood—the fictional identity he constructed for himself so that he might redeem his shameful illegitimate birth—he learned a great deal from his stepfather's daughters, who had grown up in an orphanage because John London could not support them. He also learned about the orphan—and the double—from reading literature, which he did on his own and without the encouragement of his parents, who did not appreciate books or magazines. Jack read *Oliver Twist, John Halifax, Gentleman,* and *Signa,* the last of which was published in 1875, the year before his birth, by Ouida, the pen name of the popular English novelist Marie Louise de la Ramée. By the age of eight, he identified with Signa, the poor orphan boy who becomes a great artist. He vowed to follow in Signa's footsteps — to rise from poverty to glory. Orphanhood became him, and without thinking, he would tell strangers that he had no parents, that his mother and father were dead, and that he had grown up "alone and forlorn on the streets of San Francisco." Patricide and matricide, at least in his imagination and in his tales, provided a way of working out his trauma, his rage, and his sense of the innate injustice of the world.

All through the 1870s and 1880, the impoverished London clan packed and unpacked their meager belongings, moving from one dilapidated home to another, from desolate location to wasteland, all the way to the cold, barren coast in San Mateo County, and then to Livermore, where, as Jack put it, "everything was squalid and sordid." Growing up with a sense of dislocation instilled in him two contrary impulses: to become a domesticated creature of comforts, and at the same time a wild beast roaming freely.

As a child, moving terrified him, and even as an adult, he remembered his recurring nightmares — from the age of three — in which a mad locomotive pursued him again and again, knocking him down and running him over. If only he could reach the ladder and escape to safety, all would be well, he thought. His dream of the mad locomotive, which he recounted to George Wharton James, epitomized his feeling that something immense and all-powerful — perhaps his own inexorable past — stalked him and might annihilate him. The dark nineteenth-century industrial world of machines and factories burrowed deeply and disturbingly into his subconscious, as illustrated by his brilliant short story "The Apostate" (1906). Indeed, he understood intuitively that capitalism shaped not only humanity's waking hours but also its sleeping hours — and its dreams, as well. As an adult, he remembered the sense of "horrible dread" that surrounded him as a child and that turned him into a character that might have stepped directly from the pages of Kierkegaard's *Fear and Trembling* (1843). "When I was about three years old we were moving from one part of Oakland to another," he recalled. "Up to that time I had not known fear, but this particular afternoon when I went into the house and saw the vacant rooms, the boxes and furniture moved here and there, and everything different, and suddenly realized that I was alone in the house, a deadly fear came upon me."

His fears and nightmares apparently dissipated only when he lost himself in the pages of literature and in the pulp novels of the day, replete with daring heroes like Deadwood Dick and Nick Carter, beloved by nineteenth-century American readers. He found a haven — perhaps the only true haven in all his childhood — in the Oakland Free Public Library, where he discovered a valuable resource in Ina

Coolbrith, the librarian whom he described as a "goddess." Coolbrith had been an editor, with Bret Harte, at the *Overland Monthly,* California's premier literary magazine. Middle-class bookish women—from Ina to Mabel Maude, to Anna and his wife Charmian—never failed to arouse his passion. If the women he encountered weren't bookish goddesses, they were more often than not prostitutes, and he could rage, as though drawing on his own personal experience in foreign ports, about the "monstrous female form" that "preys on sailors."

Inside the safe walls of the public library, where books were free and librarians showered their attention on him, he became a voracious reader. He disappeared into novels, biographies, and histories until he could not tell the difference between the real world and the world of fiction, the pirates on the printed page and the pirates in San Francisco Bay. He wrapped the books he read all around him and lived like a character in a book. By the time he was a teenager, his reading in pulp fiction and in the works of Herman Melville (1819–1891), Mark Twain (1835–1910), and Lafcadio Hearn (1850–1904)—the author he admired because he lived among and wrote about the enigmatic Japanese—persuaded him to become a writer and to pursue the exotic and the grotesque. His first published work, "The Story of a Typhoon off the Coast of Japan," appeared in the *San Francisco Morning Call* in 1893 under the byline "John London" when he was seventeen. The editors felt that he made an egregious mistake by writing in the present tense about the death of a worker—a bricklayer turned sailor—during a storm at sea. They promptly rewrote his story in the past tense, an experience that taught him to be wary of editors and to regard them as a class enemy. In his scheme of things, editors were bourgeois, while he was a proletarian. They cared only about sales and circulation, while he cared about art and the integrity of the artist. Though he complained bitterly about the crass ways and the hypocrisy of editors and publishers, he furnished them with the romance and the melodrama they wanted, and he demanded his money on time and not a penny less than his contracts allowed. He counted every single word in every single article and story, demanding to be paid by the word, as though he were a proletarian in a factory doing piecework. No one could exploit him or steal from him.

"The Story of a Typhoon off the Coast of Japan" showed how serious a writer he could be. A masterful imitator of the "imaginative orgies"—as he described them—in Melville's *Moby-Dick* (1851), he learned to paint pictures with words, to fill large canvases with color, and to put himself into the picture, too, as a fictional character with the name "Jack." From then on, there would be no way to keep himself out of his stories and novels. "Jack" appeared in one guise or another, sometimes appropriately, and sometimes not, as in *The Valley of the Moon* (1913), in which his presence mars the story. He could not stop looking at, and admiring, himself, and so he emerged as a kind of California narcissist, as California historian Kevin Starr has noted.

Jack's mother regarded him as a boy put on the face of the earth to make money and provide for her needs. She had urged him to enter the *Morning Call*'s competition for descriptive writing by an author under the age of twenty-five. Eager for him to receive the $25 prize for first place, she delivered his article, in person, to the editors, pausing long enough to promote her son. "John has often wished he could write about what he has seen," she explained. It seems likely that she, not he, also collected—and spent—the $25 he won for first prize. Jack felt like an exploited worker—a feeling that informs his surrealistic story "The Apostate." The $25 prize also prompted him to write more stories inspired by his own experiences. If only he could escape from manual labor and make money by selling his brainpower, not his brawn, he thought, he would be happy.

Flora drilled into him an appreciation for the dollar, and so by the age of fifteen he was keeping a notebook with a section entitled "Financial Receipts and Disbursements" in which he recorded the money that came into the household and the money that went out—to purchase ice, milk, and his mother's little pills. Keeping track of cash became a necessity for the survival of the family, and, not surprisingly, as Jack grew up, he became fixated on money; early in his career, he insisted unapologetically that he was "in pursuit of dollars, dollars, dollars." Even though he was a socialist, he offered no apology for his desire for all the luxuries that wealth could buy, things that he had grown up without: books, elegant clothes, and the latest technology and tools. At the same time, he felt that he prostituted his talent; he betrayed his art for dollars, and, as with Herman Melville, "dollars damned him." The school of "art for art's sake" did not seduce him for long, nor did the antimaterialist bohemians, though he remained friends with California bohemians—like the visionary mystical poet George Sterling (1869–1926)—and he shared their sense of community, their worship of the great outdoors, and their love of the sensual life.

"I discovered that socialism was the only way out for art and the artist," London wrote. Socialism taught him that under capitalism, literature was a commodity with a price tag, to be bought and sold, and that the transactions between writer and publisher occurred in a competitive marketplace, not in an ivory tower or in a carefree bohemian café. Socialism also provided him with a ready-made working-class audience and with radical magazines—like *Comrade*—that he could write for. Despite his attempt to be objective about writing and money, he did have illusions about success, art, publishing, and fame, believing they would make him happy and bring him love. Inevitably, he became disillusioned about the writer's life. He told that story in *Martin Eden,* a portrait of the artist as a young man in which he presented himself more honestly than anywhere else, though he denied identification with his protagonist when he defended the book against attack from an Oakland pastor.

The Reverend Charles R. Brown denounced London for having ended the novel with the suicide of its main character. In a public letter London circulated to redeem himself in the face of the pastor's charges, he wrote, "Martin Eden failed and died, in *my* parable, not because of his lack of faith in God, but because of his lack of faith in man." Further, no parallel existed between himself and his protagonist. "Martin Eden killed himself," he proclaimed. "I am still alive." They had nothing in common. Martin Eden was an individualist, while he was a socialist. Few readers were convinced, however. The novel's socialist poet Russ Brissenden tells Eden, "I'd like to see you a socialist . . . it is the one thing that will save you." But Brissenden's own brand of socialism can't and doesn't save Eden or himself. Brissenden takes his own life by shooting himself in the head.

ON THE PROTEAN ROAD

After his initial success with "The Story of a Typhoon off the Coast of Japan," London did not make a cent from writing for years, but he did not give up. In 1894, when he went on the road at the age of eighteen, he borrowed a notebook from a friend and wrote the name "John London" inside. He saw himself as a writer cultivating experiences and gathering materials for the purpose of writing about them. When he returned from his 1894 odyssey, he wrote an essay about the experience, with reflections about hobos and tramps, but no editor would publish it, and it would not see the light of day until 1905.

Part of the time, he traveled with a rag-tag contingent of politically conscious, unemployed men marching to Washington, D.C., to demand federal jobs—a formative, radicalizing time that made him feel like a part of contemporary history. Known as "Kelly's Army" because they followed the leadership of Charles T. Kelly, a radical San Francisco printer and union organizer, the out-of-work men joined forces with "Coxey's Army," another contingent marching to the capital. Their ranks grew steadily as they approached Washington, D.C., where federal troops, under orders from President Grover Cleveland, prevented them from entering the city. Eugene Victor

Debs (1855–1926)—the popular leader of the militant American Railway Union—watched the progress of the army and paid homage to it. "They walk, they ride, they float," he exclaimed, eloquently. "The storms beat upon them, their tents their skins; their couch the mother earth, their pillows stones." London basked in the glory of that army and in the glory of Debs's prose; he became a radical in part because the radical movement included inspired poetic writers like Oscar Wilde (1854–1900) and rousing orators like Debs; he caught Debs's lyrical style and made it his own. He admired Debs his whole life; his short story "The Dream of Debs" (1909) offers a tribute to the socialist leader, and Debs, in turn, admired London's work and urged socialists to read his fiction.

On the road, with only the earth for his couch and a stone for a pillow, Jack kept one foot in the army of class-conscious men who read Marx and spouted revolution. His other foot he kept firmly planted in his own army of one, unwilling to surrender his sovereignty to the cause—defining himself as a staunch individualist among collectivists. He chafed under Kelly's leadership, and, joining a group of other disaffected marchers, he begged and borrowed, turning into a thief and petty criminal, which he described in the essay "The March of Kelly's Army." This group of renegades from the army intimidated farmers and merchants, taking what they could for themselves, until the army leadership stopped them. George Speed, second in command to Kelly, noted, "Jack was never *in* the army or *of* it." Indeed, a telling photo from that time shows Jack off to the side, at a safe distance from the marchers, keeping his own company.

Soon he left the march altogether, leaving behind him the persona of heroic proletarian and taking on a new character. He followed in Huck Finn's carefree footsteps, floating down the Mississippi River all the way to Hannibal, where Mark Twain had spent his youth. Then he abruptly changed directions, traveling to Chicago, where he visited what was left of the 1893 World's Fair, collected mail and money from home, slept in a bed at the Salvation Army, and "went down amongst the Jews of South Clark St[reet] where after a great deal of wrangling & talking I bought shoes, overcoat, hat, pants & shirt"—an encounter that solidified his impression that Jews wrangled about money. Now, dressed like a respectable traveler and with money in his pocket, he visited his mother's sister in Michigan. This part of his journey he omitted from his 1907 *The Road* because it did not accord with his image of himself as a lone vagabond.

In Buffalo, New York, the police arrested him for vagrancy. A judge sentenced him, without a trial, to thirty days in the Erie County Penitentiary, where he told his jailors his name was John London and that he was a sailor and an atheist. Handcuffed to another prisoner, his possessions confiscated, his head shaved, he was thrown into a cell, which he described as a "living hell." But he learned to adapt to the loss of free-dom, applying to prison conditions lessons he'd learned on the outside. During the journey from California, he called himself "a fluid sort of organism" who enjoyed "Hobo Land," because, as he explained, "the face of life is protean—an ever changing phantasmagoria, where the impossible happens and the unexpected jumps out of the bushes at every turn."

As a hobo, he discovered how to live like a Zen Buddhist—"in the present moment"—and to appreciate "the futility of telic endeavor." That Buddhist state of mind he also cultivated behind bars. Then, too, he saw that prison mirrored society on the outside. The prisoners' system of buying, selling, and trading goods—along with the endemic corruption and abuse of power by their jailers—reproduced the economic and political laws that operated in the country as a whole. Society looked like a charade in which everyone played a part, and the criminals at the bottom were mirror images of the rich at the top. "We but patterned ourselves after our betters outside the walls, who, on a larger scale, and under the respectable disguise of merchants, bankers, and capital-ists of industry, did precisely what we were doing," he wrote. If he needed another rea-son to become a socialist, the Erie County Penitentiary provided one. He went home more self-confident and less morose than he had been for years, finding in Milton's *Paradise Lost* a sentiment he could live by: "Better to reign in hell than serve in heaven."

All through the 1890s, however, he battled depression, self-destructiveness, and suicidal impulses. Once, after Flora went to Hickmott's Cannery to collect his wages before he could spend them, he wrote melodramatically, "I could have slashed my wrists." He aimed to drown his sorrow in drink—wine, beer, and spirits in the saloons and bars of Oakland—and he would disappear in drunken stupors. At sixteen or so, while intoxicated, he tried to commit suicide by drowning himself, only to be saved by a fisherman, a story he told and retold for years to illustrate his plasticity and his ability to come back from the dead. Suicide (unlike his illegitimate birth) did not strike him as stigmatizing. He talked about it freely and found an essential connection between suicide and socialism. "I have been so blue as to have spent a day contemplat-ing suicide and gone forth in the evening to lecture before some socialist organiza-tion," he explained to a friend. "And in the battle forgot self, been lifted out of self, and in the end returned home happy, satisfied." Of course, he also found that his dark thoughts lifted and his suicidal thoughts dissipated when he lectured before a "bour-geois organization." Isolation and solitude took a heavy toll on him. Mixing with his fellows lifted his spirits, and yet he often rejected human company, retreating to his own solitary space and his own imagination.

Writing and speaking about socialism served as an elixir in 1895 and 1896, but then his own past was unexpectedly revealed to him when in 1897 he unearthed archives of the *San Francisco Chronicle* and read, at last, the lurid June 1875 story about his mother and her common-law husband, William Henry Chaney. No one took credit for informing Jack about the story, and he never assigned credit or blame. It seems likely, however, that Edward Applegarth, the English-born brother of Jack's girlfriend, Mabel, revealed the secret—perhaps to end Jack and Mabel's romantic idyll and terminate any thoughts they might have had about marriage. A bastard in the family—and a socialist at that—could hardly have been acceptable in a bourgeois household like the Applegarths'. London was devastated by the story, which described the squabbles between Flora and her husband, including Chaney's demand that she abort the fetus. Just as gruesome was the story that his mother had attempted suicide, which would also have terminated his life. "I hardly know what to write," London explained to Edward Applegarth in June 1897. "I am completely stagnated." The only uplifting news he could convey had to do with the cause. "Organized labor, headed by Debs & beginning with the American Railway Union, has commenced a change of front," he reported—though that information was not accurate. "They now strike for political power," London added. Showing that his mood wasn't entirely bleak, he wrote, "Socialist propaganda in the United States is assuming greater proportions."

One can hardly blame him for feeling at the end of his tether in June 1897. The article in the *Chronicle* brought him bad news and unquiet thoughts. To answer the inevitable questions that arose about paternity, he wrote to Chaney in Chicago— clandestinely, using Applegarth's address as his own to keep his mother and stepfather in the dark. Jack's letters to Chaney no longer exist; Chaney's to Jack survive. Addressing his interlocutor as "Dear Sir" and not "My dear boy" or even "Dear Jack," Chaney agreed to comply with the young man's "wish to observe silence and secrecy."

"For you I feel a warm sympathy," Chaney wrote on June 3, 1897, and, in what sounded like genuine sympathy, he added, "I can imagine what my emotions would be were I in your place"—a compassionate sentiment no one else had ever extended to him so directly. But just as suddenly as Chaney reached out and expressed empathy, he backed away. "I cannot be your father," he wrote. Now "past seventy-six" and "quite poor," he acknowledged that he and Flora had lived together and, though "never married," he had once felt affection for her. Still, after Flora informed him of her pregnancy, he felt a sense of desperation. "I even thought of killing her and myself," he explained to Jack.

It is no wonder, with such unstable biological parents, that he worried about heredity, and what strange mental condition might have been passed on to him. And what wonderful material for a writer his own dysfunctional family offered him! Indeed, London quickly transformed the revelations from Chaney into a science fiction story entitled "A Thousand Deaths," in which a mad scientist—with menacing African American henchmen—performs a series of cruel experiments, putting his son to death repeatedly, then bringing him back to life again, only to torture him again. That cathartic story briefly quieted Jack's tormented soul, but he went back to the source of his primal hurt repeatedly.

All through the late 1890s and then again in the first decade of the twentieth century, he returned to the father-son theme in tales like "The Story of Jees Uck" (1902), about an orphan boy and about "what waifs of the generations we are, all of us, and the strange meanderings of the seed from which we spring." He had universalized his own emotional experience, thus connecting with humanity. He also drew on his birth in "Bâtard" (1902) (French for *bastard*), a story about a mean-spirited dog who brings about the death of his mean-spirited master. Here, fiction served as a means for revenge. Of course, London could not help but create dualities, and even as he wrote stories about bad fathers, he also wrote stories about good fathers; in "An Old Soldier's Story" (1898), he presented "a real incident, which occurred in the life of the writer's father."

In July 1897, London left San Francisco for the Yukon Territory in Canada, ostensibly to hunt for gold, though he clearly felt the need to escape from his family and nurse his psychic wounds. The gold rush provided him with a cloak to carry on a mining expedition into his own soul, and when he returned home, he had worked out his birth trauma and re-created his identity. The year he spent in the "Northland"—the mythological place that he manufactured and that bore little resemblance to the real Yukon—turned him into an Anglophile, a fierce defender of the British Empire, and a fan of Rudyard Kipling's fiction. "Kipling, as no one else, has sung the hymn of the dominant bourgeoisie, the war march of the white man round the world, the triumphant paean of commercialism and imperialism," he wrote. There, too, he became more intensely aware of race and the potential for race war. He came to regard "the ubiquitous Anglo-Saxon" (read "English-speaking peoples of the world") as the fittest folk on the face of the earth. At the same time, he identified with the "Indians" of Alaska and Canada, though he assumed they were doomed to extinction because of what he regarded as their inherent racial weaknesses. He often identified with the "white race," as he constructed it, but on an unconscious level that nurtured his art, he sensed that "whiteness" meant silence, death, and fear. In his stories of the Yukon, "whiteness" often becomes emblematic of everything antithetical to life and to passion. By contrast, the red Indians pulse with vitality. But make no mistake about it, London did not want to preserve and protect the culture of the indigenous peoples who inhabited the Americas. When a California Indian chief wanted his entire tribe, the Washoe, to give up all their traditions and to become "whites," he applauded the efforts. "There have been revolutions and revolutions," he wrote in an article entitled "Washoe Indians Resolve to Be White Men." Their revolution from Indians to white men, he noted, was "as unprecedented as it is refreshing to this jaded old world."

In the Yukon, he regarded the Indians as barbarians, and as highly sexualized beings. He gazed at the "beautiful half-breed" Indian women he saw, a luxury he would not have permitted himself in white, middle-class Oakland society. In "the white silence" of the Northland, his own red-blooded passions emerged, though his misogyny also emerged, and in several stories he used the fearless female Indian characters as sticks to beat their delicate, refined white sisters. He also celebrated the "White Woman" as an archetypical figure and as an integral part of the imperial nexus. In his view, the White Woman, born of empire, bred soldiers necessary for expansion and provided emotional support for the Anglo-Saxon warriors who might be called upon to quash colonial insurrection. London felt drawn to writing stories about the beautiful half-breed Indian women and their children, in imitation of Lafcadio Hearn. At times, he wanted to leave his white companions behind and "go native," as Kipling would have said. "5 AM & everybody was up, children playing, bucks skylarking, squaws giggling & flirting," he wrote enviously of the Indians in one village. He never transcended the stereotypes of "bucks" and "squaws." In his stories, the Indian magicians were evil and grotesque, and the Indian warriors sneaky savages. Not surprisingly, London's racist images proved popular in the United States as it was becoming a colonial power at the start of the twentieth century.

To the Yukon, London brought Darwin's *On the Origin of Species* (1859)—the perfect book for a young man haunted by his own origins. In his cabin, he discussed, with the "gold hunters," the differences between animals in the wild and animals in captivity and pondered the virtues of "wildness," a concept that had fascinated him from childhood, largely through reading books like *Lost in the Jungle* (1870), by the explorer Paul du Chalu. Modeling himself after Darwin and Chalu, he wandered freely, identifying birds and animals, making field notes about what he saw and heard—always a terrible racket in the wild, and never silence, in fact, though in his stories he habitually depicted a land blanketed by silence. A Darwinian naturalist and an embryonic environmentalist, he witnessed the wanton destruction of the natural world by white men, and he provided glimpses of the ravaged Yukon landscape in stories like "Li Wan, the Fair." "The hills had been stripped of their trees, and their raw sides gored and perforated by great timber-slides and prospect holes," he wrote. He saw, too, "like a monstrous race of ants . . . an army of men — mud-covered, dirty, disheveled men . . . [who] toiled and sweated . . . men . . . digging, tearing, and scouring the face of nature." But in the next breath, he depicted the Yukon as a perfect place for colonization and a territory for capital to be invested and where laboring men might find employment, riches, and happiness. Thus the socialist London went hand in hand with the colonialist London.

HAMMERING IN THE DARK

When he returned home with $4.50 worth of gold in his pockets, he sat down immediately to write stories in which he made use of myth, symbol, and archetype. Of course, by the 1890s, readers were already attuned to myths and symbols, and so when London looked at literature, he hunted for hidden symbols and myths just under the surface of the narrative. When he wasn't reading or writing, he visited Mabel Maude; but after the Yukon, he could not pick up the pieces of their fragmented relationship. "We have no common ground," he told her. "The time is past when any John Halifax Gentleman ethics can go down with me." Dinah Mulock's *John Halifax, Gentleman* (1857), a novel about a poor orphan boy who works hard and becomes a success, had inspired him once upon a time, but no longer appealed. "If I were a woman I would prostitute myself to all men but that I would succeed," he added, as though to show how ungentlemanly he had become.

After the Yukon, he returned to socialism, even more enthusiastically than before, and wrote effusive essays about the global economic picture, the scramble for worldwide markets, and the imminent future of war and revolution, eschewing topics of local, Oakland interest. "Predatory capital wanders the world over, seeking where it may establish itself," he wrote in 1898, in "The Question of the Maximum," an essay that no editor would touch. One can understand why. He took on imperialism, describing how empires were built on colonies. Then, too, as though thinking aloud, he noted, "It is possible, considering the inertia of the masses, that the world might in time come to be dominated by a group of industrial oligarchies, or one great oligarchy." He added, "It is not probable." And yet, once the idea surfaced, he could not shake it, and so even as he advocated socialism, he feared that oligarchy and a capitalist dictatorship would inevitably precede it. Disaster loomed ahead, he cautioned. In an essay published at the start of 1900, entitled, ironically, "The Impossibility of War," he wrote incisively about the future of war, insisting that "economics and not force of arms" would decide who might win and who might lose a world war. "Behind all, ready and anxious to say the last word, looms the ominous figure of Revolution," he wrote, knowing that he had taken it upon himself to serve as a prophet for the century just then dawning. Cycles of war and peace had fueled the nineteenth century; from now on, war and revolution would propel the course of history.

As Jack London settled into his latest role as revolutionary oracle, he began an important friendship with Cloudesley Johns (1874–1948), a radical and a post-master in Harold, California. More adroitly than anyone else, Johns drew the often shy and reclusive Jack London out of his self-protective shell. Johns—Jack's first real fan—wrote effusively after reading one of London's short stories in the *Overland Monthly*. Their relationship gave London the opportunity to explore and express his convictions without censoring himself. His long and often inspired letters to Johns, all through 1899—that pivotal year in which he found his voice as a writer—provide a clear and comprehensive picture of his ideas about himself as evolving socialist and maturing fiction writer.

Publication in the *Overland Monthly*—and the acclaim that followed—provided a new sense of self-respect, self-confidence, and self-importance. In his letters to Johns, too, he developed a new sense of "self" with all the force and creativity he could muster. His best subject, he realized, might be the mysterious and enigmatic self that lurked just beneath the surface. "How I chatter—all about self," he wrote to Johns, as though shocked by the recognition, perhaps for the first time, of his preoccupation with self.

At home in Oakland, after living on the Yukon frontier, he found that nearly every-thing pent up and repressed for years gushed out of him relentlessly. "I have been writ-ing like a tiger all day," he exclaimed on September 13, 1898. All through that fall and winter, and all through the next year, he wrote ferociously at his typewriter like a jun-gle animal, "unlearning and learning anew," as he put it, and working long hours to learn what he most prized—"the art of omission." In the twelve months beginning in January 1899, he produced twenty-four artful short stories, including "In a Far County," "The God of His Fathers," and "An Odyssey of the North." The last appeared in the prestigious *Atlantic Monthly* and gave him a national reputation. He also churned out nine articles about politics, as well as dozens of poems—a few in French, in which he ventured into the realm of art for art's sake. He tried out, for size, the role of the decadent fin de siècle artist then in vogue, loath to let any role escape him.

In fiction, he turned increasingly to romance, not to the tradition of the realistic nineteenth-century English or European novel or to the naturalist school of writers, though he admired naturalists like the California-born Frank Norris (1870–1902). He favorably reviewed Norris's *The Octopus* (1901) because it captured the American West. As an escape artist liberated from the tyranny of fact, London wrote books in which readers might follow the mythological trails he carved out and, like him, escape from the real world of work, masters, and muck into the fabulous "Northland" of Indian warriors and maidens — Orientalism transported to the frozen spaces of ice and snow. Of course, in the anti-worlds he created, he meant readers to recognize the everyday worlds in which they existed. Absolute fidelity to the truth would only fetter men, he believed. The romantic imagination might free them, so what could be mattered as much to him as what was.

"The Alaskan gold hunter is proverbial, not so much for his unveracity, as for his inability to tell the precise truth," he explained in the essay "The Gold Hunters of the North." He added — with himself in mind — "in a country of exaggerations, he likewise is prone to hyperbolic descriptions of things actual." Inspired by the example of the Yukon storytellers, he exaggerated and embellished — and mastered the art of omission — and learned, too, to be freer about himself. When Ninetta Eames, his editor, invited him to the office of the *Overland Monthly,* she told him to bring his Yukon garb so he could pose for photos; he didn't hesitate, knowing that those images would sell him — especially in the East — as the real thing, and his books as the authentic article. Indeed, the black-and-white pictures made it appear that the author of "In a Far Country" lived in that "far country," not in a house in Oakland. Playing fast and loose with actuality didn't trouble him or Eames. She knew that London had prospected little in the Yukon, and had, in fact, spent most of his time reading books, listening to tall tales, and gathering information so he might write. But the magazine promoted London as an American author who has "put his own life into his books."

On a few occasions in the late 1890s, he ventured to reveal bits and pieces of himself to Mabel Maude Applegarth, who seemed to be everything he was not — British born, upper class, well mannered, and formally educated. "About the loneliest Christmas I ever faced — guess I'll write to you," he began a letter on Christmas Day, 1898. He also wrote to Applegarth, "My body and soul were starved as a child." But for the most part, he was reticent with her.

With Cloudesley Johns, he could be more himself — less guarded and less in need of rescuing. For one thing, he felt more comfortable with men. Women put him on the defensive and forced him to playact, though he enjoyed sparring with them. Had he been born in San Francisco in another age, he might have been bisexual. Although his main love interest was a woman, he admired the male body as much as if not more than the female body. Throughout his work he described the beauty of the male body, and many of his books, including *The Sea-Wolf* and *John Barleycorn,* are infused with homoeroticism. He loved the company of men—on ships, on the road, in clubs, and on teams—and he made several enduring male friendships, not only with Johns but also with Upton Sinclair and George Sterling. A part of him felt, as did Walt Whitman, that democracy derived from comradeship among men and that true brotherhood would generate real social equality.

"All my life I have sought an ideal chum," he told Johns, longingly. "From what I have learned of you, you approach as nearly as any I have met." London's letters seem unrehearsed, and he always insisted they were uninhibited and unplanned. "Haven't the slightest idea what I'm going to say when I sit down," he wrote, sounding like the Beat writer Jack Kerouac, who advocated spontaneous expression. "Just hammer it out as fast as I can," he told Johns. The hammer and hammering became two of his favorite images for writing, appropriately enough for an author who identified with workers and the working class—though hammering hardly suggests craftsmanship. "Just been hammering around in the dark till I knocked holes through here and there and caught glimpses of daylight," he told his editors at Houghton Mifflin. In fact, a large, powerful hammer in the hand of a muscular worker served as the emblem for the Socialist Labor Party. Like his fellow socialists, London celebrated the working-man with a hammer, much as Edwin Markham—one of London's favorite poets—celebrated the farmer with a hoe in "The Man with the Hoe" (1898).

To Johns, he hammered out tantalizing details about his own private life that he never revealed to another human being. He had "several scars," he said, not bothering to locate or describe them. As a child, he had a "Negress nurse," he wrote, but here, too, he declined to elaborate. When Johns wrote to ask if "Jack London" was his real name, not a pseudonym, as he suspected, Jack wrote back emphatically, "My name is Jack London." Ninetta Eames had wondered about his name, too, when the unknown writer's manuscripts came across the transom at the *Overland Monthly.* When Johns asked him to send a photo, he declined, preferring to remain more mysterious than a black-and-white snapshot might allow, but he went on to paint a self-portrait with words. "Clean face makes my age enigmatical," he wrote. His complexion was "bronzed," and he might not be taken for a white man, either, he implied. (Elam Harnish, the semi-autobiographical hero of the novel *Burning Daylight* [1910], has a bronzed complexion and looks like an Indian.) London didn't mind white men who had Indian features, if they didn't behave like "savage" Indians.

About his sexuality, he also sounded an enigmatic note. On one occasion, he wrote, he traveled with a group of friends on horseback from Fresno to Yosemite "clad in almost tropical nudity." In the heat of summer, he carried a woman's fan and silk parasol, and citizens turned out to scrutinize him and his exotic fellow travelers. "Some of my party who lagged behind, heard guesses hazarded as to whether I was male or female," Jack told Johns, delighted by his enigmatic appearance. Whatever he did, however peculiar, his friends accepted him. "It's only Jack," they would say, much to his delight. Still, despite his own libertine ways, his ideas about the roles of men and women were largely conventional. "The female is the passive, the male the active factor in the carrying on of the function of reproduction," he wrote. Marriage did not strike his fancy, he said, nor did monogamy. "I must have been created for some polygamous country," he added. He had close women friends and comrades in the socialist movement, including Emma Goldman and Charlotte Perkins Gilman (1860–1935), author of "The Yellow Wallpaper" and *Herland,* but it took him years before he finally accepted the idea of women's suffrage—and then only because the vote for women would bring about the much-needed prohibition of alcohol. As for religion, he told Johns that he was an agnostic; he had rejected the atheism he once espoused, perhaps because agnosticism fit the image of himself that he wanted to promulgate—an enigmatic individual.

In many of his letters, he described himself as a misfit and a rebel. Again and again, he referred to his "wild young days" when he "made more money in one week than I do in a year now"—through illegal means. He looked back with nostalgia at his adventures as a youth. "How educating my roving has been," he wrote. He was not to be pigeonholed, he insisted, and he had a wide array of identities to choose from. "To satisfy my various sides," he told Johns, "I should be possessed of at least a dozen astral selves." Only after he had explored all those sides would he know his "composite self."

To Johns, he also said that he was a "radical" and that he would never drift back "into the conservative ways of thinking." (On another occasion, he noted, "Once a Socialist, always a Socialist." There were few, if any, backsliders in the movement, he claimed.) But he wanted Johns, his ideal chum, to know that he did not fit the stereotype of the "fanatical" radical. He was "normal and fallible," he insisted. He had evolved gradually as a socialist, not in a sudden conversion, and he believed that social change would also take place gradually, and through "ballots not bullets." Violent revolution had failed in the past, he observed, and violent revolutionaries, like the men and women—fanatics, in his view—who created the Paris Commune of 1871, were dead and buried, along with their extreme tactics. Socialism would have to be achieved through the slow, often painstaking process of electoral politics.

Much to Johns's surprise, London noted that socialism was "not an ideal system." It would not accomplish miracles, bring about paradise, or usher in the "regeneration of mankind in a day," he stated. In a socialist society, he asserted, social inequalities would remain, and bold leaders and dynamic leadership would be needed, too. "True individualism," he explained, was impossible under capitalism, but it might well become a reality in a socialist society.

Perhaps most of all, London shocked Johns when he noted that the "first motor principle of the movement is selfishness, pure downright selfishness." He also wrote, "I do not believe in the universal brotherhood of man." Further, "I believe that my race is the salt of the earth." On the subject of wealth and possessions, he wrote, "It's money I want, or rather the things money will buy; and I never could possibly have too much." Here was an odd socialist indeed, who aspired to wealth and who disliked anyone who didn't belong to the white race. "The negro race, the mongrel races, the slavish races, the unprogressive races, are of bad blood. That is, of blood which is not qualified to permit them to successfully survive the selection by which the fittest survive," he insisted. "The black has stopped, just as the monkey has stopped." He would go on to put these very same, and similar, ideas into the mouths of his fictional characters—like Frone Weise in his first novel, *A Daughter of the Snows* (1902), who sings the praises of the white race. Near the end of his life, he would also write the novel *The Mutiny of the Elsinor* (1913), in which the white ruling-class hero and heroine suppress a rebellion by the polyglot sailors. The narrator defends the British Empire and extols the brutal repression of insurrection by colonial subjects. When one race bred with another, the whole world edged toward degeneration, London asserted. South America, he noted, was composed of inferior "bastard races."

London became Johns's mentor, advising him about the craft of fiction: plot, character development, and the expression of political ideas in literature. As a literary critic, London offered astute comments about the relationships between writers and the societies in which they were nurtured. Following in the footsteps of Marx, he forged a kind of Marxist literary criticism, tracing the relationships between economics and culture and arguing that the work of writers like Sir Walter Scott (1771–1832), Charles Dickens (1812–1870), and Rudyard Kipling (1865–1936) reflected the class values of their times. "As Scott sang the swan song of chivalry and Dickens the burger-fear of the rising merchant class, so Kipling, as no one else, has sung the hymn of the dominant bourgeoisie," he would write in "These Bones Will Rise Again" (1903). The author ought not to preach to readers, London told Johns. Advocating ideas would be appropriate in an essay or lecture, but not in a novel. Of course, he did not heed his own advice. In "The Son of the Wolf," for example, he ridiculed "the barbaric mind," though he also praised "the barbarians"—meaning the Indians—for their "instinctive poetry-love." Civilization killed a certain kind of creativity, he believed, but he had no intention of returning to a primitive past, and he even made fun of white men and women who collected Indian artifacts and romanticized Indians. In "The God of His Fathers"—aiming to be the Kipling of the Yukon—he eulogized the sons of empire who "died under the cold fire of the aurora, as did his brothers in burning sands and reeking jungles."

ROMANTIC REVOLUTIONARY

London the romantic lover and London the romantic revolutionary went hand in hand, especially in the years 1900 to 1906, when he was intimately connected with Anna Strunsky. London met Anna, the beautiful Russian-born Jewish socialist, in San Francisco in the winter of 1899 at a lecture on the Paris Commune given by his friend Austin Lewis (1865–1944), a socialist and a lawyer who wrote about the working class. London sent Strunsky a story he'd written about a Jew named Jaky, and Strunsky—an avid reader and a perceptive critic of literature—found London's story clichéd and its main character a stereotype. "Not all Jews haggle and bargain," she pointed out, and though London offered a mea culpa, he also insisted that a real Jaky did exist. He wasn't anti-Semitic, London explained to Strunsky; he had even helped Jaky and his wife learn English.

London's relationship with Strunsky—which lasted for about six years—paralleled, not coincidentally, his most passionate engagement with socialism. Indeed, he enacted a personal sexual revolution, even as he took part in a political revolution—a not uncommon pattern of behavior in radical circles, as Friedrich Engels (Marx's comrade and collaborator, 1820–1895) and others have observed. Many of London's biographers, including his wife Charmian and his daughter Joan, neglected the pivotal personal and political connections between Jack and Anna. Charmian didn't care to admit that independent, radical women like Strunsky played a vital part in her husband's life. As for Joan London, an examination of her father's relationship with Strunsky would have forced her to acknowledge the depth and sincerity of his socialism, and that she would not do. From her point of view, her father's politics were largely incoherent, if not proto-fascist. Had he lived into the 1920s, he might have become a supporter of the Italian dictator Benito Mussolini, she suggested.

Orwell thought that he might have turned into a Nazi or a Communist had he lived another decade. Given London's racist ideas, especially his belief in the superiority of white people and the cause of "the Great White Man," their ideas are not entirely far-fetched. Other biographers have also neglected London's ties to Strunsky, ignoring the ways in which the personal and the political were entwined.

Whether Anna and Jack were sexual partners or not isn't clear, though they were clearly in love with each other and physically affectionate. Of course, London was married for most of the time he and Anna were in love. Marriage was no impediment to his affairs with single women — both casual acquaintances and friends. Then, too, at least on one occasion he proposed to Strunsky, unfazed by the fact that he was already married to Bessie. "Marry me," he exclaimed, like a character in one of his own romantic novels. "Let us run away to New Zealand or Australia." Anna replied, no less romantically, "Yes, darling, with all my heart," though she quickly withdrew her acceptance. She adored Jack, but life as his wife would not bring her happiness, she knew, and Jack sulked, fumed, and resented her for refusing his hand.

More than any other woman he knew, Anna embodied "plasticity" — that ability to morph and not break; and, more than any other woman, she met him as his equal. She wrote poems for and about him, though she also served as his muse and a model for his women characters. Unlike Anna, Charmian adapted her life to his, accepted his sexual affairs with other women, and allowed herself to be his everything. She was mother, wife, secretary, muse, playmate — a situation that led to what she called "his almost childlike dependence upon me." Inevitably, she experienced a loss of identity, as she herself recognized, that left her feeling "like one enchanted, my faculties paralyzed."

A deeply committed socialist, Strunsky came from that wing of the movement about which London knew the least, and felt the most reticent, and even suspicious: the immigrant intellectual wing, largely Jewish and based in and around New York. "Ghetto socialists" he called them dismissively, though he never leveled that accusation directly against Strunsky. Together, he and she came to represent, as they both recognized, the political and cultural polarities of the socialist cause in the United States at the dawn of the twentieth century.

Their paths would probably not have crossed had it not been for the socialist movement. Indeed, the movement brought them together as it brought together rich and poor, native born and immigrants, workers and intellectuals, Jews and Gentiles, inculcating an appreciation of different races, cultures, and religions. Had it not been for socialism, and especially for Anna Strunsky, it seems likely that London would have been unable, as he occasionally did, to rise above his racial prejudices. He probably never would have embraced, as he did in 1904 and 1905, working men and women in Puerto Rico, Japan, Italy, and France as his equals. In the socialist movement, the ethnic barriers he had built up during his time in the Yukon broke down somewhat. London even came to celebrate ethnic diversity—especially in his 1905 lecture "Revolution," which marked the peak of his internationalism. Socialists preached "that passionate gospel, the Brotherhood of Man," he wrote, contradicting his own early view.

Though he was a native-born American and a celebrity, and Strunsky was an immigrant and a newcomer to the States, she often expressed herself with more self-confidence than he. English was his first language, while it was her second, after Russian, but at times she could be more at ease in English than he, and she often seemed more at home in her self than he in his self. Of the two, he seemed more fragile and vulnerable. "I am a sentient creature," he told her plaintively. "For one of my mould I realize how easily I may go to pieces." Indeed, he went to pieces repeatedly, while she held together. She married a radical British millionaire, William English Walling (1877–1936), and outlived Jack by more than half a century. Strunsky brought out the best and the worst in Jack, and in his relationship with her, he revealed even more about himself than he revealed to Johns. With no other woman was he less boyish, and more of an adult male—though he retained much of his boyish charm. Strunsky seemed to be his soul mate, and he didn't mind telling her about his immature infatuation—his "puppy love" for Mabel Maude.

At the start of their relationship, he adored her from afar, depicting himself as a supplicant, as though kneeling at her altar. "I came to you like a parched soul out of the wilderness," he wrote. "The highest and the best had been stamped out of me," he added. Anna didn't rush to heal him, though she certainly understood his fragility and pain. Unlike Jack, she came from a close-knit, loving family. Her parents supported her financially and emotionally, encouraging her to attend Stanford, read books, and become a socialist—and to be the equal of any man or woman in their lively home in San Francisco, a haven for radicals like Emma Goldman. It's no wonder that London thrived in Anna's warmth and enjoyed the company of her Russian-Jewish, socialist parents—Elias and Anna Hurowich Strunsky—and her brother Max, a doctor. The Strunsky family embraced him and enlarged his cultural and political horizons.

Jack opened himself up to Anna. He confided his ideas for stories and revealed the innermost workings of his imagination. "I am reading to write a novel to be called *The Flight of the Duchess!*" he told her. "Similar motive to Robert Browning's." Too bad he never wrote that novel, but dozens of his ideas for fiction never got off the ground. He advised Anna about publishing, educating her about the book industry, though, oddly enough, she did as much to advance his career as he did to advance hers. She reviewed glowingly—for the most part—his second book, *The God of His Fathers* (1901). A reviewer from the Smithsonian insisted insightfully that London's Indian characters were mostly white men with red faces; Strunsky didn't find flaws in London's depiction of Indians, but focused instead on his one-dimensional women characters, who seemed to her to be "built up as types rather than individuals."

Indeed, the sisters, mothers, and daughters in his fiction were usually flat characters, in part because he held conventional notions about love, marriage, sex, and the role of women. Perhaps only in *The Valley of the Moon* did he create a convincing female character—the feisty, working-class Saxon Brown, who finds "freedom from the suffocating slavery of the ironing board." Criticizing the great Jack London didn't daunt Anna, while he sometimes shied away from debate with her, afraid of hurting her feelings. Then, in a sudden reversal, he would lash out. "You will never get beyond the man-and-woman mystery," he snarled. But he also whimpered and wallowed in self-pity about his plebian origins, complaining that the poverty of his youth had destroyed his soulfulness. "I was sown on arid soil, gave vague promise of budding," he wrote. "But was crushed by the harshness of things." Over and over again, he could not escape that sense of being crushed, beaten down, and, though he never admitted that he had been beaten as a child, it's hard to imagine that he wasn't. Realistic depictions of physical beatings occur throughout his work.

Earle Labor, perhaps the most knowledgeable of London scholars, has argued that Jack found true love with Charmian Kittredge and an abiding faith in humanity in the cause of socialism. Marriage and socialism saved him from the "pessimistic disillusionment" he had known, Labor insists. But to make that case, he ignores much of the dark side of Jack London, especially in the last decade of his life, including the evidence offered by his own novels, memoirs, and letters. Oddly enough, in *The Portable Jack London,* which Labor edited, he included only one letter to Anna Strunsky—from 1899—though their correspondence was as essential for London's development as an artist and as a radical as any other in his entire life. When he sank into despair and depression, he did not hesitate to tell her. "I have been suffering from the blues," he wrote. He also told her when he felt bitter about the cause and cynical about the prospects for popular revolution. "I grow sometimes almost to hate the mass, to sneer at dreams of reform," he wrote. He added, "To be superior to the mass is to be the slave of the mass. The mass knows no slavery; it is the task master." When she objected to his going to witness the state's execution of a murderer at San Quentin, he responded passionately, "If you dare accept the gaslight on the corner then you must accept the murders the Law commits, for you are part of that Law." When he smoked "hashessh" with his friends George Sterling and Herman Whitaker—an activity that did not strike him as incompatible with radicalism—he explained that it was "a matter of *scientific* investigation." Immediately after one of his experiments with hashish—which he called the "simplest and most enticing of maidens"—he noted, "It is glorious here, more like a poppy dream than real living." To Anna, he disclosed the traits about himself that he liked the least. "There are poseurs," he wrote. "I am the most successful of them all." He also urged her to consider, and perhaps accept, ideas that she found especially abhorrent. "The paradox of social existence, to be truthful, we lie, to live true, we live untruthfully," he noted, perhaps thinking of his own lies.

Still, he was honest enough to tell her that he might use her as a character in his fiction. "I may some time steal you or certain portions of you for exploitation between covers, unless you hasten to get yourself copyrighted," he wrote, obviously enjoying the double entendres. When he felt that his work failed to meet his own standards, she was the first to know. *The People of the Abyss,* he noted, was "not constructed as a book should be constructed, but as a series of letters are written—without regard to form."

Jack's letters reach out to Anna. "I should like some time to be with you so long as to be sated; then I would not be hungry when you went away," he wrote. He envisioned a future that included her—"We shall live together, dear," he would say—but he also described a chasm between them. "You epitomize your race, as I epitomize mine," he wrote, reverting to his notions of racial determinism. He went on to enumerate all the ways they were different. "You are subjective, in the last analysis," he said. "I am objective. You toy with phantasmagoria; I grasp the living facts. You pursue mirages, insubstantialities, subtleties that are vain & worthless; I seize upon realities and hammer blindly to result." Almost all the qualities he assigned to her, he might have found in himself—had he looked closely.

The cause that brought them together as lovers and comrades also drove them apart, and they came to feud about money—about who owed whom and how much. When revolution broke out in Russia in 1905, Anna joined her Russian comrades and reported on it firsthand for American readers. Jack told her that he had other plans. He was to build a yacht—the *Snark,* named after Lewis Carroll's mythological beast—and sail around the world like an adventurous traveler. "Wish me luck," he wrote provocatively.

Then, too, soon after their rupture over money, he wrote *The Iron Heel,* his imperfect but haunting dystopian novel about the advent of a dictatorship in America and the brutal repression of radicals—as though to tell Anna and other buoyant, optimistic socialists like her that he no longer shared their faith and hope about the revolution. *The Iron Heel* reads, in part, like a farewell letter to Anna. But perhaps London also wrote the novel for himself: to wake himself up from his own mirages and phantasmagorias and remind himself that his beloved revolution remained centuries away. The masses, he made clear in *The Iron Heel,* could hardly be counted upon to enter the fray and lend their strength to the cause of socialism. He had promised—or was it a warning?—that he would "steal" Anna "for exploitation between covers," and he made good on his word, using her in large measure as the model for Avis, *The Iron Heel*'s romantic narrator, who describes the struggles between the oligarchy and the revolutionaries and the role of the abysmal masses as unthinking brutes, manipulated by the powers-that-be.

Jack's first wife, Bessie May Maddern, was not unaware of his relationship with Strunsky. In her own home, Bessie saw Jack reading Anna's letters to him and writing to Anna. Bessie also saw Jack and Anna talking intimately at Socialist Party events, picnics, and dinners. She even watched as Anna sat on Jack's lap, his arms around her, the two of them laughing amorously. When she filed for divorce, she named Anna as "the other woman"—though Anna was not, of course, the only other woman in his life. Charmian Kittredge was attractive to him because she was literary and free-spirited—a fellow orphan who was prepared to engage in amorous subterfuge. He also had an affair with the San Francisco drama and music critic Blanche Partington. For several years, it wasn't clear to anyone, including London, which woman, if any, he favored, though for a time it seemed to be Anna. "I was tangled up with Anna Strunsky," he would write in hindsight, as honest a comment as he could bring himself to make.

Naturally, newspapers reveled in the story of his divorce and ran banner headlines proclaiming, in 1905, "Jack London Sued by Wife," along with accounts of his relationship with Strunsky. By then he had achieved success with *The Call of the Wild* and *The Sea-Wolf.* He had covered the Russian-Japanese War for the *San Francisco Examiner* and published *The People of the Abyss,* his account of brutal poverty in London, England. He was one of the highest paid and perhaps the most famous of writers in America, as well as a socialist Don Juan—the first radical American author to achieve that dubious distinction. News of London's marital infidelity was bound to sell newspapers, and so, like William Henry Chaney before him, he appeared in lurid stories in the press. Headlines proclaimed, "Young Journalist Is Accused of Extreme Cruelty in Action for Legal Separation: Woman Collaborator Figures in Trouble:

Domestic Infelicity Dates Back to Time When Miss Strunsky Assisted in Writing the 'Kempton-Wace Letters.'"

Jack and Anna collaborated—London's one and only literary collaboration—on an epistolary novel on the theme of love entitled *The Kempton-Wace Letters* (1903), which was published anonymously in the first edition and with their names in the second edition. Collaborating on a novel about love provided a perfect cover for a romantic relationship; working together on their literary project, they might cuddle, kiss, and embrace. For the book, Strunsky assumed the persona of the romantic Dane Kempton, while London played the part of the rationalist Professor Herbert Wace. In the pages of fiction, they engaged in the kind of flirtation and repartee they enjoyed in real life. In the novel, Wace dismisses Kempton as a dreamer, much as Jack would dismiss Anna as unrealistic; Kempton fires back, ridiculing Wace as a Philistine. In their correspondence, they discuss their favorite romantic writers: Sappho, Schopenhauer, Whitman, and Elizabeth Barrett Browning. "It is always more important to love than to be loved," Kempton insists, while Wace boasts that he is "not in love" and "is not blinded by love madness." Jack London was madly in love with Anna, even as he wrote those lines. "Take me this way," he wrote to her, in real life, not behind the mask of his character, Professor Wace. He added, "A stray guest, a bird of passage, splashing with salt-rimed wings through a brief moment of your life—a rude and blundering bird, used to large airs and great spaces, unaccustomed to the amenities of confined existence." What woman could have resisted love letters from a man as wildly romantic and as inspired as he?

CAPTIVE COMRADE

London's socialism—like every other movement, cause, and philosophy that he embraced—never stood still. Moreover, he could be a socialist without surrendering any of the dozen different astral selves that he pursued—or so he thought. His fame and wealth went hand in hand with the cause, and he recognized no inconsistency. As a radical, he went through a series of metamorphoses: from moderate to extremist; from law-abiding Socialist Party candidate for mayor of Oakland to revolutionary firebrand who at one point advocated political assassination and, in 1905, even terrorism. "We do back up the assassinations by our comrades in Russia," he wrote. "They are not disciples of Tolstoy, nor are we. We are revolutionists." Socialism taught him that the United States was a deeply divided class society with fierce social and political antagonisms that could not be peacefully resolved—not a widely held belief at that time. At the start of the twentieth century, he was certain that class war would intensify, especially in light of the closing of the frontier and the rise of American corporations. Both of those historical changes would lead, he argued, to the loss of economic and political freedom and bring smoldering class war into the open, to the streets.

All through 1905 and again at the start of 1906, he traveled across the country with his Korean valet, lecturing on socialism, from Berkeley to Harvard and Yale, taking time out, only briefly, to go to Jamaica and Cuba on a honeymoon with Charmian. "The socialist movement is limited only by the limits of the planet," he told college students everywhere. As though to demonstrate his point, he managed to transcend his own racism and sexism, writing eloquently of women factory workers and children who toiled in textile mills, and insisting that urban American men and women were more destitute than men and women in prehistoric times. "No caveman ever starved as chronically as they starve, ever slept as vilely as they sleep, ever festered with rottenness and disease as they fester, nor ever toiled as hard and for as long hours as they toil," he wrote.

After a decade of speaking in public, he had become a seasoned orator; he knew how to inform, entertain, and appeal to the heart, as well as the head. Though he spoke in crowded halls, before audiences that he did not know, he made his talks personal and provided a sense of intimacy, forging communities of radicals wherever he went. At the podium, he became inspired and he found himself, to his delight, uttering words he had not expected to say.

"I received a letter the other day," he began the talk entitled "Revolution," which would be published as an essay in *Revolution and Other Essays* in 1910. He went on to describe an emotionally charged letter from a man in Arizona that began "Dear Comrade" and that ended "Yours for the Revolution"—salutations and farewells that he helped to popularize and that became, with his encouragement, popular in the movement. He urged socialists to think of themselves as members of a family and a tribe and to regard revolution as a living, breathing organism they might shape, nurture, and nourish. He seemed, at times, to think of revolution itself as an orphaned child, abandoned at birth by history, that he could adopt and lead into maturity—a child who, in turn, would care for him and for all humanity.

London ended his college talk, after two hours, defiantly, with the words "The revolution is here, now. Stop it who can." At Harvard, the students gave him a standing ovation and invited him to a party, while Mary Harris Jones (1830–1930), the labor organizer better known as "Mother Jones," climbed the stage and kissed him on both cheeks. In 1905 and 1906, he played the leading role in the drama of American radicalism, with Emma Goldman and Eugene Victor Debs playing supporting roles. At Yale, the college he regarded as the quintessential bastion of conservatism, London urged the students to undertake the "serious study of socialism," predicting that "every young man who will study socialism will become a convert to its doctrine." At that moment, he had no doubts. Soon after his thirtieth birthday, in January 1906, he served as the primary icon of the cause; posters for his Yale speaking engagement depicted him in a bright red sweater, which came to be part of the unmistakable London trademark. When he spoke from the podium, audience members waved small red flags as a sign of solidarity. Even the "capitalist press," as he called it, helped to further his popularity, though the *New York Times* insisted that London the poet had sacrificed himself to the cause, and become, unfortunately, a propagandist.

At thirty, he was still a committed young socialist—and he was eloquent, too. Both a poet and a propagandist, he articulated the hopes and dreams of his generation. In his society, unions would have the right to organize and strike for higher pay and better working conditions. Men and women would only work an eight-hour day. Children would not have to toil, as he had toiled as a child, in order to ensure the survival of their families. Socialism also meant equality of opportunity; he counted on socialists to create a society of equals, since, he argued, the Republicans and the Democrats were both the parties of business—big business and little business—and would never serve the working classes. All over the country, and especially on college campuses, he enjoyed planting the seeds of subversion among the elite. He enjoyed infiltrating Republican strongholds, and he succeeded beyond his dreams. The *New Haven Register* recognized, soon after his Yale speech, that he played a "useful public service" by challenging conventional opinions and by advocating heretical ideas. As he knew, heretical ideas often became orthodox ideas, and orthodox ideas discomforted him greatly. Like all genuine revolutionaries, he wrestled with the problem of how not to grow old and become conservative; perhaps he solved the problem by deciding he simply would not grow old. But he felt that it was important to leave a legacy as a radical.

In 1905, he and his friend and comrade Upton Sinclair created the Intercollegiate Socialist Society (ISS), the predecessor of Students for a Democratic Society (SDS)—the militant 1960s organizations of undergraduates that fomented cultural revolution and confrontation on college campuses. London served as the president of the ISS, and Sinclair, who had moved toward socialism in large part because of

London's influence, served as vice president. They were an odd revolutionary couple, indeed. London drank, smoked, caroused, and bombarded Sinclair with tales of his amorous adventures, including his seductions of the daughters of Oakland's bourgeoisie in the 1890s. Sinclair wouldn't touch alcohol or hold a cigarette, and about sex he had ideas that London thought were positively medieval; Jack called him a "mollycoddle." Sinclair signed copies of his books "The Author" until Jack taught him the arts of self-promotion, advertising, and public relations, which he believed were as important as knowing how to organize a strike, ride a horse, or box. Jack helped Sinclair immensely to promote his muckraking novel *The Jungle* (1906), providing a blurb in which he predicted the novel would awaken Americans to the injustice of "wage slavery" much as Harriet Beecher Stowe's *Uncle Tom's Cabin* had awakened Americans to the inhumanity of chattel slavery in the 1850s. For a moment, he seemed to understand that African Americans, who had toiled under the plantation system, were kin to workers exploited under capitalism, and that enslavement, of any race or any class, was immoral.

In 1905, when the czar's army crushed the 1905 revolution in Russia and socialist candidates failed to win elections in America, he became disillusioned, and the depression that lurked just beneath the surface reasserted itself. When he talked about socialism with millionaires, he discovered how terrified they were of popular upheaval and the thought that their own private property might be confiscated. He learned how adamantly they opposed socialism and how determined they were to fight it root and branch. He could see that it would not be easy to create a socialist society—that it would cost countless human lives and take far longer to accomplish than he had imagined—and he knew he could not wait that long.

In 1905, the same year he announced that the revolution would "confiscate all the possessions of the capitalist class," he bought 129 acres of prime real estate in Glen Ellen, California. For years, he had felt claustrophobic in Oakland, and he told friends that he would sooner slit his own throat than to live and work there forever. No writers lived in Glen Ellen, and he liked the solitude of the country; but he also invited the world to visit him. The signs on his front and his back door were as enigmatic as anything else about him, and visitors must have wondered whether he genuinely wanted their company or not. "No admittance except on business!" and "Positively No Transactions Here," the front door signs read, and on the back door: "No one admitted without knocking" and "Do not knock."

He accumulated material possessions as quickly as he could, and on his estate, Beauty Ranch, he lived a life of "conspicuous consumption"—a phrase he had read about in Thorstein Veblen's *The Theory of the Leisure Class* (1899) — replete with house servants and field-workers on lease from San Quentin. If he had wanted evidence of the elasticity and resilience of capitalism, he had only to examine himself and to recognize his own rise from poverty to wealth, as he evolved from abject toiler to avid consumer, buying up all the commodities he wanted. As Anna Strunsky and others pointed out, he wanted to "beat the capitalists at their own game" — and that, apparently, meant becoming a capitalist. In Anna's view, he was a kind of Robin Hood who took from the wealthy and gave to the poor. He invited hobos, ex-convicts, and members of the Industrial Workers of the World (IWW), the radical organization that he admired and defended, to come and live the bourgeois lifestyle with him in Sonoma County, drink martinis, and eat half-cooked duck. In an early attempt at green architecture, he set about constructing Wolf House — a mansion fit for a world-famous writer or a business tycoon — from the rock, the stone, and the redwoods on his own property.

Indeed, increasingly after 1906, the revolution he had in mind was green, not red, and long before the popular environmental slogan "Think Globally, Act Locally" took hold, London was putting it into practice at Beauty Ranch. "I see my farm in terms of the world," he asserted, "and I see the world in terms of my farm." Much of his best work in the last decade of his life — including *Burning Daylight* and *The Valley of the Moon* — depicts characters like himself who are disillusioned with urban life and who retreat to the country to start anew, close to nature. The revolution, he noted bitterly, had betrayed him; he had given it everything, and now no one appreciated him. He would show them; he would turn his back on the cause, tend his own garden, and create a socialist paradise on private property for the whole world to see. Increasingly, too, he defined himself as a Californian: a man who lived in wide open spaces away from urban centers, a continent away from New York, the city he detested. If the revolution were to erupt, he might come down from his mountain to join it, he allowed.

"I love socialism," he wrote in 1912, the year before *The Valley of the Moon* appeared in print, but "there is the other passion in me. The sky, the sea, the hills, wilds — I just love them and must have them." He embraced the wild outdoors, rode his horse, Washoe Ban, and pushed aside socialism and the working class. In his books, especially *Martin Eden,* he left political topics behind. In his last years, he seemed to retreat to that brand of individualism he had adopted before he joined the cause. He turned, once again, to a simplistic version of Nietzsche and the Nietzschean superman.

In *The Cruise of the Snark* (1911), an account of his disastrous voyage across the Pacific in a sailboat that nearly cost him, and lost him, his whole fortune to build, he dispatched an unambiguous message about radicalism. He proclaimed, "The ultimate word is I like"—counting *I* and *like* as one word. He continued, "It is I like that makes the drunkard drink and the martyr wear a hair shirt; that makes one man a reveler and another man an anchorite; that makes one man pursue fame, another gold, another love, and another God." Of course, London played all those parts: drunkard, martyr, reveler, anchorite, and seeker after gold, God, fame, love, and socialism—though socialism disappeared from the list he offered in *The Cruise of the Snark.*

In 1911, his bitterness and resentment intensified. Publishers and editors, he claimed, had put his name on a "blacklist" of the kind that factory owners used for union organizers and troublemakers—to keep them from employment. "I have been boycotted and blacklisted by stupid capitalists on account of my socialism," he insisted. "I have paid through the nose for my socialism to the tune of hundreds of thousands of dollars." But in 1911, he published four books, in 1912 three more, and in 1913, two books—hardly evidence of a vast literary conspiracy against him. He seems to have come closer to the truth about his inability to earn top dollar when he told his first wife, Bessie, that his writing had "gone out of vogue" and that he had experienced a "natural and inevitable deterioration as a writer."

His astral selves once promised a life of adventure; now they pulled him in a dozen different directions, more aimlessly than ever before. His relationships were difficult almost everywhere he turned. In Oakland, his daughter Joan—a young writer— admired her English teacher more than her father. In Hollywood, two producers— "the meanest men I ever met in my life," he wrote—fought him in court for the movie rights to his stories. In New York, Roland Phillips, one of his editors, complained that his stories had "too much meat" and needed to have much more love interest to satisfy "half a million lady readers." In the Santa Cruz mountains and elsewhere, men took his name and identity, claiming to be Jack London. And while the idea of having a "double" intrigued him, it also unnerved him, especially when the imposters signed and cashed checks with his name. It seems ironical and yet inevitable that London would inspire a real-life double. After all, he saw double nearly everywhere he looked, imagining the world as a series of dichotomies between the wild and the tame, the genuine and the fake, the rich and the poor, the proletariat and the bourgeoisie, the optimist and the pessimist, the urbanite and the country dweller, the materialist and the spiritualist, the Anglo-Saxon and the "half-breed."

As doubles proliferated, he found himself taunted almost everywhere he turned: his legitimacy as a writer was challenged, and his integrity as a socialist was questioned. In Ohio, a nineteen-year-old boy who took the pen name "Le Dare" wrote to him, "Your life has struck the groove. It runs smoothly. It needs to get out. It takes fire and vim to make the effort. Yours is burned out."

London wrote back, "You are right. I am all in . . . The last adventure remains to me—the making of my will." All his life he had been obsessed with fires, especially with starting them, and he had written brilliantly about making fires in stories and novels. Oddly enough, he even promised to set fire to Wolf House. "It will be a usable house and a beautiful house . . . It will be a happy house—or else I'll burn it down," he wrote. In 1913, Wolf House burned to the ground. London collected the insurance and went on writing, almost as if nothing had happened, though Charmian insisted that he was never the same man again, and that the fire had, in fact, burned him up, from the inside out.

Three years later, he resigned from the Socialist Party because, he insisted, it was too conservative for him. He admired the Industrial Workers of the World and their leaders, including the flamboyant William ("Big Bill") Haywood (1869–1928). Like the IWW, he believed in "direct action and in syndicalism," though he was incapable of taking any direct action of any kind. His ultra-leftism seemed an empty gesture, and his anti-Semitism flared up again as he complained once more about "ghetto socialists." When a Jewish reader complained about what he perceived as London's negative portraits of Jews, Jack replied that he could make his characters whatever nationality or ethnicity he wanted.

Socialism had once worked miracles for London. For nearly two decades, it provided a sense of home, hope, family, and connectedness to the world. It gave him friends, comrades, readers, and a reason to write. But it could not, once and for all, rid him of "the blues," "the long sickness," and his "morbid anxiety." Socialism did not and could not heal his deepest emotional wounds, and, sooner or later, it seems, he had to abandon it—and then blame it for abandoning him. Without socialism he became an orphan again. Of course, he continued to write until he died—he was a workaholic as well as an alcoholic—but his writing does not seem to have eased the agony of his last years. In her two-volume study of her husband, Charmian depicted a dark, tormented modern marriage; without her at his side, he often acted as though he were a little lost child.

After his death, his body was cremated, and his ashes were buried at his beloved Beauty Ranch, befitting a man who had written, "I would rather be ashes than dust! I would rather that my spark should burn in a brilliant blaze than it should be stifled by dry rot." Upton Sinclair, by that time a famous author, spoke at his funeral. Three other close friends also spoke: George Sterling, the bohemian poet; Frank Strawn-

Hamilton, the hobo philosopher who introduced London to Nietzsche in the 1890s; and James Hopper, who first met him during his one semester at the University of California, Berkeley, when they attended football games and cheered their team.

No one at the funeral, or in any single obituary, had the last word on London's life, death, and work, though Anna Strunsky, perhaps, came the closest of anyone in her 1917 obituary for *The Masses,* which depicted their extraordinary time together, as lovers and fellow socialists. Certainly no one—not Charmian, not Joan London, who wrote what she termed an "unconventional biography" of her father—portrayed him as compassionately and honestly as Strunsky. "Sometimes a vertigo seized him," she wrote. He literally had a fear of falling into the abyss—a fear that no one else seemed to have noticed or described. "He had never had a childhood," Anna wrote, and he "was obsessed by suicidal thoughts." She said "he was a Revolutionist," and then, in the next breath, she discussed his belief in the "inferiority of certain races" and the "biological inferiority of women to man." Strunsky reminded readers that he "came out of the abyss" with all "the strength and the virtue of its terrible and criminal vices" and that he was imbued with "youth, adventure, romance." She understood, perhaps far better than anyone else with whom he was intimate, that although he was a socialist, he was a child of capitalist society, and he remained, in many ways, a prisoner of that same society from which he wanted humanity to escape.

That contradiction, of course, was not unique to Jack London. Socialists have always been the progeny of bourgeois society. They have always struggled to create a near-perfect world that no one, neither capitalist nor socialist, has ever seen. Still, London embodied, in a grand and magnificent way, the contradictions inherent in the socialist ideal, and, in a sense, those contradictions, not his addictions to alcohol and work, killed him, as Upton Sinclair observed when he noted that American society doomed Jack London to an early death. In Anna's obituary about Jack, it wasn't an idea that she wanted to impart to readers, but rather an image and a feeling about him as fundamentally a lover of nature. Jack London—her precious Jack London—had finally found the peace that had eluded him all his life, she suggested. The warrior, the revolutionary, and the "somnambulist," as he called himself, could now sleep the sleep of the ages. Jack London had come to rest, at last, and, in death, he had surely found his final astral self. "I see him on a May morning leaning from the balustrade of a veranda sweet with honeysuckle, to watch two humming birds of beauty," Strunsky wrote. "He was a captive of beauty—the beauty of bird and Bower, of sea and sky and the icy vastness of the Arctic world."

PART I

BOY SOCIALIST

1895 – 1899

Pessimism, Optimism and Patriotism

First published in and reprinted from the Oakland High School *Aegis*, March 1, 1895.

London never graduated from Oakland High School, but as a student there in 1895 he wrote stories and essays for the school's literary magazine, the *Aegis*, an experience that gave him his first real audience and enabled him to serve an apprenticeship as a writer. In several short stories he created a character he called the " 'Frisco Kid"—a kind of latter-day Huck Finn. He brought "The Kid" back to life in *The Cruise of the Dazzler* (1902). Written for boys, his parable about a rich boy and a poor boy depicts an idyllic boyhood world in which class and class conflict don't matter.

In "Pessimism, Optimism and Patriotism" (1895) London strives to emulate the nineteenth-century essayists he admired, particularly Ralph Waldo Emerson and John Ruskin, both of whom he mentions in the text. London walks a middle ground, trying to avoid the extremes of the pessimists (the radicals) and the optimists (the conservatives). Gradually, he reveals his sympathies by defining the optimists as the "prosperous middle and autocratic classes" and the pessimists as the "anarchists, socialists and labor leaders, with the great masses which they represent." By the end, his essay has become a political manifesto condemning the inhumane working conditions that give rise to "social and moral degradation." The title hints at London's own extreme mood swings, from pessimism to optimism, and his deep-seated American patriotism. •

Three isms—but what a wealth of significance they contain, when considered relatively. Both pessimism and optimism, though diametrically opposed, embrace many followers, who, though they view the affairs of this world through different colored glasses, are working for a common cause, which, in its highest sense, is called patriotism. But does the common cause benefit by the patriotic endeavors of these two classes? Nay, they do it the greatest harm. And why? For the simple reason that the followers of optimism should be pessimists, and the followers of pessimism should be optimists. As it is, the inconsistency of their relative positions is so startlingly apparent, that it would quite nonplus Emerson, himself, if he tried to reconcile it with his almost divine law of "Compensation."

Every nation, in the written or unwritten history of the world, that has risen, declined and fallen through internal causes, fell through the antagonism of these two classes, in which pessimism always ultimately triumphed. And so, if one can read the "signs of the times" aright, in the dim future, like calamities await us through like causes. If the adherents of these two principles were to change places, or if we could wipe out, "root and branch," every optimist in the land, and become a race of pessimists, then could we prove the shadow lengthening across the American landscape to be a phantom, nothing more.

Already, I can hear the reader asking, "Who are our optimists, who should be rooted out; swept from the face of the earth; annihilated?" And I answer, They are our sleepers. They know, yet know not that they know. They are the great gray matter of our nation; those who should mould and control our progress, and not leave it to dash wildly on with its own ungovernable force. Our prosperous middle and autocratic higher classes are optimists; as are our university and collegiate bred men, who have received the "fruits of higher education." They are all, or nearly all, satisfied with the existing state of affairs. They believe that everything is for the best, and when an occasional rumble is heard, think it but a misplaced boulder, crushed beneath the Wheels of Progress.

This class reminds one of the Pompeians, who knew that in the days before Vesuvius had risen in his might on destruction bent; yet they paused not to reflect, when from far beneath, the rumbles and groans of complaining earth came to the ear.

Again, I hear the reader ask, "Who are our pessimists?" And I answer, They are the pulsing life-cells of our nation, its flesh and bones and sinews. They are those who know not, and know not that they know not. They contend and find fault (and rightly so) with existing conditions. They are our pessimists, who, if they had the brains of our optimists, would sustain, renovate and advance with healthy stimulus, the prosperity of the nation. As it is, though their motives are right, their results are decidedly wrong. While wishing to recreate, they ignorantly destroy. Our anarchists, socialists and labor leaders with the great masses which they represent, are the components of that great tidal wave of humanity, which a few of our talented observers have already taken notice of and classified as the "Coming Terror."

In the second issue of the Aegis, a pessimist asserts that "we are on the verge of destruction and anarchism." In the third, he is laughed at by an optimist, who alleges that "we are approaching the goal of universal enlightenment." And both cry, "Universal education." The pessimist says we need it; the optimist says we have it; and I say whether we have it or not, we need something more.

It has been truly said that a "little education is a dangerous thing." We cry, "Educate the masses!" and at the same time overlook the fact that the powers "that be" prevent these very masses from gaining more than a little education. Long hours, sweating systems and steadily decreasing wages are conducive to naught but social and moral degradation. As Ruskin says, "We have now a low and lower class, and who, if there is a next world, are damned; and if there is none, they are damned already."

Can we expect to attain the "goal of universal enlightenment" while the nation labors under such conditions?

You gray matter! You optimists! You cry, "Universal Education!" Then settle down and wait for the mountain to come to Mohammed. We need universal education; but we also need a first cause, which would be supplied, if our optimists would become pessimists, and with their superior intellectual abilities, break the path for the masses to tread.

Arise, ye Americans, patriots and optimists! Awake! Seize the reins of a corrupted government and educate your masses!

What Socialism Is

First published in and reprinted from the *San Francisco Examiner,* December 25, 1895.

In "What Socialism Is" London tackled the volatile subject of revolution, which was making headlines around the world. He might have written for a socialist publication, but he wanted to reach middle-class readers—not just radicals like himself—and the *San Francisco Examiner,* the leading Bay Area newspaper, suited his aims. Written poetically, and with passion, the essay illustrates London's distinctive style. Here, for the first time, he put the "stamp of self," as he called it, on the subject of social and political upheaval, depicting revolution as a storm brewing on the horizon. Oakland and San Francisco had their share of young radical writers, but few, if any, had London's élan, mystique, and gumption. At a time when most Americans regarded socialism—an alien worldview imported by immigrants—with deep suspicion, London managed to make it seem patriotic to be a socialist.

London did not directly quote Marx's *The Communist Manifesto,* available in English since 1888 and distributed widely in the United States, or refer to Marx explicitly, but Marx's influence is apparent. Borrowing Marx's metaphor of Communism as a "specter" haunting Europe, London described it as a specter haunting the Bay Area. He seems to have wanted, in part, to shock his readers with the idea of socialism haunting them on Christmas, when his article appeared in print. As a Dickensian Ghost of Christmas Present, London haunted would-be Bay Area Scrooges: "How incongruous this specter, stalking forth when all is joy and merry-making." He urged his readers to "give the reins of your imagination to your curiosity" and to "picture this dreadful monster with all the terrorism your fear may suggest."

On the same day, the *Examiner* ran a colorful profile of London as the "Boy Socialist," by A. Walter Tate, plus several pen-and-ink sketches of London by J. D. Hoffman, who depicted him in tie and jacket, looking like a young gentleman—nothing like the cliché of the bearded, bomb-throwing anarchist. Two bold headlines reinforced the positive spin: "The Boy Socialist Defines the Meaning and the Intent of the New Philosophy" and "A Youth With Up-to-date Ideas who Will Make a lasting Impression on the Twentieth Century." Sooner or later, Tate wrote, "all peoples of the world" would have to think seriously about socialism. Moreover, readers would have to shed their stereotypes of socialists "as people, who having nothing, want no one else to have anything; who are, as a rule, cutthroats, incendiaries, assassins or thieves, and whose only aim is the overthrow and destruction of the established order of things."

In "What Socialism Is," London embraces nearly everyone on the spectrum of left-wing politics: "Communists, nationalists, collectivists, Utopians and Altrurians." He only rejects nihilists and anarchists, "the twin brothers" of a "common mother." That ecumenical attitude he maintained for most of his political life—loath to engage in sectarian debates. In fact, he never took part, directly, in internal Socialist Labor Party, or Socialist Party, meetings and discussions about official policy and strategy. "I've just been a propagandist," he would say. •

Socialism and Christmas. How incongruous this specter, stalking forth when all is joy and merry-making! How it must cast a chill upon the festivities—this fearsome thing—that is abroad in our land! But close your doors, good people and draw down the blinds, so that you may not see it, and give the reins of your imagination to your curiosity; then picture this dreadful monster with all the terrorism your fear may suggest.

Alas! It has always been your policy to close the door and draw the blind when the poor fellow comes by. You have never seen him; you are ignorant of him; and yet your ignorance paints, with vivid coloring, his horrid picture.

Let us interrogate socialism, and try and obtain a more legitimate knowledge of it.

Socialism is commonly the synonym for a lawless and revolutionary scheme, projected and carried out by cut-throats, with fire and sword in the van, and carnage, destruction and chaos in the wake. This is an injustice. Anarchy and nihilism may have given cause or such an impression, but they are as far apart from socialism as are the poles. They are the extremes, but not the extreme forms. There can be no alliance of such contradictions, though we must confess that they are children of a common mother; but one is day, the other two are night.

A socialist is of necessity social—hence his name. He wishes to be social—that is, to live in a society formed of social beings like himself. And as a sequence he must conform to the laws perhaps unwritten, of such society, whether it be family, community or State. All he wishes is to better such laws. An anarchist, on the contrary, recognizes none of these laws, of every restraint. His is a scheme of pure individualism, which is impossible without perfect man, and even with perfect man all the power of co-operation and organization would be lost. His would be a golden age, such as Greek mythology depicts, but not an enlightened age of civilization, such as we would wish. His twin brother, the nihilist (trace the word) wishes nothing. But with man imperfect as he is, their schemes would bring chaos.

Still, socialism is an all-embracing term. Communists, nationalists, collectivists, idealists, Utopians and Altrurians are all socialists; but it cannot be said that socialism is any one of these, for it is all. Any man is a socialist who strives for a better form of Government than the one he is living under.

Socialism means a reconstruction of society with a more just application of labor and distribution of the returns thereof. It cries out, "Every one according to his deeds!" Its logical foundation is economic; its moral foundation, "All men are born free and equal," and its ultimate aim is pure democracy.

By "all men are born free and equal" it means born free and with equal opportunities to earn by honest labor — mental or physical — a livelihood.

By a pure democracy is meant a form of government in which the supreme power rests with and is exercised directly by the people instead of the present form, which is a republican form of democracy, in which the supreme power rests with the people, but is indirectly exercised by them, through representatives.

Representatives may be corrupted, but how could the whole people be bribed? It would be a Herculean task, and as Lincoln said, "You may fool all the people part of the time; part of the people all the time; but not all the people all the time."

Socialism is a phenomenon of this century. It is a vision of the future, while its agents are actively at work in the present. It is a product of social evolution. We have slavery, feudalism, capitalism — and socialism. It is the obvious step. Whether this generation will see it is uncertain, but "coming events cast their shadows before us," and its shadow already darkens the world. It is a cloud rising above us with increasing magnitude. The dull rumble of its thunder can be heard; its lightning flashes brighter and brighter; it is upon us. Will it bring the cooling rain to the dry, parched earth, or will it bring the devastation of the hurricane? Think friends, if you have not before. If you have, think again.

The Voters' Voice

First published in and reprinted from the *Oakland Times*, May 9, 1896.

In this essay, which won first prize in a competition for students sponsored by the Oakland People's Party, a twenty-year-old London expresses a sense of hope and optimism about American democracy. He even looks forward to the day when there might be "purity in politics." At the same time, he condemns established political parties, corporations that fund politicians, and the Electoral College. He places his faith in the people to rule themselves, intelligently. Under a republican form of government, in which citizens elect congressmen and senators, citizens have little means of redressing grievances, he argues, except to vote officeholders out of office in the next election. He insists that the people ought to have absolute control over their own sovereignty. In a genuine democracy, men of "unimpeachable integrity"—presently in short supply—would come forward, run for office, and drive out corrupt politicians. Here, London presents himself as a reformer, not a revolutionary, but he clearly wants a total transformation of society—an "awakening"—and a reign of "truth, justice and equity." For the most part, he sounds progressive, not Marxist, though he does anticipate a time when people will "escape the bondage of class rule." He also discusses the battle for bimetallism—the use of both gold and silver as monetary standards—which was a key issue in the 1896 presidential campaign in which the Democratic Party candidate William Jennings Bryant famously declared, "You shall not press down upon the brow of labor this crown of thorns, you shall not crucify mankind upon a cross of gold." This essay, like many others, shows that London not only followed but also took sides in the political debates of his time that divided the country. It shows, too, that his ideas continue to have relevance today, perhaps especially when he calls for "the overthrow of party politics" and for a sweeping effort to bring disenfranchised voters back into the electoral process. •

Of the many forms of government, democracy has been, and always will be considered the highest and best. Next to a democracy, a republican form of government is deemed best, and such is the government, we, of the United States enjoy.

The difference between a democracy and a republic is direct legislation. In a republic the sovereignty lies in the people, but is vested by them in representatives. Hence, they lose the direct exercise thereof. They cannot initiate laws; neither can they veto. They elect their officers for a term of years, and then, no matter now necessary would be the proposal and passage of a certain law, or repeal of another, they are powerless. They have surrendered their sovereignty. If their representatives are obdurate, they can do nothing; they have no control over them; they cannot discharge them. Their only recourse is to endure the evils till the next election, when they may elect new masters, who misbehave as their predecessors have done.

In a democracy where the sovereignty lies in the people and is directly exercised by them, direct legislation, through the initiative and the referendum, is their great executive instrument. Suppose, for example, they were cursed with a corrupt legislature which, controlled by rings and syndicates, found their interests to be in contradiction to those of the people. The people wish to have laws passed to remedy certain evils. Their representatives do not act. The people then initiate or propose such bills as they may wish, vote upon them, and they become laws, having been ratified by a majority of the people. Suppose the Federal legislature had passed laws detrimental to the interests of the commonwealth. The people exercise their prerogative granted by the referendum and veto them. In any event, it is the voice, the will of the people, which rules.

The control by the majority is the principle on which our government should rest, but upon which it does not at present. Our electoral college does not allow that, and neither does our system of representation. They, a minority, pass and refuse to pass, many bills, which the people, a majority, do not want or wish for.

Another of the great benefits to be derived from direct legislation, is the overthrow of party politics, and partisanship, which are the worst of the evils we suffer under today. Loyalty to the nation is forgotten in the allegiance to party, and the talents of the best of our public men are prostituted to the furtherance of party designs and powers.

To-day our most talented citizens refuse to come forward and enter public life, because there is no opening for such a career save through a party. Such men are crushed out by the professional politicians and office seekers. If we had direct legislation we would choose for our representatives men of ability, principle and unimpeachable integrity. As it is, we chose such as may happen to have their names on a party ticket, no matter how unprincipled and corrupt they may be. We have but one resource if such a proceeding is distasteful, and that is, not to vote at all, which is certainly unpatriotic. But we do vote, for the man is forgotten for the party.

A good illustration of the beneficial working of direct legislation may be found in the Silver Question.

Many of out citizens have reason to believe that great good will accrue from the adoption of a bi-metallic standard. They propose to effect such a standard. Now, witness the laborious method by which they have to strive in the endeavor to obtain it. They have to agitate; they hold conventions; they try to get their plank inserted in the platform of some party; and, failing in this, form a party of their own. Their work has but begun, though it has taken many weary months. Then, year after year, campaign after campaign, they must struggle in the political arena till success crowns their efforts and they have a majority in the House and Senate. Then, they adopt the bi-metallic standard. But hold, it is not yet a law, for Mr. President has still to attach his signature. If he is a mono-metallist he refuses. The bill goes back to the House whence it originated, where the same battles must be fought anew, and this time with a hand-icap, for they needs must have a two-thirds, instead of a simple majority. If they have not got it, they must pocket their disappointment and wait for a change in the admin-istration. And so the years roll by.

If direct legislation had been in vogue, how quick would the matter have been set-tled! The laborious formation of a party would have been useless, for the people would have initiated it, and if it pleased the majority, it would have become a law. But if a majority had shown their minds by voting against it, it would have been equally decisive. The majority vote of the people is emphatic.

And surely the people are competent to manage their own affairs. Of a verity, they would be more honest than the classes that at present rule. They will, they must be honest to themselves, for it is to their interests to be so. But it is not so with their rep-resentatives. To be true to their own interests they must be false to those of their con-stituents for with a lobby backed by the money rings, corporations and syndicates, emolument is theirs—if they will but reciprocate.

It has been objected that the people are incompetent to rule themselves; but Sismonde most truly says, "If pure democracy is a bad form of government, represen-tative democracy cannot be worth more." What an increased interest in pubic affairs! What a revival of patriotism! What an awakening would ensure, if direct legislation were adopted! The people, no longer forced to hire servants to do their thinking for them; the people eager to exercise their sovereignty; the people glad to escape the bondage of class rule; would spring into the arena, buckle on their armor, and do their own thinking, voting and vetoing. Then would the disenfranchised welcome enfran-chisement, while our party tyrants were relegated to obscurity, and the nation, with renewed vigor, resume her triumphant progress. Then would our honest men enter into public life; then would "purity in politics" be not only the watchword, but the accomplished fact; then would truth, justice and equity reign.

Socialistic Views

First published in and reprinted from the *Oakland Times,* August 12, 1896.

Soon after he read *The Communist Manifesto,* London discovered Karl Marx's magnum opus, *Das Kapital.* In an August 1896 letter to the *Oakland Times,* he urged readers to study it and discover the economics of socialism. He'd gleaned from Marx's work the notion that capitalist society could be viewed in terms of two antithetical forces: capital and labor. In "Socialistic Views," he applied, to the particular circumstances of Oakland's rival water companies, the lessons he'd learned from Marx. Here, as almost everywhere he turned, he saw unrelenting warfare. London argues that in place of competition, monopoly, and ever higher utility bills, citizens might opt for public ownership of water.

Several weeks earlier, in another letter to the *Oakland Times,* he'd written that "the Socialists of Germany, France, Italy, Spain, Belgium and other European countries, will not fuse—will not set aside their doctrines for mere palliatives." He added, "The main issue is public ownership of all the facilities of production and distribution, and they will never drift away from it to measures, which are mere temporary alleviations and not permanent cures."

This passage shows why he called himself a "radical." Temporary relief of social ills he disdained; instead, he favored fundamental, permanent solutions to problems posed by unequal production and distribution of commodities. He also suggested that his arguments about water could be applied to the railroad industry in California.

"Socialistic Views" shows London's ability to adapt European socialist demands to American circumstances, as well as his ability to use examples that ordinary, working-class Americans would easily understand. He offers the example of the "shell game," arguing that citizens are easily tricked into believing that free-market competition will benefit them. He also uses the example of the opium addict, asserting that competition, like opium, is a drug; it may provide the illusion of temporary relief, but as soon as the initial phase wears off, the consumer is addicted—and poorer than ever before.   •

A word on competition, both local and national. Competition is the life of trade; it gives incentive to capital and labor and benefits the consumer. It stimulates business and is the index of the nation's prosperity. It quickens in to life the latent energies of a people; develops the resources of a country; and bequeaths to a nation, as a necessary heirloom, both individual and collective independence.

This, and very much more, is the result—or is said to be the result—of competition. The people, the great seething masses, believe it, hence it must be so. But the people have been, are, and can be deceived. As an illustration, take the shell game. It is simple—the pea, the shells, the manipulator are before one's very eyes. Yet how many men have come to grief on attempting the petty feat of pointing out under which shell the pea is? Still, they decide just as hastily on the merits and demerits of competition, which is a myriad fold more intricate. If every citizen would give it an honest, thoughtful analysis, how different would be his conclusion.

Let us analyze, taking for example the merely local affair presented to us by Oakland's rival water companies. The Contra Costa Water Company, but a short time ago supplied all Oakland with water. It was a monopoly, and hence distasteful to the citizens and damaging to their interests. They clamored for a change, and the great elixir, competition, was offered them. They took the dose and are happy—happy as the opium eater under the sway of his subtle drug. But when its effects have passed away and the reaction comes, how miserable the opium eater is! So it is with the people of Oakland; they are now experiencing the action; the reaction is yet to come.

The Contra Costa Water Company had the necessary water supply, the necessary facilities for distributing it, and as a logical conclusion, the necessary capital to operate it with. It is obvious that further capital was not needed to furnish Oakland with water. The Oakland Water Company sprang into existence, and twice the capital was now required to give Oakland water. It paralleled the older company's pipes, tore up our streets anew, and dug, tunneled and dammed in our hills to obtain the precious commodity. Then the war began and rates were cut ruinously, while our citizens enjoyed the spectacle and saved their pockets at the same time. They forgot that tomorrow always comes. With such a competition duly inaugurated and a rate war in progress there can be three, and only three results.

In the first place, selling water at a loss, the company with the smallest capital, being less capacitated to stand the strain, will go under. The other company will now be a monopoly and its first move will be to retrench. It will make the Oaklanders who enjoyed the low rates sweat, by raising them.

In the second place, the fight may be so bitter and show such signs of long continuance, that the wealthier company will buy out the poorer one. What follows? It has been forced to double its invested capital and to obtain a dividend on the same, equivalent to its previous dividend it will have to double the previous rates, Also, having lost money during the period of competition, it will further raise the rates in order to reimburse itself.

In the third place, if both companies have about equal strength, they may continue the war till both are on the verge of bankruptcy. Then they will awake to the dangers of the situation. They will confer with each other and come to the conclusion that if it is properly managed, both may reap good dividends on the investment. They will then pool interests and mutually raise the rates to any height agreed upon. Since double the capital is now invested, double the interest is required and that the old rates will be doubled to obtain it, is a foregone conclusion.

Outside of these three, there is no other way in which the competition of the Oakland water companies can be settled. The reaction will have come—the opium eater will have awakened!

The Valley railroad can be thus analyzed, and so, in fact, can every similar scheme. If one company is ably fitted to perform its business, the eruption of a second can but end in one of the ways I have mentioned. If the company is too small to handle the business required of it and another small company appears on the scene, there can be very little competition for neither will be in the position to grasp the other's trade, while, if the new company is of sufficient magnitude, it will freeze the older one out.

If, in a community of 100 workers, all of them are at work legitimately producing the necessaries and luxuries of life, one would decide that it were more prosperous than a second community of 100 workers, in which twenty were engaged in the unremunerative task of pumping the ocean dry. Suppose [William J.] Dingee [president of the Oakland Water Company] employed 500 men for one year of 300 working days, the day's labor being ten hours. Then the 1,500,000 hours at labor have been useless, spuriously expended, since the Contra Costa Water Company was well able to supply Oakland with water.

It seems apparent that such competition necessitates a waste of labor and capital, and always results in monopoly. Is there any path out of the wilderness? Can the reader suggest a remedy for Oakland's rival water companies? If he cannot, I would ask him if he has ever heard of municipal ownership?

The Road

First published in and reprinted from *Jack London Reports: War Correspondence, Sports Articles, and Miscellaneous Writings,* edited by King Hendricks and Irving Shepard (Garden City, NY: Doubleday, 1970).

London probably wrote the essay "The Road" in 1896 or 1897 at the age of twenty or twenty-one. His records indicate that he sent it to the *San Francisco Examiner* as well as to several magazines in 1897, and that they all rejected it. In 1899, the *Arena,* a Boston magazine, accepted it, but the next year returned it to the author unpublished. It remained unpublished until 1970, when King Hendricks and Irving Shepard included it in *Jack London Reports,* an anthology of his writings on diverse subjects.

London based "The Road" on his experiences traveling by railroad across the Sierras in the summer of 1892, when he was sixteen, and again when he went across the country in 1894. A few salient phrases that appear in his 1894 journal crop up in the essay, and he carried through on his initial intention of writing "character studies" of the men he observed. In "The Road," however, he omits all of his own personal experiences, which would have made the piece more saleable. Though he had been present in 1894 at Council Bluffs, Iowa, and had observed the encampment of Kelly's army of unemployed workers marching to the nation's capital, he expunges all mention of himself in "The Road." Clearly, London wanted to cast himself not as a tramp but as a scholar and as a student of tramp life—a controversial and timely subject in the late 1890s.

In 1897, Walter Augustus Wyckoff (1865–1908), a Princeton University sociologist, published the first of a two-volume study entitled *The Workers: An Experiment in Reality,* based on his own experiences with, and direct observations of, itinerant American laborers. In 1899, Josiah Flint Willard, a former hobo, published *Tramping with Tramps, Studies and Sketches of the Vagabond Life,* under the pseudonym Josiah Flynt. Of the two authors, London preferred Willard/Flynt's account, because he was a tramp first and a writer second, not a professor who took on the disguise of the hobo to write a book. "Josiah Flynt is the tramp authority," London told his friend Cloudesley Johns. "Wyckoff knows only the working-man."

London's 1896 essay would have added to the fast-growing body of literature about hobos. A decade later, he returned to the subject of tramps, but this time he wisely cast himself as the central figure in the story, presenting himself as the archetypal hobo in *The Road* (1907), a full-length book about his experiences.

"The Road" reads like the work of a "tyro," as London described himself. The language is sometimes flowery and stilted. Still, it has strengths. At the end of the essay, London deciphers the hobo argot, ably describing the caste system operating in "Trampland." At the start of the essay, London invites readers to look at the tramp through the eyes of the Victorian lady and gentleman. He uses the pronoun "we" as though he's middle class himself. "We have met him everywhere, even desecrating the sanctity of our back stoop, where he ate of the crumbs of our table," he writes of the tramp. As a hobo, London had eaten crumbs at back stoops, but in writing his essay, he took on the persona of the citizen handing out those crumbs.

In "The Road," he only hints at his own personal experience. He writes about "romantic and unruly boys" who take to the road to "escape parental discipline"—probably thinking about himself. But he never leads readers behind the scenes and never shows himself as one of those unruly boys in rebellion against his parents. Still, he manages to convey real empathy for the vagrant who lives "on the ragged edge of nonentity" and who experiences "the negation of being"—an apt phrase that sounds like it might come from the pages of the French existentialists.

London's racist ideas surface in "The Road," perhaps for the first time. There's a derisive tone to his comment about Jews, and African Americans are depicted as "incubuses" and "passive," while he praises the "indomitability of the Teuton." These racial ideas would later come to the fore in his writings about Indians and Anglo-Saxons in the Yukon. "The Road" shows that he held racial stereotypes and ethnic clichés before he left California. London makes fun of men who, in his view, take on feminine traits. In his lexicon they're "squawmen"—not real men at all. The essay also seems flawed because of its many florid generalizations about the human race, as in sentences like "Man, vicious and corrupt, the incarnation of all that is vile and loathsome, is a melancholy object"; or again, on the subject of "boy tramps," he writes, "They are cast out, by the cruel society which gave them birth, into a nether world of outlawry and darkness." Here as in many of his early essays, he ends with a question, rather than an affirmation, as though feeling tentative about himself and his place in the world. •

The "Road," the hog-train, or for brevity's sake, the hog: It is a realm almost as unexplored as fairyland, yet hardly as impregnable. Nay, in fact, destiny not only entices but forces world-weary mortals into its embrace. It entices romantic and unruly boys, who venture along its dangerous ways in search of fortune or in rash attempt to escape parental discipline. It seizes with relentless grip the unfortunate who drifts with, or struggles against the tide of human affairs. Those who cannot go whither must come thither, all hope behind. It is the river of oblivion, of which the soul-wanderer, shuddering with coward's heart (or religious scruple) at self-destruction, must drink. Henceforth all identity is lost. Though with many aliases, not even the semirespectable number of the convict is his. He has but one designation; they all have it:—Tramp. But the law aids him, however, if reputation grows with syllables, for under it he is known as vagrant. Yet herein is a double injustice done. While all tramps are vagrant, all vagrants are not tramps. Many are worse, a thousand times worse than the tramp. And again, the small bit of respectability which may yet linger about his former name is destroyed. He is a vagrant: It is shortened to "Vag." Three letters, two consonants and a vowel, stand between him and the negation of being. He is on the ragged edge of nonentity.

We all know the tramp—that is, we have seen him and talked with him. And what an eyesore he has always been! Perhaps, when hurrying home through the rainy night, all comfortable in mackintosh, umbrella and overshoes, he has dawned upon us like a comet, malignant of aspect. Wet, shivering, and miserable, whining for the price of a bed or a meal, he casts his baleful influence over us: Nor can hastily given largess or abrupt refusal overcome it. Our comfort seems out of place, actually jars upon us. We are thrown out of our good humor and rudely awakened from the anticipatory dream we have dreamed all day at the office — the snug little home, all cheery, bright and warm; the smiling wife and her affectionate greeting; the laughing children, or perhaps the one little crowing tot, the son and heir. We have met him in the park, always occupying the best benches; on the overland and summer excursions; at the springs and at the seaside: In short, we have met him everywhere, even desecrating the sanctity of our back stoop, where he ate of the crumbs of our table. Still, his land is an unknown region, and we are less conversant with his habits and thoughts than with those of the inhabitants of the Cannibal Islands.

One astonishing thing about Trampland is its population. Variously estimated by equally competent authorities at from 500,000 to 1,500,000 it will be found that 1,000,000 is not far out of the way. A million! It seems impossible, yet it is a fact. If a Stanley may be lost in Africa, cannot such a number be lost in the United States? This is rendered easy because of the breadth of country and the evenness of their distribution. Every town, village, railroad station, watering-tank and siding, has its proportion; in the great metropolises their numbers mount into the tens of thousands; while each county and city jail has its due quota, supported by the taxpayer. It is only when concentrated that their abundance is manifested. One example will suffice. On a rainy morning in the spring of '94, an army of them, 2,000 strong, marched out of Council Bluffs. They had, as an organization, already traveled two thousand miles and their numbers were augmenting at every step. At their head rode their leader on a handsome black charger, presented him by an enthusiastic farmer. They were marshaled in divisions and companies and had staff officers, couriers, aid-de-campes, buglers, banner-bearers, army physicians and fully equipped medical department, a fife and drum corps, a healthy strong-box, and efficient police service, a commissary, and above all, the best of discipline. The stationary Negro population is often called the incubus of the South; but is not this increasing, shifting, tramp population, not passive like the Negro but full of the indomitability of the Teuton, equally worthy of consideration, and by the whole race?

Strange as it may seem, in this outcast world the sharp lines of caste are as rigorously drawn as in the world from which it has evolved. There are several prominent divisions. The Simon-pure tramp, hence professional, calls himself "The Profesh." He is not the one we meet with so profusely in *Judge* or *Puck*. The only resemblance lies in that he never works. He does not carry a tomato-can on a string, wear long hair, or manifest his calling in his dress. His clothes are almost always good, never threadbare, torn and dirty. In fact, with him, the comb, cake of soap, looking-glass and clothes brush are indispensables. He lives better and more easily than the average working-man. Having reduced begging to a fine art, he scorns back stoops and kitchen tables, patronizes the restaurant, and always has the price of the drinks about him. His is the class most to be feared. Many of them have "done time" and are capable and worthy of doing more. They will commit, under stress of circumstances and favorable opportunity, every crime on the calendar, and then, just a few more besides. Perhaps the simile is unjust, but they are looked up to as the aristocracy of their underworld.

The largest class is that of the working tramp. That is, the tramp who looks for work and is not afraid of it when he finds it. He usually carries his blankets and is somewhat akin to his more respectable Australian compatriot, who strikes off into the "bush" with his "swag" and "billy-can." Because of his predilection to carrying his bed with him, he is known in trampland as the "bindle stiff." The etymology of this phrase is simple. Any tramp is a "stiff," and the blanket in a bundle is a "bindle." These are the men, who, in New York, travel into the Genesee county to the hops; in the Dakotas, to the harvests; in Michigan, to the berry-picking; and in California, to the vintage, hops and harvest.

The "Stew Bum" is the most despised of his kind. He is the *Canaille,* the *Sans-culotte,* the fourth estate of trampland. Of such stuff are squawmen made. It is he who is the prototype of the individual aforementioned, who graces the pages of our humorous periodicals. He is not supremely wicked nor degraded; deep-sunk in a state of languorous lassitude, he passively exists, viewing the active world with philosophic soul. His own ambition, one dream, one ideal is stew: Hence his only evil trait — an electric affinity which always draws him and chicken roosts into close conjunctions.

A curious class, closely connected in career with the Chinatown bum who drinks cheap gin and fills an early grave, is that of the "Alki Stiffs." "Alki" is the argot for alcohol. They travel in gangs and are a close approach to communists, only differing in that they have no community of goods. The reason for this is simple: They have no goods. But the ideal commune could not vie with them in a community of drink. Every penny, begged or stolen, goes to the purchase of their fiery beverage, of which all may drink. The finest mixer of the "cocktail route" cannot approach them in the art of diluting alcohol with water. Too much water and it is spoiled; Too little, and they are spoiled, for then and there is much devastation done to the linings of their stomachs. Masters there are among them, but they have seldom served a long appren-ticeship: Death comes too soon for that. In the world, when a man falls, he takes to drink: In trampland, to the "white line," as they tritely call it. Somehow, one never meets a gang of these poor devils lying in the grass and wild flowers of the country wayside, sleeping and drowsing in the depths of debauch, without being reminded of Tennyson's *Lotus Eaters,* who swore and kept an oath: —

> In the hollow lotus-land to live and lie reclined
> On the hills like gods together, careless of mankind.

The cripples, usually traveling in pairs, often are to be met with in gangs of twenty or more. A universal custom with such groups is to have two or three of the most bru-tal of the "profesh" as bodyguard. These fight their battles, run their errands, handle their money, and take care of them when they are drunk. In return, these mercenar-ies are given their meal and drink money. It is amusing to witness the meeting of two stranger cripples. Each will solicitously inquire as to how the other lost his limb. Then will follow a detailed account of its amputation, with criticism of the surgeons who officiated and their methods, the conversation usually terminating with an adjourn-ment to some secluded spot, where, with all the fondness of paternal affection, they compare stumps. One touch of amputation makes all cripples kin.

Then there is a transient class, a sort of general miscellany, composed of all kinds of men temporarily down in their luck. Among these the most interesting character studies may be made. Strikingly diverse and powerful individualities are here found, all bound in a mesh of pathos and ludicrity *[sic]*. Most of them are the men whose money has given out and who are forced to make their way home as best they can. Farmer-boys, turning their backs on the city; city-bred men, turning away from the country; men who have been fleeced and are too proud to write or wire for help; oth-ers, fleeing from justice; some who have been indiscreet; many who have tried to cut too brilliant a dash; broken down actors, sports and tinhorns; and even some (a small percentage) who, parsimoniously inclined, wish to save their railroad fare. Nearly all of them are possessed of a little money and furnish rich plucking to mean railroad men and the "profesh." They are to be known at a glance. Their ignorance of the cus-toms and unwritten rules of the "road" paint their greenness as vividly as does the unsophistication and lack of conventionality of our friend the "hayseed," when he comes to town. They are wanderers in a strange land and the scrapes and pitfalls they stumble into, are laughable yet often tragic.

Another division, which is merely a sub-class and closely allied to the "profesh," is that of the "Fakirs." These are tinkers, umbrella menders, locksmiths, tattooers, tooth-pullers, quack doctors, corn doctors, horse doctors — in short, a lengthy list. Some sell trinkets and gew gaws and others, "fakes." These "fakes" are as curious and interesting as they are innumerable. We all remember the Frenchman who made flea powder out of pulverized brick — this is the nature of the "fake." Here is a sample, as simple as it is successful: — The prudent housewife meets at the door a glib young individual, who shows her a piece of tin, so closely perforated with tiny holes that is almost a gauze. He gives a rambling a [sic] very impressive disquisition on the principles of the kerosene lamp, then explains that this tin, fitted to the top of the wick, will give twice the flame, burn less oil, and never burn the wick which will thus last forever. He even volunteers to attach it to her oldest lamp and if she be not convinced it costs her noth-ing; if convinced, only fifteen cents. She brings from some top shelf an old lamp, long since fallen into disuse. Very business-like, he produces pinchers and snippers and sets to work, volubly chattering all the while. Examining the ancient burner and deftly opening the clogged flues and air vents, he attaches his tin. Then he lights it and the admiring housewife beholds a flame, larger and more luminous than that of her best parlor lamp. After receiving his fifteen cents, he advises her to give it a trial for that night and promises to call next day. He duplicates this operation in the whole neigh-borhood. In the evening, the wondrous flame is the center of interest in the family cir-cle — "So saving! And so cheap! Father, we must have them on all the lamps." Next day the young man reappears and puts his little "fake" on every burner in the house. He receives anywhere from fifty cents to a dollar for a couple of cents worth of low grade tin, and vanishes for ever, as Carlyle would say, "Into outer darkness." But O, 'tis passing fair. Two days suffice: The tin drops off.

Saddest of all, is the training school of the "Road." Man, vicious and corrupt, the incarnation of all that is vile and loathsome, is a melancholy object; but how much more, is innocent youth, rapidly becoming so! Modification by environment — O pregnant term! In it lies all the misery and all the joy of mankind, all the purest and all the most degraded soul-development, all the noblest and foulest attributes and deeds. Man, blindly-groping, with weak, finite conception, personifies these antithe-ses in the powers of light and darkness: Yet, even to man, poor earthworm, is given the power to qualify these personifications of his through *modification by environment*. Still, we, Americans, and partakers of the science and culture of our tremendous civ-ilization, cognizant of all this, allow in our midst the annual prostitution of tens of thousands of souls. Boy tramps or "Road-kids" abound in our land. They are children, embryonic souls—the most plastic of fabrics. Flung into existence, ready to tear aside the veil of the future; with the mighty pulse of dawning twentieth century throbbing about him; with the culminating forces of the thousand dead and the one living civilization effervescing in the huge world-caldron, they are cast out, by the cruel society which gave them birth, into a nether world of outlawry and darkness.

But to the "Road-kids." Many are run-aways, who through romantic dreaming or undue harshness, have left comfortable homes for the stern vicissitudes of tramp life. The romantic always return, but of those who have been cruelly treated, virtually none. These cases may be sad, but there is still a second division—the children, begotten of ignorance, poverty and sin. Uncultivated, with no helping hand to guide their faltering footsteps, with the brand of Cain upon their brows, and they raise their moan in silent brute-anguish to a cold world and drift into trampland, the scapegoats of their generation. To become what? "Alki Stiffs" and "Stew Bums"? Perhaps; but almost always to become of the "Profesh" the most professional. Inscrutable scheme of life! Cast out and scourged by society, their mother, they return, the scourge of their mother, society. We have all wept for little Oliver Twist; nor have we failed to reserve a copious draught for Nancy Sikes—she was a woman; but the artful dodger, who weeps for him? Yet his is the saddest of all.

Though sometimes journeying in gangs, they often travel with members of the "Profesh." A gang of them, composed of the more intrepid and vicious, is a terrible thing to meet. They are wolves in human guise. Besides committing all sorts of sly and petty depredations, they hunt higher game. "Rolling a stiff," as they call robbing a drunken man, is a mere pastime; but they do not refrain from attacking sober ones. Like wolves, they fly at the throat, giving what is known as the "strong arm." This is applied from behind, the large bone of the wrist and the victim's windpipe coming into painful and dangerous juxtaposition. Those who travel with the "Profesh" are serving their criminal apprenticeship. They are very useful, and in some crimes even indispensable. It is a hard school and they learn rapidly, soon finding the proper field for the exercise of their peculiar talents. The faithfulness of the "Road-kids" for their teachers or "pals" and vice-versa, is often pathetic. The self-sacrifice, hardship and punishment they will undergo for each other, is astonishing—a sure index to the latent nobility of soul which lurks within, dwarfed instead of developed. Poor devils! With the hand of society raised against them, it is the only opening through which the shrunken higher parts of their nature may be manifested.

Clothing, eating, and sleeping are not so difficult to obtain in trampland; but of the three, a comfortable place to sleep is the hardest. In the cities and large towns, a goodly portion buy their meals with money begged on the street. Others, not so bold, go from house to house, "slamming gates," as they picturesquely describe it. When at a back door, eatables are given them wrapped in paper, they call it a "poke-out" or "hand-out." This is not prized so highly as a "set-down" (going into the kitchen.) Above all the tramp likes his "java" (coffee.) Especially in the morning after a cold night, they, all-benumbed, prefer it to all the "hand-outs" in Christendom. As to clothes: Some, being lazy, wait till their very delapidation calls forth a voluntary contribution of cast-off garments; others, possessed with energy and love of neatness, ask for them whenever necessary. Nay, the "Profesh" make many a pretty penny on clothes thus obtained, which they sell to workingmen and Jews.

When out on the "Road," away from cities, the "Profesh" can always be told by their manner of sleeping. Realizing the worth of a good "front" (appearance), it behooves them to take good care of their apparel, so they have recourse to the newspaper blanket: Wherever they may select to sleep, they spread a newspaper or two on which to lie. Sleeping on the "road" in cold weather, the "Bindle Stiff" is the only comfortable tramp. The "Profesh," "Alki Stiffs," "Road-kids," etc. scorn carrying a "bindle" and needs must pay the consequence. But if a warm nook is to be had, trust them to find it. A favorite trick is their method of utilizing a refrigerator car. The walls of such a car are a foot thick, the doors fasten hermetically, and there is little or no ventilation. Once inside with the door closed, they make a bonfire of newspapers. As the heat cannot escape, they sleep comfortably, and in the morning when they open the door, the inner is much warmer than the outer atmosphere.

The circulation of this great mass of human beings is an interesting phenomenon with which few of the upper world are conversant. Every spring the slums of the cities, the jails, poor houses, hospitals—the holes and dens in which the winter has been spent—give up their denizens who take to the "Road." This is the flux. All summer they wander, covering thousands upon thousands of miles, and with fall, crawl back to their holes and dens again—the ebb. Many blow whither they listeth: Many have definite plans. For instance, a tramp winters in New York City; starts out in the spring and travels to the north and west among the mining states; in the fall, goes south to Florida for the winter. Next summer finds him in Canada and the following winter in California. A third summer's wandering through the west and the south, concludes with the warm weather of Mexico, where he laughs at winter terrors. This ebb and flow is also noticeable in the rushes to the great catastrophes, such as the Johnston flood, the Charleston earthquake, the Chicago fire, and the St. Louis cyclone. There is also the periodic rush to the harvests and to the great fairs. At these places, for the

"Profesh," is to be found rich loot; for the laboring tramp, work. Most pathetic is the return of the "Bindle Stiffs" from the harvest. They journey up into the Dakotas, and even into Manitoba, by the thousands, paying the brakemen half a dollar a division for the privilege of riding in empty box cars. They are essentially honest, hard-working laborers. All through the harvest they toil from dawn till dark, and at the season's close, are possessed of from one to three hundred dollars. They return in the same; but now they encounter the "Profesh," veritable beasts of the jungle. Perhaps half a dozen of them, having tipped the trainmen, are in a box car. Enter one or two "Profesh," who, at the pistol point, rob them of their year's wages. In the good old times, a single "Profesh" has often returned from three weeks of such work with two or three thousand dollars. This form of robbery is still perpetuated, but more rarely and with less remuneration. The resident population has increased, and fewer "Bindle Stiffs" are needed; while those who do earn money, usually send it back by mail or Wells Fargo.

Their *argot* is peculiar study. While in some instance it resembles that of "Chimmie Faden," in most, it is widely different. Truly has [Victor] Hugo said of *argot*, "Each accursed race has deposited its stratum, each suffering has dropped its stone, each heart has given its pebble." The sources of much are easily to be traced. *Kibosh* means utter discomfiture, from the Chinook; *galway*—priest—from the Gaelic; *bobbie*—policeman—transplanted from Cockney *argot; monica*—cognomen—a distorted version, both in form and meaning, of monogram; *star-route*—a "side jump" away from railroads—can be traced to the asterisks which denote Pony Express stations, and to steering and traveling by the heavenly constellations, when from the latter it is usually called a *star-light. Sou-markee* is a distorted combination from two root languages. It is a hyperbolical synonym for the smallest absolute coin and is used thus:—I haven't a *sou-markee*. The derivation is obvious. *Pounding the ear* means to sleep; *gondola,* flat car; *pogy,* poor house; *jerk,* a branch road or one little traveled; *glam,* steal; *gat,* gun; *shiv,* knife; *faune,* false; *crimpy,* cold; *dorse* or *kip,* to sleep; queens, *women; punk* or *dummy,* bread. One may understand the ordinary tramp, but it is often impossible to even comprehend the very "Profesh." Attempt to translate this:—*De stem? Nit! Yaeggin's o the sugar train. Hit a fly on the main-drag for a light piece; de bull snared me; got a t'ree hour blin'.* Here is a free version:—The street for begging? It is worthless. On the main street I begged a policeman in citizen's clothes for a small sum, but he (fly) (bull) (policeman) arrested me and the judge gave me three hours in which to leave town.

The tramp problem opens a vast field of study. In our high civilization it is a phenomenon, unique and paradoxical. Cause and cure have received countless explanations; but of one thing we must all be certain; and that, that work is not to be had for them. If they were annihilated, our industries would not suffer—nay, our army of unemployed would still be so large that wages would not rise. Capital being crystallized labor, it is axiomatic that labor produces more than it consumes. Hence, many must be idle; and, since through invention the efficiency of labor is constantly increasing, so must this army of idlers increase—of course, fluctuating as trade fluctuates. Is this true or is it not? Can the tramp be abolished or can he not? Is he an attendant evil on our civilization in certain stages of development or a permanent one? This is the problem: Is it to be solved?

The Question of the Maximum

First published in and reprinted from *War of the Classes* (New York: Macmillan, 1905).

"The Question of the Maximum" was written in 1898 and then delivered as a speech before the Oakland section of the Socialist Labor Party on November 25, 1899. Several editors accepted the essay but then declined to publish it. It appeared in print for the first time in *War of the Classes*. In this essay, London offers, for the first time, a global perspective on industry, commerce, and trade; he writes about civilizations, not simply nations, presenting a broad historical point of view. "The Question of the Maximum" describes the industrial revolutions of the nineteenth century, the development of capitalism around the world, the rise and the gradual decline of the British Empire, and the intense competition unleashed between rival imperial powers—Germany, France, Russia, Japan, and the United States. London writes about "the shrinkage of the planet"—a topic he would take up again later in an essay with that title in which he would also describe the concentration of economic and political power in the imperial capitals of the world.

Technology, he explains, has made it possible to communicate globally more quickly than ever before. News travels faster, and remote parts of the world are linked to European and American capitals by telegraph, railroad, and ship. "Each morning, every part [of the world] knows what every other part is thinking, contemplating, or doing," he writes. Perhaps that was an exaggeration in London's day. Today, in the age of the Internet and the cell phone, it's a commonplace. London does not use the word *imperialism*, but the world he describes here is that of twentieth-century imperialism, in which colonies are essential for the economic and political hegemony of the European powers. V. I. Lenin would have praised London's savvy.

London sees a time when rival empires will reach the tipping point of economic development. At that point, he argues, the world will be faced with a choice: oligarchy or social-ism, dictatorship or democracy. For the first time—in 1898—he uses the image of "the iron heel" to characterize oligarchy. A decade later, he would use this phrase again for the title of his dystopian novel, *The Iron Heel* (1908). In "The Question of the Maximum" he expresses the hope that the citizens of the world will choose socialism and that an era of the common man will come into existence, but he does not rule out the possibility of a global dictatorship.

A voracious reader, London studied the key controversial works of his day that explored politics, finance, banking, and the military. Everything he read, he absorbed quickly and integrated into his own thought. In "The Question of the Maximum," he men-tions nearly a half-dozen writers—some conservatives, others radicals—whose work and ideas he pondered. He refers to and quotes from three well-known American thinkers in the 1890s: Brook Adams (1848–1927), author of the influential *The Law of Civilization* (1898) and student of the rise and fall of empires; Henry Demarest Lloyd (1847–1903), muckraking journalist, foe of monopoly capitalism, and author of the classic *Wealth against Commonwealth* (1894); and Charles Arthur Conant (1861–1915), a whiz on banks and inter-national finance. London also refers to Lord Charles Beresford (1846–1919), whose career in the military and Parliament reflected the trajectories of the British Empire. Finally, he borrows the ideas of Pierre Paul Leroy-Beaulieu (1843–1916), the French expert on the modern state and colonialism. London's reading is impressive, as is his marshaling of data, including those on imports and exports. Perhaps most impressive and moving is London's mastery of the art of persuasion. His style is seductive, his sentences powerful, his images striking. London turns economics and politics into a global drama with money and capital-ists as the leading players. Karl Marx, himself a master stylist in *The Communist Manifesto,* would have been carried along by London's rhetoric; indeed, "The Question of the Maximum" echoes the *Manifesto.* "Battles will be waged," London writes, "not for honor and glory, nor for thrones and sceptres, but for dollars and cents and for marts and exchanges." By the end of the essay, readers may well feel they have a front row seat in the global the-ater of war, revolution, and empire. Readers will see that he could be as adept in the world of fact as in the world of fiction and that he could be as much at home with statistics as with intangible ghosts, goblins, and the human soul. •

For any social movement or development there must be a maximum limit beyond which it cannot proceed. That civilization which does not advance must decline, and so, when the maximum of development has been reached in any given direction, soci-ety must either retrograde or change the direction of its advance. There are many families of men that have failed, in the critical period of their economic evolution, to effect a change in direction, and were forced to fall back. Vanquished at the moment of their maximum, they have dropped out of the whirl of the world. There was no room for them. Stronger competitors have taken their places, and they have either rotted into oblivion or remain to be crushed under the iron heel of the dominant races in as remorseless a struggle as the world has yet witnessed. But in this struggle fair women and chivalrous men will play no part. Types and ideals have changed. Helens and Launcelots are anachronisms. Blows will be given and taken, and men fight and die, but not for faiths and altars. Shrines will be desecrated, but they will be the shrines, not of temples, but market-places. Prophets will arise, but they will be the prophets of prices and products. Battles will be waged, not for honor and glory, nor for thrones and sceptres, but for dollars and cents and for marts and exchanges. Brain and not brawn will endure, and the captains of war will be commanded by the captains of industry. In short, it will be a contest for the mastery of the world's commerce and for industrial supremacy.

It is more significant, this struggle into which we have plunged, for the fact that it is the first struggle to involve the globe. No general movement of man has been so wide-spreading, so far-reaching. Quite local was the supremacy of any ancient people; likewise the rise to empire of Macedonia and Rome, the waves of Arabian valor and fanaticism, and the mediaeval crusades to the Holy Sepulchre. But since those times the planet has undergone a unique shrinkage.

The world of Homer, limited by the coast-lines of the Mediterranean and Black seas, was a far vaster world than ours of today, which we weigh, measure, and compute as accurately and as easily as if it were a child's play-ball. Steam has made its parts accessible and drawn them closer together. The telegraph annihilates space and time. Each morning, every part knows what every other part is thinking, contemplating, or doing. A discovery in a German laboratory is being demonstrated in San Francisco within twenty-four hours. A book written in South Africa is published by simultaneous copyright in every English-speaking country, and on the day following is in the hands of the translators. The death of an obscure missionary in China, or of a whiskey-smuggler in the South Seas, is served, the world over, with the morning toast. The wheat output of Argentine or the gold of Klondike are known wherever men meet and trade. Shrinkage, or centralization, has become such that the humblest clerk in any metropolis may place his hand on the pulse of the world. The planet has indeed grown very small; and because of this, no vital movement can remain in the clime or country where it takes its rise.

And so today the economic and industrial impulse is world-wide. It is a matter of import to every people. None may be careless of it. To do so is to perish. It is become a battle, the fruits of which are to the strong, and to none but the strongest of the strong. As the movement approaches its maximum, centralization accelerates and competition grows keener and closer. The competitor nations cannot all succeed. So long as the movement continues its present direction, not only will there not be room for all, but the room that is will become less and less; and when the moment of the maximum is at hand, there will be no room at all. Capitalistic production will have overreached itself, and a change of direction will then be inevitable.

Divers queries arise: What is the maximum of commercial development the world can sustain? How far can it be exploited? How much capital is necessary? Can sufficient capital be accumulated? A brief resume of the industrial history of the last one hundred years or so will be relevant at this stage of the discussion. Capitalistic production, in its modern significance, was born of the industrial revolution in England in the latter half of the eighteenth century. The great inventions of that period were both its father and its mother, while, as Mr. Brooks Adams has shown, the looted treasure of India was the potent midwife. Had there not been an unwonted increase of capital, the impetus would not have been given to invention, while even steam might have languished for generations instead of at once becoming, as it did, the most prominent factor in the new method of production. The improved application of these inventions in the first decades of the nineteenth century mark the transition from the domestic to the factory system of manufacture and inaugurated the era of capitalism. The magnitude of this revolution is manifested by the fact that England alone had invented the means and equipped herself with the machinery whereby she could overstock the world's markets. The home market could not consume a tithe of the home product. To manufacture this home product she had sacrificed her agriculture. She must buy her food from abroad, and to do so she must sell her goods abroad.

But the struggle for commercial supremacy had not yet really begun. England was without a rival. Her navies controlled the sea. Her armies and her insular position gave her peace at home. The world was hers to exploit. For nearly fifty years she dominated the European, American, and Indian trade, while the great wars then convulsing society were destroying possible competitive capital and straining consumption to its utmost. The pioneer of the industrial nations, she thus received such a start in the new race for wealth that it is only today the other nations have succeeded in overtaking her. In 1820 the volume of her trade (imports and exports) was 68,000,000 pounds. In 1899 it had increased to 815,000,000 pounds,—an increase of 1200 per cent in the volume of trade.

For nearly one hundred years England has been producing surplus value. She has been producing far more than she consumes, and this excess has swelled the volume of her capital. This capital has been invested in her enterprises at home and abroad, and in her shipping. In 1898 the Stock Exchange estimated British capital invested abroad at 1,900,000,000 pounds. But hand in hand with her foreign investments have grown her adverse balances of trade. For the ten years ending with 1868, her average yearly adverse balance was 52,000,000 pounds; ending with 1878, 81,000,000 pounds; ending with 1888, 101,000,000 pounds; and ending with 1898, 133,000,000 pounds. In the single year of 1897 it reached the portentous sum of 157,000,000 pounds.

But England's adverse balances of trade in themselves are nothing at which to be frightened. Hitherto they have been paid from out the earnings of her shipping and the interest on her foreign investments. But what does cause anxiety, however, is that, relative to the trade development of other countries, her export trade is falling off, without a corresponding diminution of her imports, and that her securities and foreign holdings do not seem able to stand the added strain. These she is being forced to sell in order to pull even. As the London Times gloomily remarks, "We are entering the twentieth century on the down grade, after a prolonged period of business activity, high wages, high profits, and overflowing revenue." In other words, the mighty grasp England held over the resources and capital of the world is being relaxed. The control of its commerce and banking is slipping through her fingers. The sale of her foreign holdings advertises the fact that other nations are capable of buying them, and, further, that these other nations are busily producing surplus value.

The movement has become general. Today, passing from country to country, an ever-increasing tide of capital is welling up. Production is doubling and quadrupling upon itself. It used to be that the impoverished or undeveloped nations turned to England when it came to borrowing, but now Germany is competing keenly with her in this matter. France is not averse to lending great sums to Russia, and Austria-Hungary has capital and to spare for foreign holdings.

Nor has the United States failed to pass from the side of the debtor to that of the creditor nations. She, too, has become wise in the way of producing surplus value. She has been successful in her efforts to secure economic emancipation. Possessing but 5 per cent of the world's population and producing 32 per cent of the world's food supply, she has been looked upon as the world's farmer; but now, amidst general consternation, she comes forward as the world's manufacturer. In 1888 her manufactured exports amounted to $130,300,087; in 1896, to $253,681,541; in 1897, to $279,652,721; in

1898, to $307,924,994; in 1899, to $338,667,794; and in 1900, to $432,000,000. Regarding her growing favorable balances of trade, it may be noted that not only are her imports not increasing, but they are actually falling off, while her exports in the last decade have increased 72.4 per cent. In ten years her imports from Europe have been reduced from $474,000,000 to $439,000,000; while in the same time her exports have increased from $682,000,000 to $1,111,000,000. Her balance of trade in her favor in 1895 was $75,000,000; in 1896, over $100,000,000; in 1897, nearly $300,000,000; in 1898, $615,000,000; in 1899, $530,000,000; and in 1900, $648,000,000.

In the matter of iron, the United States, which in 1840 had not dreamed of entering the field of international competition, in 1897, as much to her own surprise as any one else's, undersold the English in their own London market. In 1899 there was but one American locomotive in Great Britain; but, of the five hundred locomotives sold abroad by the United States in 1902, England bought more than any other country. Russia is operating a thousand of them on her own roads today. In one instance the American manufacturers contracted to deliver a locomotive in four and one-half months for $9250, the English manufacturers requiring twenty-four months for delivery at $14,000. The Clyde shipbuilders recently placed orders for 150,000 tons of plates at a saving of $250,000, and the American steel going into the making of the new London subway is taken as a matter of course. American tools stand above competition the world over. Ready-made boots and shoes are beginning to flood Europe, — the same with machinery, bicycles, agricultural implements, and all kinds of manufactured goods. A correspondent from Hamburg, speaking of the invasion of American trade, says: "Incidentally, it may be remarked that the typewriting machine with which this article is written, as well as the thousands — nay, hundreds of thousands — of others that are in use throughout the world, were made in America; that it stands on an American table, in an office furnished with American desks, bookcases, and chairs, which cannot be made in Europe of equal quality, so practical and convenient, for a similar price."

In 1893 and 1894, because of the distrust of foreign capital, the United States was forced to buy back American securities held abroad; but in 1897 and 1898 she bought back American securities held abroad, not because she had to, but because she chose to. And not only has she bought back her own securities, but in the last eight years she has become a buyer of the securities of other countries. In the money markets of London, Paris, and Berlin she is a lender of money. Carrying the largest stock of gold in the world, the world, in moments of danger, when crises of international finance loom large, looks to her vast lending ability for safety.

Thus, in a few swift years, has the United States drawn up to the van where the great industrial nations are fighting for commercial and financial empire. The figures of the race, in which she passed England, are interesting:

Year	United States Exports	United Kingdom Exports
1875	$497,263,737	$1,087,497,000
1885	673,593,506	1,037,124,000
1895	807,742,415	1,100,452,000
1896	986,830,080	1,168,671,000
1897	1,079,834,296	1,139,882,000
1898	1,233,564,828	1,135,642,000
1899	1,253,466,000	1,287,971,000
1900	1,453,013,659	1,418,348,000

As Mr. Henry Demarest Lloyd has noted, "When the news reached Germany of the new steel trust in America, the stocks of the iron and steel mills listed on the Berlin Bourse fell." While Europe has been talking and dreaming of the greatness which was, the United States has been thinking and planning and doing for the greatness to be. Her captains of industry and kings of finance have toiled and sweated at organizing and consolidating production and transportation. But this has been merely the developmental stage, the tuning-up of the orchestra. With the twentieth century rises the curtain on the play,—a play which shall have much in it of comedy and a vast deal of tragedy, and which has been well named The Capitalistic Conquest of Europe by America. Nations do not die easily, and one of the first moves of Europe will be the erection of tariff walls. America, however, will fittingly reply, for already her manufacturers are establishing works in France and Germany. And when the German trade journals refused to accept American advertisements, they found their country flamingly bill-boarded in buccaneer American fashion.

M. Leroy-Beaulieu, the French economist, is passionately preaching a commercial combination of the whole Continent against the United States,—a commercial alliance which, he boldly declares, should become a political alliance. And in this he is not alone, finding ready sympathy and ardent support in Austria, Italy, and Germany. Lord Rosebery said, in a recent speech before the Wolverhampton Chamber of Commerce: "The Americans, with their vast and almost incalculable resources, their acuteness and enterprise, and their huge population, which will probably be 100,000,000 in twenty years, together with the plan they have adopted for putting accumulated wealth into great cooperative syndicates or trusts for the purpose of carrying on this great commercial warfare, are the most formidable . . . rivals to be feared."

The London Times says: "It is useless to disguise the fact that Great Britain is being outdistanced. The competition does not come from the glut caused by miscalculation as to the home demand. Our own steel-makers know better and are alarmed. The threatened competition in markets hitherto our own comes from efficiency in production such as never before has been seen." Even the British naval supremacy is in danger, continues the same paper, "for, if we lose our engineering supremacy, our naval supremacy will follow, unless held on sufferance by our successful rivals."

And the Edinburgh Evening News says, with editorial gloom: "The iron and steel trades have gone from us. When the fictitious prosperity caused by the expenditure of our own Government and that of European nations on armaments ceases, half of the men employed in these industries will be turned into the streets. The outlook is appalling. What suffering will have to be endured before the workers realize that there is nothing left for them but emigration!"

That there must be a limit to the accumulation of capital is obvious. The downward course of the rate of interest, notwithstanding that many new employments have been made possible for capital, indicates how large is the increase of surplus value. This decline of the interest rate is in accord with Bohm-Bawerk's law of "diminishing returns." That is, when capital, like anything else, has become over-plentiful, less lucrative use can only be found for the excess. This excess, not being able to earn so much as when capital was less plentiful, competes for safe investments and forces down the interest rate on all capital. Mr. Charles A. Conant has well described the keenness of the scramble for safe investments, even at the prevailing low rates of interest. At the close of the war with Turkey, the Greek loan, guaranteed by Great Britain, France, and Russia, was floated with striking ease. Regardless of the small return, the amount offered at Paris, (41,000,000 francs), was subscribed for twenty-three times over. Great Britain, France, Germany, Holland, and the Scandinavian States, of recent years, have all engaged in converting their securities from 5 per cents to 4 per cents, from 4.5 per cents to 3.5 per cents, and the 3.5 per cents into 3 per cents.

Great Britain, France, Germany, and Austria-Hungary, according to the calculation taken in 1895 by the International Statistical Institute, hold forty-six billions of capital invested in negotiable securities alone. Yet Paris subscribed for her portion of the Greek loan twenty-three times over! In short, money is cheap. Andrew Carnegie and his brother bourgeois kings give away millions annually, but still the tide wells up.

These vast accumulations have made possible "wild-catting," fraudulent combinations, fake enterprises, Hooleyism; but such stealings, great though they be, have little or no effect in reducing the volume. The time is past when startling inventions, or revolutions in the method of production, can break up the growing congestion; yet this saved capital demands an outlet, somewhere, somehow.

When a great nation has equipped itself to produce far more than it can, under the present division of the product, consume, it seeks other markets for its surplus products. When a second nation finds itself similarly circumstanced, competition for these other markets naturally follows. With the advent of a third, a fourth, a fifth, and of divers other nations, the question of the disposal of surplus products grows serious. And with each of these nations possessing, over and beyond its active capital, great and growing masses of idle capital, and when the very foreign markets for which they are competing are beginning to produce similar wares for themselves, the question passes the serious stage and becomes critical.

Never has the struggle for foreign markets been sharper than at the present. They are the one great outlet for congested accumulations. Predatory capital wanders the world over, seeking where it may establish itself. This urgent need for foreign markets is forcing upon the world-stage an era of great colonial empire. But this does not stand, as in the past, for the subjugation of peoples and countries for the sake of gaining their products, but for the privilege of selling them products. The theory once was, that the colony owed its existence and prosperity to the mother country; but today it is the mother country that owes its existence and prosperity to the colony. And in the future, when that supporting colony becomes wise in the way of producing surplus value and sends its goods back to sell to the mother country, what then? Then the world will have been exploited, and capitalistic production will have attained its maximum development.

Foreign markets and undeveloped countries largely retard that moment. The favored portions of the earth's surface are already occupied, though the resources of many are yet virgin. That they have not long since been wrested from the hands of the barbarous and decadent peoples who possess them is due, not to the military prowess of such peoples, but to the jealous vigilance of the industrial nations. The powers hold one another back. The Turk lives because the way is not yet clear to an amicable division of him among the powers. And the United States, supreme though she is, opposes the partition of China, and intervenes her huge bulk between the hungry nations and the mongrel Spanish republics. Capital stands in its own way, welling up and welling up against the inevitable moment when it shall burst all bonds and sweep resistlessly across such vast stretches as China and South America. And then there will be no more worlds to exploit, and capitalism will either fall back, crushed under its own weight, or a change of direction will take place which will mark a new era in history.

The Far East affords an illuminating spectacle. While the Western nations are crowding hungrily in, while the Partition of China is commingled with the clamor for the Spheres of Influence and the Open Door, other forces are none the less potently at work. Not only are the young Western peoples pressing the older ones to the wall, but the East itself is beginning to awake. American trade is advancing, and British trade is losing ground, while Japan, China, and India are taking a hand in the game themselves.

In 1893, 100,000 pieces of American drills were imported into China; in 1897, 349,000. In 1893, 252,000 pieces of American sheetings were imported against 71,000 British; but in 1897, 566,000 pieces of American sheetings were imported against only 10,000 British. The cotton goods and yarn trade (which forms 40 per cent of the whole trade with China) shows a remarkable advance on the part of the United States. During the last ten years America has increased her importation of plain goods by 121 per cent in quantity and 59.5 per cent in value, while that of England and India combined has decreased 13.75 per cent in quantity and 8 per cent in value. Lord Charles Beresford, from whose "Break-up of China" these figures are taken, states that English yarn has receded and Indian yarn advanced to the front. In 1897, 140,000 piculs of Indian yarn were imported, 18,000 of Japanese, 4500 of Shanghai-manufactured, and 700 of English.

Japan, who but yesterday emerged from the mediaeval rule of the Shogunate and seized in one fell swoop the scientific knowledge and culture of the Occident, is already today showing what wisdom she has acquired in the production of surplus value, and is preparing herself that she may tomorrow play the part to Asia that England did to Europe one hundred years ago. That the difference in the world's affairs wrought by those one hundred years will prevent her succeeding is manifest; but it is equally manifest that they cannot prevent her playing a leading part in the industrial drama which has commenced on the Eastern stage. Her imports into the port of Newchang in 1891 amounted to but 22,000 taels; but in 1897 they had increased to 280,000 taels. In manufactured goods, from matches, watches, and clocks to the rolling stock of railways, she has already given stiff shocks to her competitors in the Asiatic markets; and this while she is virtually yet in the equipment stage of production. Erelong she, too, will be furnishing her share to the growing mass of the world's capital.

As regards Great Britain, the giant trader who has so long overshadowed Asiatic commerce, Lord Charles Beresford says: "But competition is telling adversely; the energy of the British merchant is being equalled by other nationals . . . The competition of the Chinese and the introduction of steam into the country are also combining to produce changed conditions in China." But far more ominous is the plaintive note he sounds when he says: "New industries must be opened up, and I would especially direct the attention of the Chambers of Commerce (British) to . . . the fact that the more the native competes with the British manufacturer in certain classes of trade, the more machinery he will need, and the orders for such machinery will come to this country if our machinery manufacturers are enterprising enough."

The Orient is beginning to show what an important factor it will become, under Western supervision, in the creation of surplus value. Even before the barriers which restrain Western capital are removed, the East will be in a fair way toward being exploited. An analysis of Lord Beresford's message to the Chambers of Commerce discloses, first, that the East is beginning to manufacture for itself; and, second, that there is a promise of keen competition in the West for the privilege of selling the required machinery. The inexorable query arises: *What is the West to do when it has furnished this machinery?* And when not only the East, but all the now undeveloped countries, confront, with surplus products in their hands, the old industrial nations, capitalistic production will have attained its maximum development.

But before that time must intervene a period which bids one pause for breath. A new romance, like unto none in all the past, the economic romance, will be born. For the dazzling prize of world-empire will the nations of the earth go up in harness. Powers will rise and fall, and mighty coalitions shape and dissolve in the swift whirl of events. Vassal nations and subject territories will be bandied back and forth like so many articles of trade. And with the inevitable displacement of economic centres, it is fair to presume that populations will shift to and fro, as they once did from the South to the North of England on the rise of the factory towns, or from the Old World to the New. Colossal enterprises will be projected and carried through, and combinations of capital and federations of labor be effected on a cyclopean scale. Concentration and organization will be perfected in ways hitherto undreamed. The nation which would keep its head above the tide must accurately adjust supply to demand, and eliminate waste to the last least particle. Standards of living will most likely descend for millions of people. With the increase of capital, the competition for safe investments, and the consequent fall of the interest rate, the principal which today earns a comfortable income would not then support a bare existence. Saving toward old age would cease among the working classes. And as the merchant cities of Italy crashed when trade slipped from their hands on the discovery of the new route to the Indies by way of the Cape of Good Hope, so will there come times of trembling for such nations as have failed to grasp the prize of world-empire. In that given direction they will have attained their maximum development, before the whole world, in the same direction, has attained its. There will no longer be room for them. But if they can survive the shock of being flung out of the world's industrial orbit, a change in direction may then be easily effected. That the decadent and barbarous peoples will be crushed is a fair presumption; likewise that the stronger breeds will survive, entering upon the transition stage to which all the world must ultimately come.

This change of direction must be either toward industrial oligarchies or socialism. Either the functions of private corporations will increase till they absorb the central government, or the functions of government will increase till it absorbs the corporations. Much may be said on the chance of the oligarchy. Should an old manufacturing nation lose its foreign trade, it is safe to predict that a strong effort would be made to build a socialistic government, but it does not follow that this effort would be successful. With the moneyed class controlling the State and its revenues and all the means of subsistence, and guarding its own interests with jealous care, it is not at all impossible that a strong curb could be put upon the masses till the crisis were past. It has been done before. There is no reason why it should not be done again. At the close of the last century, such a movement was crushed by its own folly and immaturity. In 1871 the soldiers of the economic rulers stamped out, root and branch, a whole generation of militant socialists.

Once the crisis were past, the ruling class, still holding the curb in order to make itself more secure, would proceed to readjust things and to balance consumption with production. Having a monopoly of the safe investments, the great masses of unremunerative capital would be directed, not to the production of more surplus value, but to the making of permanent improvements, which would give employment to the people, and make them content with the new order of things. Highways, parks, public buildings, monuments, could be builded; nor would it be out of place to give better factories and homes to the workers. Such in itself would be socialistic, save that it would be done by the oligarchs, a class apart. With the interest rate down to zero, and no field for the investment of sporadic capital, savings among the people would utterly cease, and old-age pensions be granted as a matter of course. It is also a logical necessity of such a system that, when the population began to press against the means of subsistence, (expansion being impossible), the birth rate of the lower classes would be lessened. Whether by their own initiative, or by the interference of the rulers, it would have to be done, and it would be done. In other words, the oligarchy would mean the capitalization of labor and the enslavement of the whole population. But it would be a fairer, juster form of slavery than any the world has yet seen. The per capita wage and consumption would be increased, and, with a stringent control of the birth rate, there is no reason why such a country should not be so ruled through many generations.

On the other hand, as the capitalistic exploitation of the planet approaches its maximum, and countries are crowded out of the field of foreign exchanges, there is a large likelihood that their change in direction will be toward socialism. Were the theory of collective ownership and operation then to arise for the first time, such a movement would stand small chance of success. But such is not the case. The doctrine of socialism has flourished and grown throughout the nineteenth century; its tenets have been preached wherever the interests of labor and capital have clashed; and it has received exemplification time and again by the State's assumption of functions which had always belonged solely to the individual.

When capitalistic production has attained its maximum development, it must confront a dividing of the ways; and the strength of capital on the one hand, and the education and wisdom of the workers on the other, will determine which path society is to travel. It is possible, considering the inertia of the masses, that the whole world might in time come to be dominated by a group of industrial oligarchies, or by one great oligarchy, but it is not probable. That sporadic oligarchies may flourish for definite periods of time is highly possible; that they may continue to do so is as highly improbable. The procession of the ages has marked not only the rise of man, but the rise of the common man. From the chattel slave, or the serf chained to the soil, to the highest seats in modern society, he has risen, rung by rung, amid the crumbling of the divine right of kings and the crash of falling sceptres. That he has done this, only in the end to pass into the perpetual slavery of the industrial oligarch, is something at which his whole past cries in protest. The common man is worthy of a better future, or else he is not worthy of his past.

NOTE.—The above article was written as long ago as 1898. The only alteration has been the bringing up to 1900 of a few of its statistics. As a commercial venture of an author, it has an interesting history. It was promptly accepted by one of the leading magazines and paid for. The editor confessed that it was "one of those articles one could not possibly let go of after it was once in his possession." Publication was voluntarily promised to be immediate. Then the editor became afraid of its too radical nature, forfeited the sum paid for it, and did not publish it. Nor, offered far and wide, could any other editor of bourgeois periodicals be found who was rash enough to publish it. Thus, for the first time, after seven years, it appears in print.

PART II

COMRADE WHITE MAN

The Economics of the Klondike

First published in and reprinted from the *American Monthly Review of Reviews,* January 1900.

In the summer of 1898, when he went to the Klondike, London brought with him, in addition to his gear, a lively interest in Marx and a critical perspective on the workings of capitalist society. For the most part, however, the Klondike took him away from Marxism, socialism, and the radicalism he'd practiced since 1895. The Klondike interrupted his political journey toward revolution, complicating not only his life but also his outlook. In "The Economics of the Klondike," published a year and a half after his return to California, he looks at the region from an economist's point of view, suggesting that in the long run it will be ideal for empire building. The article shows that London knew a great deal about the history, geography, and climate of the Klondike, and, when one compares it to his short stories, one sees the extent to which he mythologized the place in the pages of his fiction.

In the first part of the article, he shows how difficult it would be for the lone miner to make a fortune by hunting for gold in the Klondike. It reads like a warning to dreamers who want to get rich quick. More money will go into the Klondike than the prospector will take out in gold, London insists. Always good with numbers, he crunches them in "The Economics of the Klondike," showing that digging for gold didn't pay, except for a few wealthy mine owners. "If the newcomers succeeded in possessing one claim out of each twenty staked they did well," he writes. "And since not one claim in twenty developed pay dirt, the amount of dust taken out by the newcomers is practically *nil*."

In the second part of the article, London paints a cheerful picture of the Klondike as a territory for commercial development; the article does an abrupt about-face, becoming a glowing advertisement aimed at investors. "The new Klondike, the Klondike of the future, will present remarkable contrasts with the Klondike of the past," he writes. "Natural obstacles will be cleared away or surmounted, primitive methods abandoned, and hardship of toil and travel reduced to the smallest possible minimum."

London wrote critically of capitalism in the industrial world—in England, France, and the United States—but he was largely uncritical of capitalism in the colonial world, including the Yukon. In Europe and the United States, he saw the damage that capitalism wrought, especially in the lives of the working classes. But when he looked at capitalism as it played itself out in Africa, Asia, Latin America—and in the Yukon—he saw inevitable development, progress, and economic advancement for workers as well as capitalists. The fate of the indigenous population did not figure in his calculations, and in "The Economics of the Klondike" he does not once mention Native Americans or the land that was taken from them.

Jack London the Marxist could also be Jack London the imperialist. For most of the 1890s, he greatly admired the British Empire, and in the Yukon, his appreciation of imperial England and its colonial agents soared, perhaps because of the influence of Rudyard Kipling, the bard of empire, whose works he read and admired. •

Now that the rush to the northland Eldorado is a thing of the past, one may contemplate with sober vision its promises and their fulfillment. Who has profited? Who has lost? How much gold has gone into it? And finally, what will be the ultimate outcome of this great shifting of energy, this intense concentration of capital and labor upon one of the hitherto unexplored portions of the earth's surface?

In 1897, between the middle of July and the first of September, fully 25,000 argonauts attempted to enter the Yukon country. Of these the great majority failed, being turned back at the head of the Lynn Canal and at St. Michaels by the early advent of winter and the consequent closing of navigation on the Yukon. The spring of 1898 found 100,000 more on the various trails leading to the Klondike, chief among which were Skagnay and Dyea, the Stickeen route, beginning at Fort Wragell, the "all-Canadian" route by Edmonton, and the all-water route by way of Bering Sea. To all of these had been iterated and reiterated the warning of the old-timers: Don't dream of venturing north with less than $600. The more the better. One thousand dollars will be none too much.

A few bold spirits were not to be deterred that they did not possess the required amount, but in the main $600 was, if anything, under the average sum buckled about each pilgrim's waist. But taking $600 as a fair estimate of individual expense, for 125,000 men it makes an outlay of $75,000,000. Now, it is unimportant whether all or none of them reached the goal—these $75,000,000 were expended in the attempt. The railroad, the ocean transportation companies, and the outfitting cities of Puget Sound received probably $35,000,000; the remainder was dropped on the trail. The majority of those who succeeded in getting through had barely the $10 necessary for a miner's license; a few were able to pay the $15 required for the recording of the first claim they staked; many were penniless.

Since the transportation and outfitting companies certainly profited, the question arises: Did the Yukon district return to the gold-seekers the equivalent of what they spent in getting there? This may be decided by a brief review of the gold discoveries which have been made. In the fall of 1896 the first news of MacCormack's strike went down the Yukon and across the border to the established Alaskan mining camps of Forty Mile and Circle City. A stampede resulted and the Eldorado, Bonanza, and Hunker Creeks were staked. That winter the news crept out to "salt water" and civilization. But no excitement was created, no rush precipitated. The world proper took no notice of it.

In the summer of 1897 a stampede from the three creeks mentioned went over the divide back of Eldorado and staked Dominion Creek, a tributary of the Indian River. At this very moment the first gold shipments were reaching the Pacific Coast and the first seeds of the gold rush being sown by the newspapers. During this period and the early fall, Sulphur, Bear, and Gold Run Creeks were being staked in a desultory fashion — as of course were many others which have since proved worthless. Regardless of glowing reports and the ubiquitous "wildcats," and with the exception of a very small number of bench claims, there have been no more paying creeks discovered in the Klondike. And this must be noted and emphasized: All the paying creeks above named were located before the people arrived who were hurrying in from the outside.

It is thus clearly demonstrated that those who participated in the fall rush of 1898 were shut out from the only creeks which would even pay expenses. But, the stay-at-home at once exclaims, were there not other ways of playing even? How about the benches and the "lays"?

Let the "benches" be first considered. A bench claim is a hillside claim as distinguished from a creek claim. The Skookum bench strike was made prior to the influx from the outside, and consequent to it came the discovery of the French Hill and Gold Hill benches, situated between Skookum and Eldorado. These last two are the only strikes in which the newcomers could have taken part. But at this point two factors arise limiting their participation. In the first place, not more than a score of French Hill and Gold Hill bench claims are rich, and not one will turn out more than $100,000. In the second place, these benches were right in the heart of the old workings, where the old-timers were on the ground, not five minutes' walk away. If the newcomers succeeded in possessing one claim out of each twenty staked they did well; and since not one claim in twenty developed pay dirt, the amount of dust taken out by the newcomers is practically *nil.*

Now as to the "lays." In the winter of 1896 the lay men did well. But at that time conditions were entirely different from those of the following winter. The importance of the Klondike strike was not appreciated, the value of the gold in the gravel problematical, grub was scarce, and the demand greatly in excess of the labor supply. Under these circumstances it was easy for men to obtain profitable lays. But in 1897 these favorable conditions had disappeared. The owners knew the true worth of their holdings, grub was plentiful, and the labor market stocked. Now, no mine owner was silly enough to let a lay to a man which would clear that man $50,000, when he (the mine owner) could work that same man on wages the same length of time for $2,000. However, many newcomers, with an ignorance really pathetic, took such lays as were offered, used their own tools and "grub," worked hard all winter, and at the wash-up found that they would have been better off had they idled in their cabins. It is a fact that hundreds of lay men on various creeks refused to put their winter's dumps through the sluices. It is thus evident that the Yukon returned no equivalent to the gold-seekers who expended $75,000,000.

It is an old miner's maximum that two dollars go into the ground for each dollar that comes out. This the Klondike has not failed to exemplify, and a startling balance-sheet may be struck between the cost of effort and the value of the reward. On the one side legitimate effort alone must be considered; on the other the actual gold taken from the earth.

Scores of new transportation and trading companies, formed during the excitement with an enterprise only equaled by their ignorance, lost in wrecked river and ocean-going craft and in collapse several millions of dollars. The men in the country before the rush—the mine owners, middlemen, and prospectors—between their expenses and their labor form an important item, as do also the expenditures of the Canadian and American governments. But disregarding these items and many minor ones, the result will still be sufficiently striking. Consider only the 125,000 gold-seekers, each of whom on an average, in getting or in trying to get into the Klondike, spent a year of his life. In view of the hardship and the severity of their toil, $4 per day per man would indeed be a cheap purchase of their labor. One and all, they would refuse in a civilized country to do the work they did do at such a price. And let them be granted 65 resting days in the twelvemonth. Still the effort expended by these 125,000 men in the course of the year is worth in the aggregate $150,000,000. To this let there be added the $75,000,000 they spent in cash, and we have for one side of the balance the sum of $225,000,000—or, roughly $220,000,000.

The other side is easily constructed. The spring wash-up of 1898 was $8,000,000; of 1899, $14,000,000. In the absence of the full reports this latter is a liberal estimate, allowing an increment of $4,000,000 and considering the fact that no new discoveries have since been made. The figures stand for themselves; $220,000,000 have been spent in extracting $22,000,000 from the ground.

Such a result would seem pessimistic were not the ultimate result capable of a reasonable anticipation. While this sudden and immense application of energy proved disastrous to those involved, it has been of inestimable benefit to the Yukon country, to those who will remain in it, and to those yet to come.

Perhaps more than all other causes combined the food shortage has been the greatest detriment in the development of that region. From the first explorer down to and including the winter of 1897 the land has been in a chronic state of famine. But a general shortage of supplies is now a thing of the past. About 1874 George Holt was the first white man to penetrate the country avowedly in quest of gold. In 1880 Edward Bean headed a party of twenty-five from the Sitka to the Hootalinqua River, and from then on small parties of gold-seekers constantly filtered into the Yukon Valley. But these men had to depend wholly upon what provisions they could carry in with them by the most primitive methods. Consequently thorough prospecting was out of the question, for they were always forced back to the coast through lack of food. Then the Alaska Commercial Company, in addition to maintaining its trading posts scattered along the river, began to freight in provisions to sell to the miners who wished to winter in the country. But so many men remained that a food shortage was inevitable. With every steamer that was added more men hurried over the passes and wintered; and as a result demand always increased faster than supply. Every winter found the miners on the edge of famine, and every spring, with the promise of more steamers, more men rushed in.

But henceforth famine will only be a tradition in the land. The Klondike rush placed hundreds of steamers on the Yukon, opened the navigation of its upper reaches and the lakes, put tramways around the unnavigable Box Canon and White Horse Rapids, and built a railroad from salt water at Skaguay across the White Pass to the head of steamboat traffic on Lake Bennett.

With the dwindling of population caused by the collapse of the rush, these transportation facilities will be, if anything greater than the need of the country demands. The excessive profits will be cut down and only the best-equipped and most efficient companies remain in operation. Conditions will become normal and the Klondike just enter upon its true development. With the necessaries and luxuries of life cheap and plentiful, with the importation of the machinery which will cheapen many enterprises and render many others possible, with easy traveling and quick communication between it and the world and between its parts, the resources of the Yukon district will be opened up and developed in a steady, business-like way.

Living expenses being normal, a moderate wage will be possible. Nor will laborers fail to hasten there from the congested labor markets of the older countries. This, in turn, will permit the Employment on a large scale of much of the world's restless capital now seeking investment. On the White River, eighty miles south of Dawson, great deposits of copper are to be found. Coal, so essential to the country's exploitation, has already been discovered at various places along the Yukon, from "MacCormack's Houses" above the Five Finger Rapids down to Rampart City and the Koyukuk in Alaska. There is small doubt that iron will eventually be unearthed, and with equal certainty the future gold-mining will be mainly quartz.

As to the ephemeral placers, the outlook cannot be declared bad. It is fair to suppose that many new ones will be discovered, but outside of this there is much else that is favorable. While there are very few "paying" creeks, it must be understood that nothing below a return of $10 a day per man under the old expensive conditions has been considered "pay." But when a sack of flour may be bought for a dollar instead of fifty, and all other things in proportion, it is apparent how great a fall the scale of pay can sustain. In California gravel containing 5 cents of gold to the cubic yard is washed at a profit; but hitherto in the Klondike gravel yielding less than $10 to the cubic yard has been ignored as unprofitable. That is to say, the old conditions in the Klondike made it impossible to wash dirt which was not at least two hundred times richer than that washed in California. But this will not be true henceforth. There are immense quantities of these cheaper gravels in the Yukon, and it is inevitable that they yield to the enterprise of brains and capital.

In short, though many of its individuals have lost, the world will have lost nothing by the Klondike. The new Klondike, the Klondike of the future, will present remarkable contrasts with the Klondike of the past. Natural obstacles will be cleared away or surmounted, primitive methods abandoned, and hardship of toil and travel reduced to the smallest possible minimum. Exploration and transportation will be systematized. There will be no waste energy, no harum-scarum carrying on of industry. The frontiersman will yield to the laborer, the prospector to the mining engineer, the dog-driver to the engine driver, the trader and speculator to the steady-going modern man of business; these are the men in whose hands the destiny of the Klondike will be entrusted.

Incarnation of Push and Go

First published in and reprinted from the *Los Angeles Challenge*, February 27, 1901.

London joined the Socialist Labor Party (SLP) in 1896, and though he gave speeches before the organization, he did not attend regular meetings or take part in the fierce debates—about how, when, and where to make the revolution—within its ranks or the ranks of the Socialist Party of America, which was formed in 1901. That year, along with most of the members of the Oakland branch of the SLP, he joined the Socialist Party of America (SPA), which also gained members from the recently formed Social Democratic Party (SDP). The ideological differences between these three radical organizations mattered dearly to some socialists, but not to London, and in 1901, at the age of twenty-five, he accepted the nomination of the brand new Social Democratic Party as its candidate for mayor of Oakland, his hometown. SPA members also supported him, and he felt sanguine about his own chances for victory, though he only received 245 votes. In 1904, he wrote an ebullient essay entitled "Explanation of the Great Socialist Vote of 1904," published in William Randolph Hearst's *San Francisco Examiner* soon after election day. "That the working class shall conquer (mark the note of fatalism), is as certain as the rising of the sun," he noted. "Just as the merchant class of the eighteenth century wanted democracy applied to politics, so the working class of the twentieth century wants democracy applied to industry, and to this end they organize the working classes into a political party that is a party of revolt." In 1905, he ran again for mayor of Oakland, and though he only received 981 votes, he continued to express optimism and hope about the inevitable triumph of socialism in America. In the upbeat, energetic essay "Incarnation of Push and Go," he accepts his party's nomination as candidate for mayor. Published in February 1901, in the *Los Angeles Challenge*—a publication owned by the socialist millionaire H. Gaylord Wilshire—it reads like a campaign speech for public office. London condemns the Republicans and the Democrats alike, though he does not once mention the names of those two parties. Both are opportunistic and hypocritical, he insists, and they both buttress the capitalist system. London notes that socialists have moved the political agenda of the nation to the left, and that public ownership of utilities—long one of his pet projects—has been co-opted by the major parties. They thereby "unwittingly" aided the socialists "in the education of the people."

Without economic equality, London argues in "Incarnation of Push and Go," there can be no real social or political equality in America, and the socialists alone demand equality of economic opportunity. Not once in this essay does he mention his own character, personality, or work as a creative writer. The political and economic issues are what matter to him. Justice matters, too, and as he explains, "The law is many-sided," and "that which it measures to the poor man is not always what it measures, under precisely the same circumstances, to the rich corporation." •

Dear [H. Gaylord] Wilshire—Am two months behind in all my work, sleeping five-and-one-half in the twenty-four, and trying to catch up, so I can't find time and space to write anything original for The Challenge. However, find herewith, if it can be of any use to you, my letter of acceptance of nomination for mayor.

My God, The Challenge goes along with a rush! It seems the incarnation of the push and go of the period.

Oakland, Cal., February 16, 1901

Good luck, Jack London

1130 East Fifteenth Street, Oakland, Cal., Jan. 29

Mr. J. H. Eustice, Secretary,
City Executive Committee, the Social Democratic Party:

Dear Sir—In accepting the nomination for mayor at the hands of the Social Democratic party, I feel constrained to add a few words concerning the forthcoming election.

A striking feature of recent municipal elections has been the remarkable similarity in the platforms of the various parties. All the platforms, not omitting the Social Democrats, have contained strong demands for the municipalization of public utilities. So expressed, it would seem, therefore, that the common wish of the community was for municipal ownership. And it would seem, furthermore, since all parties have demanded it, that long ere this a fair share of the public utilities had passed into the hands of the people of Oakland.

So, it seems, but as a matter of fact, not so. There has been some hemming and hawing, no doubt; and that was all that was to be expected. It could not have been otherwise, considering the parties into whose keeping were entrusted the affairs of the city. They could have done nothing more than they have done; nor is it in the nature of things that they should.

Between the national creed and the municipal creed of either of the old parties there is little or nothing in common. The little in common is, in the last analysis, that they are capitalists. The interests of capitalism are their interests, and that is all. On the other hand, there is much in conflict. When a party nationally champions gold, expansion, the trusts, and the big capitalists, it is certainly very inconsistent for the same party to municipally champion public ownership, to the detriment of the large capitalist and the benefit of the proletariat. The same holds for the other party, when it goes into municipal politics; for, though it opposed gold, expansion, the trusts, and the large capitalists, it cries out unavailingly for the salvation, not of the proletariat, but of the small capitalist who is being crushed out by the inexorable industrial evolution. So, election after election, we see the same inconsistency flourish, the same paradox, which strive as they will, cannot be fused into the honest truism.

But the municipal platform of the Social Democratic Party does not stand, unrelated, as something different from the national platform; for, after all, it is merely a part of a great world philosophy—an economic, political and social philosophy, reared on sound ethical and humanely ethical foundations. Its one great demand is justice, or, in other words, an equal chance for all men. Just as we today have civil equality before the law, and political equality at the polls, so it is a matter of simple justice that we should also have equality of opportunity in industrial life. For without the last, the first and the second often come to naught. The law is many-sided. That which it measures to the poor man is not always what it measures, under precisely the same circumstances, to the rich corporation. Of this here is no discussion. It has been substantiated, under oath, before too many a congressional and State investigation committee. As regards political equality, it is much the same. One vote counts as much as another, true; but the machine counts for something more, and when the wealth of the country is back of the machine, the equality of the unorganized incoherent, moneyless working class vanishes in thin air.

So, when we Social Democrats draft our municipal platform, we demand that which our national platform demands, that which we demand the world over, namely, equality of opportunity. True, our immediate municipal demands partake of the nature of palliatives; but on the other hand, they are consistent with our great fundamental demand. This cannot be said of the old parties.

Incidentally, in closing, it is meet that we congratulate ourselves for the work we have already done. For it is we, the Socialists, working as a leaven throughout society, who are responsible for the great and growing belief in municipal owner-ship. It is we, the Socialists, by our propaganda, who have forced the old parties to throw as sops to the popular unrest, like demands, and unwittingly to aid us in the education of the people.

Fraternally yours, Jack London.

The Salt of the Earth

First published in *Anglo-American Magazine,* August 1902; reprinted from the typescript at the Huntington Library.

This essay, never before available to the general public, reveals London at his most jingoistic, racist, and strident. For London, the "salt of the earth" are the Anglo-Saxons—"the English-speaking people of the world" who acknowledge "English traditions." Every other nationality and ethnic group, in his view, is doomed to extinction and extermination, including the French, whom he describes as effete. Taking the vantage point of the empire builder, London characterizes the world at the start of the twentieth century in terms of bloodshed and conquest, a "scramble for markets and resources," and political domination by England and the United States.

London, of course, was not alone in articulating an imperialist perspective at the end of the nineteenth century and the start of the twentieth. In fact, he reflected popularly held notions—many of them expressed by leading scientists and learned professors of biology and history—about the superiority of the white race over the brown, yellow, and black races, which were, of course, described as inferior and "unfit," a concept that enticed Jack London. "I am first of all a white man and only then a socialist," he said. Indeed, his sense of identity as a white person goes back to his earliest years, preceding his reading in both socialism and the racist and imperialist literature of the day, including Kipling, Herbert Spencer, and Benjamin Kidd, the author of *Social Evolution* (1894)—an international bestseller—and *Control of the Tropics* (1898). Indeed, in "The Salt of the Earth," London repeats the kinds of ideas about race that Kidd, who believed in the superiority of the English, expressed in the mid and late 1890s. In a sense, London agreed with the African American intellectual and scholar W. E. B. DuBois, who wrote in *The Souls of Black Folk*—published in 1903, a year after the essay "The Salt of the Earth"—that "the problem of the twentieth century is the problem of the color line." Except that London and DuBois stood on opposite sides of the color line.

In the distant future, London allows in "The Salt of the Earth," the laws of evolution may turn against the white Anglo-Saxon, unseating him from power, but in the immediate future, he will prevail. Evolution, he explains, serves no moral purpose and is neither wrong nor right; the fittest races survive and thrive, while the weaker races degenerate and perish. "The Negro" in the American South, he notes indifferently, is "disenfranchised and reduced to an economic slavery." The inhabitants of Tasmania are disappearing so that a "superior race" can take over. "The dominant races are robbing and slaying in every quarter of the globe," he observes coolly. From London's perspective, this carnage is not only inevitable but also beneficial for the progress of humanity.

He may sound cold and heartless, he says; the modern age demands it. "There is no longer the naïve faith in rosy dreams and reverence for hoary tradition." Viewing the world stage from a perspective infused with social Darwinism, London is blind to the global eco-nomic forces that would lead to World War I, as well as the embryonic anticolonial move-ments that would sweep the world as the British Empire disintegrated. It would not be racial or ethnic factors—as he suggested—that would dismantle that empire, but economic and political forces. Moreover, London's narrow perspective on the British Empire in India eclipses the brutal effects of colonialism.

Though London deleted this essay from his 1905 anthology of essays *War of the Classes,* the originally intended title for which was *The Salt of the Earth,* he held on to the views that he expressed here. Glorification of empire and fear of nonwhite races surface in other essays, including "These Bones Shall Rise Again," another paean to empire and the Anglo-Saxon race, and "The Yellow Peril," his warning to the white race about the ris-ing power of China and the Chinese. Other ideas found in the present selection also appear elsewhere, including the notions that "the history of civilization is a history of wan-dering," that civilization is a "very thin veneer," and that underneath the surface, modern man is as "savage and elemental and barbarous" as his primitive ancestors.

What's perhaps most distressing about "The Salt of the Earth"—and so much at odds with London's socialist ideals of equality—is the hardness of heart, and the indifference, London expresses on the subject of genocide. He reduces millions to the status of insects: "In the last century, nineteenth of its era, millions of human beings were destroyed through contact with superior civilization," he writes. To those who protest, crying out with "reckless reverence" words like "liberty," "equality," and "universal brotherhood," he says, "eternal inequality is the iron rule of life."

Perhaps London should be given credit, though, for looking at the economic and polit-ical situation of the world honestly, and not through rose-colored glasses. Indeed, one of his main points is that people did not face the naked facts of the twentieth century—a century born of violence and bloodshed. London argues that people make pious state-ments and invoke a pure morality, but they don't do much if anything to change the lam-entable situations they condemn—often even adding to the problem. In short, he says, modern humans are hypocrites—an attitude he shares with George Orwell, among others. People offer "wise and virtuous maxims" while their own country invades and destroys less powerful nations. They talk about equality and then compete fiercely with and exploit their own neighbors. Then, too, he notes that idealists and enlightened citizens like to insist that all people have the right to sovereignty, but don't act to stop or slow the "robbing and slay-ing" by powerful nations that goes on all around the world. Humanity has not progressed very far from prehistoric times, London insists in "The Salt of the Earth." Men murder one another. They torture one another; they rape and pillage. Those who live by the sword die by the sword, he says; but those who reject the sword also die by it. Near the end of this long essay, London offers a quotation from Aline Gorren, the author of *Anglo-Saxons and Others* (1900) and an editor at Scribner's, as well as an insightful literary critic: "To know

what life is you must live it, face it squarely, take hold of it with both hands, shoulder its burdens, without asking whether they are pleasant or unpleasant exactly as they present
themselves." Gorren's words might be read as London's motto, and though he did not
always live by it, he certainly tried. •

The movement of human thought from the particular to the universal has caused
many changes in the attitude of man toward himself and this his world. Definiteness,
and still greater definiteness, characterize this movement. The dim perceptions and
vague phantasms of the old theology have flickered and vanished in the clear white
light of science. Darwin horrified the world, but to-day our remote relationship with
the anthropoid apes is not repulsive. Our cave and arboreal ancestors, hairy of body
and prognathous of jaw, have taken their place on the witness stand, and false Adam's
lineal claim has been thrown out of court. We are for the greater frankness to-day. We
demand an honest statement of fact. No matter how it hurts, the truth must be spo-
ken. Truth — not of the heart's ardent logic but of the head's colder reasoning.
Credulity has little place in the present age. There is no longer the naïve faith in rosy
dreams and reverence for hoary tradition. Let us hear the evidence, we say. If there be
none, fling them out!

Disguise it as we may, though a good world it is yet a brutal one. For nineteen hundred years the teachings of Christ have been multiplied and spread over all the earth.
And in the year just ended, the nations of the earth, as of yore, went up against one
another in their harness. In that same time, in the United States, there were 14,000
murders. We are not unaccustomed to a community burning one of its members at
the stake and carrying off to its homes choice slices of roasted flesh, heat-crinkled ears,
and shriveled fingerjoints. We kill men, individually and collectively; we put to the
torture; nor is it unusual for the females of our species to be ravished much in the
same way the wife-stealing exogamists did in the forgotten past. So we must confess
the truth: our civilization has not yet proved itself aught but a veneer, and a very thin
veneer. Underneath we are as savage and elemental and barbarous as primitive man.

More than ever to-day is the race to the swift, the battle to the strong. Nor have the
meek and lowly yet come to inherit the earth. In the struggle for food and shelter, for
place and power, the weak and less efficient are crowded back and trampled under as
they always have been. We have captains of industry who live in palaces and control
revenues more colossal than those controlled by the wearers of the Roman or
Babylonian purple. And we have wage slaves of field and sweatshop, and paupers as

empty-bellied and cadaverous, as any who have raised the wail of the miserable and the despised down all the past. It is the same old game of natural selection, ruthlessly being played out. From era to era the rules change somewhat, but at bottom it is the same, the survival of the fittest. Among the ancient forbears of the race, it was the physically strong who triumphed and gathered to them an unequal portion of material comfort and glory. Later, it was those who were strong both physically and intellectually. To-day it is the intellectually strong. But through all its guises, through all its differences of time and space, it is the strong who triumph, and more usually, the strongest of the strong. Just as sure as in the past lower and weaker types have given way to higher and stronger types, just so sure, to-day and to-morrow, will the higher and stronger types take to themselves the earth and its treasures. And their tenure shall be a tenure of strength. Should they weaken, or should yet stronger types arise, they will be dispossessed and crushed.

Evolution is an expression which we use for convenience to describe the play and interplay of force and matter. We do not know whether there is a vast directing intelligence behind this process. We do know that it deals only with the things that are; that never yet has it been known to produce a result other than that predicated by the forces and matter at work. If the sum of the forces of a given environment lay a premium upon the ugly and vile and a handicap upon the beautiful and good, the ugly and vile will survive and the beautiful and good be blotted out. To happen otherwise is unthinkable. It would take away whatever rational sanction for thought we may possess; for the stupendous fabric of knowledge we have reared crashes to chaos if there is no such thing as persistence of phenomena.

So evolution deals with force and matter. It has no concern with human right and wrong. And this fact is one well worth the notice of those who would read moral purposes into the evolutionary process. Such sentimental ethicists, heart-reasoners and dreamers, fail to note the difference between precept and practice, between preached ethics and practiced ethics. They spell out, with reckless reverence, such phrases as "liberty," "equality," "natural rights," and "universal brotherhood," seemingly unaware of the fact that eternal difference and eternal inequality is the iron rule of life. They preach the gospel of the weak, and straightway take a mortgage on their neighbor's goods and chattels, or undercut or outbid their competitors in business or labor. While they talk idle words of right and wrong and of what ought to be, *what is* is taking place. While they are saying, "the abused negro, give him a chance," the negro is being disenfranchised and reduced to an economic slavery as severe as the chattel slavery he endured a generation back. They speak of the right of a people to its native soil, forgetting that all peoples are trespassers; and even as they speak, the dominant races are robbing and slaying in every quarter of the globe.

Evolution does not hold in leash its mighty forces till pigmy man has determined the right and wrong of the next step. Nor has it a chosen people. In the surface strata of the earth rot the wrecks of myriads of species which were, but which are not. For a time they held their own in the forefront of the fight for life, then vanished before stronger competitors like summer mist in the prime of day. The story of man is likewise filled with such disaster. We speculate on that early race whose records we read in the Nile mud, and which had disappeared ere the ancient Egyptian dynasties were founded. The Celt, who overshadowed Europe in the morning of history, wretchedly survives in a few isolate regions. And what of that dark skinned race which held the soil even before he came? And in our own day we have witnessed the melancholy spectacle of the Tasmanian passing away in order that a superior race might find room. Yet the passing of these peoples is no manifestation of retributive justice. They did no sin. The Celt was not emasculated by luxury. He was not eaten with the canker of degeneration. He was strong, and vigorous, and healthy. But a new and stronger race burst upon the stage he trod, and he was hustled ignominiously off.

By the ethics we hold to-day, this hurling out of existence of unsinning races is unjust. None the less they have been hurled out, they are being hurled out. And there lies the crux of the whole question. In the struggle of type with type, it is ethnics which determines, not ethics. Under a given environment the race which survives is that best fitted to survive; and it is best fitted to survive because in its evolution it has developed characters which better enable it to cope with the given environment than can the race it displaces.

On the other hand, it may be said that this is all very true of the past, but that in the present, man, actuated by higher ideals and a broader humanity, softens the rigor of the struggle of type with type. The possession of certain moral concepts is a safeguard against a repetition of the cruelties of the past. Maxims and axioms have become potent factors in the new evolution. In other words, ethical formulae have the power to mould and determine social growth, even in the face of and contrary to the whole previous biological and social growth. But is this true? A hundred years ago, they hit upon a few such formulas in France. It was the settled opinion that by the instilling of wise and virtuous maxims a whole people would become wise and virtuous. But they had failed to figure upon their own composition, and the scheme of social regeneration went gloriously to pieces. To-day we own many wise and virtuous maxims. Yet the world holds its hands and watches Great Britain trounce little

Transvaal. We of the United States have proclaimed for a century and a quarter that life, liberty and the pursuit happiness are inalienable rights; yet, when our economic development was ripe, we denied some millions of people over on the other side of the world the right to live and pursue happiness otherwise than by the sacrifice of their liberty. And the sociologist, hammering together the ribs of his skeleton science, confesses that the time has not yet arrived when man may intellectually impel as well as direct the society in which he lives.

Preach as we may, dream as we may, the struggle between man and man, and between families of men, still goes on. Heart-reasoners and idealizers do not retard one jot or tittle the passing of the Alaskan Indian—an erstwhile mighty race now crooning its death-song over the cold ashes of dead fires. Nor do these heart-reasoners and idealizers stop for an instant the political and commercial exploitation of the continent of Africa. In the disposition of China, with her four hundred millions of souls, they have no say. And in the clamor and tumult of the marshalling of the races and the apportionment of the globe, their voices are not heard.

There are breeds and breeds of men, some stronger than others, some more efficient. The present world-era is a machine era and commercial era. And in such an era, the best inventors, cheapest producers, and keenest traders, are the fittest breeds for survival, provided, certainly, that they are also possessed of commensurate organization and political genius. And in this connection it is of interest to speculate upon which of the breeds is pre-eminently fittest to live in this our world in these first decades of the twentieth century. Which breed, from the evidence at hand, bids highest for the material wealth and resources of the globe? Which breed, for to-day and the immediate to-morrow, is it that may be called "The Salt of the Earth?"

At first glance, and on closer scrutiny, the evidence preponderates in favor of the Anglo-Saxon. In lands, in wealth, in population (including tributary population), in commercial and political prestige, and in peculiar fitness to cope with the forces of this present world-era, it stands second to none. Consider the British Empire. It is four times the size of Europe, containing between eleven and twelve millions of square miles of territory. Its population approximates four hundred millions. In this day, when a world-power must be a sea-power, it possesses far and away the strongest navy in the world. In wealth and power and structure it is like to nothing in all the past. It is the mightiest and most prodigious empire the world has yet witnessed. And like unto none in all the past, a confederation of democracies such as it is, it carries within itself the capacity for growth and adaptation. It is the most successful political adventure man has yet achieved.

But this tight little island on the rim of the Western Ocean, with is dependencies, is not the Anglo-Saxon race. Beyond that Western Ocean, stretching forth its arms from the East Indies to the Antilles, is the United States. What figure does it make among the nations? The United States has a larger population than any European country save Russia; while, measured by its standard of living, by its wealth, education, and productive capacity, in real greatness it is far beyond the land of the White Tsar. In the last ten years its increase of thirteen millions of population was greater than that of any country; while of that portion of its increase brought about by immigration practically all is assimilable. By the machinery it has cunningly devised, and by its efficient organization of industry, its seventy-five millions are equal in productive power to one hundred and fifty millions of Europeans. It has rushed into the world-market with such zest and vigor that the other manufacturing countries have not yet caught their breaths. And it has shot up to the van of the creditor nations, and even now is lending its money to every power in Europe. But this is not the Anglo-Saxon race.

Words are subject to growth, and such growth necessarily involves a change in the connotation. While the Angles, Jutes, and Saxons settled Britain, it chanced that of the three names, that of the Angles was chosen to designate the land—Angle-land in that early day. Later, for convenience of thought, in order to differentiate between the salient features of the people of Angle-land and those of other lands, the people of England were called Anglo-Saxons. The word soon lost this signification. The Englishman of the last few hundred years, what of the Celt, Scandinavian, and Norman in him, could not be literally called an Anglo-Saxon, yet he was so called, for the connotation had changed. And of recent times it has undergone yet greater change. To-day, "Anglo-Saxon" stands for the English-speaking people of the world, who, in forms and institutions and traditions, are more peculiarly and definitely English than anything else.

As Aline Gorren has pointed out, there is no need to quarrel with the label "Anglo-Saxon." A better label might have been chosen, but it was not. Our own country might better have been named after Columbus. "Anglo-Saxon," then, has come to stand for the race, to stand for the civilization England has given to the world. Let it go at that. The name does not alter the fact, while the fact is of vaster importance. "Anglo-American" would be, perhaps, a little nearer the mark. But, "Anglo" and "American" are both literal misnomers, and the difficulty only grown more complicate. So, in default of better and in line with custom, we employ "Anglo-Saxon" to designate that portion of the human family which speaks the English tongue, acknowledges English traditions, and which, in traits and characteristics, is more nearly English than anything else.

A common fellowship, a common tongue, and a common goal, to say nothing of the commercial and political hatred of Europe, knit the whole race together. It is not daring too much to say that never again will the Anglo-Saxon race go to war with itself. What if the Australian Confederation is growing lustily down there in the Antipodes? What if the center of economic exchanges (and with it necessarily the seat of empire), is crossing the Atlantic? What if the island of Britain is to become, in the words of Mr. William Clarke, "the Athens for the Greater England?" Angle-land, the historic home of the race? The outpost of the Anglo-Saxon civilization facing the frontier of Europe when the Pacific has become an Anglo-Saxon sea? Blood of one blood, bone of one bone, they draw closer together in the hastening years, and the old sea-mother does not forget her virile progeny, sea-farmers themselves and empire-builders to the ends of the earth.

Is this a dream? There are men who say there is room in the world for all, that there is no need of shoving, that race-pride is insular prejudice and empire-building a lust and an abomination. Nonetheless the facts point the other way. The population of the world *is* increasing, and, what of man's recent great conquests of force and matter, the increase is just beginning to accelerate. As for empire-building, it is a function which the times demand shall be performed. Those peoples that build no empires are losing ground. When Alfred the Great intermittently ruled and ran in England, the population was approximately two millions. Scandinavia, at that date, possessed about the same. To-day, the population of all Scandinavia is about eight millions, while that of England alone is forty-one millions, without taking into account the millions it has flung broadcast over the earth, or the seventy-five millions in the United States. To solve this interesting problem would be to become involved, first, in an intricate mesh of causes; but on the face of it, England has toiled and sweated at empire-building, while Scandinavia has not. But of what moral value, may be asked, is this prolificacy of breed?—of a breed which blunders brutally through the world, beating down the lesser breeds to its own gross aggrandizement? Ah! but moral values have nothing to do with it. The strong breeds *are* stamping hungrily over the earth; they *are* devouring the weak; they *are* surviving, they and their progeny.

Concerning population, we must not forget Malthus of old time, whose memorable "Law" has been somewhat derided of late. Insofar as it related to the human, because the human was capable of modifying its environment, Malthus' law of population was considered extreme. But today there are many who have swung to the opposite extreme and deny the possibility of there ever being a pressure of population. Such men hold that man has been increasing his control over nature and production faster than he himself has been increasing. But that does not disprove the inevitability of a pressure of population, sometime, somewhere. In the first place, society has just been passing through a developmental stage of production. The means of subsistence have kept ahead of population. But that they can, indefinitely, continue to keep ahead, is absurd. There must come a time when man shall attain his maximum productivity. Again, the world is only so large , and it cannot be populated to infinity. And yet again, the rise in the standard of living requires a greater subsistence for a given population.

Japan, China, and India, on a small scale but precisely similar to a world-scale, have endured pressure of population. By large colonies of hetairae, by infanticide and destruction of malformed infants, and by famine, pestilence and the thousand and one ills of excessive crowding, they have kept their numbers stationary. Introduce the machinery and organization of the Western world into stifling China, and her four hundred millions would become eight hundred millions in a very short time. Japan has undergone this experience, somewhat, and her erstwhile stationary population is now increasing at the rate of half a million yearly.

The Western world is increasing for a like reason. The figures are interesting. At the beginning of the last century the population of Europe was one hundred and sixty millions, at the close, three hundred and seventy millions. In the United States, the city of New York, alone, has half a million more souls than did all the thirteen colonies in 1776; while the country, in one hundred years, has increased from five millions to seventy-five millions. At the present rate of increase of eighteen per cent we shall have, roughly, a round half-billion in the year 2000. One hundred years ago the population of Europe and of countries whose people were of European origin was one hundred and sixty-three millions; to-day the same stock is five hundred millions; and at present rate of increase, one hundred years from now it will be fifteen hundred millions.

Then there are those who draw wrong conclusions from the biological law that, other things being equal, the higher the organism the less fertile it is. They contend, with the rise in the plane of living caused by the mastery of production, that man will not only intentionally check the birth rate, but that he will become organically less fertile.

In the first instance, let France be considered. Did she cease to expand because of the check she put upon her birth rate? Or, rather, did she not put the check upon her birth rate because she had ceased to expand and was beginning to feel the pressure of population against subsistence? The facts seem to bear out the latter explanation. England had shut France out from the sea; Russia and the Continental alliances from the land. Perforce, she recoiled upon herself. She did not have room. Nor has she been blind to the cause of her misfortune. Paul Leroy-Beaulieu, writing in 1882, in tone similar to scores of writers and statesmen, says: "From now on, our colonial expansion must occupy the first place in our national consciousness . . . We must found a great French Empire in Africa and in Asia; else of the great role which France has played in the past there will remain nothing but the memory, and that dying out as the days pass . . . Colonization is a question of life or death for France. Either we must found an African Empire, or in one hundred years we shall have sunk to the level of a second-rate power." It is a fair supposition, had France continued to expand, that her population would have continued its upward sweep. Recoiling upon herself, unable to maintain her standard of living and at the same time permit her natural increase, she chose, consciously or not, to limit her birth rate. Had she chosen otherwise, her population most probably would have increased, but inevitably her standard of living would have fallen. 'Twixt the devil and the deep sea, as it were.

The decline in the average organic fertility of a species does not proceed from within, out. External forces, operating through a long period of time, may produce a highly organized type, such as man, capable of reacting, within certain limits, upon his natural environment. By so reacting, the tenure of life is made more secure. With the tenure of life more secure, with a reduced mortality and an increased lifetime of the generation, the degree of his previous fertility is no longer necessary to maintain his species constant. Without going into the discussion of how it is brought about, let it suffice to say, that man, multiplying until he presses against the means of subsistence and the bounds of his habitat, must then undergo a decline in organic fertility. *But the point is: not until after he presses against the means of subsistence and the bounds of his habitat.*

In a society, where industry is stationary, production must balance with consumption. And in such a society, which is also not expanding, mortality must balance with fertility. As long as production is increasing, or habitat expanding, just so long may births exceed deaths; but when a society becomes stationary in both these matters, it must speedily, in one way or another, bring about a balance between fertility and mortality. In short, the artificial and natural checks upon fertility must operate from without, in.

To return. So far as we may know, never before in the history of the world has the production of wealth been so high. And production to-day is not stationary. It is still increasing at prodigious leaps and bounds. Never before has the population of the world increased so rapidly. And never before has there been such an expansion of the superior races. For the first time, it is a world-expansion. The poles and naked space alone are its limits. As regards the human, there is no longer such a thing as geographical distribution. The whole earth is the habitat of man, and the possible habitat for the superior races alone. That the superior races, engaged as they are in overrunning the earth, should suddenly stop short, is impossible. That the inferior races must undergo destruction or some humane form of economic slavery, is inevitable.

This position is not without its ethical side; but its ethics are practical ethics, and are not related to the heart. The future, when man shall come to intellectually impel as well as intellectually direct society in its affairs, may bring forth some new law of development; but the old law of development is—that the strong and fit, and their progeny, shall have a better chance for survival than the weak and less fit and the progeny of the weak and less fit. This is the acknowledged basis of American society to-day. In other words, equality of opportunity, so that every member of society, within certain race limits, may enter the lists without social handicap. We do not yet possess complete equality of opportunity, but the whole trend of society is in that direction. The practical, practiced ethics within the social organism, deny the slothful, improvident, weak, or vicious individual the best rewards society can give. This individual, if he starts with nothing but his heredity, either dies or remains a hewer of wood and drawer of water to the end of his days. If he starts, possessed of a bit of land or a business left him by his progenitors, he is quickly crowded out and becomes a tenant or wage slave to his stronger competitors. The real ethical significance of this is that the race progresses and wins a higher average of strength and efficiency

However, this practical ethical concept cannot stop at its application to the individual. If, within a society, the slothful give way to the energetic, the weak to the strong, then without, between societies, the improvident and weak must give way to the strong and energetic. This is practical and consistent. It is actual. Not only does the strong individual expropriate the weak individual, but the strong society expropriates the weak society, the strong breeds the weak breeds.

This history of civilization is a history of wandering—a wandering, sword in hand, of strong breeds, clearing away and hewing down the weak and less fit. In the misty younger world, peoples, nobody knows whence or whither, rise up in blood-red splendor, conquering and slaying, and like phantoms, conquered and slain, pass away. True, those who rise by the sword perish by the sword; but be it remembered, in that day as in this, that those who foreswear the sword none the less perish by the sword. It is the history of all life. In the meadowgrass, sun-kissed and dew-kissed, flower-scattered and fragrant, this fearful struggle goes on. The drifting butterflies, the droning bees, the flute-throated warblers, the very fragrances, are potent weapons in the carnage. Selection, though the intensest struggle, is the keynote of progress. As primordial man dispossessed the ape, so has latter-day man dispossessed primordial man; and in like fashion are the barbarous and decadent people being dispossessed to-day.

There is such a thing as natural selection among races. In the last century, nineteenth of its era, millions of human beings were destroyed through contact with superior civilization. Unable to assimilate, or be assimilated, they perished. They were less fitted for organization, government, and the exploitation of nature. Nor were they able to imitate these things. The strain which the dominant races to-day place upon their members, was too great. The pace was too hot. They were unable to stand the concentration and sustained effort which pre-eminently mark the races best fitted to live in this our world. And so they perished, and so they are perishing, for no reason under the sun save that they are so made. Call it murder. The name does not affect the case. The fact is, it *was* done, it *is* being done. And it were well that this fact be taken into consideration by those who cast, in large black capitals, the horoscope of man.

The twentieth century dawns in blood. In this it no wise differs from the previous centuries. But the times have changed, somewhat. We no longer think in feudatories and provinces, but in continents. But while we think in continents, the minutest fragments of continents have place in our thought. As Lord Rosebery has said, "Every mile of unoccupied territory, every tribe of naked savages is wrangled over as if it were situated in the center of Europe."

In another way the times have changed. The nations gird up their loins and go forth, not primarily for militant conquest, but for industrial conquest. This is the machine age, the industrial age, the commercial age; in token whereof, the captains of war are commanded by the captains of industry. The scramble for the world is the scramble for markets and resources, and to this end are bent the sword, the hammer and the mace. King's mistresses, for insults real or fancied, no longer hurl nations into conflict; nor do sacred sepulchers or holy Meccas sweep waves of armed men across the astonished earth; but a squabble over iron mines, borax deposits, or coaling stations, is cause sufficient for the loosing of the most splendid fighting machines our modern civilization can boast.

Every manufacturing country is striving feverishly to deal with the momentous problem of "surplus product." In all industrial processes, labor, receiving in wages, roughly, half of the net product, cannot possibly buy back more than that proportion of the product. Nor can the capitalist or parasite classes consume the remainder. None the less it must be sold and consumed, somewhere, somehow, and the foreign market is the only vent. Then again, the countries with the richer natural resources can rush their goods more cheaply into the foreign market; and thus it behooves the manufacturing countries with the poorer natural recourses to go forth in search of richer foreign natural resources. And still again, the countries with the richer home resources must countercheck this move, or, in turn, be thrust out of the foreign market by their competitors who have become better equipped. For this reason the powers close hungrily in on China, which possesses great, if not the greatest virgin mineral deposits of the world; and for this reason, whether blindly or with foresight, the United States opposes the partition of that most unfit empire.

So it goes, and natural selection, in new guise, still continues to operate. What its guise will be somewhere in the future, matters not. Only those peoples that survive now, will be permitted to undergo some future different form of the selective process. And now, in the immediate present, the industrial conquest of the world is at hand. The period of development for the struggle is well-nigh past. Everything is prepared. The machinery has been invented, industry organized, and capital massed. Railroads and waterways have made the parts of all the earth accessible, and the telephone and telegraph drawn them closely together.

But there is another phase of the struggle which must be taken into consideration — nationalism. The growing consciousness of nationality has peculiarly marked the nineteenth century, and to-day, as never before, is there an avowed marshalling of the races. Up to the Renaissance, men dreamed of a world-state; but since then nationalism has become a dominant force. Napoleon failed whenever he came in conflict with this force. This is the force which drove Austria out of the German Confederation, which cemented the North German states into *national* empire, which Garibaldi and the House of Savoy called to their aid in the unification of Italy. The mere massing of jarring nationalities does not to-day make a power of the first class. There must be assimilation. But for assimilation there must be a common ancestry somewhere in the past. The Teuton, the Celt and the Slav may assimilate one another under favorable conditions; but none of them may actually assimilate the black, brown or yellow races. Long separated branches of the one stock may grow together again and learn a common tongue and a common tradition; but widely differentiated stocks, though they may learn a common tongue, cannot learn the tradition which accompanies that tongue, nor assimilate, one way or the other, the different blood. Blood has proved itself thicker than water, and the nation which would play a leading part in the new drama, must be one where those within the blood are dearer than those without.

And now, when the marshalling races proceed to the task of settling the planetary problem, how stands the Anglo-Saxon? Undeniably, he is the most significant figure on the world-stage. There is no country with large ambitions which does not regard him with gloomy respect. M. Edmond Demoulins, preaching a passionate gospel to the French, says: "They (the Anglo-Saxons) are overrunning the earth at this hour, cultivating it, colonizing it, driving out everywhere the adherents of the old social system, and accomplishing these prodigies through the forces of private initiative alone, by the sole triumphant power of men left to their own devices." And Sig. Guglielmo Ferrero, in "Young Europe", strives to show the Latins wherein they lack much which is essential, and which the Angle-Saxon possesses. He has done these things, and is doing them, they say, because of his initiative, will, energy, self-determination, and enterprise, because of his personal pride, and of his personal independence, which has been called "the great Teutonic legacy to the world."

And it is for these things, and the place and power they have brought him, that the Angle-Saxon is hated. He is prosperous wherever he goes, and he goes everywhere. And what more natural than that his push, energy, and aggressiveness should stir up enmity? The sin of possessing fair lands and fat revenues is a sin which merely human governments cannot condone. That the Englishman is well and widely hated on the Continent, is an open fact; and equally open was the display of Europe's hatred for the United States during the late Spanish-American war. The Fashoda incident and the Kaiser's telegram to Kruger are events of yesterday; and today the agitation for a Continental alliance is frankly hostile. M. Leroy-Beaulieu, French economist and member of the French Institute, writes, in a letter to the Vienna *Tageblatt:* "The United States is on the point of becoming the most important economic factor in the world. It may henceforth be regarded as the first industrial nation, and its superiority will become more strikingly evident, year by year." Then he proceeds to advocate an economic alliance between the Continental nations for the purpose of barring out American goods by high customs duties, while establishing lower rates among themselves—an economic alliance, in his own words, *"which may possibly and desirably develop into a political alliance."*

Nor are they to be blamed, these Continental peoples. It is instinctive. They cannot but wish to endure. But tariff walls and political alliances will not help them against the Anglo-Saxon, if they cannot attain a like economy of production. They must make their labor and machinery as efficient as that of the Anglo-Saxon, and at home and abroad they must throw more of his "sheer nerve" in their enterprise. They must take the pace the Anglo-Saxon is setting, and it is confessedly a hot one. And not only must they take his pace, but they must *overtake* him. Not only must they learn from him the principles of the new colonization, but they must put a stop to his own tremendous colonizing, else there will be nothing left for them.

This question of colonization is illuminating. The maritime nations which emerged from the middle ages turned naturally to colonization. And of these, worthy of note, were Spain, Portugal, France, Holland and England. Martin V, on the principle that all countries under the sun are subject to the papacy, had given then King of Portugal a clear title to all lands whatsoever between Cape Boarder and the East Indies. And likewise Pope Alexander VI, by the bull of May 4, 1493, had presented the King and Queen of Spain with all lands "west and south of a line drawn from the Arctic to the Antarctic pole, one hundred leagues west of the Azores." Even so. But Spain and Portugal, holding these great areas in fee-simple from the Almighty, could not prevail. The Netherlands took over the Eastern Empire of Portugal. Spain committed suicide, and her colonies were divided up in a wild scramble. The Netherlands, though doing fair colonizing work in New Amsterdam, speedily knocked under, and it remained for England and France, like Rome and Carthage of old-time, to grapple for the world. France was militant and romantic; England industrial and hard-headed; and at the cost of enormous treasure and blood, she hurled France back from the sea and the lands in the midst of the sea.

Since that time England has well demonstrated her peculiar colonizing fitness. Not only has she been the greatest colonizer, but she has been the most successful. She has made her colonies pay, which is something no other country can boast, with the exception of Holland's island of Java which is merely a government plantation. And this colonial empire of hers is a thing so colossal as to dwarf Rome of the ancient world, and sufficient to cause Alexander the Macedonian to weep fresh tears could he arise from the grave and look about.

And England has conquered, sword in hand, every foot of this vast dominion, and at the same time put down piracy, cleared away the slavers, and held the sea for her highway—"incarnadined the multitudinous seas with the blood of her enemies and her own blood," as some joyous writer puts it. And after conquering it, with her managerial genius she has organized and developed it. And with her political genius she has held it together and given it far greater measure of order and justice. And not only has she done all this, but she did it in pure pioneer fashion, breaking new trails, working things out for herself and aping none of the other nations—they, "sweating and stealing" many a year behind.

Of the political genius of the Anglo-Saxon, John Fiske writes: "The task of organizing society politically so that immense communities might grow up peacably, preserving their liberties and affording ample opportunity for the varied exercise of the human faculties, is a task which baffled the splendid talents of ancient Greece, and in which the success of the Romans was but partial and short lived. We believe that the men who use the mingled speech of Alfred and of William the Norman have solved the great political problem better than others have solved it. If we except the provinces of the Netherlands, the Swiss cantons, and such tiny city states as Monaco and San Marino, which retain their ancient institutions, there is not a nation on earth, making any pretence to freedom and civilization, which has not a constitution in great measure copied, within the present century, either from England or from the United States."

As for managerial genius, there is no more brilliant an achievement than that of the Indian Empire. And to-day, seven thousand miles from home, one hundred thousand Anglo-Saxons rule, two hundred heterogeneous millions of natives and set them their daily tasks. At plowing and sowing, at bridge-building and road-making, these swarming millions do the bidding of the mere handful of white masters, marshalling under their banner, fighting for them and dying for them.

If ever there was a race mastered by the verb: "to do" it is the Anglo-Saxon. Under a blind compulsion, in bitter sweat and hardship, unwitting of what he did so long as he did something, "in a fit of absent mind he has conquered and peopled half the world." The record of the work done by the people of the United States is a proud one. As Josiah Strong has pointed out, in one hundred years, 6,000,000 people have built homes for 75,000,000. "For forty years there was an average of 16,0000 acres of wild land subdued daily." Five and three-quarter million farms have been put under plough and harrow, half a myriad of cities built, 750,000 miles of telephone strung and 800,000 of telegraph. Railways have been built which would parallel every line in all Europe, and with the remainder the globe could be girdled at the equator. In 1895, Mulhall estimated our energy at 129,306,000,000 foot-tons daily—more than twice as much as that of Great Britain, and almost as much as that of Great Britain, Germany, and France combined. Containing only 5% of the world's population, the United States furnishes 32% of the world's food supply, while it has virtually just commenced to manufacture on a like cyclopean scale. A remarkable contrast to this is furnished by South America, with its political dictatorships, its impotency, and its wanton poverty which flourishes in the midst of its vast untouched natural wealth.

So it must be granted that the Anglo-Saxon is a race of mastery and achievement. It has done things, and it is doing things. And it is the worker and doer to-day who is best fitted for survival—the worker and doer strong in his muscles and strong in his life, hard-headed and practical, properly respectful of common things and unafraid of great things. The attitude of the Anglo-Saxon toward life, Aline Gorren well quotes: "To know what life is you must live it, face it squarely, take hold of it with both hands, shoulder its burdens, without asking whether they are pleasant or unpleasant exactly as they present themselves. Do the Will, in short;—and perhaps—you may learn the Doctrine. But do the Will, in any case, and the Will is that a man shall tell the truth, and have some care as to the purity of his ways, and not wish for strange gods, nor juggle with intellectual phantasmagoria; and above all, that he shall depend upon his own resources and help himself."

And not only is the Anglo-Saxon a worker and doer, but there is an unrest in his blood which the mere mechanism of life (a thing he thoroughly understands), cannot satisfy. With a wholesome regard for material comfort, he settles himself down in waste places and makes the soil fruitful and the sea prosperous. He destroys the wild and forbidding things, establishes law and order, devises machinery to lighten his labor, and builds himself bridges and roads and houses. But when he has done all this, he is not content to rest and enjoy it and let the world wag on. He has still an interest in that world. The unrest and the adventurousness have not departed from him. He cannot shut his ears to the call of the far-journeyer, and the wander-lust lays him by the heels till he turns his back upon the comfort he has created and fares forth empty-handed to accomplish his destiny.

And as befits one born to place and power in a brutal world, the Anglo-Saxon is brutal. By that brutality much that he has achieved has been made possible. As readily as the other breeds, he strips his culture from him and steps forth in primal nakedness. And at other times, none the less brutal, with stern and rugged temper, fanatically sincere, he does harsh things in the belief that it is his God-given task to Anglicize the world. The scenes in London following the capture of Cronje and the relief of Mafeking, are not yet forgotten. They were brutal—brutal and honestly disgraceful to a moral civilization. But none the less they are facts. When Kipling sings his savage song of sweat and moil and blood-welter, the race as savagely responds. This also is a fact—one of many of its kind—and one most necessary to be taken into consideration by those who dream that in the dawning of the twentieth century lions and lambs may be persuaded to lie down peacably together.

So, in the noon of the world, as in the morning, fitness and strength determine place and power. With population surging upward and the families of men increasing faster than ever before, there cannot possibly be room for all the families of men. Not only will there not be room for the barbarous and decadent peoples, but there will not be room for all the developed and healthy. One by one they must depart to the limbo of the forgotten or vaguely remembered races. At the best, they may leave some scrawl on the page of history, some token in the institutions of those that endure. And for place among those that endure, the Anglo-Saxon makes his bid. As a machinist and an inventor of machines, as a governor and an inventor of governments, as a trader and a maker of trade, he is unmatched. In numbers, and resources, and strength, he is head and shoulders above the press. And in an age when to foreswear the sword is to perish, he acknowledges the sword and is unafraid of the sword.

But he did not spring, full-grown, from the earth. Nor did he climb down out of the sky. It so happens, like the camel or the cuttlefish or any other creature, that he has brought down out of the past certain characters differing in whole or degree from those of other men. And it further happens that these characters are all-potent in the present world-era. Just now, evolution, which has no chosen people, favors him. How long he may continue to be so favored is beyond foresight. A new force in his environment, or a new combination of forces, and evolution may turn upon him and destroy him. He may, after all, soften under his comfortable civilization. Master of matter, he may be mastered by matter. A conqueror of the environment, he may succeed in putting into operation some new law of development, some highly moral selective process, which, in turn, may emasculate him and leave him the defenseless prey of some other of the dominant northern races. He may divide the world with the Slav; he may give the world up to the Slav. All these things are possible, but just now, to-day and in the promise of the immediate tomorrow, he stands forth the most prominent figure among the races and the highest bidder for the world.

The People of the Abyss, Chapter 1 : The Descent

First published in and reprinted from *The People of the Abyss* (New York: Macmillan, 1903).

"The abyss"—that very real, tangible place—rarely felt far away to Jack London, and he wrote much of his best work, including *The People of the Abyss,* when he situated himself literally in the depths of society. *The People of the Abyss* depicts the impoverished human beings who lived, just barely, in the East End of London at the start of the twentieth century. London himself is the main character in the story, as well as the narrator, and he's almost always in the picture. He's the participant and the observer, a student of British culture and civilization, and a gadfly who means to wake sleeping citizens and rouse their collective conscience. More than a hundred years later, his first-person eyewitness account remains a powerfully grim and depressing testimony to the human wreckage that he saw before him. One might well call London the father of gonzo journalism and a precursor of Hunter S. Thompson, author of *Fear and Loathing in Las Vegas,* and Ted Conover, author of *Coyotes* and *Newjack.* Like them, he lived firsthand the stories he wrote about and wrote impassioned prose, too.

The experience of living for several months in the East End, in the midst of poverty, homelessness, hunger, and hopelessness, certainly surprised and depressed Jack London. He had been an admirer of the British Empire, and of British civilization, and now, at "the very uttermost heart of the empire," he saw a way of life that seemed more backward than that of cave dwellers in prehistoric times. In frequent comparisons between England and his native habitat of California, the latter always outshines the former. At the heart of the book, London depicts the contrast between the sumptuous pomp and ceremony at the coronation of King Edward VII and "the rags and tatters" of the invisible men and women at the bottom of British society. Still, despite the grim reality, the author's exhilaration—his sense of awe and wonder at the spectacle before him—is apparent. Indeed, in "The Abyss," he seems to come fully alive. His compassion emerges, and he creates a gallery of compelling human characters—outcasts from their own society, many broken beyond repair, who share their lives with him and to whom he grants a kind of immortality in the pages of his work. Of London's many books, this may be the most free of racist comments and derogatory observations about ethnic groups. He doesn't disparage the Jews, and in Chapter 12, "Coronation Day," he lists the races and nationalities that are represented—"all the breeds of all the world"—coming as near to the spirit of egalitarianism as he could muster.

To write the book, London did what he enjoyed most of all: playing a role, wearing a disguise, taking on a different identity. He had done just that repeatedly in his life; now he did it as a professional reporter on paid assignment. He describes the shedding of his skin as a prosperous American, taking on the skin of an impoverished Englishman. A born listener—a kind of human tape recorder with a knack for hearing and imitating dialect—London attends closely to the inhabitants of the East End of London, and, in his narrative, he plays back, precisely, the words he hears. In face-to-face conversations, he allows the people to tell their own stories, and their voices ring true. The chapter has many wonderful details: buying clothes and assembling his "costume," learning the slang of the ghetto and "gripping hold of the vernacular," sewing a gold coin into his clothes in case of emergency, and blending into the crowd.

The People of the Abyss—a forerunner of the "new journalism" of the 1960s, made famous by Norman Mailer, Tom Wolfe, and Joan Didion—describes London's "descent," as he calls it in the first chapter, and then his journey through "the inferno." On every page, there's a sense of gritty realism. London gathers facts and figures, presenting documentary evidence to buttress his case against the wealthy and the powerful, and to indict the British ruling class for gross mismanagement of the whole society. In that sense, *The People of the Abyss* comes as close to the art of muckraking—and the muckrakers, whom he admired—as any of London's books. Lincoln Steffens, perhaps America's leading muckraking reporter, wrote about "the shame of American cities" in a series of articles for *McClure's* that appeared in 1902 and 1903—and as a book in 1904—in which he described the largely unseen poverty and invisible corruption in Minneapolis, St. Louis, and Pittsburgh. *The People of the Abyss* describes the shame of the city of London, which becomes a character—a "monster," the author calls it—in its own right. By describing the shame of London, England—the financial capital of the world in 1902—Jack London casts shame on the civilized world. Each chapter—there are twenty-eight in all—addresses a particular social problem or aspect of life in "the abyss," covering topics such as unemployment, alcohol, marriage and children, domestic violence and crime, suicide, and diet. The back-and-white photographs in the book—London took them himself—contribute to its gritty, documentary feel.

At the same time, he conveys the sense that he's on a mythic journey that takes him down, deeper and deeper into the underworld. Soon after he finished the book, he complained that *The People of the Abyss* lacked shape; yet it reads like a literary work in which the author has been closely attentive to matters of style. Each chapter begins with a quotation that sets the tone—from Thomas Carlyle, Ralph Waldo Emerson, Abraham Lincoln, William Morris, Oscar Wilde—and that shows how thoroughly steeped London was in the literature of the nineteenth century as well as how deeply influenced he was by the Victorian and Pre-Raphaelite critics of capitalism.

The People of the Abyss also radiates a sense of spirituality; London offers quotations from the Old Testament and talks about the "sociology of Jesus Christ." In the chapter entitled "A Vision of the Night," he offers a vision of the poor, who crawl, like beasts, "out of their dens and lairs," much like the peasants and workers who appeared, seemingly out of nowhere, to storm the Bastille at the start of the French Revolution. Mostly, however, London does not urge revolution or even predict revolution. Reform from within seems to be what he has in mind. "Society must be reorganized, and a capable management put at the head," he writes in "The Management"—the last chapter. "It is inevitable that this management, which has grossly and criminally mismanaged, shall be swept away."

To the end of his days, *The People of the Abyss* would remain one of London's favorite works, which is understandable since it came from his innermost heart. The chapter included here—"The Descent"—reflects his inimitable style and his seminal ideas, and it contains some of his most inspired writing. This chapter also suggests that by living in and writing about "the abyss," London overcame his fear of the same, and so, like all of his best work, *The People of the Abyss* is deeply and profoundly autobiographical—an exploration of his own self and "the abyss" within. •

> Christ look upon us in this city,
> And keep our sympathy and pity
> Fresh, and our faces heavenward,
> Lest we grow hard.
> Thomas Ashe.

"But you can't do it, you know," friends said, to whom I applied for assistance in the matter of sinking myself down into the East End of London. "You had better see the police for a guide," they added, on second thought, painfully endeavoring to adjust themselves to the psychological processes of a madman who had come to them with better credentials than brains.

"But I don't want to see the police," I protested. "What I wish to do, is to go down into the East End and see things for myself. I wish to know how those people are living there, and why they are living there, and what they are living for. In short, I am going to live there myself."

"You don't want to *live* down there!" everybody said, with disapprobation writ large upon their faces. "Why, it is said there are places where a man's life isn't worth tu'pence."

"The very places I wish to see," I broke in.

"But you can't, you know," was the unfailing rejoinder.

"Which is not what I came to see you about," I answered brusquely, somewhat nettled by their incomprehension. "I am a stranger here, and I want you to tell me what you know of the East End, in order that I may have something to start on."

"But we know nothing of the East End. It is over there, somewhere." And they waved their hands vaguely in the direction where the sun on rare occasions may be seen to rise.

"Then I shall go to Cook's," I announced.

"Oh, yes," they said, with relief. "Cook's will be sure to know."

But O Cook, O Thomas Cook & Son, pathfinders and trail-clearers, living signposts to all the world and bestowers of first aid to bewildered travelers—unhesitatingly and instantly, with ease and celerity, could you send me to Darkest Africa or

Innermost Thibet, but to the East End of London, barely a stone's throw distant from Ludgate Circus, you know not the way!

"You can't do it, you know," said the human emporium of routes and fares at Cook's Cheapside branch. "It is so—ahem—so unusual."

"Consult the police," he concluded authoritatively, when I persisted. "We are not accustomed to taking travellers to the East End; we receive no call to take them there, and we know nothing whatsoever about the place at all."

"Never mind that," I interposed, to save myself from being swept out of the office by his flood of negations. "Here's something you can do for me. I wish you to understand in advance what I intend doing, so that in case of trouble you may be able to identify me."

"Ah, I see; should you be murdered, we would be in position to identify the corpse."

He said it so cheerfully and cold-bloodedly that on the instant I saw my stark and mutilated cadaver stretched upon a slab where cool waters trickle ceaselessly, and him I saw bending over and sadly and patiently identifying it as the body of the insane American who *would* see the East End.

"No, no," I answered; "merely to identify me in case I get into a scrape with the 'bobbies.'" This last I said with a thrill; truly, I was gripping hold of the vernacular.

"That," he said, "is a matter for the consideration of the Chief Office."

"It is so unprecedented, you know," he added apologetically.

The man at the Chief Office hemmed and hawed. "We make it a rule," he explained, "to give no information concerning our clients."

"But in this case," I urged, "it is the client who requests you to give the information concerning himself."

Again he hemmed and hawed.

"Of course," I hastily anticipated, "I know it is unprecedented, but—"

"As I was about to remark," he went on steadily, "it is unprecedented, and I don't think we can do anything for you."

However, I departed with the address of a detective who lived in the East End, and took my way to the American consul-general. And here, at last, I found a man with whom I could "do business." There was no hemming and hawing, no lifted brows, open incredulity, or blank amazement. In one minute I explained myself and my project, which he accepted as a matter of course. In the second minute he asked my age, height, and weight, and looked me over. And in the third minute, as we shook hands at parting, he said: "All right, Jack. I'll remember you and keep track."

I breathed a sigh of relief. Having built my ships behind me, I was now free to plunge into that human wilderness of which nobody seemed to know anything. But at once I encountered a new difficulty in the shape of my cabby, a gray-whiskered and eminently decorous personage, who had imperturbably driven me for several hours about the "City."

"Drive me down to the East End," I ordered, taking my seat.

"Where, sir?" he demanded with frank surprise.

"To the East End, anywhere. Go on."

The hansom pursued an aimless way for several minutes, then came to a puzzled stop. The aperture above my head was uncovered, and the cabman peered down perplexedly at me.

"I say," he said, "wot plyce yer wanter go?"

"East End," I repeated. "Nowhere in particular. Just drive me around, anywhere."

"But wot's the haddress, sir?"

"See here!" I thundered. "Drive me down to the East End, and at once!"

It was evident that he did not understand, but he withdrew his head and grumblingly started his horse.

Nowhere in the streets of London may one escape the sight of abject poverty, while five minutes' walk from almost any point will bring one to a slum; but the region my hansom was now penetrating was one unending slum. The streets were filled with a new and different race of people, short of stature, and of wretched or beer-sodden appearance. We rolled along through miles of bricks and squalor, and from each cross street and alley flashed long vistas of bricks and misery. Here and there lurched a drunken man or woman, and the air was obscene with sounds of jangling and squabbling. At a market, tottery old men and women were searching in the garbage thrown in the mud for rotten potatoes, beans, and vegetables, while little children clustered like flies around a festering mass of fruit, thrusting their arms to the shoulders into the liquid corruption, and drawing forth morsels, but partially decayed, which they devoured on the spot.

Not a hansom did I meet with in all my drive, while mine was like an apparition from another and better world, the way the children ran after it and alongside. And as far as I could see were the solid walls of brick, the slimy pavements, and the screaming streets; and for the first time in my life the fear of the crowd smote me. It was like the fear of the sea; and the miserable multitudes, street upon street, seemed so many waves of a vast and malodorous sea, lapping about me and threatening to well up and over me.

"Stepney, sir; Stepney Station," the cabby called down.

I looked about. It was really a railroad station, and he had driven desperately to it as the one familiar spot he had ever heard of in all that wilderness.

"Well?" I said.

He spluttered unintelligibly, shook his head, and looked very miserable. "I'm a strynger 'ere," he managed to articulate. "An' if yer don't want Stepney Station, I'm blessed if I know wotcher do want."

"I'll tell you what I want," I said. "You drive along and keep your eye out for a shop where old clothes are sold. Now, when you see such a shop, drive right on till you turn the corner, then stop and let me out."

I could see that he was growing dubious of his fare, but not long afterward he pulled up to the curb and informed me that an old clothes shop was to be found a bit of the way back.

"Won'tcher py me?" he pleaded. "There's seven an' six owin' me."

"Yes," I laughed, "and it would be the last I'd see of you."

"Lord lumme, but it'll be the last I see of you if yer don't py me," he retorted.

But a crowd of ragged onlookers had already gathered around the cab, and I laughed again and walked back to the old clothes shop.

Here the chief difficulty was in making the shopman understand that I really and truly wanted old clothes. But after fruitless attempts to press upon me new and impossible coats and trousers, he began to bring to light heaps of old ones, looking mysterious the while and hinting darkly. This he did with the palpable intention of letting me know that he had 'piped my lay,' in order to bulldoze me, through fear of exposure, into paying heavily for my purchases. A man in trouble, or a high-class criminal from across the water, was what he took my measure for—in either case, a person anxious to avoid the police.

But I disputed with him over the outrageous difference between prices and values, till I quite disabused him of the notion, and he settled down to drive a hard bargain with a hard customer. In the end I selected a pair of stout though well-worn trousers, a frayed jacket with one remaining button, a pair of brogans which had plainly seen service where coal was shovelled, a thin leather belt, and a very dirty cloth cap. My underclothing and socks, however, were new and warm, but of the sort that any American waif, down in his luck, could acquire in the ordinary course of events.

"I must sy yer a sharp 'un," he said, with counterfeit admiration, as I handed over the ten shillings finally agreed upon for the outfit. "Blimey, if you ain't ben up an' down Petticut Lane afore now. Yer trouseys is wuth five bob to hany man, an' a docker'ud give two an' six for the shoes, to sy nothin' of the coat an' cap an' new stoker's singlet an' hother things."

"How much will you give me for them?" I demanded suddenly. "I paid you ten bob for the lot, and I'll sell them back to you, right now, for eight. Come, it's a go!"

But he grinned and shook his head, and though I had made a good bargain, I was unpleasantly aware that he had made a better one.

I found the cabby and a policeman with their heads together, but the latter, after looking me over sharply and particularly scrutinizing the bundle under my arm, turned away and left the cabby to wax mutinous by himself. And not a step would he budge till I paid him the seven shillings and sixpence owing him. Whereupon he was willing to drive me to the ends of the earth, apologizing profusely for his insistence, and explaining that one ran across queer customers in London Town.

But he drove me only to Highbury Vale, in North London, where my luggage was waiting for me. Here, next day, I took off my shoes (not without regret for their lightness and comfort), and my soft, gray travelling suit, and, in fact, all my clothing; and proceeded to array myself in the clothes of the other and unimaginable men, who must have been indeed unfortunate to have had to part with such rags for the pitiable sums obtainable from a dealer.

Inside my stoker's singlet, in the armpit, I sewed a gold sovereign (an emergency sum certainly of modest proportions); and inside my stoker's singlet I put myself. And then I sat down and moralized upon the fair years and fat, which had made my skin soft and brought the nerves close to the surface; for the singlet was rough and raspy as a hair shirt, and I am confident that the most rigorous of ascetics suffer no more than did I in the ensuing twenty-four hours.

The remainder of my costume was fairly easy to put on, though the brogans, or brogues, were quite a problem. As stiff and hard as if made of wood, it was only after a prolonged pounding of the uppers with my fists that I was able to get my feet into them at all. Then, with a few shillings, a knife, a handkerchief, and some brown papers and flake tobacco stowed away in my pockets, I thumped down the stairs and said good-by to my foreboding friends. As I passed out the door, the 'help,' a comely middle-aged woman, could not conquer a grin that twisted her lips and separated them till the throat, out of involuntary sympathy, made the uncouth animal noises we are wont to designate as "laughter."

No sooner was I out on the streets than I was impressed by the difference in status effected by my clothes. All servility vanished from the demeanor of the common people with whom I came in contact. Presto! in the twinkling of an eye, so to say, I had become one of them. My frayed and out-at-elbows jacket was the badge and advertisement of my class, which was their class. It made me of like kind, and in place of the fawning and too-respectful attention I had hitherto received, I now shared with them a comradeship. The man in corduroy and dirty neckerchief no longer addressed me as "sir" or "governor." It was "mate," now—and a fine and hearty word, with a tingle to it, and a warmth and gladness, which the other term does not possess. Governor! It smacks of mastery, and power, and high authority—the tribute of the man who is under to the man on top, delivered in the hope that he will let up a bit and ease his weight. Which is another way of saying that it is an appeal for alms.

This brings me to a delight I experienced in my rags and tatters which is denied the average American abroad. The European traveller from the States, who is not a Croesus, speedily finds himself reduced to a chronic state of self-conscious sordidness by the hordes of cringing robbers who clutter his steps from dawn till dark, and deplete his pocketbook in a way that puts compound interest to the blush.

In my rags and tatters I escaped the pestilence of tipping, and encountered men on a basis of equality. Nay, before the day was out I turned the tables, and said, most gratefully, "Thank you, sir," to a gentleman whose horse I held, and who dropped a penny into my eager palm.

Other changes I discovered were wrought in my condition by my new garb. In crossing crowded thoroughfares I found I had to be, if anything, more lively in avoiding vehicles, and it was strikingly impressed upon me that my life had cheapened in direct ratio with my clothes. When before, I inquired the way of a policeman, I was usually asked, "Buss or 'ansom, sir?" But now the query became, "Walk or ride?" Also, at the railway stations it was the rule to be asked, "First or second, sir?" Now I was asked nothing, a third-class ticket being shoved out to me as a matter of course.

But there was compensation for it all. For the first time I met the English lower classes face to face, and knew them for what they were. When loungers and workmen, on street corners and in public houses, talked with me, they talked as one man to another, and they talked as natural men should talk, without the least idea of getting anything out of me for what they talked or the way they talked.

And when at last I made into the East End, I was gratified to find that the fear of the crowd no longer haunted me. I had become a part of it. The vast and malodorous sea had welled up and over me, or I had slipped gently into it, and there was nothing fearsome about it—with the one exception of the stoker's singlet.

How I Became a Socialist

First published in *Comrade,* March 1903; reprinted from *War of the Classes* (New York: Macmillan, 1905).

London became a socialist in the 1890s, but he waited nearly a decade before he explained, publicly, how and why he did so. Oddly enough, he does not mention Marx or Marxism in this essay, though both played a significant role in his radicalization. London could have written several essays entitled "How I Became a Socialist," all with different perspectives. Indeed, he wrote several successive versions about his political conversion, including the autobiographical preface to *War of the Classes* (1905) and his personal essay "What Life Means to Me" (1906). When John Spargo, an editor at *Comrade,* asked him to account for his own political journey, he replied, "Shall be glad to tell how I became a socialist, & I think it may differ very interestingly from the causes given by most men." Soon after the founding of *Comrade* in 1901, he wrote, "My congratulations on your note-worthy first number. What with the *International Socialist Review* and *Comrade,* I really feel a respectable member of society, able to say to the most finicky: 'Behold the literature of my Party!'"

In "How I Became a Socialist," London explains the crucial role that fear played in his conversion. He also notes how thoroughly bourgeois he had been as a youth and how con-servative his outlook had been. For a time, he admits, he revered Nietzsche, espoused indi-vidualism, and accepted the basic competitive values of capitalist society. He might have become a strikebreaker, he says, not a supporter of unions and striking workers. Autobiographical accounts of conversions to socialism had been a staple of international socialist literature ever since William Morris (1834–1896)—an English artist and writer from a wealthy family—published his story in 1894. Eugene V. Debs (1855–1926), the militant union organizer and perennial Socialist Party candidate for public office, published his impassioned "How I Became a Socialist" in *Comrade* in 1902. The topic continued to fasci-nate American radicals throughout the twentieth century, and a series of writers, including Helen Keller, described their conversions. By the late 1940s and early 1950s, the "how-I-became-a-socialist" essay had largely been replaced by the "how-communism-betrayed-me" and "the-god-that-failed" political confession. London planned to write an essay about how the god of socialism failed him, but never did. •

It is quite fair to say that I became a Socialist in a fashion somewhat similar to the way in which the Teutonic pagans became Christians—it was hammered into me. Not only was I not looking for Socialism at the time of my conversion, but I was fighting it. I was very young and callow, did not know much of anything, and though I had never even heard of a school called "Individualism," I sang the paean of the strong with all my heart.

This was because I was strong myself. By strong I mean that I had good health and hard muscles, both of which possessions are easily accounted for. I had lived my childhood on California ranches, my boyhood hustling newspapers on the streets of a healthy Western city, and my youth on the ozone-laden waters of San Francisco Bay and the Pacific Ocean. I loved life in the open, and I toiled in the open, at the hardest kinds of work. Learning no trade, but drifting along from job to job, I looked on the world and called it good, every bit of it. Let me repeat, this optimism was because I was healthy and strong, bothered with neither aches nor weaknesses, never turned down by the boss because I did not look fit, able always to get a job at shovelling coal, sailorizing, or manual labor of some sort.

And because of all this, exulting in my young life, able to hold my own at work or fight, I was a rampant individualist. It was very natural. I was a winner. Wherefore I called the game, as I saw it played, or thought I saw it played, a very proper game for MEN. To be a MAN was to write man in large capitals on my heart. To adventure like a man, and fight like a man, and do a man's work (even for a boy's pay) — these were things that reached right in and gripped hold of me as no other thing could. And I looked ahead into long vistas of a hazy and interminable future, into which, playing what I conceived to be MAN'S game, I should continue to travel with unfailing health, without accidents, and with muscles ever vigorous. As I say, this future was interminable. I could see myself only raging through life without end like one of Nietzsche's *blond beasts,* lustfully roving and conquering by sheer superiority and strength.

As for the unfortunates, the sick, and ailing, and old, and maimed, I must confess I hardly thought of them at all, save that I vaguely felt that they, barring accidents, could be as good as I if they wanted to real hard, and could work just as well. Accidents? Well, they represented FATE, also spelled out in capitals, and there was no getting around FATE. Napoleon had had an accident at Waterloo, but that did not dampen my desire to be another and later Napoleon. Further, the optimism bred of a stomach which could digest scrap iron and a body which flourished on hardships did not permit me to consider accidents as even remotely related to my glorious personality.

I hope I have made it clear that I was proud to be one of Nature's strong-armed noblemen. The dignity of labor was to me the most impressive thing in the world. Without having read Carlyle, or Kipling, I formulated a gospel of work which put theirs in the shade. Work was everything. It was sanctification and salvation. The pride I took in a hard day's work well done would be inconceivable to you. It is almost inconceivable to me as I look back upon it. I was as faithful a wage slave as ever capitalist exploited. To shirk or malinger on the man who paid me my wages was a sin, first, against myself, and second, against him. I considered it a crime second only to treason and just about as bad.

In short, my joyous individualism was dominated by the orthodox bourgeois ethics. I read the bourgeois papers, listened to the bourgeois preachers, and shouted at the sonorous platitudes of the bourgeois politicians. And I doubt not, if other events had not changed my career, that I should have evolved into a professional strike-breaker, (one of President Eliot's American heroes), and had my head and my earning power irrevocably smashed by a club in the hands of some militant trades-unionist.

Just about this time, returning from a seven months' voyage before the mast, and just turned eighteen, I took it into my head to go tramping. On rods and blind baggages I fought my way from the open West where men bucked big and the job hunted the man, to the congested labor centres of the East, where men were small potatoes and hunted the job for all they were worth. And on this new *blond-beast* adventure I found myself looking upon life from a new and totally different angle. I had dropped down from the proletariat into what sociologists love to call the "submerged tenth," and I was startled to discover the way in which that submerged tenth was recruited.

I found there all sorts of men, many of whom had once been as good as myself and just as blond-beastly; sailor-men, soldier-men, labor-men, all wrenched and distorted and twisted out of shape by toil and hardship and accident, and cast adrift by their masters like so many old horses. I battered on the drag and slammed back gates with them, or shivered with them in box cars and city parks, listening the while to life-histories which began under auspices as fair as mine, with digestions and bodies equal to and better than mine, and which ended there before my eyes in the shambles at the bottom of the Social Pit.

And as I listened my brain began to work. The woman of the streets and the man of the gutter drew very close to me. I saw the picture of the Social Pit as vividly as though it were a concrete thing, and at the bottom of the Pit I saw them, myself above them, not far, and hanging on to the slippery wall by main strength and sweat. And I confess a terror seized me. What when my strength failed? when I should be unable to work shoulder to shoulder with the strong men who were as yet babes unborn? And there and then I swore a great oath. It ran something like this: *All my days I have worked hard with my body, and according to the number of days I have worked, by just that much am I nearer the bottom of the Pit. I shall climb out of the pit, but not by the muscles of my body shall I climb out. I shall do no more hard work, and may God strike me dead if I do another day's hard work with my body more than I absolutely have to do.* And I have been busy ever since running away from hard work.

Incidentally, while tramping some ten thousand miles through the United States and Canada, I strayed into Niagara Falls, was nabbed by a fee-hunting constable, denied the right to plead guilty or not guilty, sentenced out of hand to thirty days' imprisonment for having no fixed abode and no visible means of support, handcuffed and chained to a bunch of men similarly circumstanced, carted down country to Buffalo, registered at the Erie County Penitentiary, had my head clipped and my budding mustache shaved, was dressed in convict stripes, compulsorily vaccinated by a medical student who practised on such as we, made to march the lock-step, and put to work under the eyes of guards armed with Winchester rifles—all for adventuring in *blond-beastly* fashion. Concerning further details deponent sayeth not, though he may hint that some of his plethoric national patriotism simmered down and leaked out of the bottom of his soul somewhere—at least, since that experience he finds that he cares more for men and women and little children than for imaginary geographical lines.

To return to my conversion. I think it is apparent that my rampant individualism was pretty effectively hammered out of me, and something else as effectively hammered in. But, just as I had been an individualist without knowing it, I was now a Socialist without knowing it, withal, an unscientific one. I had been reborn, but not renamed, and I was running around to find out what manner of thing I was. I ran back to California and opened the books. I do not remember which ones I opened first. It is an unimportant detail anyway. I was already It, whatever It was, and by aid of the books I discovered that It was a Socialist. Since that day I have opened many books, but no economic argument, no lucid demonstration of the logic and inevitableness of Socialism affects me as profoundly and convincingly as I was affected on the day when I first saw the walls of the Social Pit rise around me and felt myself slipping down, down, into the shambles at the bottom.

What Shall Be Done with This Boy?

First published in and reprinted from the *San Francisco Examiner*, June 21, 1903.

London looked at society as a sociologist and wrote about social types: the criminal, the hobo, the scab, and the plutocrat, to name a few. He also looked at the world from a philosophical point of view and wrote about Man, with a capital M, and about eternal verities like Truth and Fate. In the article "What Shall Be Done with This Boy?" he showed that he could also write compassionately about a single individual—a poor, troubled eleven-year-old juvenile delinquent in San Francisco—not all boys, or Boyhood in the abstract. When he visited Edgar Sonne in June 1903 at the Boys' and Girls' Aid Society in San Francisco, it seems likely that he remembered his own troubled boyhood and that he recalled his own behavior as a hoodlum. In the not-too-distant past, Jack might have been in Edgar's shoes. Moreover, Sonne's particular case probably stirred up London's long-simmering ideas about heredity and the environment. It certainly enabled him to clarify his thinking about crime and punishment, individual responsibility, and the responsibility of society to the individual. After meeting and talking with Sonne, London concluded that the boy had not been born a criminal or innately antisocial, but had been made into a criminal by society, and by his own mother, who had neglected to raise him properly, and as a healthy child. London painstakingly explains that sentimentality plays no part in his diagnosis of Sonne's case. From a practical, business point of view, he insists, society would do well to feed, heal, and reform Sonne, not punish him. "Policemen, detectives, judges, superintendents of aid societies, patrol wagons and what not, have run up a pretty item in society's expense account," London writes. "And, worst of all, nothing has been gained." Today, his outlook would probably be described as "liberal." He believed that society can and should take the initiative to reform, not punish, its deviant citizens. At the same time, London does not excuse Sonne's burglaries and thefts. He holds him responsible for his own actions. He also argues that society must be protected from deviant individuals like Sonne. Utilitarianism—which he defines as "the greatest good to the greatest number" of people—provides London with an ethical yardstick to measure Sonne's case. Not surprisingly, he concludes that for the benefit and welfare of society as a whole, boys like Sonne must be helped to begin life anew.

In the preface to this article, the *Examiner* noted that London was eminently qualified to write about Edgar Sonne, and to judge him, too. "His recent experience in the slums of London . . . and his rugged life as a sailor before the mast and a traveler on the Dawson trail, have given him an intimate knowledge of human nature and the lower social stratum," the editors of the paper wrote. They also noted that the case of Sonne was important "to every thoughtful person concerned with good citizenship." Clearly, the *Examiner* regarded Sonne as emblematic of the troubled boys and girls in San Francisco at the birth of the twentieth century. Half a century later, boys like Sonne would be described by sociologists as "juvenile delinquents." They would join gangs—and movies and musicals would be made about them. Still later, they would become taggers. By writing about Sonne, London paved the way for a long succession of reporters who would investigate and depict the lives of "troubled youth" in the twentieth century. Credit, too, goes to the newspaper.

To send Sonne to prison for the rest of his life would be to deny him the possibility of rehabilitation, while setting him free would only "give full reign to his misguided instincts," the *Examiner's* editors wrote. How to avoid both those pitfalls and to find a solution to the problem was the daunting task they assigned London. From the start, they felt that his article would be characterized by "accuracy and impartiality." They were not disappointed.

The *Examiner* also published, on the same page as London's article, a sidebar entitled "How to Cure a Child of Bad Temper," in which it offered practical suggestions to parents with difficult children. Physical punishment would not achieve the desired end, the author of the sidebar wrote. "Kindness" and "calm firmness" were highly recommended. •

At the Boys' and Girls' Aid Society is an eleven-year-old boy, Edgar Sonne, whose past is already black and historic for it has made him a pariah in his own neighborhood and household. It is sufficient to state his immediate record of the past few weeks to interest not only those with a penchant for criminal sociology, but every person who is concerned with good government, good citizenship, and good social morality, and whose ethical concepts and hopes for humanity are fine and high.

In two weeks this child of eleven years has been guilty of the following depredations upon society: daylight burglary of the residence of Mrs. Woodman, 433 Capp Street; arrested for the Woodman burglary; committed by the juvenile court to the custody of his mother; theft of twenty dollars from home during his mother's absence; arrested for theft from home; committed by juvenile court to the custody of the Boys' and Girls' Aid Society; escaped from Boys' and Girls' Aid Society with a cleverness worthy of an adult and experienced criminal; burglary of mother's home during the night; arrested for burglary of mother's home and returned by juvenile court to the custody of the Boys' and Girls' Aid Society.

Questions at once swarm into the mind. What is to become of such a boy? What is to become of society if it does not deal correctly with such a boy and all of his kind? How did such a boy happen to be? And how did society let such a boy happen to be?

In the first place, no matter what extenuating conditions, Edgar Sonne's welfare must be secondary to the welfare of society. He is a deviation from the normal type of the human; he is, in short abnormal. And since the majority of individuals composing society are normal, it is not only logical, but right, that they be protected from the depredations of the minority which is abnormal. So far, so good. Edgar Sonne is first and above all responsible to society. He will not be punished in the old retributive sense, but in the new and saner sense his freedom may be interfered with and he be put into social quarantine. By the application of the just and democratic aphorism, "The greatest good to the greatest number," he may be put to much pain and discomfort.

On the other hand, there is a responsibility which society owes to Edgar Sonne. It is a fact that all men are, at one time or another, tempted to commit crime. The normal men do not yield to the temptation. They have sufficient self-control to abstain. And this is the distinction between them and the abnormal men who do yield. The question at once arises: is this yielding due to some inherent weakness of the constitution itself, which cannot be cured? Or is it due to an acquired and non-essential weakness of the constitution which can be cured?

And right here enters Edgar Sonne and society's responsibility to Edgar Sonne. Society must determine, first, whether or not he is curable. If incurable, if the stuff of his life is too malformed and rotten, then society's responsibility to itself demands that he shall be put away where he can do no harm. But if he be curable, if the stuff of his life may be cleansed and made wholesome, then society's responsibility to Edgar Sonne demands that every effort be made to effect a cure. And if society does not make every effort, it will be guilty of a sin vastly more grievous than any sin Edgar Sonne can commit.

With this reasoning in mind, I went to the Boys' and Girls' Aid Society to see what manner of boy Edgar Sonne was. His record had prepared me for the regular type of born criminal or degenerate, but my disappointment was agreeable when I found that he was just an ordinary-looking boy, exceptionally thin, head well-shaped, and face not at all bad or remarkably vicious. His eyes were large, and without much character, while the lines of his face betrayed weakness — but no greater weakness than that of countless men who are respectable members of society.

Rottenness and irregularity of the teeth, an abnormally shaped roof of the mouth, and certain other minor peculiarities were all that might possibly be classed as stigmata of degeneracy, but which, in themselves alone, signified no more than signify the notable teeth of our strenuous President.

Edgar Sonne did not appear to be an hereditary criminal or degenerate. The stuff of his life had not been marred in making. Of this, not only am I convinced, but Mr. H. W. Lewis, the kindly Superintendent, is likewise convinced.

Edgar Sonne talked readily, and we were soon deep in a recital of his boyish impulses, struggles and wrongs. He has a lively sense of wrong, which argues well for him, in spite of the wrong that he has done. The "Lictor Boy" who kept him out late at night, compelling him to go without supper, and to sell four papers in order to earn a nickel, struck him as especially unfair — likewise his mother, when she swept the bunch of keys into the ash-barrel, charged him with stealing them, and whipped him with a leather trace such as is used to harness a horse to a wagon. Resenting this injustice, and seeking as men have always sought, and as they still continue to seek by means of civil suits, compensation for injury, "to get even," in his own language, he promptly robbed his mother of twenty dollars and went off on a good time.

But let no mistake be made. His crimes have not all been of this simple, innocent order. Burglaries and thefts he told me of, where the impulse was not emotional or passionate, but cold-blooded and acquisitive. He made it plain, unconsciously, of course, that it was easier for him to steal and rob than not to steal or rob. He moved along the line of least resistance, which, to him, was in the direction of crime.

As we talked, further glimpses were given of the forces which had moulded the stuff of his life into what it was. Such things as home environment and mother's love may be imagined from the following data:

"Been here two weeks," he sobbed, once, when he broke down, "an' she ain't been here to see me."

"She put me in the Youth's Directory when she was movin' house and I was there for months."

"She laughed when she saw the policeman had me."

"And what did you do with the money you earned by selling papers?" I asked him.

"Took it home to my mother."

"Always?"

"No," he said. "She'd ask me for it, and I'd say, 'I ain't sellin' no papers.' If she found out she'd beat me. That's the only thing she can do."

"The only thing she can do!" From our conversation it seemed the only thing she had ever done. Many nights, he said, he slept out in the backyard; nor in the morning did his mother ever ask him where he had been. "She don't care," was the way he put it.

But there was more to come in the process of finding out how the stuff of his life had been marred, not in the making, but after it had been made.

Mr. Lewis put his hand over the boy's mouth, completely covering it, and told him to blow out through his nose. He obeyed, but no air was expelled. His hand went up to the crown of his head. It hurt him there, he said, whenever he tried to blow air through his nose. Directed by Mr. Lewis, I looked into his mouth. The tonsils were so enlarged that the passage between them was no more than an eighth of an inch wide. The palate, instead of hanging down, was thrust by the tonsils straight out to the front at right angles to its normal position.

An examination had been made by a surgeon, I learned, who had found the postnasal cavity entirely filled with a growth of adenoids or tumors. Not only did this adenoidal growth absolutely close the nose to the passage of air, but it exerted an ascertained pressure on the brain itself. Deafness was also beginning to come on.

In answer to a question from me, he admitted that he could not run so far, or fast, or long as other boys. "It makes my heart beat," he said, indicating its action by a fluttery motion of his hand.

It was patent that he did not get sufficient air into his lungs. Instead of breathing down to his stomach, as a healthy boy should, he breathed high up in his chest—higher up than any woman breathes. As a result, his blood lacked oxygen, was impoverished. In consequence of this, the whole physical organization was impoverished, starved. Body and brain were in an anaemic condition. He rolled up his sleeve, exposing a scrawny, emaciated arm, sharp at the elbow and with no more than a faint semblance of the biceps, which reminded one forcibly of the famine pictures of starving children in India.

If this were the condition for this body, resulting from impoverished blood, what, from the same cause, must be the condition of his brain and mind? His record is the answer. As emaciation was the result of his starved body, so was criminality the result of his starved brain. For there is a direct and intimate relation between the body and brain, between the flesh and the spirit. If dyspepsia is capable of giving a bias to a good man's soul to such an extent that it is impossible for anything less than an angel or a martyr to live with him, then the condition of Edgar Sonne's mind and soul can be readily imagined.

"Not pre-natal at all," said Mr. Lewis, referring to the adenoid growths. "Contracted after birth, like warts, from bad physical surroundings, such as insufficient ventilation, or from so simple a thing as sleeping continuously with the head under the covers."

"Can these growths be removed? I asked. "And can these enlarged tonsils be reduced so that sufficient air may find its way to the lungs?"

"Certainly," said Mr. Lewis.

"And could all this have been done years ago?"

Mr. Lewis was emphatic in his affirmation.

Here, then, was criminality prior to the criminality of Edgar Sonne—the criminality, first, of his mother, in permitting the diseased condition to go unattended; and the criminality, second, of society for the same reason. For if society arrogates to itself the punishment of youthful offenders, then it must take upon itself the responsibility for the making of youthful offenders. If society provides jails and policemen for children, it should likewise provide physical examinations and physicians.

This is not a sentimental consideration. It is eminently business-like and practical. Had society taken hold of Edgar Sonne years ago and amended his moral nature by enabling him to breathe properly, it would have saved money. As it is, policemen, detectives, judges, superintendents of aid societies, patrol wagons and what not, have run up a pretty item in society's expense account. And, worst of all, nothing has been gained. Society has still to doctor Edgar Sonne, and it will be a more expensive and serious doctoring than it would have been had his disease been checked and cured in its commencement.

"Every neglected child is a menace to society and the State," says Judge R. S. Tuthill. And Jacob Riis, "Just in proportion to the neglect of them now will be the smart of them hereafter."

But to return to Edgar Sonne. His whole history and development seem clear and plain. The stuff of his life was apparently normal in the making. It promised a multitude of potentialities, the uses or abuses of which his adventure into the world would determine. With these potentialities, the gifts of heredity, he came into the world, a soft and pulpy infant, to be moulded by the physical and social forces which would bear upon him. What these forces were, we have seen. An unchecked, untreated disease, which impoverished and caused an abnormal condition of mind and body; and a harsh, unlovely and unsympathetic home and neighborhood environment which gave the criminal bias to the sickly body and brain and moral nature.

What is to be done?

Mr. Lewis answers this question most eloquently.

"First, we will give him a tonic treatment of the body; build up and strengthen him as much as possible. Then we will operate upon him, reduce the tonsils and remove the adenoids. Then, and not until then, will we be able to treat the mind. And it will be a tonic treatment, too. The abnormal condition removed, plenty of fresh pure blood surging through the brain, and we will build up the mind and the moral nature until they become healthy, wholesome and good.

"Give me three months," he added, with sparkling eyes, and with a certitude born of intimate experience with all manner of youthful offenders. "Give me three months of a healthy brain to which to make mental and moral appeal, and I'll show you a transformed boy."

"The outcome of the operation and of Mr. Lewis' efforts will be eagerly awaited."

Japanese Officers Consider Everything a Military Secret

First published in and reprinted from the *San Francisco Examiner,* June 26, 1904.

London wrote passionately about modern warfare. His nearly two dozen articles for the *San Francisco Examiner* about the Russian-Japanese War of 1904 show real brilliance, though some of them—not all—are also seriously marred by his deep-seated racism. Clichés about Asians abound. "The Asiatic does not value life as we do," he noted in one article. "Justice is a characteristic belonging to the white man," he commented in another, adding, "From the white man only is it [justice] obtainable." In yet another article he wrote, "The Korean is spiritless . . . He is soft and effeminate . . . a coward." After covering the war from February to May 1904, he concluded, "Beware the Japanese." He did not trust "brown men," and this mistrust only deepened as a result of his experience as a war reporter. In his defense, a year later he would call Japanese socialists his comrades and his equals.

London did much more than spew racial hatred, however, in his 1904 *Examiner* articles. He also wrote insightfully about the nature of war in the twentieth century: how it had changed radically since the origins of war eons before, when cave dwellers battled one another. He learned, too, how difficult it had become to report war honestly and accurately. He saw that the Japanese carried out their own public relations campaign about the war, intended to make friends and allies, and he saw that military officials staged events for reporters, holding press conferences to disseminate the official version of the war. Again and again, he found himself in impossible situations in which officially, everything was allowed, but in fact nothing was allowed. "Correspondents may witness all military operations," the Japanese informed reporters, though they were not allowed to directly witness any military operations.

London himself figures largely as a character in many of his articles. As a war reporter, he became a crucial part of the story. By writing about himself, he was able to describe the war of words that accompanied the actual combat—the battle to win the hearts and minds of newspaper readers around the world. The frustration London expressed in 1904 would be echoed by war reporters for the next hundred years—including embedded reporters who covered the invasion of Iraq in 2003. On one occasion, Japanese military officials escorted him, along with other western reporters, to the battlefront. "We saw what we were permitted to see, and the chief duty of the officers looking after us was to keep us from seeing anything," he noted in frustration and indignation. "No war correspondent can see of his own eyes all that is taking place."

Here, as elsewhere in his life, Jack London followed a familiar pattern; at the start of the war, having read Stephen Crane's and Rudyard Kipling's accounts about the lives of soldiers and about majestic battles, he held romantic illusions about the heroic reporter. By the end of his stay, he had become disillusioned about the possibilities of covering a modern war at all, and he went home with a sense that he had failed to get the big story he'd set out to get. Indeed, he did not watch men fighting in close combat. But he did learn that modern warfare often meant long-distance warfare, with big guns and chemical weapons, and he recognized much of the madness and absurdity of war. "The theory seems to be to pump lead at the landscape in such quantities that there are bound to be some lucky accidents," he observed. His articles might also be read as antiwar tracts. London certain did not glorify war in any way. The aim of war, he concludes, is "to kill, to kill swiftly and to kill the uttermost." Never mind justice, freedom, and democracy.

London's June 26, 1904, article "Japanese Officers Consider Everything a Military Secret" sums up his experiences. He describes a visit to a location where a skirmish had taken place. "How many Japanese were killed?" he asks. "I cannot tell you. It is a military secret," he is told. When he does obtain and record facts, he must submit them to a censor and then wait for them to be "emasculated" and approved before they can be sent, via telegraph, to the United States. Much the same story would be played out decades later in Vietnam, Iraq, Afghanistan, and wherever soldiers clashed with one another.

London also took photographs, many of which were confiscated because they were deemed military secrets. Denied access to the front and forced to show his stories to the censor, he felt that he would never get the kind of scoop he had hoped for. By the time his reports reached San Francisco, they were of little value, he noted. Of course, London might have pretended that he had unlimited access to the front and that he had scooped all the other reporters. Though he had gone with heroic aspirations fueled by Crane and Kipling, he was committed to writing the truth about what he saw (and didn't see).

A decade later, in 1914, his articles on the U.S. military intervention in Mexico were little more than racist pro-American propaganda. It was the "duty" of the United States to interfere in nations with "millions of mismanaged and ill-treated subjects," London insisted, and he argued that the United States, as an "enlightened nation," ought to "police, organize, and manage Mexico." •

Antung (First Japanese Army) June 2 — It is all very well, this long-range fighting; but if the range continues to increase, and if other armies are as solicitous for the welfare of the correspondents as are the Japanese, war correspondence will become a lost art and there will be a lot of war correspondents entering new professions late in life.

In the first place, when the front of battle extends for miles and miles, no correspondent can see of his own eyes all that is taking place. What is happening to the right, miles away, behind the mountains where the Yalu curls into the east, and what is happening to the left, miles away, behind the mountains where the Yalu curls into the west, is beyond him. He cannot understand what is taking place before his eyes (or his field-glasses, rather, for his eyes show him nothing), without knowing what is taking place on left and right; and there is no one to tell him what is taking place on right and left. The officers may not tell him, because, in their parlance, it would be an exposure of a military secret.

This would not be so bad if they did not consider practically everything a military secret. A propos of this, a correspondent, on his way up country, arrives at the village of Kasan. A skirmish had once taken place at Kasan. A month had passed. The front had moved up a hundred miles. The correspondent saw a few graves on the hillside. "How many Japanese were killed?" he asked an officer. The officer was a major. He replied, "I cannot tell you. It is a military secret."

This may seem far-fetched, but it is not. It is merely typical. On every side is the military secret. The correspondent is hedged by military secrets. He may not move about for fear he will pop on a military secret, though what he may do with a military secret only the Japanese know. First, in order to get a military secret out of the country, he must show it to the censor and get permission. This obtained, he must dispatch it by Korean runners to Ping-yang, a couple of hundred miles to the south, where it may be telegraphed by his agent to Seoul and from there be cabled, via Japan, to his paper. But granting that the military secret has survived all the vicissitudes of the journey to Ping-yang and not lost in its time-value, it is not yet out of the country. Seven or eight days later a runner arrives with a note from his Ping-yang agent telling him that all cables are being held up. So the military secret, like the peasant who started out for Carcosonne, dies unobtrusively of old age upon the way.

The position of the correspondent in the Japanese army is an anomalous one of interloper and honored guest. The restrictions which stultify all his efforts show the one, the solicitude of his hosts shows the second. If a skirmish or demonstration is to be made, word is sent to him to that effect—also, a further word to the effect that he is to assemble with his colleagues at a certain place and proceed and be directed under the management of an army officer told off for the purpose. He is further warned that neither he nor his colleagues may go individually. Still further, he has fresh in his mind the previous day's instructions from headquarters as, for instance, those of April 29th, from which I quote the following:

"There is no official news to communicate concerning military operations now proceeding or pending."

"Headquarters (unofficially) is aware that artillery has been engaged on both sides of the river.

"For the present and until further notice the transmission of any dispatches from the front where wireless telegraphy is employed is forbidden. The necessary steps are being taken to see that this order is obeyed.

"It may be found necessary to enforce a still stricter censorship than that already existing.

"From to-day and until further notice, it is forbidden to take photographs or make sketches of any kind within the area now occupied by the Japanese troops. It is useless to apply for permission to do so, as applications of this kind will not be entertained.

"Correspondents may witness all military operations. They must keep well in the rear of the firing line. They are forbidden to approach certain (unspecified) works."

The peculiar force of this last order lies in that the correspondent who ventures out for a "look see" all by himself finds that just about everything in the landscape is unspecifiedly forbidden. The nearest I have succeeded in getting to a Japanese battery, and one not in action either, was when I crawled to the top of a hill about half a mile to the rear and gazed upon it through field glasses in fear and trembling.

Even before the taking of photographs was absolutely forbidden I once had the temerity to take a snap of an army farrier and his bellows. "Here at last was something that was not a military secret," I had thought in my innocence. Fifteen minutes ride away I was stopped by a soldier who could not speak English. I showed my credentials and on my arm the official insignia of my position in the Japanese army. But it was no use. Something serious was pending. I was ordered to remain where I was, and while I waited I cudgeled my brain in an endeavor to find what military secret had crept in unawares.

I did not know of any, but I was confident that one was there somewhere. After much delay an officer was brought to me. He was a captain, and his English was excellent—a great deal purer and better than my own.

"You have taken a photograph of an army blacksmith," he said accusingly and reproachfully.

With a sinking heart I nodded my head to acknowledge my guilt.

"You must give it up," he said.

"It is ridiculous," I burst out.

"You must give it up," he repeated.

Then, after some discussion with the soldiers, he said I might keep it; but he added that the road was one of the unspecified forbidden places, and that I must go back.

Back I went, but the field telephone must have beaten me, for they knew all about my transgression at headquarters before I got there.

The function of the war correspondent, so far as I can ascertain, is to sit up on the reverse slopes of hills where honored guests cannot be injured, and from there to listen to the crack of rifles and vainly search the dim distance for the men who are doing the shooting; to receive orders from headquarters as to what he may or may not do; to submit daily to the censor his conjectures and military secrets, and to observe article 4 of the printed First Army Regulations — to wit:

"Press correspondents should look and behave decently, and never should do anything disorderly, and should never enter the office rooms of the headquarters."

With one exception, the correspondents with the first army are what is called "cable" men. Theirs is the task to cable, telegraph, use runners and whatever means to hand to get news out of the country as quickly as possible. There is the censor to begin with. What little news they do manage to glean is pretty well emasculated by him before it is allowed to start. At the very earliest it will arrive in Japan five days later. From Japan it radiates to the rest of the world. But the headquarters is connected directly with Tokyo by wire. That is to say, the headquarters news beats the correspondents' news to Tokyo by five days. Not only that, for it has full details and is correct. In addition, the powers that be at Tokyo are more liberal than the first army censor, so that Tokyo makes public to the world a fuller account five days before the "cable" men's accounts begin to arrive. If other nations in future wars imitate the Japanese in this, the "cable" men would cease to exist. There would be no reason for them to exist. The regular newsgatherers in the capitals of the contending countries would serve the purpose just as well and a great deal better.

Remains the writing man. Long range fighting, supervising officers who lead him about in the rear as Cook's tourists are led about Rome and Paris, military secrets, and censors do for him. When he has described two or three invisible battles and has had his conjectures trimmed down by the censor, he is done for. He can't go on describing the sounds of rifles and guns; the bursting of shell and shrapnel, and the occasional moving specks for a whole campaign. Nor can he go on describing the transport trains in the rear; the only things he sees too much of and which as yet have not been placed under the taboo of military secret.

Personally, I entered upon this campaign with the most gorgeous conceptions of what a war correspondent's work in the world must be. I knew that the mortality of war correspondents was said to be greater, in proportion to numbers, than the mortality of soldiers. I remembered, during the siege of Kartoum and the attempted relief by Wolseley the deaths in battle of a number of correspondents. I had read "The Light that Failed." I remembered Stephen Crane's descriptions of being under fire in Cuba. I had heard—God what was there aught I had not heard? of all sorts and conditions of correspondents in all sorts of battles and skirmishes, right in the thick of it, where life was keen and immortal moments were being lived. In brief, I came to war expecting to get thrills. My only thrills have been those of indignation and irritation.

Revolution

First published in *Contemporary Review*, January 1908; reprinted from *Revolution and Other Essays* (New York: Macmillan, 1910).

"Revolution" was delivered as a speech to the student body at the University of California, Berkeley, in January 1905, and then all across the country that year, culminating at Harvard in December. In the decade between 1895, when he wrote for the Oakland High School *Aegis,* and 1905, when he served as the poster boy for American radicalism, London underwent a dramatic metamorphosis. As the socialist cause grew stronger, he became more defiant, and, in turn, he helped to swell the ranks of the revolution. In those ten years, he moved from a moderate version of socialism that emphasized public ownership of utilities to an extreme position on the left that endorsed violent upheaval, the confiscation of private property, and the redistribution of wealth. In 1895 and 1896, in Oakland, London urged voters to go to the polls and cast their ballots for socialist candidates and measures. In 1905, he traveled across the United States to denounce capitalism, calling upon students, teachers, and workers to rebel against the system—with arms.

London also went through a revolution in his personal life during this decade. He become a world-famous wealthy writer. He moved from Oakland to Glen Ellen, in rural Sonoma County. He married and divorced his first wife, Bessie. He traveled everywhere with his Korean servant, Manyoungi, whom he had hired in 1904 while covering the war between Russia and Japan. A peripatetic and colorful figure, London was the focus of much attention from the press.

On college campuses, London's lectures were sponsored by the Intercollegiate Socialist Society (ISS), the organization of radical students that he had helped to start with Upton Sinclair. He also spoke in churches and to civic groups, as well as to gatherings of millionaires who wanted to meet and debate with the legendary Jack London. At off-campus events, he was paid as much as $500. As always, his idea was to make money even while he aimed to further the revolution, and he liked to boast that he was the only money-making socialist author in America. For the most part, his socialist friends admired him for his ability to take money from the bourgeoisie while denouncing it for its material-ism. When he returned to Oakland from his national tour, he was introduced to packed audiences as "our comrade" and as a conquering hero. Audiences loved him.

During his travels across the country, and especially in the East, London encountered American millionaires who, he realized, were not about to relinquish their wealth or their power—and who argued with him about the revolution. This eye-opening experience altered his political outlook. Socialism, he sensed, probably would not become a reality in his own lifetime. But he did not give up on socialism or the revolution. He was always loath to let go of an idea, surrender a passion, or discontinue a literary line once he started it. So, even as he generated new and different interests from 1906 to the end of his life, he continued to write from a radical stance, albeit with a darker, more somber mood.

In "Revolution," London personalizes the socialist cause. He makes it tangible, connect-ing it to the lives of real working men, women, and children suffering under capitalism in the United States and around the world. He characterizes socialism as a movement "lim-ited only by the limits of the planet" that "transcends race prejudice." In 1904, he'd sounded the alarm about Japanese militarism. In "Revolution," he writes warmly about the Japanese people—his Japanese comrades—and speaks proudly about "international solidarity."

London captures the epic sweep of history—from Xerxes to Napoleon, from the American Revolution of 1776 to the French Revolution of 1789 and the Russian Revolution of 1905. He also focuses on individuals, nowhere more poignantly than when he quotes verbatim from the diary of W. G. Robbins, an unemployed American who, unable to find food or work, committed suicide. He even rejected the idea of "the survival of the fittest," which he had long held sacrosanct, as bourgeois and outmoded.

In *The People of the Abyss* (1903) London indicts the British ruling class for "misman-agement." In "Revolution" he indicts the "blind and greedy" American capitalist class for "mismanagement," too—for creating a society with hunger, homelessness, poverty, and people "living miserably . . . segregated in slum ghettos." No one ever recorded "Revolution," but reading it, one can hear London's heartfelt passion, especially for the child laborer working twelve hours a day. His outrage about political repression is also clearly appar-ent—the use of scabs and strikebreakers, court injunctions, and civil lawsuits. "Antagonism never lulled revolution," he insists. The more repression, the more resistance, he argues. London also describes the cause as a religious movement with the "fervor in it of Paul and Christ." He ends his talk defiantly and provocatively: "The revolution is here, now. Stop it who can." Now, more than one hundred years after he wrote it, "Revolution" remains a clas-sic in the literature of American radicalism. •

"The present is enough for common souls,
Who, never looking forward, are indeed
Mere clay, wherein the footprints of their age
Are petrified forever."

I received a letter the other day. It was from a man in Arizona. It began, "Dear
Comrade." It ended, "Yours for the Revolution." I replied to the letter, and my letter
began, "Dear Comrade." It ended, "Yours for the Revolution." In the United States
there are 400,000 men, of men and women nearly 1,000,000, who begin their letters
"Dear Comrade," and end them "Yours for the Revolution." In Germany there are
3,000,000 men who begin their letters "Dear Comrade" and end them "Yours for the
Revolution"; in France, 1,000,000 men; in Austria, 800,000 men; in Belgium,
300,000 men; in Italy, 250,000 men; in England, 100,000 men; in Switzerland,
100,000 men; in Denmark, 55,000 men; in Sweden, 50,000 men; in Holland, 40,000
men; in Spain, 30,000 men — comrades all, and revolutionists.

These are numbers which dwarf the grand armies of Napoleon and Xerxes. But
they are numbers not of conquest and maintenance of the established order, but of
conquest and revolution. They compose, when the roll is called, an army of 7,000,000
men, who, in accordance with the conditions of to-day, are fighting with all their
might for the conquest of the wealth of the world and for the complete overthrow of
existing society.

There has never been anything like this revolution in the history of the world.
There is nothing analogous between it and the American Revolution or the French
Revolution. It is unique, colossal. Other revolutions compare with it as asteroids compare with the sun. It is alone of its kind, the first world revolution in a world whose
history is replete with revolutions. And not only this, for it is the first organized
movement of men to become a world movement, limited only by the limits of the
planet.

This revolution is unlike all other revolutions in many respects. It is not sporadic.
It is not a flame of popular discontent, arising in a day and dying down in a day. It is
older than the present generation. It has a history and traditions, and a martyr-roll
only less extensive possibly than the martyr-roll of Christianity. It has also a literature
a myriad times more imposing, scientific, and scholarly than the literature of any previous revolution.

They call themselves "comrades," these men, comrades in the socialist revolution.
Nor is the word empty and meaningless, coined of mere lip service. It knits men

together as brothers, as men should be knit together who stand shoulder to shoulder under the red banner of revolt. This red banner, by the way, symbolizes the brotherhood of man, and does not symbolize the incendiarism that instantly connects itself with the red banner in the affrighted bourgeois mind. The comradeship of the revolutionists is alive and warm. It passes over geographical lines, transcends race prejudice, and has even proved itself mightier than the Fourth of July, spread-eagle Americanism of our forefathers. The French socialist workingmen and the German socialist workingmen forget Alsace and Lorraine, and, when war threatens, pass resolutions declaring that as workingmen and comrades they have no quarrel with each other. Only the other day, when Japan and Russia sprang at each other's throats, the revolutionists of Japan addressed the following message to the revolutionists of Russia: "Dear Comrades—Your government and ours have recently plunged into war to carry out their imperialistic tendencies, but for us socialists there are no boundaries, race, country, or nationality. We are comrades, brothers and sisters, and have no reason to fight. Your enemies are not the Japanese people, but our militarism and so-called patriotism. Patriotism and militarism are our mutual enemies."

In January, 1905, throughout the United States the socialists held mass-meetings to express their sympathy for their struggling comrades, the revolutionists of Russia, and, more to the point, to furnish the sinews of war by collecting money and cabling it to the Russian leaders.

The fact of this call for money, and the ready response, and the very wording of the call, make a striking and practical demonstration of the international solidarity of this world revolution: "Whatever may be the immediate results of the present revolt in Russia, the socialist propaganda in that country has received from it an impetus unparalleled in the history of modern class wars. The heroic battle for freedom is being fought almost exclusively by the Russian working-class under the intellectual leadership of Russian socialists, thus once more demonstrating the fact that the class-conscious workingmen have become the vanguard of all liberating movements of modern times."

Here are 7,000,000 comrades in an organized, international, world-wide, revolutionary movement. Here is a tremendous human force. It must be reckoned with. Here is power. And here is romance—romance so colossal that it seems to be beyond the ken of ordinary mortals. These revolutionists are swayed by great passion. They have a keen sense of personal right, much of reverence for humanity, but little reverence, if any at all, for the rule of the dead. They refuse to be ruled by the dead. To the bourgeois mind their unbelief in the dominant conventions of the established order is startling. They laugh to scorn the sweet ideals and dear moralities of bourgeois society. They intend to destroy bourgeois society with most of its sweet ideals and dear moralities, and chiefest among these are those that group themselves under such heads as private ownership of capital, survival of the fittest, and patriotism—even patriotism.

Such an army of revolution, 7,000,000 strong, is a thing to make rulers and ruling classes pause and consider. The cry of this army is, "No quarter! We want all that you possess. We will be content with nothing less than all that you possess. We want in our hands the reins of power and the destiny of mankind. Here are our hands. They are strong hands. We are going to take your governments, your palaces, and all your purpled ease away from you, and in that day you shall work for your bread even as the peasant in the field or the starved and runty clerk in your metropolises. Here are our hands. They are strong hands."

Well may rulers and ruling classes pause and consider. This is revolution. And, further, these 7,000,000 men are not an army on paper. Their fighting strength in the field is 7,000,000. To-day they cast 7,000,000 votes in the civilized countries of the world.

Yesterday they were not so strong. To-morrow they will be still stronger. And they are fighters. They love peace. They are unafraid of war. They intend nothing less than to destroy existing capitalist society and to take possession of the whole world. If the law of the land permits, they fight for this end peaceably, at the ballot-box. If the law of the land does not permit, and if they have force meted out to them, they resort to force themselves. They meet violence with violence. Their hands are strong and they are unafraid. In Russia, for instance, there is no suffrage. The government executes the revolutionists. The revolutionists kill the officers of the government. The revolutionists meet legal murder with assassination.

Now here arises a particularly significant phase which would be well for the rulers to consider. Let me make it concrete. I am a revolutionist. Yet I am a fairly sane and normal individual. I speak, and I *think,* of these assassins in Russia as "my comrades." So do all the comrades in America, and all the 7,000,000 comrades in the world. Of what worth an organized, international, revolutionary movement if our comrades are not backed up the world over! The worth is shown by the fact that we do back up the assassinations by our comrades in Russia. They are not disciples of Tolstoy, nor are we. We are revolutionists.

Our comrades in Russia have formed what they call "The Fighting Organization." This Fighting Organization accused, tried, found guilty, and condemned to death, one Sipiaguin, Minister of Interior. On April 2 he was shot and killed in the Maryinsky Palace. Two years later the Fighting Organization condemned to death and executed another Minister of Interior, Von Plehve. Having done so, it issued a document, dated July 29, 1904, setting forth the counts of its indictment of Von Plehve and its responsibility for the assassination. Now, and to the point, this document was sent out to the socialists of the world, and by them was published everywhere in the magazines and newspapers. The point is, not that the socialists of the world were unafraid to do it, not that they dared to do it, but that they did it as a matter of routine, giving publication to what may be called an official document of the international revolutionary movement.

These are high lights upon the revolution granted, but they are also facts. And they are given to the rulers and the ruling classes, not in bravado, not to frighten them, but for them to consider more deeply the spirit and nature of this world revolution. The time has come for the revolution to demand consideration. It has fastened upon every civilized country in the world. As fast as a country becomes civilized, the revolution fastens upon it. With the introduction of the machine into Japan, socialism was introduced. Socialism marched into the Philippines shoulder to shoulder with the American soldiers. The echoes of the last gun had scarcely died away when socialist locals were forming in Cuba and Porto Rico. Vastly more significant is the fact that of all the countries the revolution has fastened upon, on not one has it relaxed its grip. On the contrary, on every country its grip closes tighter year by year. As an active movement it began obscurely over a generation ago. In 1867, its voting strength in the world was 30,000. By 1871, its vote had increased to 100,000. Not till 1884 did it pass the half-million point. By 1889, it had passed the million point. It had then gained momentum. In 1892 the socialist vote of the world was 1,798,391; in 1893, 2,585,898; in 1895, 3,033,718; in 1898, 4,515,591; in 1902, 5,253,054; in 1903, 6,285,374; and in the year of our Lord 1905 it passed the seven-million mark.

Nor has this flame of revolution left the United States untouched. In 1888, there were only 2,068 socialist votes. In 1902, there were 127,713 socialist votes. And in 1904, 435,040 socialist votes were cast. What fanned this flame? Not hard times. The first four years of the twentieth century were considered prosperous years, yet in that time more than 300,000 men added themselves to the ranks of the revolutionists, flinging their defiance in the teeth of bourgeois society and taking their stand under the blood-red banner. In the state of the writer, California, one man in twelve is an avowed and registered revolutionist.

One thing must be clearly understood. This is no spontaneous and vague uprising of a large mass of discontented and miserable people—a blind and instinctive recoil from hurt. On the contrary, the propaganda is intellectual; the movement is based upon economic necessity and is in line with social evolution; while the miserable people have not yet revolted. The revolutionist is no starved and diseased slave in the shambles at the bottom of the social pit, but is, in the main, a hearty, well-fed work-ingman, who sees the shambles waiting for him and his children and recoils from the descent. The very miserable people are too helpless to help themselves. But they are being helped, and the day is not far distant when their numbers will go to swell the ranks of the revolutionists.

Another thing must be clearly understood. In spite of the fact that middle-class men and professional men are interested in the movement, it is nevertheless a distinctly working-class revolt. The world over, it is a working-class revolt. The workers of the world, as a class, are fighting the capitalists of the world, as a class. The so-called great middle class is a growing anomaly in the social struggle. It is a perishing class (wily statisticians to the contrary), and its historic mission of buffer between the capitalist- and working-classes has just about been fulfilled. Little remains for it but to wail as it passes into oblivion, as it has already begun to wail in accents Populistic and Jeffersonian-Democratic. The fight is on. The revolution is here now, and it is the world's workers that are in revolt.

Naturally the question arises: Why is this so? No mere whim of the spirit can give rise to a world revolution. Whim does not conduce to unanimity. There must be a deep-seated cause to make 7,000,000 men of the one mind, to make them cast off allegiance to the bourgeois gods and lose faith in so fine a thing as patriotism. There are many counts of the indictment which the revolutionists bring against the capitalist class, but for present use only one need be stated, and it is a count to which capital has never replied and can never reply.

The capitalist class has managed society, and its management has failed. And not only has it failed in its management, but it has failed deplorably, ignobly, horribly. The capitalist class had an opportunity such as was vouchsafed no previous ruling class in the history of the world. It broke away from the rule of the old feudal aristocracy and made modern society. It mastered matter, organized the machinery of life, and made possible a wonderful era for mankind, wherein no creature should cry aloud because it had not enough to eat, and wherein for every child there would be opportunity for education, for intellectual and spiritual uplift. Matter being mastered, and the machinery of life organized, all this was possible. Here was the chance, God-given, and the capitalist class failed. It was blind and greedy. It prattled sweet ideals and dear moralities, rubbed its eyes not once, nor ceased one whit in its greediness, and smashed down in a failure as tremendous only as was the opportunity it had ignored.

But all this is like so much cobwebs to the bourgeois mind. As it was blind in the past, it is blind now and cannot see nor understand. Well, then, let the indictment be stated more definitely, in terms sharp and unmistakable. In the first place, consider the caveman. He was a very simple creature. His head slanted back like an orang-utan's and he had but little more intelligence. He lived in a hostile environment, the prey of all manner of fierce life. He had no inventions nor artifices. His natural efficiency for food-getting was, say, 1. He did not even till the soil. With his natural efficiency of 1, he fought off his carnivorous enemies and got himself food and shelter. He must have done all this, else he would not have multiplied and spread over the earth and sent his progeny down, generation by generation, to become even you and me.

The caveman, with his natural efficiency of 1, got enough to eat most of the time, and no caveman went hungry all the time. Also, he lived a healthy, open-air life, loafed and rested himself, and found plenty of time in which to exercise his imagination and invent gods. That is to say, he did not have to work all his waking moments in order to get enough to eat. The child of the caveman (and this is true of the children of all savage peoples) had a childhood, and by that is meant a happy childhood of play and development.

And now, how fares modern man? Consider the United States, the most prosperous and most enlightened country of the world. In the United States there are 10,000,000 people living in poverty. By poverty is meant that condition in life in which, through lack of food and adequate shelter, the mere standard of working efficiency cannot be maintained. In the United States there are 10,000,000 people who have not enough to eat. In the United States, because they have not enough to eat, there are 10,000,000 people who cannot keep the ordinary measure of strength in their bodies. This means that these 10,000,000 people are perishing, are dying, body and soul, slowly, because they have not enough to eat. All over this broad, prosperous, enlightened land, are men, women, and children who are living miserably. In all the great cities, where they are segregated in slum ghettos by hundreds of thousands and by millions, their misery becomes beastliness. No caveman ever starved as chronically as they starve, ever slept as vilely as they sleep, ever festered with rottenness and disease as they fester, nor ever toiled as hard and for as long hours as they toil.

In Chicago there is a woman who toiled sixty hours per week. She was a garment worker. She sewed buttons on clothes. Among the Italian garment workers of Chicago, the average weekly wage of the dressmakers is 90 cents, but they work every week in the year. The average weekly wage of the pants finishers is $1.31, and the average number of weeks employed in the year is 27.85. The average yearly earnings of the dressmakers is $37.00; of the pants finishers, $42.41. Such wages means no childhood for the children, beastliness of living, and starvation for all.

Unlike the caveman, modern man cannot get food and shelter whenever be feels like working for it. Modern man has first to find the work, and in this he is often unsuccessful. Then misery becomes acute. This acute misery is chronicled daily in the newspapers. Let several of the countless instances be cited.

In New York City lived a woman, Mary Mead. She had three children: Mary, one year old; Johanna, two years old; Alice, four years old. Her husband could find no work. They starved. They were evicted from their shelter at 160 Steuben Street. Mary Mead strangled her baby, Mary, one year old; strangled Alice, four years old; failed to strangle Johanna, two years old, and then herself took poison. Said the father to the police: "Constant poverty had driven my wife insane. We lived at No. 160 Steuben Street until a week ago, when we were dispossessed. I could get no work. I could not even make enough to put food into our mouths. The babies grew ill and weak. My wife cried nearly all the time."

"So overwhelmed is the Department of Charities with tens of thousands of applications from men out of work that it finds itself unable to cope with the situation." —*New York Commercial,* January 11, 1905.

In a daily paper, because he cannot get work in order to get something to eat, modern man advertises as follows:

"Young man, good education, unable to obtain employment, will sell to physician and bacteriologist for experimental purposes all right and title to his body. Address for price, box 3466, *Examiner.*"

"Frank A. Mallin went to the central police station Wednesday night and asked to be locked up on a charge of vagrancy. He said he had been conducting an unsuccessful search for work for so long that he was sure he must be a vagrant. In any event, he was so hungry he must be fed. Police judge Graham sentenced him to ninety days' imprisonment." —*San Francisco Examiner.*

In a room at the Soto House, 32 Fourth Street, San Francisco, was found the body of W. G. Robbins. He had turned on the gas. Also was found his diary, from which the following extracts are made:

"March 3.—No chance of getting anything here. What will I do?

"March 7.—Cannot find anything yet.

"March 8.—Am living on doughnuts at five cents a day.

"March 9.—My last quarter gone for room rent.

"March 10.—God help me. Have only five cents left. Can get nothing to
  do. What next? Starvation or—? I have spent my last nickel
  to-night. What shall I do? Shall it be steal, beg, or die? I have
  never stolen, begged, or starved in all my fifty years of life, but
  now I am on the brink—death seems the only refuge.

"March 11.—Sick all day—burning fever this afternoon. Had nothing
  to eat to-day or since yesterday noon. My head, my head.
  Good-by, all."

How fares the child of modern man in this most prosperous of lands? In the city of New York 50,000 children go hungry to school every morning. From the same city on January 12, a press despatch was sent out over the country of a case reported by Dr. A. E. Daniel, of the New York Infirmary for Women and Children. The case was that of a babe, eighteen months old, who earned by its labor fifty cents per week in a tenement sweat-shop.

"On a pile of rags in a room bare of furniture and freezing cold, Mrs. Mary Gallin, dead from starvation, with an emaciated baby four months old crying at her breast, was found this morning at 513 Myrtle Avenue, Brooklyn, by Policeman McConnon of the Flushing Avenue Station. Huddled together for warmth in another part of the room were the father, James Gallin, and three children ranging from two to eight years of age. The children gazed at the policeman much as ravenous animals might have done. They were famished, and there was not a vestige of food in their comfortless home."—*New York Journal,* January 2, 1902.

In the United States 80,000 children are toiling out their lives in the textile mills alone. In the South they work twelve-hour shifts. They never see the day. Those on the night shift are asleep when the sun pours its life and warmth over the world, while those on the day shift are at the machines before dawn and return to their miserable dens, called "homes," after dark. Many receive no more than ten cents a day. There are babies who work for five and six cents a day. Those who work on the night shift are often kept awake by having cold water dashed in their faces. There are children six years of age who have already to their credit eleven months' work on the night shift. When they become sick, and are unable to rise from their beds to go to work, there are men employed to go on horseback from house to house, and cajole and bully them into arising and going to work. Ten per cent of them contract active consumption. All are puny wrecks, distorted, stunted, mind and body. Elbert Hubbard says of the child-laborers of the Southern cotton-mills: —

"I thought to lift one of the little toilers to ascertain his weight. Straightaway through his thirty-five pounds of skin and bones there ran a tremor of fear, and he struggled forward to tie a broken thread. I attracted his attention by a touch, and offered him a silver dime. He looked at me dumbly from a face that might have belonged to a man of sixty, so furrowed, tightly drawn, and full of pain it was. He did not reach for the money—he did not know what it was. There were dozens of such children in this particular mill. A physician who was with me said that they would all be dead probably in two years, and their places filled by others—there were plenty more. Pneumonia carries off most of them. Their systems are ripe for disease, and when it comes there is no rebound—no response. Medicine simply does not act— nature is whipped, beaten, discouraged, and the child sinks into a stupor and dies."

So fares modern man and the child of modern man in the United States, most prosperous and enlightened of all countries on earth. It must be remembered that the instances given are instances only, but that they can be multiplied myriads of times. It must also be remembered that what is true of the United States is true of all the civilized world. Such misery was not true of the caveman. Then what has happened? Has the hostile environment of the caveman grown more hostile for his descendants? Has the caveman's natural efficiency of 1 for food-getting and shelter-getting diminished in modern man to one-half or one-quarter?

On the contrary, the hostile environment of the caveman has been destroyed. For modern man it no longer exists. All carnivorous enemies, the daily menace of the younger world, have been killed off. Many of the species of prey have become extinct. Here and there, in secluded portions of the world, still linger a few of man's fiercer enemies. But they are far from being a menace to mankind. Modern man, when he wants recreation and change, goes to the secluded portions of the world for a hunt. Also, in idle moments, he wails regretfully at the passing of the "big game," which he knows in the not distant future will disappear from the earth.

Nor since the day of the caveman has man's efficiency for food-getting and shelter-getting diminished. It has increased a thousand fold. Since the day of the caveman, matter has been mastered. The secrets of matter have been discovered. Its laws have been formulated. Wonderful artifices have been made, and marvellous inventions, all tending to increase tremendously man's natural efficiency of 1 in every food-getting, shelter-getting exertion, in farming, mining, manufacturing, transportation, and communication.

From the caveman to the hand-workers of three generations ago, the increase in efficiency for food and shelter-getting has been very great. But in this day, by machinery, the efficiency of the hand-worker of three generations ago has in turn been increased many times. Formerly it required 200 hours of human labor to place 100 tons of ore on a railroad car. To-day, aided by machinery, but two hours of human labor is required to do the same task. The United States Bureau of Labor is responsible for the following table, showing the comparatively recent increase in man's food- and shelter-getting efficiency:

	Machine Hours	Hand Hours
Barley (100 bushels)	9	211
Corn (50 bushels shelled, stalks, husks, and Blades cut into fodder)	34	228
Oats (160 bushels)	28	265
Wheat (50 bushels)	7	160
Loading ore (loading 100 tons iron ore on cars)	2	200
Unloading coal (transferring 200 tons from canal-boats to bins 400 feet distant)	20	240
Pitchforks (50 pitchforks, 12-inch tines)	12	200
Plough (one landside plough, oak beams and handles)	3	118

According to the same authority, under the best conditions for organization in farming, labor can produce 20 bushels of wheat for 66 cents, or 1 bushel for 3⅓ cents. This was done on a bonanza farm of 10,000 acres in California, and was the average cost of the whole product of the farm. Mr. Carroll D. Wright says that to-day 4,500,000 men, aided by machinery, turn out a product that would require the labor of 40,000,000 men if produced by hand. Professor Herzog, of Austria, says that 5,000,000 people with the machinery of to-day, employed at socially useful labor, would be able to supply a population of 20,000,000 people with all the necessaries and small luxuries of life by working 1½ hours per day.

This being so, matter being mastered, man's efficiency for food- and shelter-getting being increased a thousand fold over the efficiency of the caveman, then why is it that millions of modern men live more miserably than lived the caveman? This is the question the revolutionist asks, and he asks it of the managing class, the capitalist class. The capitalist class does not answer it. The capitalist class cannot answer it.

If modern man's food- and shelter-getting efficiency is a thousand fold greater than that of the caveman, why, then, are there 10,000,000 people in the United States to-day who are not properly sheltered and properly fed? If the child of the caveman did not have to work, why, then, to-day, in the United States, are 80,000 children working out their lives in the textile factories alone? If the child of the caveman did not have to work, why, then, to-day, in the United States, are there 1,752,187 child-laborers?

It is a true count in the indictment. The capitalist class has mismanaged, is to-day mismanaging. In New York City 50,000 children go hungry to school, and in New York City there are 1320 millionnaires. The point, however, is not that the mass of mankind is miserable because of the wealth the capitalist class has taken to itself. Far from it. The point really is that the mass of mankind is miserable, not for want of the wealth taken by the capitalist class, *but for want of the wealth that was never created.* This wealth was never created because the capitalist class managed too wastefully and irrationally. The capitalist class, blind and greedy, grasping madly, has not only not made the best of its management, but made the worst of it. It is a management prodigiously wasteful. This point cannot be emphasized too strongly.

In face of the facts that modern man lives more wretchedly than the caveman, and that modern man's food- and shelter-getting efficiency is a thousand fold greater than the caveman's, no other solution is possible than that the management is prodigiously wasteful.

With the natural resources of the world, the machinery already invented, a rational organization of production and distribution, and an equally rational elimination of waste, the able-bodied workers would not have to labor more than two or three hours per day to feed everybody, clothe everybody, house everybody, educate everybody, and give a fair measure of little luxuries to everybody. There would be no more material want and wretchedness, no more children toiling out their lives, no more men and women and babes living like beasts and dying like beasts. Not only would matter be mastered, but the machine would be mastered. In such a day incentive would be finer and nobler than the incentive of to-day, which is the incentive of the stomach. No man, woman, or child would be impelled to action by an empty stomach. On the contrary, they would be impelled to action as a child in a spelling match is impelled to action, as boys and girls at games, as scientists formulating law, as inventors applying law, as artists and sculptors painting canvases and shaping clay, as poets and statesmen serving humanity by singing and by statecraft. The spiritual, intellectual, and artistic uplift consequent upon such a condition of society would be tremendous. All the human world would surge upward in a mighty wave.

This was the opportunity vouchsafed the capitalist class. Less blindness on its part, less greediness, and a rational management, were all that was necessary. A wonderful era was possible for the human race. But the capitalist class failed. It made a shambles of civilization. Nor can the capitalist class plead not guilty. It knew of the opportunity. Its wise men told it of the opportunity, its scholars and its scientists told it of the opportunity. All that they said is there to-day in the books, just so much damning evidence against it. It would not listen. It was too greedy. It rose up (as it rises up to-day), shamelessly, in our legislative halls, and declared that profits were impossible without the toil of children and babes. It lulled its conscience to sleep with prattle of sweet ideals and dear moralities, and allowed the suffering and misery of mankind to continue and to increase. In short, the capitalist class failed to take advantage of the opportunity.

But the opportunity is still here. The capitalist class has been tried and found wanting. Remains the working-class to see what it can do with the opportunity. "But the working-class is incapable," says the capitalist class. "What do you know about it?" the working-class replies. "Because you have failed is no reason that we shall fail. Furthermore, we are going to have a try at it, anyway. Seven millions of us say so. And what have you to say to that?"

And what can the capitalist class say? Grant the incapacity of the working-class. Grant that the indictment and the argument of the revolutionists are all wrong. The 7,000,000 revolutionists remain. Their existence is a fact. Their belief in their capacity, and in their indictment and their argument, is a fact. Their constant growth is a fact. Their intention to destroy present-day society is a fact, as is also their intention to take possession of the world with all its wealth and machinery and governments. Moreover, it is a fact that the working-class is vastly larger than the capitalist class.

The revolution is a revolution of the working-class. How can the capitalist class, in the minority, stem this tide of revolution? What has it to offer? What does it offer? Employers' associations, injunctions, civil suits for plundering of the treasuries of the labor unions, clamor and combination for the open shop, bitter and shameless opposition to the eight-hour day, strong efforts to defeat all reform child-labor bills, graft in every municipal council, strong lobbies and bribery in every legislature for the purchase of capitalist legislation, bayonets, machine-guns, policemen's clubs, professional strike-breakers, and armed Pinkertons—these are the things the capitalist class is dumping in front of the tide of revolution, as though, forsooth, to hold it back.

The capitalist class is as blind to-day to the menace of the revolution as it was blind in the past to its own God-given opportunity. It cannot see how precarious is its position, cannot comprehend the power and the portent of the revolution. It goes on its placid way, prattling sweet ideals and dear moralities, and scrambling sordidly for material benefits.

No overthrown ruler or class in the past ever considered the revolution that overthrew it, and so with the capitalist class of to-day. Instead of compromising, instead of lengthening its lease of life by conciliation and by removal of some of the harsher oppressions of the working-class, it antagonizes the working-class, drives the working-class into revolution. Every broken strike in recent years, every legally plundered trades-union treasury, every closed shop made into an open shop, has driven the members of the working-class directly hurt over to socialism by hundreds and thousands. Show a workingman that his union fails and he becomes a revolutionist. Break a strike with an injunction or bankrupt a union with a civil suit, and the workingmen hurt thereby listen to the siren song of the socialist and are lost forever to the *political capitalist* parties.

Antagonism never lulled revolution, and antagonism is about all the capitalist class offers. It is true, it offers some few antiquated notions which were very efficacious in the past, but which are no longer efficacious. Fourth-of-July liberty in terms of the Declaration of Independence and of the French Encyclopedists is scarcely apposite to-day. It does not appeal to the workingman who has had his head broken by a policeman's club, his union treasury bankrupted by a court decision, or his job taken away from him by a labor-saving invention. Nor does the Constitution of the United States appear so glorious and constitutional to the workingman who has experienced a bull pen or been unconstitutionally deported from Colorado. Nor are this particular workingman's hurt feelings soothed by reading in the newspapers that both the bull pen and the deportation were preeminently just, legal, and constitutional. "To hell, then, with the Constitution!" says he, and another revolutionist has been made—by the capitalist class.

In short, so blind is the capitalist class that it does nothing to lengthen its lease of life, while it does everything to shorten it. The capitalist class offers nothing that is clean, noble, and alive. The revolutionists offer everything that is clean, noble, and alive. They offer service, unselfishness, sacrifice, martyrdom—the things that sting awake the imagination of the people, touching their hearts with the fervor that arises out of the impulse toward good and which is essentially religious in its nature.

But the revolutionists blow hot and blow cold. They offer facts and statistics, economics and scientific arguments. If the workingman be merely selfish, the revolutionists show him, mathematically demonstrate to him, that his condition will be bettered by the revolution. If the workingman be the higher type, moved by impulses toward right conduct, if he have soul and spirit, the revolutionists offer him the things of the soul and the spirit, the tremendous things that cannot be measured by dollars and cents, nor be held down by dollars and cents. The revolutionist cries out upon wrong and injustice, and preaches righteousness. And, most potent of all, he sings the eternal song of human freedom—a song of all lands and all tongues and all time.

Few members of the capitalist class see the revolution. Most of them are too ignorant, and many are too afraid to see it. It is the same old story of every perishing ruling class in the world's history. Fat with power and possession, drunken with success, and made soft by surfeit and by cessation of struggle, they are like the drones clustered about the honey vats when the worker-bees spring upon them to end their rotund existence.

President Roosevelt vaguely sees the revolution, is frightened by it, and recoils from seeing it. As he says: "Above all, we need to remember that any kind of class animosity in the political world is, if possible, even more wicked, even more destructive to national welfare, than sectional, race, or religious animosity."

Class animosity in the political world, President Roosevelt maintains, is wicked. But class animosity in the political world is the preachment of the revolutionists. "Let the class wars in the industrial world continue," they say, "but extend the class war to the political world." As their leader, Eugene V. Debs, says: "So far as this struggle is concerned, there is no good capitalist and no bad workingman. Every capitalist is your enemy and every workingman is your friend."

Here is class animosity in the political world with a vengeance. And here is revolution. In 1888 there were only 2000 revolutionists of this type in the United States; in 1900 there were 127,000 revolutionists; in 1904, 435,000 revolutionists. Wickedness of the President Roosevelt definition evidently flourishes and increases in the United States. Quite so, for it is the revolution that flourishes and increases.

Here and there a member of the capitalist class catches a clear glimpse of the revolution, and raises a warning cry. But his class does not heed. President Eliot of Harvard raised such a cry: "I am forced to believe there is a present danger of socialism never before so imminent in America in so dangerous a form, because never before imminent in so well organized a form. The danger lies in the obtaining control of the trades-unions by the socialists." And the capitalist employers, instead of giving heed to the warnings, are perfecting their strikebreaking organization and combining more strongly than ever for a general assault upon that dearest of all things to the trades-unions, — the closed shop. In so far as this assault succeeds, by just that much will the capitalist class shorten its lease of life. It is the old, old story, over again and over again. The drunken drones still cluster greedily about the honey vats.

Possibly one of the most amusing spectacles of to-day is the attitude of the American press toward the revolution. It is also a pathetic spectacle. It compels the onlooker to be aware of a distinct loss of pride in his species. Dogmatic utterance from the mouth of ignorance may make gods laugh, but it should make men weep. And the American editors (in the general instance) are so impressive about it! The old "divide-up," "men-are-not-born-free-and-equal" propositions are enunciated gravely and sagely, as things white-hot and new from the forge of human wisdom. Their feeble vaporings show no more than a schoolboy's comprehension of the nature of the revolution. Parasites themselves on the capitalist class, serving the capitalist class by moulding public opinion, they, too, cluster drunkenly about the honey vats.

Of course, this is true only of the large majority of American editors. To say that it is true of all of them would be to cast too great obloquy upon the human race. Also, it would be untrue, for here and there an occasional editor does see clearly — and in his case, ruled by stomach-incentive, is usually afraid to say what he thinks about it. So far as the science and the sociology of the revolution are concerned, the average editor is a generation or so behind the facts. He is intellectually slothful, accepts no facts until they are accepted by the majority, and prides himself upon his conservatism. He is an instinctive optimist, prone to believe that what ought to be, is. The revolutionist gave this up long ago, and believes not that what ought to be, is, but what is, is, and that it may not be what it ought to be at all.

Now and then, rubbing his eyes vigorously, an editor catches a sudden glimpse of the revolution and breaks out in naive volubility, as, for instance, the one who wrote the following in the *Chicago Chronicle:* "American socialists are revolutionists. They know that they are revolutionists. It is high time that other people should appreciate the fact." A white-hot, brand-new discovery, and he proceeded to shout it out from the housetops that we, forsooth, were revolutionists. Why, it is just what we have been doing all these years — shouting it out from the housetops that we are revolutionists, and stop us who can.

The time should be past for the mental attitude: "Revolution is atrocious. Sir, there is no revolution." Likewise should the time be past for that other familiar attitude: "Socialism is slavery. Sir, it will never be." It is no longer a question of dialectics, theories, and dreams. There is no question about it. The revolution is a fact. It is here now. Seven million revolutionists, organized, working day and night, are preaching the revolution — that passionate gospel, the Brotherhood of Man. Not only is it a cold-blooded economic propaganda, but it is in essence a religious propaganda with a fervor in it of Paul and Christ. The capitalist class has been indicted. It has failed in its management and its management is to be taken away from it. Seven million men of the working-class say that they are going to get the rest of the working-class to join with them and take the management away. The revolution is here, now. Stop it who can.

PART III

APOSTATE REVOLUTIONARY

1906 – 1912

The Apostate

First published in *Woman's Home Companion* with the subtitle "A Child Labor Parable," September 1906; reprinted from *When God Laughs and Other Stories* (New York: Macmillan, 1911).

"The Apostate"—perhaps the most heartfelt and authentic rendering of working-class life of London's short stories—describes the surreal life of Johnny, a teenage boy who is growing up in an unnamed city that might be anywhere in the dreary industrial world. For the most part, London wrote about working men and women who were unemployed—hobos, tramps, and migrant laborers in search of jobs—and about "scabs," those workers who were hired by employers during a strike, with the explicit purpose of breaking the union and its cause. Here, in "The Apostate," he offers a change of pace and writes about a young man who toils at a machine all day. Johnny is a casualty in the class struggle that preoccupied London his entire life. The story surely draws on the author's own experiences, and especially his *feelings*—though not necessarily the facts—about his own boyhood. In his essay "How I Became a Socialist," London describes his hatred of hard physical labor and explains, "I have been busy ever since running away from hard work." In the character of Johnny, he re-created his own flight from toil. Had Edgar Allan Poe lived to write about factories, he might have written this story, or something very much like it, and had Franz Kafka started out in an American working-class city, not Prague, he might have written something like it, too. In "The Apostate," London offers a grotesque, macabre, and fantastic parable about the ills of labor and laboring men—and a remedy of sorts, too.

Born on the floor of a jute mill, and thus both literally and figuratively a child of the machine age, London's hero, Johnny, has never known childhood or boyhood. Raised in a world of machines and machinery, without nature, Johnny evolves into "the perfect worker" and then "the perfect machine"; his most intimate relationships are not with other human beings, but with machinery; he's a stranger to himself as well as to his family members. Alienation is the keynote here.

Much of the story takes place in the jute mill that is sucking the life out of Johnny. Part of the story is set in his family's impoverished home, where the dramatic conflict derives in large part from Johnny's raging battles with his unnamed mother, who grabs him, shakes him, and deceives him, all with one purpose: to force him, against his will, to work. In addition to his heartless mother, he has a younger brother who has grown uncannily powerful, in geometrical proportion to Johnny's growing powerlessness. Appropriately, his name is Will, and he's a kind of double, or twin. The father is long since departed.

The story coveys realistic details of working-class life—the noise of the flying shuttles in the mill, the stink from the "filthy sink," and the unappetizing "small piece of cold pork" Johnny eats for breakfast. His world is also tinged with the surreal. Johnny has a single memory of his father: his "savage and pitiless feet." London takes readers inside his raucous head, which resounds with "the shrieking, pounding, crashing, roaring of a million looms" and where "all space" is "filled with flying shuttles." Though he's a child laborer and clearly exploited, he doesn't join a union or complain to the factory overseer about working conditions: "it seemed to him as useless to oppose the overseer as to defy the will of a machine."

Still, the boy's existence is not without purpose. London suggests that Johnny's whole life is a cry of "infinite protest." He calls his character an "apostate," but he doesn't use the word in its ordinary sense to mean a renegade from organized religion. London's Johnny is an apostate because he becomes a fugitive from wage slavery, escaping from the capitalist system with its worship of all-mighty work and its gospel of obedience to assembly-line production. One day, he refuses to work—"blasphemy," London calls it. Johnny loses himself "in a great communion with himself" and then shambles—he can't even walk—away from home, "a sickly ape." Johnny's own journey as a grotesque everyman illuminates the descent of the human species in industrial society; devolution, not evolution, is described in these pages. Still, Johnny manages to escape; he climbs aboard a freight train and disappears in the darkness, smiling enigmatically.

In this period of his life, London focused on the theme of apostasy. He returned to it in another short story—albeit only outlined and not completed—about a socialist man who loses the love of his life when she joins the cause just as he abandons it and becomes what she detests—an apostate. •

Now I wake me up to work;
I pray the Lord I may not shirk.
If I should die before the night,
I pray the Lord my work's all right.

Amen.

"If you don't git up, Johnny, I won't give you a bite to eat!"

The threat had no effect on the boy. He clung stubbornly to sleep, fighting for its oblivion as the dreamer fights for his dream. The boy's hands loosely clenched themselves, and he made feeble, spasmodic blows at the air. These blows were intended for his mother, but she betrayed practised familiarity in avoiding them as she shook him roughly by the shoulder.

"Lemme 'lone!"

It was a cry that began, muffled, in the deeps of sleep, that swiftly rushed upward, like a wail, into passionate belligerence, and that died away and sank down into an inarticulate whine. It was a bestial cry, as of a soul in torment, filled with infinite protest and pain.

But she did not mind. She was a sad-eyed, tired-faced woman, and she had grown used to this task, which she repeated every day of her life. She got a grip on the bed-clothes and tried to strip them down; but the boy, ceasing his punching, clung to them desperately. In a huddle, at the foot of the bed, he still remained covered. Then she tried dragging the bedding to the floor. The boy opposed her. She braced herself. Hers was the superior weight, and the boy and bedding gave, the former instinctively following the latter in order to shelter against the chill of the room that bit into his body.

As he toppled on the edge of the bed it seemed that he must fall head-first to the floor. But consciousness fluttered up in him. He righted himself and for a moment perilously balanced. Then he struck the floor on his feet. On the instant his mother seized him by the shoulders and shook him. Again his fists struck out, this time with more force and directness. At the same time his eyes opened. She released him. He was awake.

"All right," he mumbled.

She caught up the lamp and hurried out, leaving him in darkness.

"You'll be docked," she warned back to him.

He did not mind the darkness. When he had got into his clothes, he went out into the kitchen. His tread was very heavy for so thin and light a boy. His legs dragged with their own weight, which seemed unreasonable because they were such skinny legs. He drew a broken-bottomed chair to the table.

"Johnny!," his mother called sharply.

He arose as sharply from the chair, and, without a word, went to the sink. It was a greasy, filthy sink. A smell came up from the outlet. He took no notice of it. That a sink should smell was to him part of the natural order, just as it was a part of the nat-ural order that the soap should be grimy with dish-water and hard to lather. Nor did he try very hard to make it lather. Several splashes of the cold water from the running faucet completed the function. He did not wash his teeth. For that matter he had never seen a toothbrush, nor did he know that there existed beings in the world who were guilty of so great a foolishness as tooth washing.

"You might wash yourself wunst a day without bein' told," his mother complained.

She was holding a broken lid on the pot as she poured two cups of coffee. He made no remark, for this was a standing quarrel between them, and the one thing upon which his mother was hard as adamant. "Wunst" a day it was compulsory that he should wash his face. He dried himself on a greasy towel, damp and dirty and ragged, that left his face covered with shreds of lint.

"I wish we didn't live so far away," she said, as he sat down. "I try to do the best I can. You know that. But a dollar on the rent is such a savin', an' we've more room here. You know that."

He scarcely followed her. He had heard it all before, many times. The range of her thought was limited, and she was ever harking back to the hardship worked upon them by living so far from the mills.

"A dollar means more grub," he remarked sententiously. "I'd sooner do the walkin' an' git the grub."

He ate hurriedly, half chewing the bread and washing the unmasticated chunks down with coffee. The hot and muddy liquid went by the name of coffee. Johnny thought it was coffee — and excellent coffee. That was one of the few of life's illusions that remained to him. He had never drunk real coffee in his life.

In addition to the bread, there was a small piece of cold pork. His mother refilled his cup with coffee. As he was finishing the bread, he began to watch if more was forthcoming. She intercepted his questioning glance.

"Now, don't be hoggish, Johnny," was her comment. "You've had your share. Your brothers an' sisters are smaller'n you."

He did not answer the rebuke. He was not much of a talker. Also, he ceased his hungry glancing for more. He was uncomplaining, with a patience that was as terrible as the school in which it had been learned. He finished his coffee, wiped his mouth on the back of his hand, and started to rise.

"Wait a second," she said hastily. "I guess the loaf kin stand you another slice — a thin un."

There was legerdemain in her actions. With all the seeming of cutting a slice from the loaf for him, she put loaf and slice back in the bread box and conveyed to him one of her own two slices. She believed she had deceived him, but he had noted her sleight-of-hand. Nevertheless, he took the bread shamelessly. He had a philosophy that his mother, because of her chronic sickliness, was not much of an eater anyway.

She saw that he was chewing the bread dry, and reached over and emptied her coffee cup into his.

"Don't set good somehow on my stomach this morning," she explained.

A distant whistle, prolonged and shrieking, brought both of them to their feet. She glanced at the tin alarm-clock on the shelf. The hands stood at half-past five. The rest of the factory world was just arousing from sleep. She drew a shawl about her shoulders, and on her head put a dingy hat, shapeless and ancient.

"We've got to run," she said, turning the wick of the lamp and blowing down the chimney.

They groped their way out and down the stairs. It was clear and cold, and Johnny shivered at the first contact with the outside air. The stars had not yet begun to pale in the sky, and the city lay in blackness. Both Johnny and his mother shuffled their feet as they walked. There was no ambition in the leg muscles to swing the feet clear of the ground.

After fifteen silent minutes, his mother turned off to the right.

"Don't be late," was her final warning from out of the dark that was swallowing her up.

He made no response, steadily keeping on his way. In the factory quarter, doors were opening everywhere, and he was soon one of a multitude that pressed onward through the dark. As he entered the factory gate the whistle blew again. He glanced at the east. Across a ragged sky-line of housetops a pale light was beginning to creep. This much he saw of the day as he turned his back upon it and joined his work gang.

He took his place in one of many long rows of machines. Before him, above a bin filled with small bobbins, were large bobbins revolving rapidly. Upon these he wound the jute-twine of the small bobbins. The work was simple. All that was required was celerity. The small bobbins were emptied so rapidly, and there were so many large bobbins that did the emptying, that there were no idle moments.

He worked mechanically. When a small bobbin ran out, he used his left hand for a brake, stopping the large bobbin and at the same time, with thumb and forefinger, catching the flying end of twine. Also, at the same time, with his right hand, he caught up the loose twine-end of a small bobbin. These various acts with both hands were performed simultaneously and swiftly. Then there would come a flash of his hands as he looped the weaver's knot and released the bobbin. There was nothing difficult about weaver's knots. He once boasted he could tie them in his sleep. And for that matter, he sometimes did, toiling centuries long in a single night at tying an endless succession of weaver's knots.

Some of the boys shirked, wasting time and machinery by not replacing the small bobbins when they ran out. And there was an overseer to prevent this. He caught Johnny's neighbour at the trick, and boxed his ears.

"Look at Johnny there—why ain't you like him?" the overseer wrathfully demanded.

Johnny's bobbins were running full blast, but he did not thrill at the indirect praise. There had been a time . . . but that was long ago, very long ago. His apathetic face was expressionless as he listened to himself being held up as a shining example. He was the perfect worker. He knew that. He had been told so, often. It was a commonplace, and besides it didn't seem to mean anything to him any more. From the perfect worker he had evolved into the perfect machine. When his work went wrong, it was with him as with the machine, due to faulty material. It would have been as possible for a perfect nail-die to cut imperfect nails as for him to make a mistake.

And small wonder. There had never been a time when he had not been in intimate relationship with machines. Machinery had almost been bred into him, and at any rate he had been brought up on it. Twelve years before, there had been a small flutter of excitement in the loom room of this very mill. Johnny's mother had fainted. They stretched her out on the floor in the midst of the shrieking machines. A couple of elderly women were called from their looms. The foreman assisted. And in a few minutes there was one more soul in the loom room than had entered by the doors. It was Johnny, born with the pounding, crashing roar of the looms in his ears, drawing with his first breath the warm, moist air that was thick with flying lint. He had coughed that first day in order to rid his lungs of the lint; and for the same reason he had coughed ever since.

The boy alongside of Johnny whimpered and sniffed. The boy's face was convulsed with hatred for the overseer who kept a threatening eye on him from a distance; but every bobbin was running full. The boy yelled terrible oaths into the whirling bobbins before him; but the sound did not carry half a dozen feet, the roaring of the room holding it in and containing it like a wall.

Of all this Johnny took no notice. He had a way of accepting things. Besides, things grow monotonous by repetition, and this particular happening he had witnessed many times. It seemed to him as useless to oppose the overseer as to defy the will of a machine. Machines were made to go in certain ways and to perform certain tasks. It was the same with the overseer.

But at eleven o'clock there was excitement in the room. In an apparently occult way the excitement instantly permeated everywhere. The one-legged boy who worked on the other side of Johnny bobbed swiftly across the floor to a bin truck that stood empty. Into this he dived out of sight, crutch and all. The superintendent of the mill was coming along, accompanied by a young man. He was well dressed and wore a starched shirt—a gentleman, in Johnny's classification of men, and also, "the Inspector."

He looked sharply at the boys as he passed along. Sometimes he stopped and asked questions. When he did so, he was compelled to shout at the top of his lungs, at which moments his face was ludicrously contorted with the strain of making himself heard. His quick eye noted the empty machine alongside of Johnny's, but he said nothing. Johnny also caught his eye, and he stopped abruptly. He caught Johnny by the arm to draw him back a step from the machine; but with an exclamation of surprise he released the arm.

"Pretty skinny," the superintendent laughed anxiously.

"Pipe stems," was the answer. "Look at those legs. The boy's got the rickets — incipient, but he's got them. If epilepsy doesn't get him in the end, it will be because tuberculosis gets him first."

Johnny listened, but did not understand. Furthermore he was not interested in future ills. There was an immediate and more serious ill that threatened him in the form of the inspector.

"Now, my boy, I want you to tell me the truth," the inspector said, or shouted, bending close to the boy's ear to make him hear. "How old are you?"

"Fourteen," Johnny lied, and he lied with the full force of his lungs. So loudly did he lie that it started him off in a dry, hacking cough that lifted the lint which had been settling in his lungs all morning.

"Looks sixteen at least," said the superintendent.

"Or sixty," snapped the inspector.

"He's always looked that way."

"How long?" asked the inspector, quickly.

"For years. Never gets a bit older."

"Or younger, I dare say. I suppose he's worked here all those years?"

"Off and on — but that was before the new law was passed," the superintendent hastened to add.

"Machine idle?" the inspector asked, pointing at the unoccupied machine beside Johnny's, in which the part-filled bobbins were flying like mad.

"Looks that way." The superintendent motioned the overseer to him and shouted in his ear and pointed at the machine. "Machine's idle," he reported back to the inspector.

They passed on, and Johnny returned to his work, relieved in that the ill had been averted. But the one-legged boy was not so fortunate. The sharp-eyed inspector held him out at arms length from the bin truck. His lips were quivering, and his face had all the expression of one upon whom was fallen profound and irremediable disaster. The overseer looked astounded, as though for the first time he had laid eyes on the boy, while the superintendent's face expressed shock and displeasure.

"I know him," the inspector said. "He's twelve years old. I've had him discharged from three factories inside the year. This makes the fourth."

He turned to the one-legged boy. "You promised me, word and honor, that you'd go to school."

The one-legged boy burst into tears. "Please, Mr. Inspector, two babies died on us, and we're awful poor."

"What makes you cough that way?" the inspector demanded, as though charging him with crime.

And as in denial of guilt, the one-legged boy replied: "It ain't nothin'. I jes' caught a cold last week, Mr. Inspector, that's all."

In the end the one-legged boy went out of the room with the inspector, the latter accompanied by the anxious and protesting superintendent. After that monotony settled down again. The long morning and the longer afternoon wore away and the whistle blew for quitting time. Darkness had already fallen when Johnny passed out through the factory gate. In the interval the sun had made a golden ladder of the sky, flooded the world with its gracious warmth, and dropped down and disappeared in the west behind a ragged sky-line of housetops.

Supper was the family meal of the day—the one meal at which Johnny encountered his younger brothers and sisters. It partook of the nature of an encounter, to him, for he was very old, while they were distressingly young. He had no patience with their excessive and amazing juvenility. He did not understand it. His own childhood was too far behind him. He was like an old and irritable man, annoyed by the turbulence of their young spirits that was to him arrant silliness. He glowered silently over his food, finding compensation in the thought that they would soon have to go to work. That would take the edge off of them and make them sedate and dignified—like him. Thus it was, after the fashion of the human, that Johnny made of himself a yardstick with which to measure the universe.

During the meal, his mother explained in various ways and with infinite repetition that she was trying to do the best she could; so that it was with relief, the scant meal ended, that Johnny shoved back his chair and arose. He debated for a moment between bed and the front door, and finally went out the latter. He did not go far. He sat down on the stoop, his knees drawn up and his narrow shoulders drooping forward, his elbows on his knees and the palms of his hands supporting his chin.

As he sat there, he did no thinking. He was just resting. So far as his mind was concerned, it was asleep. His brothers and sisters came out, and with other children played noisily about him. An electric globe at the corner lighted their frolics. He was peevish and irritable, that they knew; but the spirit of adventure lured them into teasing him. They joined hands before him, and, keeping time with their bodies, chanted in his face weird and uncomplimentary doggerel. At first he snarled curses at them — curses he had learned from the lips of various foremen. Finding this futile, and remembering his dignity, he relapsed into dogged silence.

His brother Will, next to him in age, having just passed his tenth birthday, was the ringleader. Johnny did not possess particularly kindly feelings toward him. His life had early been embittered by continual giving over and giving way to Will. He had a definite feeling that Will was greatly in his debt and was ungrateful about it. In his own playtime, far back in the dim past, he had been robbed of a large part of that playtime by being compelled to take care of Will. Will was a baby then, and then, as now, their mother had spent her days in the mills. To Johnny had fallen the part of little father and little mother as well.

Will seemed to show the benefit of the giving over and the giving way. He was well-built, fairly rugged, as tall as his elder brother and even heavier. It was as though the life-blood of the one had been diverted into the other's veins. And in spirits it was the same. Johnny was jaded, worn out, without resilience, while his younger brother seemed bursting and spilling over with exuberance.

The mocking chant rose louder and louder. Will leaned closer as he danced, thrusting out his tongue. Johnny's left arm shot out and caught the other around the neck. At the same time he rapped his bony fist to the other's nose. It was a pathetically bony fist, but that it was sharp to hurt was evidenced by the squeal of pain it produced. The other children were uttering frightened cries, while Johnny's sister, Jennie, had dashed into the house.

He thrust Will from him, kicked him savagely on the shins, then reached for him and slammed him face downward in the dirt. Nor did he release him till the face had been rubbed into the dirt several times. Then the mother arrived, an anaemic whirlwind of solicitude and maternal wrath.

"Why can't he leave me alone?" was Johnny's reply to her upbraiding. "Can't he see I'm tired?"

"I'm as big as you," Will raged in her arms, his face a mass of tears, dirt, and blood. "I'm as big as you now, an' I'm goin' to git bigger. Then I'll lick you — see if I don't."

"You ought to be to work, seein' how big you are," Johnny snarled. "That's what's the matter with you. You ought to be to work. An' it's up to your ma to put you to work."

"But he's too young," she protested. "He's only a little boy."

"I was younger'n him when I started to work."

Johnny's mouth was open, further to express the sense of unfairness that he felt, but the mouth closed with a snap. He turned gloomily on his heel and stalked into the house and to bed. The door of his room was open to let in warmth from the kitchen. As he undressed in the semi-darkness he could hear his mother talking with a neighbour woman who had dropped in. His mother was crying, and her speech was punctuated with spiritless sniffles.

"I can't make out what's gittin' into Johnny," he could hear her say. "He didn't used to be this way. He was a patient little angel."

"An' he is a good boy," she hastened to defend. "He's worked faithful, an' he did go to work too young. But it wasn't my fault. I do the best I can, I'm sure."

Prolonged sniffling from the kitchen, and Johnny murmured to himself as his eyelids closed down, "You betcher life I've worked faithful."

The next morning he was torn bodily by his mother from the grip of sleep. Then came the meagre breakfast, the tramp through the dark, and the pale glimpse of day across the housetops as he turned his back on it and went in through the factory gate. It was another day, of all the days, and all the days were alike.

And yet there had been variety in his life — at the times he changed from one job to another, or was taken sick. When he was six, he was little mother and father to Will and the other children still younger. At seven he went into the mills — winding bobbins. When he was eight, he got work in another mill. His new job was marvellously easy. All he had to do was to sit down with a little stick in his hand and guide a stream of cloth that flowed past him. This stream of cloth came out of the maw of a machine, passed over a hot roller, and went on its way elsewhere. But he sat always in one place, beyond the reach of daylight, a gas-jet flaring over him, himself part of the mechanism.

He was very happy at that job, in spite of the moist heat, for he was still young and in possession of dreams and illusions. And wonderful dreams he dreamed as he watched the steaming cloth streaming endlessly by. But there was no exercise about the work, no call upon his mind, and he dreamed less and less, while his mind grew torpid and drowsy. Nevertheless, he earned two dollars a week, and two dollars represented the difference between acute starvation and chronic underfeeding.

But when he was nine, he lost his job. Measles was the cause of it. After he recovered, he got work in a glass factory. The pay was better, and the work demanded skill. It was piecework, and the more skilful he was, the bigger wages he earned. Here was incentive. And under this incentive he developed into a remarkable worker.

It was simple work, the tying of glass stoppers into small bottles. At his waist he carried a bundle of twine. He held the bottles between his knees so that he might work with both hands. Thus, in a sitting position and bending over his own knees, his narrow shoulders grew humped and his chest was contracted for ten hours each day. This was not good for the lungs, but he tied three hundred dozen bottles a day.

The superintendent was very proud of him, and brought visitors to look at him. In ten hours three hundred dozen bottles passed through his hands. This meant that he had attained machine-like perfection. All waste movements were eliminated. Every motion of his thin arms, every movement of a muscle in the thin fingers, was swift and accurate. He worked at high tension, and the result was that he grew nervous. At night his muscles twitched in his sleep, and in the daytime he could not relax and rest. He remained keyed up and his muscles continued to twitch. Also he grew sallow and his lint-cough grew worse. Then pneumonia laid hold of the feeble lungs within the contracted chest, and he lost his job in the glass-works.

Now he had returned to the jute mills where he had first begun with winding bobbins. But promotion was waiting for him. He was a good worker. He would next go on the starcher, and later he would go into the loom room. There was nothing after that except increased efficiency.

The machinery ran faster than when he had first gone to work, and his mind ran slower. He no longer dreamed at all, though his earlier years had been full of dreaming. Once he had been in love. It was when he first began guiding the cloth over the hot roller, and it was with the daughter of the superintendent. She was much older than he, a young woman, and he had seen her at a distance only a paltry half-dozen times. But that made no difference. On the surface of the cloth stream that poured past him, he pictured radiant futures wherein he performed prodigies of toil, invented miraculous machines, won to the mastership of the mills, and in the end took her in his arms and kissed her soberly on the brow.

But that was all in the long ago, before he had grown too old and tired to love. Also, she had married and gone away, and his mind had gone to sleep. Yet it had been a wonderful experience, and he used often to look back upon it as other men and women look back upon the time they believed in fairies. He had never believed in fairies nor Santa Claus; but he had believed implicitly in the smiling future his imagination had wrought into the steaming cloth stream.

He had become a man very early in life. At seven, when he drew his first wages, began his adolescence. A certain feeling of independence crept up in him, and the relationship between him and his mother changed. Somehow, as an earner and breadwinner, doing his own work in the world, he was more like an equal with her. Manhood, full-blown manhood, had come when he was eleven, at which time he had gone to work on the night shift for six months. No child works on the night shift and remains a child.

There had been several great events in his life. One of these had been when his mother bought some California prunes. Two others had been the two times when she cooked custard. Those had been events. He remembered them kindly. And at that time his mother had told him of a blissful dish she would sometime make—"floating island," she had called it, "better than custard." For years he had looked forward to the day when he would sit down to the table with floating island before him, until at last he had relegated the idea of it to the limbo of unattainable ideals.

Once he found a silver quarter lying on the sidewalk. That, also, was a great event in his life, withal a tragic one. He knew his duty on the instant the silver flashed on his eyes, before even he had picked it up. At home, as usual, there was not enough to eat, and home he should have taken it as he did his wages every Saturday night. Right conduct in this case was obvious; but he never had any spending of his money, and he was suffering from candy hunger. He was ravenous for the sweets that only on red-letter days he had ever tasted in his life.

He did not attempt to deceive himself. He knew it was sin, and deliberately he sinned when he went on a fifteen-cent candy debauch. Ten cents he saved for a future orgy; but not being accustomed to the carrying of money, he lost the ten cents. This occurred at the time when he was suffering all the torments of conscience, and it was to him an act of divine retribution. He had a frightened sense of the closeness of an awful and wrathful God. God had seen, and God had been swift to punish, denying him even the full wages of sin.

In memory he always looked back upon that as the one great criminal deed of his life, and at the recollection his conscience always awoke and gave him another twinge. It was the one skeleton in his closet. Also, being so made, and circumstanced, he looked back upon the deed with regret. He was dissatisfied with the manner in which he had spent the quarter. He could have invested it better, and, out of his later knowledge of the quickness of God, he would have beaten God out by spending the whole quarter at one fell swoop. In retrospect he spent the quarter a thousand times, and each time to better advantage.

There was one other memory of the past, dim and faded, but stamped into his soul everlasting by the savage feet of his father. It was more like a nightmare than a remembered vision of a concrete thing—more like the race-memory of man that makes him fall in his sleep and that goes back to his arboreal ancestry.

This particular memory never came to Johnny in broad daylight when he was wide awake. It came at night, in bed, at the moment that his consciousness was sinking down and losing itself in sleep. It always aroused him to frightened wakefulness, and for the moment, in the first sickening start, it seemed to him that he lay crosswise on the foot of the bed. In the bed were the vague forms of his father and mother. He never saw what his father looked like. He had but one impression of his father, and that was that he had savage and pitiless feet.

His earlier memories lingered with him, but he had no late memories. All days were alike. Yesterday or last year were the same as a thousand years—or a minute. Nothing ever happened. There were no events to mark the march of time. Time did not march. It stood always still. It was only the whirling machines that moved, and they moved nowhere—in spite of the fact that they moved faster.

When he was fourteen, he went to work on the starcher. It was a colossal event. Something had at last happened that could be remembered beyond a night's sleep or a week's pay-day. It marked an era. It was a machine Olympiad, a thing to date from. "When I went to work on the starcher," or, "after," or "before I went to work on the starcher," were sentences often on his lips.

He celebrated his sixteenth birthday by going into the loom room and taking a loom. Here was an incentive again, for it was piece-work. And he excelled, because the clay of him had been moulded by the mills into the perfect machine. At the end of three months he was running two looms, and, later, three and four.

At the end of his second year at the looms he was turning out more yards than any other weaver, and more than twice as much as some of the less skilful ones. And at home things began to prosper as he approached the full stature of his earning power. Not, however, that his increased earnings were in excess of need. The children were growing up. They ate more. And they were going to school, and school-books cost money. And somehow, the faster he worked, the faster climbed the prices of things. Even the rent went up, though the house had fallen from bad to worse disrepair.

He had grown taller; but with his increased height he seemed leaner than ever. Also, he was more nervous. With the nervousness increased his peevishness and irritability. The children had learned by many bitter lessons to fight shy of him. His mother respected him for his earning power, but somehow her respect was tinctured with fear.

There was no joyousness in life for him. The procession of the days he never saw. The nights he slept away in twitching unconsciousness. The rest of the time he worked, and his consciousness was machine consciousness. Outside this his mind was a blank. He had no ideals, and but one illusion; namely, that he drank excellent coffee. He was a work-beast. He had no mental life whatever; yet deep down in the crypts of his mind, unknown to him, were being weighed and sifted every hour of his toil, every movement of his hands, every twitch of his muscles, and preparations were making for a future course of action that would amaze him and all his little world.

It was in the late spring that he came home from work one night aware of unusual tiredness. There was a keen expectancy in the air as he sat down to the table, but he did not notice. He went through the meal in moody silence, mechanically eating what was before him. The children um'd and ah'd and made smacking noises with their mouths. But he was deaf to them.

"D'ye know what you're eatin'?" his mother demanded at last, desperately.

He looked vacantly at the dish before him, and vacantly at her.

"Floatin' island," she announced triumphantly.

"Oh," he said.

"Floating island!" the children chorussed loudly.

"Oh," he said. And after two or three mouthfuls, he added, "I guess I ain't hungry to-night."

He dropped the spoon, shoved back his chair, and arose wearily from the table. "An' I guess I'll go to bed."

His feet dragged more heavily than usual as he crossed the kitchen floor. Undressing was a Titan's task, a monstrous futility, and he wept weakly as he crawled into bed, one shoe still on. He was aware of a rising, swelling something inside his head that made his brain thick and fuzzy. His lean fingers felt as big as his wrist, while in the ends of them was a remoteness of sensation vague and fuzzy like his brain. The small of his back ached intolerably. All his bones ached. He ached everywhere. And in his head began the shrieking, pounding, crashing, roaring of a million looms. All space was filled with flying shuttles. They darted in and out, intricately, amongst the stars. He worked a thousand looms himself, and ever they speeded up, faster and faster, and his brain unwound, faster and faster, and became the thread that fed the thousand flying shuttles.

He did not go to work next morning. He was too busy weaving colossally on the thousand looms that ran inside his head. His mother went to work, but first she sent for the doctor. It was a severe attack of la grippe, he said. Jennie served as nurse and carried out his instructions.

It was a very severe attack, and it was a week before Johnny dressed and tottered feebly across the floor. Another week, the doctor said, and he would be fit to return to work. The foreman of the loom room visited him on Sunday afternoon, the first day of his convalescence. The best weaver in the room, the foreman told his mother. His job would be held for him. He could come back to work a week from Monday.

"Why don't you thank 'im, Johnny?" his mother asked anxiously.

"He's ben that sick he ain't himself yet," she explained apologetically to the visitor.

Johnny sat hunched up and gazing steadfastly at the floor. He sat in the same position long after the foreman had gone. It was warm outdoors, and he sat on the stoop in the afternoon. Sometimes his lips moved. He seemed lost in endless calculations.

Next morning, after the day grew warm, he took his seat on the stoop. He had pencil and paper this time with which to continue his calculations, and he calculated painfully and amazingly.

"What comes after millions?" he asked at noon, when Will came home from school. "An' how d'ye work 'em?"

That afternoon finished his task. Each day, but without paper and pencil, he returned to the stoop. He was greatly absorbed in the one tree that grew across the street. He studied it for hours at a time, and was unusually interested when the wind swayed its branches and fluttered its leaves. Throughout the week he seemed lost in a great communion with himself. On Sunday, sitting on the stoop, he laughed aloud, several times, to the perturbation of his mother, who had not heard him laugh for years.

Next morning, in the early darkness, she came to his bed to rouse him. He had had his fill of sleep all the week, and awoke easily. He made no struggle, nor did he attempt to hold on to the bedding when she stripped it from him. He lay quietly, and spoke quietly.

"It ain't no use, ma."

"You'll be late," she said, under the impression that he was still stupid with sleep.

"I'm awake, ma, an' I tell you it ain't no use. You might as well lemme alone. I ain't goin' to git up."

"But you'll lose your job!" she cried.

"I ain't goin' to git up," he repeated in a strange, passionless voice.

She did not go to work herself that morning. This was sickness beyond any sickness she had ever known. Fever and delirium she could understand; but this was insanity. She pulled the bedding up over him and sent Jennie for the doctor.

When that person arrived, Johnny was sleeping gently, and gently he awoke and allowed his pulse to be taken.

"Nothing the matter with him," the doctor reported. "Badly debilitated, that's all. Not much meat on his bones."

"He's always been that way," his mother volunteered.

"Now go 'way, ma, an' let me finish my snooze."

Johnny spoke sweetly and placidly, and sweetly and placidly he rolled over on his side and went to sleep.

At ten o'clock he awoke and dressed himself. He walked out into the kitchen, where he found his mother with a frightened expression on her face.

"I'm goin' away, ma," he announced, "an' I jes' want to say good-bye."

She threw her apron over her head and sat down suddenly and wept. He waited patiently.

"I might a-known it," she was sobbing.

"Where?" she finally asked, removing the apron from her head and gazing up at him with a stricken face in which there was little curiosity.

"I don't know—anywhere."

As he spoke, the tree across the street appeared with dazzling brightness on his inner vision. It seemed to lurk just under his eyelids, and he could see it whenever he wished.

"An' your job?" she quavered.

"I ain't never goin' to work again."

"My God, Johnny!" she wailed, "don't say that!"

What he had said was blasphemy to her. As a mother who hears her child deny God, was Johnny's mother shocked by his words.

"What's got into you, anyway?" she demanded, with a lame attempt at imperativeness.

"Figures," he answered. "Jes' figures. I've ben doin' a lot of figurin' this week, an' it's most surprisin'."

"I don't see what that's got to do with it," she sniffled.

Johnny smiled patiently, and his mother was aware of a distinct shock at the persistent absence of his peevishness and irritability.

"I'll show you," he said. "I'm plum' tired out. What makes me tired? Moves. I've ben movin' ever since I was born. I'm tired of movin', an' I ain't goin' to move any more. Remember when I worked in the glass-house? I used to do three hundred dozen a day. Now I reckon I made about ten different moves to each bottle. That's thirty-six thousan' moves a day. Ten days, three hundred an' sixty thousan' moves. One month, one million an' eighty thousan' moves. Chuck out the eighty thousan'"—he spoke with the complacent beneficence of a philanthropist—"chuck out the eighty thousan', that leaves a million moves a month—twelve million moves a year.

"At the looms I'm movin' twic'st as much. That makes twenty-five million moves a year, an' it seems to me I've ben a movin' that way 'most a million years.

"Now this week I ain't moved at all. I ain't made one move in hours an' hours. I tell you it was swell, jes' settin' there, hours an' hours, an' doin' nothin'. I ain't never ben happy before. I never had any time. I've ben movin' all the time. That ain't no way to be happy. An' I ain't going to do it any more. I'm jes' goin' to set, an' set, an' rest, an' rest, and then rest some more."

"But what's goin' to come of Will an' the children?" she asked despairingly.

"That's it, 'Will an' the children,'" he repeated.

But there was no bitterness in his voice. He had long known his mother's ambition for the younger boy, but the thought of it no longer rankled. Nothing mattered any more. Not even that.

"I know, ma, what you've ben plannin' for Will—keepin' him in school to make a book-keeper out of him. But it ain't no use, I've quit. He's got to go to work."

"An' after I have brung you up the way I have," she wept, starting to cover her head with the apron and changing her mind.

"You never brung me up," he answered with sad kindliness. "I brung myself up, ma, an' I brung up Will. He's bigger'n me, an' heavier, an' taller. When I was a kid, I reckon I didn't git enough to eat. When he come along an' was a kid, I was workin' an' earnin' grub for him too. But that's done with. Will can go to work, same as me, or he can go to hell, I don't care which. I'm tired. I'm goin' now. Ain't you goin' to say good-bye?"

She made no reply. The apron had gone over her head again, and she was crying. He paused a moment in the doorway.

"I'm sure I done the best I knew how," she was sobbing.

He passed out of the house and down the street. A wan delight came into his face at the sight of the lone tree. "Jes' ain't goin' to do nothin'," he said to himself, half aloud, in a crooning tone. He glanced wistfully up at the sky, but the bright sun dazzled and blinded him.

It was a long walk he took, and he did not walk fast. It took him past the jute-mill. The muffled roar of the loom room came to his ears, and he smiled. It was a gentle, placid smile. He hated no one, not even the pounding, shrieking machines. There was no bitterness in him, nothing but an inordinate hunger for rest.

The houses and factories thinned out and the open spaces increased as he approached the country. At last the city was behind him, and he was walking down a leafy lane beside the railroad track. He did not walk like a man. He did not look like a man. He was a travesty of the human. It was a twisted and stunted and nameless piece of life that shambled like a sickly ape, arms loose-hanging, stoop-shouldered, narrow-chested, grotesque and terrible.

He passed by a small railroad station and lay down in the grass under a tree. All afternoon he lay there. Sometimes he dozed, with muscles that twitched in his sleep. When awake, he lay without movement, watching the birds or looking up at the sky through the branches of the tree above him. Once or twice he laughed aloud, but without relevance to anything he had seen or felt.

After twilight had gone, in the first darkness of the night, a freight train rumbled into the station. When the engine was switching cars on to the side-track, Johnny crept along the side of the train. He pulled open the side-door of an empty box-car and awkwardly and laboriously climbed in. He closed the door. The engine whistled. Johnny was lying down, and in the darkness he smiled.

Something Rotten in Idaho: The Tale of the Conspiracy against Moyer, Pettibone and Haywood

First published in the *Chicago Daily Socialist,* November 4, 1906; reprinted from *Jack London: American Rebel—A Collection of His Special Writings with an Extensive Study of the Man and His Times,* edited by Philip S. Foner (New York: Citadel Press, 1947).

In this article, London roundly defends three imprisoned members of the Western Federation of Miners who were also vital American labor leaders: Charles Moyer, William "Bill Big" Haywood, and George Pettibone. The trial of Moyer, Pettibone, and Haywood shook the whole nation; even President Theodore Roosevelt—with whom London tangled, in print, on several occasions—became involved, using the power of the White House to campaign against Haywood and his co-defendants. Eugene Debs, who was often prone to hyperbole, called it "the greatest legal battle in American history." Still, he was not far from the mark. The trial reflected deep class divisions in American society and intensified the antagonisms between radicals and conservatives. Jack London felt impelled to add his sentiments to the national debate—to combat the propaganda from the leading newspapers and politicians of the day with his own war of words. He attacked the wealthy and the powerful, defending the miners, their union, and their working-class allies.

As a miner in the Yukon, albeit briefly, London knew the hardships of mining, and he empathized with the striking miners in the American West. In "Something Rotten in Idaho" London lambastes the mine owners and a cabal of western politicians. London's readers would have been familiar, of course, with the line from Shakespeare—"Something is rotten in the state of Denmark." "Something," London writes, was "rotten" in the state of Idaho—where Moyer, Haywood, and Pettibone were behind bars—and that something was the "conspiracy," as he called it, between officials of the state government and the plutocrats of the capitalist class to break the back of the union and working-class solidarity.

London followed the battles in the "labor war" that raged wildly in Idaho and Colorado beginning in 1903 and reaching a climax in 1905, when a bomb killed ex–Idaho governor Frank Steunenberg, a fierce foe of the miners and their union. The police arrested Harry Orchard, a longtime criminal accused of making and planting the bomb, and Orchard, in exchange for a promise of leniency, accused Moyer, Haywood, and Pettibone of planning Steunenberg's execution.

London compares Orchard's confession to the Pinkerton Detective Agency to Judas's betrayal of Jesus to the Romans—a reference that would have reverberated with readers. "Human nature has not changed since that day," London writes. Moyer, Pettibone, and Haywood were arrested in Colorado and transported, secretly, to the Idaho State Penitentiary in Boise, where they were charged with conspiracy to commit murder. Denied bail, they appealed their case all the way to the U.S. Supreme Court. London's widely reprinted, widely read article appeared at that critical juncture in the legal proceedings.

Maxim Gorky, the acclaimed Russian novelist whose work London touted to American readers, joined the international cause that rallied around the imprisoned union leaders, and socialist leader Eugene V. Debs exclaimed in *Appeal to Reason* that "if they attempt to murder Moyer, Haywood and their brothers, a million revolutionists will meet them with guns." London does not sound nearly as provocative as Debs. In fact, he wanted radicals to know that they were up against a formidable enemy, arguing that the mine owners were so powerful and well connected politically that they would continue unimpeded to act illegally and immorally. "The capitalist organization is trying to hang the labor leaders," he writes tersely. "It will profit by exterminating the labor organization."

At the nationally publicized trial that took place in Boise in 1907, Clarence Darrow, the legendary, charismatic libertarian lawyer, defended Haywood, Moyer, and Pettibone, and they were acquitted. To London, however, the case stood out not as a resounding victory for labor, but as a sign of the conspiracy of the rich and powerful, and it informed his vision of "the iron heel"—the dictatorship he warned against in 1908. It's no wonder that he reached this conclusion when General Sherman Bell said, "To hell with habeas corpus!" and the governor of Idaho said, "To hell with the people!" •

Up in the State of Idaho, at the present moment, are three men lying in jail. Their names are Moyer, Haywood, and Pettibone. They are charged with the murder of Governor Steunenberg. Incidentally they are charged with thirty, sixty, or seventy other atrocious murders. Not alone are they labor leaders and murderers, but they are anarchists. They are guilty, and they should be swiftly and immediately executed. It is to be regretted that no severer and more painful punishment than hanging awaits them. At any rate, there is consolation in the knowledge that these three men will surely be hanged.

The foregoing epitomizes the information and belief possessed by the average farmer, lawyer, professor, clergyman, and businessman in the United States. His belief is based upon this information he has gained by reading the newspapers. Did he possess different information, he might possibly believe differently. It is the purpose of this article to try to furnish information such as is not furnished by ninety-nine percent of the newspapers of the United States.

In the first place, Moyer, Haywood & Pettibone were not even in the State of Idaho at the time the crime with which they are charged was committed. In the second place, they are at present in jail in the State of Idaho because of the perpetuation of lawless acts by officers of the law, from the chief of the state executives down to the petty deputy chiefs—and this in collusion with mine-owners' associations and railroad companies.

Here is conspiracy self-confessed and openly flaunted. And it is conspiracy and violation of law on the part of the very men who claim that they are trying to bring punishment for conspiracy and violation of law. This is inconsistency, to say the least. It may be added that it is criminal inconsistency. Two wrongs have never been known to make a right. Yet the mine owners begin their alleged crusade for the right by committing wrong.

This is a bad beginning, and it warrants investigation and analysis of the acts, motives and characters of the mine owners; and incidentally an examination of the evidence they claim to have against Moyer, Haywood, and Pettibone.

The evidence against these labor leaders is contained in the confession of one Harry Orchard. It looks bad on the face of it, when a man confesses that at the instigation of another, and for money received from that other, he has committed murder. This is what Harry Orchard confesses.

But this is not the first time these same labor leaders have been charged with murder; and this is not the first confession implicating them. Colorado is a fertile soil for confessions. Moyer, in particular, has been in jail many times charged with other murders. At least five men have solemnly sworn that at his instigation they have committed murder. Now it is a matter of history that when the tool confesses, the principal swings.

Moyer gives the lie to history. In spite of the many confessions, he has never been convicted. This would make it look bad for the confessions. Not only does it make the confessions look rotten, but the confessions, in turn, cast a doubt on the sweetness and purity of the present confession of Harry Orchard. In a region noted for the rottenness of its confession-fruit, it should be indeed remarkable to find this latest sample clean and wholesome.

When a man comes into the court to give testimony, it is well to know what his character is, what his previous acts are, and whether or not self-interest enters into the case. Comes the mine-owners' association of Colorado and Idaho to testify against Moyer, Haywood, and Pettibone. Well, then, what sort of men are these mine-owners? What have they done in the past?

That the mine owners have violated the laws countless times there is no discussion. That they have robbed thousands of voters of their suffrage is common knowledge. That they have legalized lawlessness is history. But these things have only a general bearing on the matter at issue.

In particular, during and since the labor war that began in Colorado in 1903, the mine owners have charged the members of the Western Federation of Miners with all manner of crimes. There have been many trials, and in every trial the verdict has been acquittal. The testimony at these trials has been given by hired Pinkertons and spies. Yet the Pinkertons and spies, masters in the art of gathering evidence, have always failed to convict in the courts. This looks bad for the sort of evidence that grows in the fertile Colorado soil.

But it is worse than that. While the hired Pinkertons and spies have proved poor evidence-farmers—they have demonstrated that they are good criminals. Many of them have been convicted by the courts and sent to jail for the commission of crimes ranging from theft to manslaughter.

Are the mine-owners law-abiding citizens? Do they believe in the law? Do they

uphold the law? "To hell with the Constitution!" was their clearly enunciated statement in Colorado in 1903. Their military agent, General Sherman Bell, said, "To hell
with habeas corpus! We'll give them post mortems instead!" Governor Gooding, the
present governor of Idaho has recently said, "To hell with the people!"

Now it is but natural to question the good citizenship of an organization of men
that continuously and consistently consigns to hell the principle of habeas corpus, the
people and the Constitution. In Chicago, a few years ago, some men were hanged for
uttering incendiary language, not half so violent as this. But they were mere workingmen. The mine-owners of Colorado and Idaho are the chief executives, or capitalists.
They will not be hanged. On the contrary, they have their full liberty, such liberty
they are exercising in an effort to hang some other men whom they do not like.

Why do the mine-owners dislike Moyer, Haywood, and Pettibone? Because these
men stand between the mine-owners and a pot of money. These men are leaders of
organized labor. They plan and direct the efforts of the workingmen to get better
wages and shorter hours. The operation of their mines will be more expensive. The
higher the running expenses the smaller the profits. If the mine-owners could disrupt
the Western Federation of Miners, they would increase the hours of labor, lower
wages, and thereby gain millions of dollars. This is the pot of money.

It is a fairly respectable pot of money. Judas betrayed Christ to crucifixion for
thirty pieces of silver. Human nature has not changed since that day, and it is conceiv-
able that Moyer, Haywood, and Pettibone may be hanged for the sake of a few millions of dollars. Not that the mine owners have anything personally against Moyer,
Haywood and Pettibone (Judas had nothing against Christ), but because the mine-
owners want the pot of money. Judas wanted the thirty pieces of silver.

That the foregoing is not merely surprising, it would be well to state that the mine-
owners have frequently and outspokenly announced that it is their intention to exter-
minate the Western Federation of Miners. Here is motive clearly shown and
expressed. It merits consideration on the part of every thoughtful and patriotic
citizen.

In brief, the situation at present in Idaho is as follows: following a long struggle
between capital and labor, the capitalist organization has jailed the leaders of the
labor organization. The capitalist organization is trying to hang the labor leaders. It
has tried to do this before, but its evidence and its "confessions" were always too rotten and corrupt. Its hired spies and Pinkertons have themselves been sent to prison for
the commission of all manner of crimes, while they have never succeeded in sending
one labor leader to prison.

The capitalist organization has been incendiary in speech, and by unlawful acts has lived up to its speech. It will profit by exterminating the labor organization. The capitalist organization has a bad character. It has never hesitated at anything to attain its ends. By sentiment and act is has behaved unlawfully, as have its agents whom it hired. The situation in Idaho? There can be but one conclusion—THERE IS SOMETHING ROTTEN IN IDAHO!

The Pen

First published in *Cosmopolitan Magazine*, August 1907; reprinted from *The Road* (New York: Macmillan, 1907).

Jack London's thirty-day sentence in New York State's Erie County Penitentiary made him a foe of prisons and a friend to prisoners for his whole life, and he denounced the American penal system until the day he died. In 1894, after the joys of the open road, his sudden loss of freedom hit him hard, and he recounted the experience in the "The Pen," the pivotal chapter of *The Road*, his memoir about his boyhood journey across the country and his incarceration as an inmate. For London, the open road and the prison house defined the polarities of American society: its freedom and its tyranny. Written in a lean, sinewy prose, and with an appreciation for literary form, the book as a whole shows how the prison, as an institution, casts a dark shadow on the nation itself and how it oppresses the lives of people not only inside but outside its walls. After a decade of fictionalizing his life and using himself as a model for his literary characters, London wrote directly about his own experience, casting himself as the hero of his story. "I was the American Hobo," he writes, as though he had become the representative of a whole way of life.

London journeyed across the United States in 1894 at the age of eighteen, and while he described his adventures from time to time, he didn't write about them fully until 1906, at the age of thirty, when he could afford to travel by railroad and stay in luxury hotels— not riding the rails and sleeping in barns and open fields. While he worked on *The Road*, he also devoted time and energy to *White Fang*, his novel about a feral wolf who becomes domesticated and lives happily ever after, and *The Iron Heel*, his dark, dystopian tale about dictatorship and the unhappiness it imposes. *The Road* shares both the joys of the dog story and the gloom of political fiction, swinging from elation to despair. Before it saw print as a book, chapters appeared in *Cosmopolitan Magazine* in 1907, several of them under different titles. "The Pen" appeared as "The Pen, long days in a country penitentiary," and the chapter entitled "Road Kids and Gay Cats" only appeared in the finished book.

That London would run afoul of the law and be incarcerated probably did not shock or surprise his readers. After all, he had lived as an outlaw all across the country, riding the rails for free and escaping the hands of the police repeatedly. In the first chapter, "Confession," London sets the stage for the incarceration yet to come. Alerting readers to the presence of the ever-vigilant police—"John Law"—he explains that he intends to keep out of their way at all cost, and out of prison, too. In the third chapter, "Pictures," he lauds tramp life for its boundless freedom—"an ever changing phantasmagoria"—but there's also a graphic description of a man with a whip who lashes a woman, without provocation. "I had seen women beaten before," London writes. "But never had I seen such a beating as this." Clearly, brutality without public protest occurs outside as well as inside prison walls. In "Pinched," he depicts his arrest in Buffalo, New York, his appearance before a judge, his sentencing—without a trial—and his journey to the Erie County Penitentiary, handcuffed to a fellow prisoner. London describes prison as a "living hell," and he explores his own journey into its innermost circles.

"I saw there in the prison, things unbelievable and monstrous," he writes, though he never describes what he actually saw, leaving it to the imagination of his readers. As always, London depicts his own ability to adapt, even in prison. "I am a fluid sort of organism, with sufficient kinship with life to fit myself in 'most anywhere," he writes. He learns the ways of the prison system, makes his way up the prison hierarchy, and helps to reproduce, inside the prison, the same economic patterns that obtain outside. At the end of the chapter, the guards release him, and, after stopping briefly in a saloon for a drink, he jumps a freight train and vanishes in the night—like the character Johnny in "The Apostate." In "Bulls," the last chapter in *The Road,* he returns to the subject of the police, reminding readers of his own arrest and incarceration.

"I'll never get over it," he says, and he never did. His novel *The Star Rover* (1915) condemns the inhumanity of the prison system. Decades after its publication, *The Road* inspired a generation of writers, including Nelson Algren, James Farrell, and, of course, Jack Kerouac, who followed in London's footsteps and whose novel *On the Road* continues the American literary tradition London began. •

For two days I toiled in the prison-yard. It was heavy work, and, in spite of the fact that I malingered at every opportunity, I was played out. This was because of the food. No man could work hard on such food. Bread and water, that was all that was given us. Once a week we were supposed to get meat; but this meat did not always go around, and since all nutriment had first been boiled out of it in the making of soup, it didn't matter whether one got a taste of it once a week or not.

Furthermore, there was one vital defect in the bread-and-water diet. While we got plenty of water, we did not get enough of the bread. A ration of bread was about the size of one's two fists, and three rations a day were given to each prisoner. There was one good thing, I must say, about the water — it was hot. In the morning it was called "coffee," at noon it was dignified as "soup," and at night it masqueraded as "tea." But it was the same old water all the time. The prisoners called it "water bewitched." In the morning it was black water, the color being due to boiling it with burnt bread-crusts. At noon it was served minus the color, with salt and a drop of grease added. At night it was served with a purplish-auburn hue that defied all speculation; it was darn poor tea, but it was dandy hot water.

We were a hungry lot in the Erie County Pen. Only the "long-timers" knew what it was to have enough to eat. The reason for this was that they would have died after a time on the fare we "short-timers" received. I know that the long-timers got more substantial grub, because there was a whole row of them on the ground floor in our hall, and when I was a trusty, I used to steal from their grub while serving them. Man cannot live on bread alone and not enough of it.

My pal delivered the goods. After two days of work in the yard I was taken out of my cell and made a trusty, a "hall-man." At morning and night we served the bread to the prisoners in their cells; but at twelve o'clock a different method was used. The convicts marched in from work in a long line. As they entered the door of our hall, they broke the lock-step and took their hands down from the shoulders of their line-mates. Just inside the door were piled trays of bread, and here also stood the First Hall-man and two ordinary hall-men. I was one of the two. Our task was to hold the trays of bread as the line of convicts filed past. As soon as the tray, say, that I was holding was emptied, the other hall-man took my place with a full tray. And when his was emptied, I took his place with a full tray. Thus the line tramped steadily by, each man reaching with his right hand and taking one ration of bread from the extended tray.

The task of the First Hall-man was different. He used a club. He stood beside the tray and watched. The hungry wretches could never get over the delusion that sometime they could manage to get two rations of bread out of the tray. But in my experience that sometime never came. The club of the First Hall-man had a way of flashing out — quick as the stroke of a tiger's claw — to the hand that dared ambitiously. The First Hall-man was a good judge of distance, and he had smashed so many hands with that club that he had become infallible. He never missed, and he usually punished the offending convict by taking his one ration away from him and sending him to his cell to make his meal off of hot water.

And at times, while all these men lay hungry in their cells, I have seen a hundred or so extra rations of bread hidden away in the cells of the hall-men. It would seem absurd, our retaining this bread. But it was one of our grafts. We were economic masters inside our hall, turning the trick in ways quite similar to the economic masters of civilization. We controlled the food-supply of the population, and, just like our brother bandits outside, we made the people pay through the nose for it. We peddled the bread. Once a week, the men who worked in the yard received a five-cent plug of chewing tobacco. This chewing tobacco was the coin of the realm. Two or three rations of bread for a plug was the way we exchanged, and they traded, not because they loved tobacco less, but because they loved bread more. Oh, I know, it was like taking candy from a baby, but what would you? We had to live. And certainly there should be some reward for initiative and enterprise. Besides, we but patterned ourselves after our betters outside the walls, who, on a larger scale, and under the respectable disguise of merchants, bankers, and captains of industry, did precisely what we were doing. What awful things would have happened to those poor wretches if it hadn't been for us, I can't imagine. Heaven knows we put bread into circulation in the Erie County Pen. Ay, and we encouraged frugality and thrift . . . in the poor devils who forewent their tobacco. And then there was our example. In the breast of every convict there we implanted the ambition to become even as we and run a graft. Saviours of society — I guess yes.

Here was a hungry man without any tobacco. Maybe he was a profligate and had used it all up on himself. Very good; he had a pair of suspenders. I exchanged half a dozen rations of bread for it — or a dozen rations if the suspenders were very good. Now I never wore suspenders, but that didn't matter. Around the corner lodged a long-timer, doing ten years for manslaughter. He wore suspenders, and he wanted a pair. I could trade them to him for some of his meat. Meat was what I wanted. Or perhaps he had a tattered, paper-covered novel. That was treasure-trove. I could read it and then trade it off to the bakers for cake, or to the cooks for meat and vegetables, or to the firemen for decent coffee, or to some one or other for the newspaper that occasionally filtered in, heaven alone knows how. The cooks, bakers, and firemen were prisoners like myself, and they lodged in our hall in the first row of cells over us.

In short, a full-grown system of barter obtained in the Erie County Pen. There was even money in circulation. This money was sometimes smuggled in by the short-timers, more frequently came from the barber-shop graft, where the newcomers were mulcted, but most of all flowed from the cells of the long-timers — though how they got it I don't know.

What of his preeminent position, the First Hall-man was reputed to be quite wealthy. In addition to his miscellaneous grafts, he grafted on us. We farmed the general wretchedness, and the First Hall-man was Farmer-General over all of us. We held our particular grafts by his permission, and we had to pay for that permission. As I say, he was reputed to be wealthy; but we never saw his money, and he lived in a cell all to himself in solitary grandeur.

But that money was made in the Pen I had direct evidence, for I was cell-mate quite a time with the Third Hall-man. He had over sixteen dollars. He used to count his money every night after nine o'clock, when we were locked in. Also, he used to tell me each night what he would do to me if I gave away on him to the other hall-men. You see, he was afraid of being robbed, and danger threatened him from three different directions. There were the guards. A couple of them might jump upon him, give him a good beating for alleged insubordination, and throw him into the "solitaire" (the dungeon); and in the mix-up that sixteen dollars of his would take wings. Then again, the First Hall-man could have taken it all away from him by threatening to dismiss him and fire him back to hard labor in the prison-yard. And yet again, there were the ten of us who were ordinary hall-men. If we got an inkling of his wealth, there was a large liability, some quiet day, of the whole bunch of us getting him into a corner and dragging him down. Oh, we were wolves, believe me — just like the fellows who do business in Wall Street.

He had good reason to be afraid of us, and so had I to be afraid of him. He was a huge, illiterate brute, an ex-Chesapeake-Bay-oyster-pirate, an "ex-con" who had done five years in Sing Sing, and a general all-around stupidly carnivorous beast. He used to trap sparrows that flew into our hall through the open bars. When he made a capture, he hurried away with it into his cell, where I have seen him crunching bones and spitting out feathers as he bolted it raw. Oh, no, I never gave away on him to the other hall-men. This is the first time I have mentioned his sixteen dollars.

But I grafted on him just the same. He was in love with a woman prisoner who was confined in the "female department." He could neither read nor write, and I used to read her letters to him and write his replies. And I made him pay for it, too. But they were good letters. I laid myself out on them, put in my best licks, and furthermore, I won her for him; though I shrewdly guess that she was in love, not with him, but with the humble scribe. I repeat, those letters were great.

Another one of our grafts was "passing the punk." We were the celestial messengers, the fire-bringers, in that iron world of bolt and bar. When the men came in from work at night and were locked in their cells, they wanted to smoke. Then it was that we restored the divine spark, running the galleries, from cell to cell, with our smouldering punks. Those who were wise, or with whom we did business, had their punks all ready to light. Not every one got divine sparks, however. The guy who refused to dig up, went sparkless and smokeless to bed. But what did we care? We had the immortal cinch on him, and if he got fresh, two or three of us would pitch on him and give him "what-for."

You see, this was the working-theory of the hall-men. There were thirteen of us. We had something like half a thousand prisoners in our hall. We were supposed to do the work, and to keep order. The latter was the function of the guards, which they turned over to us. It was up to us to keep order; if we didn't, we'd be fired back to hard labor, most probably with a taste of the dungeon thrown in. But so long as we maintained order, that long could we work our own particular grafts.

Bear with me a moment and look at the problem. Here were thirteen beasts of us over half a thousand other beasts. It was a living hell, that prison, and it was up to us thirteen there to rule. It was impossible, considering the nature of the beasts, for us to rule by kindness. We ruled by fear. Of course, behind us, backing us up, were the guards. In extremity we called upon them for help; but it would bother them if we called upon them too often, in which event we could depend upon it that they would get more efficient trusties to take our places. But we did not call upon them often, except in a quiet sort of way, when we wanted a cell unlocked in order to get at a refractory prisoner inside. In such cases all the guard did was to unlock the door and walk away so as not to be a witness of what happened when half a dozen hall-men went inside and did a bit of manhandling.

As regards the details of this man-handling I shall say nothing. And after all, man-handling was merely one of the very minor unprintable horrors of the Erie County Pen. I say "unprintable"; and in justice I must also say "unthinkable." They were unthinkable to me until I saw them, and I was no spring chicken in the ways of the world and the awful abysses of human degradation. It would take a deep plummet to reach bottom in the Erie County Pen, and I do but skim lightly and facetiously the surface of things as I there saw them.

At times, say in the morning when the prisoners came down to wash, the thirteen of us would be practically alone in the midst of them, and every last one of them had it in for us. Thirteen against five hundred, and we ruled by fear. We could not permit the slightest infraction of rules, the slightest insolence. If we did, we were lost. Our own rule was to hit a man as soon as he opened his mouth — hit him hard, hit him with anything. A broom-handle, end-on, in the face, had a very sobering effect. But that was not all. Such a man must be made an example of; so the next rule was to wade right in and follow him up. Of course, one was sure that every hall-man in sight would come on the run to join in the chastisement; for this also was a rule. Whenever any hall-man was in trouble with a prisoner, the duty of any other hall-man who happened to be around was to lend a fist. Never mind the merits of the case—wade in and hit, and hit with anything; in short, lay the man out.

I remember a handsome young mulatto of about twenty who got the insane idea into his head that he should stand for his rights. And he did have the right of it, too; but that didn't help him any. He lived on the topmost gallery. Eight hall-men took the conceit out of him in just about a minute and a half—for that was the length of time required to travel along his gallery to the end and down five flights of steel stairs. He travelled the whole distance on every portion of his anatomy except his feet, and the eight hall-men were not idle. The mulatto struck the pavement where I was standing watching it all. He regained his feet and stood upright for a moment. In that moment he threw his arms wide apart and emitted an awful scream of terror and pain and heartbreak. At the same instant, as in a transformation scene, the shreds of his stout prison clothes fell from him, leaving him wholly naked and streaming blood from every portion of the surface of his body. Then he collapsed in a heap, unconscious. He had learned his lesson, and every convict within those walls who heard him scream had learned a lesson. So had I learned mine. It is not a nice thing to see a man's heart broken in a minute and a half.

The following will illustrate how we drummed up business in the graft of passing the punk. A row of newcomers is installed in your cells. You pass along before the bars with your punk. "Hey, Bo, give us a light," some one calls to you. Now this is an advertisement that that particular man has tobacco on him. You pass in the punk and go your way. A little later you come back and lean up casually against the bars. "Say, Bo, can you let us have a little tobacco?" is what you say. If he is not wise to the game, the chances are that he solemnly avers that he hasn't any more tobacco. All very well. You condole with him and go your way. But you know that his punk will last him only the rest of that day. Next day you come by, and he says again, "Hey, Bo, give us a light." And you say, "You haven't any tobacco and you don't need a light." And you don't give him any, either. Half an hour after, or an hour or two or three hours, you will be passing by and the man will call out to you in mild tones, "Come here, Bo." And you come. You thrust your hand between the bars and have it filled with precious tobacco. Then you give him a light.

Sometimes, however, a newcomer arrives, upon whom no grafts are to be worked. The mysterious word is passed along that he is to be treated decently. Where this word originated I could never learn. The one thing patent is that the man has a "pull." It may be with one of the superior hall-men; it may be with one of the guards in some other part of the prison; it may be that good treatment has been purchased from grafters higher up; but be it as it may, we know that it is up to us to treat him decently if we want to avoid trouble.

We hall-men were middle-men and common carriers. We arranged trades between convicts confined in different parts of the prison, and we put through the exchange. Also, we took our commissions coming and going. Sometimes the objects traded had to go through the hands of half a dozen middle-men, each of whom took his whack, or in some way or another was paid for his service.

Sometimes one was in debt for services, and sometimes one had others in his debt. Thus, I entered the prison in debt to the convict who smuggled in my things for me. A week or so afterward, one of the firemen passed a letter into my hand. It had been given to him by a barber. The barber had received it from the convict who had smuggled in my things. Because of my debt to him I was to carry the letter on. But he had not written the letter. The original sender was a long-timer in his hall. The letter was for a woman prisoner in the female department. But whether it was intended for her, or whether she, in turn, was one of the chain of go-betweens, I did not know. All that I knew was her description, and that it was up to me to get it into her hands.

Two days passed, during which time I kept the letter in my possession; then the opportunity came. The women did the mending of all the clothes worn by the convicts. A number of our hall-men had to go to the female department to bring back huge bundles of clothes. I fixed it with the First Hall-man that I was to go along. Door after door was unlocked for us as we threaded our way across the prison to the women's quarters. We entered a large room where the women sat working at their mending. My eyes were peeled for the woman who had been described to me. I located her and worked near to her. Two eagle-eyed matrons were on watch. I held the letter in my palm, and I looked my intention at the woman. She knew I had something for her; she must have been expecting it, and had set herself to divining, at the moment we entered, which of us was the messenger. But one of the matrons stood within two feet of her. Already the hall-men were picking up the bundles they were to carry away. The moment was passing. I delayed with my bundle, making believe that it was not tied securely. Would that matron ever look away? Or was I to fail? And just then another woman cut up playfully with one of the hall-men—stuck out her foot and tripped him, or pinched him, or did something or other. The matron looked that way and reprimanded the woman sharply. Now I do not know whether or not this was all planned to distract the matron's attention, but I did know that it was my opportunity. My particular woman's hand dropped from her lap down by her side. I stooped to pick up my bundle. From my stooping position I slipped the letter into her hand, and received another in exchange. The next moment the bundle was on my shoulder, the matron's gaze had returned to me because I was the last hall-man, and I was hastening to catch up with my companions. The letter I had received from the woman I turned over to the fireman, and thence it passed through the hands of the barber, of the convict who had smuggled in my things, and on to the long-timer at the other end.

Often we conveyed letters, the chain of communication of which was so complex that we knew neither sender nor sendee. We were but links in the chain. Somewhere, somehow, a convict would thrust a letter into my hand with the instruction to pass it on to the next link. All such acts were favors to be reciprocated later on, when I should be acting directly with a principal in transmitting letters, and from whom I should be receiving my pay. The whole prison was covered by a network of lines of communication. And we who were in control of the system of communication, naturally, since we were modelled after capitalistic society, exacted heavy tolls from our customers. It was service for profit with a vengeance, though we were at times not above giving service for love.

And all the time I was in the Pen I was making myself solid with my pal. He had done much for me, and in return he expected me to do as much for him. When we got out, we were to travel together, and, it goes without saying, pull off "jobs" together. For my pal was a criminal — oh, not a jewel of the first water, merely a petty criminal who would steal and rob, commit burglary, and, if cornered, not stop short of murder. Many a quiet hour we sat and talked together. He had two or three jobs in view for the immediate future, in which my work was cut out for me, and in which I joined in planning the details. I had been with and seen much of criminals, and my pal never dreamed that I was only fooling him, giving him a string thirty days long. He thought I was the real goods, liked me because I was not stupid, and liked me a bit, too, I think, for myself. Of course I had not the slightest intention of joining him in a life of sordid, petty crime; but I'd have been an idiot to throw away all the good things his friendship made possible. When one is on the hot lava of hell, he cannot pick and choose his path, and so it was with me in the Erie County Pen. I had to stay in with the "push," or do hard labor on bread and water; and to stay in with the push I had to make good with my pal.

Life was not monotonous in the Pen. Every day something was happening: men were having fits, going crazy, fighting, or the hall-men were getting drunk. Rover Jack, one of the ordinary hall-men, was our star "oryide." He was a true "profesh," a "blowed-in-the-glass" stiff, and as such received all kinds of latitude from the hall-men in authority. Pittsburg Joe, who was Second Hall-man, used to join Rover Jack in his jags; and it was a saying of the pair that the Erie County Pen was the only place where a man could get "slopped" and not be arrested. I never knew, but I was told that bromide of potassium, gained in devious ways from the dispensary, was the dope they used. But I do know, whatever their dope was, that they got good and drunk on occasion.

Our hall was a common stews, filled with the ruck and the filth, the scum and dregs, of society—hereditary inefficients, degenerates, wrecks, lunatics, addled intelligences, epileptics, monsters, weaklings, in short, a very nightmare of humanity. Hence, fits flourished with us. These fits seemed contagious. When one man began throwing a fit, others followed his lead. I have seen seven men down with fits at the same time, making the air hideous with their cries, while as many more lunatics would be raging and gibbering up and down. Nothing was ever done for the men with fits except to throw cold water on them. It was useless to send for the medical student or the doctor. They were not to be bothered with such trivial and frequent occurrences.

There was a young Dutch boy, about eighteen years of age, who had fits most frequently of all. He usually threw one every day. It was for that reason that we kept him on the ground floor farther down in the row of cells in which we lodged. After he had had a few fits in the prison-yard, the guards refused to be bothered with him any more, and so he remained locked up in his cell all day with a Cockney cell-mate, to keep him company. Not that the Cockney was of any use. Whenever the Dutch boy had a fit, the Cockney became paralyzed with terror.

The Dutch boy could not speak a word of English. He was a farmer's boy, serving ninety days as punishment for having got into a scrap with some one. He prefaced his fits with howling. He howled like a wolf. Also, he took his fits standing up, which was very inconvenient for him, for his fits always culminated in a headlong pitch to the floor. Whenever I heard the long wolf-howl rising, I used to grab a broom and run to his cell. Now the trusties were not allowed keys to the cells, so I could not get in to him. He would stand up in the middle of his narrow cell, shivering convulsively, his eyes rolled backward till only the whites were visible, and howling like a lost soul. Try as I would, I could never get the Cockney to lend him a hand. While he stood and howled, the Cockney crouched and trembled in the upper bunk, his terror-stricken gaze fixed on that awful figure, with eyes rolled back, that howled and howled. It was hard on him, too, the poor devil of a Cockney. His own reason was not any too firmly seated, and the wonder is that he did not go mad.

All that I could do was my best with the broom. I would thrust it through the bars, train it on Dutchy's chest, and wait. As the crisis approached he would begin swaying back and forth. I followed this swaying with the broom, for there was no telling when he would take that dreadful forward pitch. But when he did, I was there with the broom, catching him and easing him down. Contrive as I would, he never came down quite gently, and his face was usually bruised by the stone floor. Once down and writhing in convulsions, I'd throw a bucket of water over him. I don't know whether cold water was the right thing or not, but it was the custom in the Eric County Pen. Nothing more than that was ever done for him. He would lie there, wet, for an hour or so, and then crawl into his bunk. I knew better than to run to a guard for assistance. What was a man with a fit, anyway?

In the adjoining cell lived a strange character — a man who was doing sixty days for eating swill out of Barnum's swill-barrel, or at least that was the way he put it. He was a badly addled creature, and, at first, very mild and gentle. The facts of his case were as he had stated them. He had strayed out to the circus ground, and, being hungry, had made his way to the barrel that contained the refuse from the table of the circus people. "And it was good bread," he often assured me; "and the meat was out of sight." A policeman had seen him and arrested him, and there he was.

Once I passed his cell with a piece of stiff thin wire in my hand. He asked me for it so earnestly that I passed it through the bars to him. Promptly, and with no tool but his fingers, he broke it into short lengths and twisted them into half a dozen very creditable safety pins. He sharpened the points on the stone floor. Thereafter I did quite a trade in safety pins. I furnished the raw material and peddled the finished product, and he did the work. As wages, I paid him extra rations of bread, and once in a while a chunk of meat or a piece of soup-bone with some marrow inside.

But his imprisonment told on him, and he grew violent day by day. The hall-men took delight in teasing him. They filled his weak brain with stories of a great fortune that had been left him. It was in order to rob him of it that he had been arrested and sent to jail. Of course, as he himself knew, there was no law against eating out of a barrel. Therefore he was wrongly imprisoned. It was a plot to deprive him of his fortune.

The first I knew of it, I heard the hall-men laughing about the string they had given him. Next he held a serious conference with me, in which he told me of his millions and the plot to deprive him of them, and in which he appointed me his detective. I did my best to let him down gently, speaking vaguely of a mistake, and that it was another man with a similar name who was the rightful heir. I left him quite cooled down; but I couldn't keep the hall-men away from him, and they continued to string him worse than ever. In the end, after a most violent scene, he threw me down, revoked my private detectiveship, and went on strike. My trade in safety pins ceased. He refused to make any more safety pins, and he peppered me with raw material through the bars of his cell when I passed by.

I could never make it up with him. The other hall-men told him that I was a detective in the employ of the conspirators. And in the meantime the hall-men drove him mad with their stringing. His fictitious wrongs preyed upon his mind, and at last he became a dangerous and homicidal lunatic. The guards refused to listen to his tale of stolen millions, and he accused them of being in the plot. One day he threw a pannikin of hot tea over one of them, and then his case was investigated. The warden talked with him a few minutes through the bars of his cell. Then he was taken away for examination before the doctors. He never came back, and I often wonder if he is dead, or if he still gibbers about his millions in some asylum for the insane.

At last came the day of days, my release. It was the day of release for the Third Hall-man as well, and the short-timer girl I had won for him was waiting for him outside the wall. They went away blissfully together. My pal and I went out together, and together we walked down into Buffalo. Were we not to be together always? We begged together on the "main-drag" that day for pennies, and what we received was spent for "shupers" of beer—I don't know how they are spelled, but they are pronounced the way I have spelled them, and they cost three cents. I was watching my chance all the time for a get-away. From some bo on the drag I managed to learn what time a certain freight pulled out. I calculated my time accordingly. When the moment came, my pal and I were in a saloon. Two foaming shupers were before us. I'd have liked to say good-by. He had been good to me. But I did not dare. I went out through the rear of the saloon and jumped the fence. It was a swift sneak, and a few minutes later I was on board a freight and heading south on the Western New York and Pennsylvania Railroad.

The Iron Heel, Chapter 23

First published in and reprinted from *The Iron Heel* (New York: Macmillan, 1908).

For years, London ridiculed psychics and seers who claimed they could foretell the future. But in 1906, at the age of thirty, he set for himself the task of predicting how the world would look in the twentieth century and for centuries afterward. He might have written a series of essays, or a work of nonfiction; instead he chose to write a novel in which he presented a kaleidoscopic series of moving pictures depicting the collapse of democracy in the United States and a bloody civil war that rages in the streets of America's cities.

In *The Iron Heel,* London became a "sociological seer." For inspiration, he turned to H. G. Wells's futuristic novel *The Time Machine* (1898). From the start, London had the title for his book and its dominant image: an iron boot heel. Midway though the novel, a conservative millionaire tells revolutionary hero Ernest Everhard, "We will grind you revolutionists down under our heel, and we shall walk on your faces." That vivid image—and the sadistic impulse behind it—inspired George Orwell when he wrote his dystopian novel *Nineteen Eighty-Four.*

Writing a novel enabled London to reach a wide audience. Moreover, by couching his novel as a romantic love story, he appealed to middle-class women readers. London made his narrator, Avis Everhard, a young woman so madly in love that she rejects her comfortable life in Berkeley to follow her man blindly into the ranks of the revolution. Avis's own melodramatic account of the rise of the "iron heel" and the defeat of the revolution constitutes the heart of the novel. Not surprisingly, her voice echoes Anna Strunsky's, and indeed, it's not a stretch of the imagination to see Anna behind Avis.

"This is the Revolution of Revolutions, the beginning of the wonderful end," Anna Strunsky wrote to London in 1906, from Russia, where she and her husband observed the political upheaval firsthand. "You see how my love brings me closer and closer with the world . . . This is not a theory; this is reality. This is the character of the man who loves me."

In *The Iron Heel,* London took aim at comrades like Strunsky and her husband, William English Walling, who believed in the imminent arrival of the revolution in America. He wrote his novel as a wake-up call, a warning and an alarm to them and to the glib socialists of his day. If he had one clear, unambiguous message, it was this: beware the oligarchy in the United States that is even now secretly preparing to seize control of the government, curtail civil liberties, turn citizens into serfs, and rule by brute force. London also meant *The Iron Heel* to be a response to *The Industrial Republic* (1906), a utopian novel by Upton Sinclair predicting that William Randolph Hearst would usher in a socialist society in America. No such thing, London insisted.

In *The Iron Heel,* the tumultuous events are viewed through Avis's idealistic eyes, but the novel also offers a series of caustic footnotes that provide a gloss on her comments, serving as a brake on her romanticism. In short, pithy sentences, the footnotes describe the greed and the corruption of London's own day, and so, even as *The Iron Heel* presents a grim picture of the future of America, it also offers a portrait of nineteenth- and early twentieth-century American society.

In a footnote to the word *utopian,* for example, which appears in chapter 5, London notes insightfully that "the people of that age were phrase slaves . . . So befuddled and chaotic were their minds that the utterance of a single word could negate the generalizations of a lifetime of serious research and thought. Such a word was the adjective *Utopian.*" In our own age, of course, words like *liberal, terrorist, socialist,* and even *utopian*—as well as phrases like "cut and run"—have immense power, through the mass media, over people, and are used to befuddle, confuse, and intimidate. George Orwell covered much the same ground in his seminal essay "Politics and the English Language" (1946). He even noted that London's phrase "the iron heel" had come to be used, unthinkingly, by political zombies. "When one watches some tired hack on the platform mechanically repeating the familiar phrases—*bestial atrocities, iron heel, bloodstained tyranny, free peoples of the world, stand shoulder to shoulder*—one often has a curious feeling that one is not watching a live human being but some kind of dummy," Orwell wrote. "A feeling which suddenly becomes stronger at moments when the light catches the speaker's spectacles and turns them into blank discs which seem to have no eyes behind them."

London delighted in writing the footnotes, though he attributes them to Anthony Meredith, a fictional historian who lives seven hundred years in the future, in a utopian society called the "Brotherhood of Man." In the guise of Meredith, London introduces Avis's manuscript—her "false document," to borrow E. L. Doctorow's useful phrase for describing a work of fiction that presents itself as fact. Avis's account has no value as to the historical record, Meredith explains, but immense value about feelings—a distinction that illustrates London's appreciation of the power of memoir as a genre.

London based his predictions for the future on his close observation of the class conflicts and political battles around him. He saw the Pinkerton Detective Agency as a sign of the surveillance society yet to come. The trials of American radicals, especially the leaders of the Industrial Workers of the World (IWW), struck him as the start of the mass persecution of radicals. He knew of the Russian Cossacks and thought that the future oligarchy would have a Cossack-like army of mercenaries. The defeat of the 1905 Russian Revolution provided grist for his political imagination, and the 1906 earthquake and fire in San Francisco, which he witnessed firsthand, offered a reservoir of images of urban chaos that he used when writing about the oligarchy and disorder in the streets of Chicago. He funneled all sorts of information into *The Iron Heel.*

London's knowledge of nineteenth-century history—from the revolutions of 1848 to the Paris Commune of 1871—also helped in the writing of the novel. To create his hero, Ernest Everhard, London drew on the life of his friend, fellow socialist—and a translator of Marx into English—Ernest Untermann. He also borrowed from his own experiences as a lecturer in 1905 and 1906. When Everhard debates the conservatives of his day, he expresses London's ideas. Unfortunately, he sounds trite. London's speeches from 1905 and 1906 have vitality; when the author puts his ideas into Everhard's mouth, they lose their force. Everhard himself becomes a stick figure and all too self-righteous to be a likable character, though he has a modicum of charm.

Many of London's predictions focus on economics and politics, though there are also comments on the arts, the media, and religion. In London's future world, power and wealth are concentrated in fewer and fewer hands. The oligarchy rules with absolute power. (In a footnote London explains that in the early twentieth century "the great mass of people" believed that "they ruled the country by virtue of their ballots. In reality, the country was ruled by what were called *political machines*.") Under "the iron heel," the middle class vanishes, a caste of well-paid workers (an "aristocracy of labor") comes into existence, and small farmers become extinct. Agri-business takes over. The masses live in ghettos, while the super-rich live in isolated majestic cities, surrounded by beauty.

News is censored, radical books suppressed. The oligarchy monitors its citizens and eliminates privacy, and public school education vanishes. Right-wing mobs roam city streets, intimidating citizens, and conspiracies lurk everywhere, making it impossible to trust anyone. Priests denounce the revolution, radicals are assassinated—or go underground, taking on new identities and creating a clandestine network for survival. "A time of madness" takes over America, and unreason presides.

London's prophecies have come true, in part, especially his prediction of a fractured, polarized society in which both sides—the left and the right—are driven by a sense of "righteousness." The oligarchs believe that "they are doing right"—no matter what injustices they perpetuate and no matter what atrocities they commit. The revolutionaries are no less self-righteous. In the last chapters of the novel, London provides a vivid description of "warfare in that modern jungle, a great city." There are street battles and "mid-air fighting," machine gun attacks, the slaughter of civilians, and the burning of whole neighborhoods. The government controls the media, which reports only good news.

Since 1899, he had been of two diametrically opposed minds about the future. In 1903, when he read William J. Ghent's *Our Benevolent Feudalism* and John Graham Brooks's *The Social Unrest*—reviewing them for the *International Socialist Review*—he explored both perspectives. He could accept Ghent's view that the capitalist class would rise to "dominate the state and the working class," and he could also accept Brooks's thesis that the working class would rise "to dominate the state and the capitalist class." When he began to write *The Iron Heel* he retained these two opposing ideas; by the time he finished the book he still had not resolved the debate between the two "contradictory teachers," as he called Ghent and Brooks. In *The Iron Heel* he allows for both futures. The oligarchs, with their dictatorship, reign for four hundred years; only afterward do the "Brotherhood of Man" and socialism come into existence.

"I should like to have socialism, yet I know that socialism is not the next step," he wrote in 1901. "I know that capitalism must live its life first." In *The Iron Heel* he gave capitalism a long, virulent life. Not surprisingly, the official socialist movement condemned or ignored London's predictions. His dark vision of the future was one radicals did not want to see or accept. The novel did not become the marketplace success that he had hoped for, though he knew it would never match the sales of *The Call of the Wild* or *The Sea-Wolf.*

"*The Iron Heel* is an attack on the bourgeoisie and all the bourgeoisie stands for," he writes. "It will not make me any friends." The *Oakland World* published selections from the novel in April and May 1908, but no major magazine expressed interest in serializing it. The fact that London left the United States in 1907 to sail around the world on the *Snark* seemed to undercut the dire message of the novel. Indeed, readers wondered why they ought to heed a prophet who had the time, money, and inclination for a world cruise.

Beginning in the 1920s, *The Iron Heel* was widely read and appreciated. The French Nobel Prize–winning author Anatole France praised it, as did Leon Trotsky, who saw it as a prediction of the coming of fascism. In the 1960s, American radicals and Vietnamese scholars hailed it as a denunciation of American imperialism. In the introduction to a 1981 edition of the novel, the critic H. Bruce Franklin characterized *The Iron Heel* as "timely" and "vital," asserting that "London understood better than any of his American intellectual contemporaries the utter ruthlessness and ferocity that the capitalist class would display if it felt its survival at stake."

Today, the novel might be appreciated for its depiction of urban guerrilla warfare and terrorism. The last chapter, "The Terrorists," describes the birth of a worldwide terrorist movement. "Many terrorist organizations unaffiliated with us sprang into existence and caused us much trouble," Avis observes. Meredith, the futuristic historian, adds, in a footnote, "The members of the terroristic organizations were careless of their own lives and hopeless about the future." Ending his story with global terrorism shows London's prescience; it was also a stroke of literary genius to conclude Avis's narrative in mid-sentence, without closure. "The magnitude of the task may be understood when it is taken into"—her unfinished thought suggests the unfinished historical record itself and also adds a sense of mystery to the story. A footnote to the last, incomplete sentence explains that the narrator "breaks off abruptly" because she "must have received warning of the coming of the Mercenaries, for she had time to hide the Manuscript before she fled or was captured."

I have included here "The People of the Abyss," the climactic twenty-third of the novel's twenty-five chapters. With all the talent of a great movie director, London captures the dramatic action of guerrilla warfare in a modern city. Two revolutionary comrades, Hartman and Garthwaite, join Avis as she makes her way through the rubble and the rioting. Bombs burst and machine guns spray bullets, while snipers fire their weapons from towering skyscrapers. The working-class ghetto goes up in flames, and "a devilish pandemonium" reigns in Chicago. Avis and Garthwaite hide briefly under a pile of dead bodies. They're attacked by the "people of the abyss"—a whole population of grotesque individuals: "crooked, twisted, misshapen monsters blasted with the ravages of disease . . . the refuse and the scum of life, a raging, screaming, screeching, demoniacal horde." London certainly doesn't romanticize the mob. Avis, of course, escapes from Chicago and makes her way to California, where, in hiding, she writes her memoir.

In London's revolution, the masses do not play a pivotal role; in the battle for Chicago, an elite corps of soldiers confronts an elite group of fervid revolutionaries. Avis, one of London's elitist revolutionaries, sees death and slaughter everywhere, but she doesn't lose her faith. "The Cause for this one time was lost," she proclaims. "But the Cause would be here to-morrow." When the mercenaries stop and question her, she knows how to deflect their suspicions. "Oh, I'm going to be married," she says. •

Suddenly a change came over the face of things. A tingle of excitement ran along the air. Automobiles fled past, two, three, a dozen, and from them warnings were shouted to us. One of the machines swerved wildly at high speed half a block down, and the next moment, already left well behind it, the pavement was torn into a great hole by a bursting bomb. We saw the police disappearing down the cross-streets on the run, and knew that something terrible was coming. We could hear the rising roar of it.

"Our brave comrades are coming," Hartman said.

We could see the front of their column filling the street from gutter to gutter, as the last war-automobile fled past. The machine stopped for a moment just abreast of us. A soldier leaped from it, carrying something carefully in his hands. This, with the same care, he deposited in the gutter. Then he leaped back to his seat and the machine dashed on, took the turn at the corner, and was gone from sight. Hartman ran to the gutter and stooped over the object.

"Keep back," he warned me.

I could see he was working rapidly with his hands. When he returned to me the sweat was heavy on his forehead.

"I disconnected it," he said, "and just in the nick of time. The soldier was clumsy. He intended it for our comrades, but he didn't give it enough time. It would have exploded prematurely. Now it won't explode at all."

Everything was happening rapidly now. Across the street and half a block down, high up in a building, I could see heads peering out. I had just pointed them out to Hartman, when a sheet of flame and smoke ran along that portion of the face of the building where the heads had appeared, and the air was shaken by the explosion. In places the stone facing of the building was torn away, exposing the iron construction beneath. The next moment similar sheets of flame and smoke smote the front of the building across the street opposite it. Between the explosions we could hear the rattle of the automatic pistols and rifles. For several minutes this mid-air battle continued, then died out. It was patent that our comrades were in one building, that

Mercenaries were in the other, and that they were fighting across the street. But we could not tell which was which—which building contained our comrades and which the Mercenaries.

By this time the column on the street was almost on us. As the front of it passed under the warring buildings, both went into action again—one building dropping bombs into the street, being attacked from across the street, and in return replying to that attack. Thus we learned which building was held by our comrades, and they did good work, saving those in the street from the bombs of the enemy.

Hartman gripped my arm and dragged me into a wide entrance.

"They're not our comrades," he shouted in my ear.

The inner doors to the entrance were locked and bolted. We could not escape. The next moment the front of the column went by. It was not a column, but a mob, an awful river that filled the street, the people of the abyss, mad with drink and wrong, up at last and roaring for the blood of their masters. I had seen the people of the abyss before, gone through its ghettos, and thought I knew it; but I found that I was now looking on it for the first time. Dumb apathy had vanished. It was now dynamic—a fascinating spectacle of dread. It surged past my vision in concrete waves of wrath, snarling and growling, carnivorous, drunk with whiskey from pillaged warehouses, drunk with hatred, drunk with lust for blood—men, women, and children, in rags and tatters, dim ferocious intelligences with all the godlike blotted from their features and all the fiendlike stamped in, apes and tigers, anaemic consumptives and great hairy beasts of burden, wan faces from which vampire society had sucked the juice of life, bloated forms swollen with physical grossness and corruption, withered hags and death's heads bearded like patriarchs, festering youth and festering age, faces of fiends, crooked, twisted, misshapen monsters blasted with the ravages of disease and all the horrors of chronic innutrition—the refuse and the scum of life, a raging, screaming, screeching, demoniacal horde.

And why not? The people of the abyss had nothing to lose but the misery and pain of living. And to gain?—nothing, save one final, awful glut of vengeance. And as I looked the thought came to me that in that rushing stream of human lava were men, comrades and heroes, whose mission had been to rouse the abysmal beast and to keep the enemy occupied in coping with it.

And now a strange thing happened to me. A transformation came over me. The fear of death, for myself and for others, left me. I was strangely exalted, another being in another life. Nothing mattered. The Cause for this one time was lost, but the Cause would be here to-morrow, the same Cause, ever fresh and ever burning. And there-after, in the orgy of horror that raged through the succeeding hours, I was able to take a calm interest. Death meant nothing, life meant nothing. I was an interested specta-tor of events, and, sometimes swept on by the rush, was myself a curious participant. For my mind had leaped to a star-cool altitude and grasped a passionless transvalua-tion of values. Had it not done this, I know that I should have died.

Half a mile of the mob had swept by when we were discovered. A woman in fan-tastic rags, with cheeks cavernously hollow and with narrow black eyes like burning gimlets, caught a glimpse of Hartman and me. She let out a shrill shriek and bore in upon us. A section of the mob tore itself loose and surged in after her. I can see her now, as I write these lines, a leap in advance, her gray hair flying in thin tangled strings, the blood dripping down her forehead from some wound in the scalp, in her right hand a hatchet, her left hand, lean and wrinkled, a yellow talon, gripping the air con-vulsively. Hartman sprang in front of me. This was no time for explanations. We were well dressed, and that was enough. His fist shot out, striking the woman between her burning eyes. The impact of the blow drove her backward, but she struck the wall of her on-coming fellows and bounced forward again, dazed and helpless, the bran-dished hatchet falling feebly on Hartman's shoulder.

The next moment I knew not what was happening. I was overborne by the crowd. The confined space was filled with shrieks and yells and curses. Blows were falling on me. Hands were ripping and tearing at my flesh and garments. I felt that I was being torn to pieces. I was being borne down, suffocated. Some strong hand gripped my shoulder in the thick of the press and was dragging fiercely at me. Between pain and pressure I fainted. Hartman never came out of that entrance. He had shielded me and received the first brunt of the attack. This had saved me, for the jam had quickly become too dense for anything more than the mad gripping and tearing of hands.

I came to in the midst of wild movement. All about me was the same movement. I had been caught up in a monstrous flood that was sweeping me I knew not whither. Fresh air was on my cheek and biting sweetly in my lungs. Faint and dizzy, I was vaguely aware of a strong arm around my body under the arms, and half-lifting me and dragging me along. Feebly my own limbs were helping me. In front of me I could see the moving back of a man's coat. It had been slit from top to bottom along the centre seam, and it pulsed rhythmically, the slit opening and closing regularly with every leap of the wearer. This phenomenon fascinated me for a time, while my senses were com-ing back to me. Next I became aware of stinging cheeks and nose, and could feel blood dripping on my face. My hat was gone. My hair was down and flying, and from the stinging of the scalp I managed to recollect a hand in the press of the entrance that had torn at my hair. My chest and arms were bruised and aching in a score of places.

My brain grew clearer, and I turned as I ran and looked at the man who was holding me up. He it was who had dragged me out and saved me. He noticed my movement.

"It's all right!" he shouted hoarsely. "I knew you on the instant."

I failed to recognize him, but before I could speak I trod upon something that was alive and that squirmed under my foot. I was swept on by those behind and could not look down and see, and yet I knew that it was a woman who had fallen, and who was being trampled into the pavement by thousands of successive feet.

"It's all right," he repeated. "I'm Garthwaite."

He was bearded and gaunt and dirty, but I succeeded in remembering him as the stalwart youth that had spent several months in our Glen Ellen refuge three years before. He passed me the signals of the Iron Heel's secret service, in token that he, too, was in its employ.

"I'll get you out of this as soon as I can get a chance," he assured me. "But watch your footing. On your life don't stumble and go down."

All things happened abruptly on that day, and with an abruptness that was sickening the mob checked itself. I came in violent collision with a large woman in front of me (the man with the split coat had vanished), while those behind collided against me. A devilish pandemonium reigned—shrieks, curses, and cries of death, while above all rose the churning rattle of machine-guns and the put-a-put, put-a-put of rifles. At first I could make out nothing. People were falling about me right and left. The woman in front doubled up and went down, her hands on her abdomen in a frenzied clutch. A man was quivering against my legs in a death-struggle.

It came to me that we were at the head of the column. Half a mile of it had disappeared—where or how I never learned. To this day I do not know what became of that half-mile of humanity—whether it was blotted out by some frightful bolt of war, whether it was scattered and destroyed piecemeal, or whether it escaped. But there we were, at the head of the column instead of in its middle, and we were being swept out of life by a torrent of shrieking lead.

As soon as death had thinned the jam, Garthwaite, still grasping my arm, led a rush of survivors into the wide entrance of an office building. Here, at the rear, against the doors, we were pressed by a panting, gasping mass of creatures. For some time we remained in this position without a change in the situation.

"I did it beautifully," Garthwaite was lamenting to me. "Ran you right into a trap. We had a gambler's chance in the street, but in here there is no chance at all. It's all over but the shouting. Vive la Revolution!"

Then, what he expected, began. The Mercenaries were killing without quarter. At first, the surge back upon us was crushing, but as the killing continued the pressure was eased. The dead and dying went down and made room. Garthwaite put his mouth to my ear and shouted, but in the frightful din I could not catch what he said. He did not wait. He seized me and threw me down. Next he dragged a dying woman over on top of me, and, with much squeezing and shoving, crawled in beside me and partly over me. A mound of dead and dying began to pile up over us, and over this mound, pawing and moaning, crept those that still survived. But these, too, soon ceased, and a semi-silence settled down, broken by groans and sobs and sounds of strangulation.

I should have been crushed had it not been for Garthwaite. As it was, it seemed inconceivable that I could bear the weight I did and live. And yet, outside of pain, the only feeling I possessed was one of curiosity. How was it going to end? What would death be like? Thus did I receive my red baptism in that Chicago shambles. Prior to that, death to me had been a theory; but ever afterward death has been a simple fact that does not matter, it is so easy.

But the Mercenaries were not content with what they had done. They invaded the entrance, killing the wounded and searching out the unhurt that, like ourselves, were playing dead. I remember one man they dragged out of a heap, who pleaded abjectly until a revolver shot cut him short. Then there was a woman who charged from a heap, snarling and shooting. She fired six shots before they got her, though what damage she did we could not know. We could follow these tragedies only by the sound. Every little while flurries like this occurred, each flurry culminating in the revolver shot that put an end to it. In the intervals we could hear the soldiers talking and swearing as they rummaged among the carcasses, urged on by their officers to hurry up.

At last they went to work on our heap, and we could feel the pressure diminish as they dragged away the dead and wounded. Garthwaite began uttering aloud the signals. At first he was not heard. Then he raised his voice.

"Listen to that," we heard a soldier say. And next the sharp voice of an officer. "Hold on there! Careful as you go!"

Oh, that first breath of air as we were dragged out! Garthwaite did the talking at first, but I was compelled to undergo a brief examination to prove service with the Iron Heel.

"Agents-provocateurs all right," was the officer's conclusion. He was a beardless young fellow, a cadet, evidently, of some great oligarch family.

"It's a hell of a job," Garthwaite grumbled. "I'm going to try and resign and get into the army. You fellows have a snap."

"You've earned it," was the young officer's answer. "I've got some pull, and I'll see if it can be managed. I can tell them how I found you."

He took Garthwaite's name and number, then turned to me.

"And you?"

"Oh, I'm going to be married," I answered lightly, "and then I'll be out of it all."

And so we talked, while the killing of the wounded went on. It is all a dream, now, as I look back on it; but at the time it was the most natural thing in the world. Garthwaite and the young officer fell into an animated conversation over the difference between so-called modern warfare and the present street-fighting and skyscraper fighting that was taking place all over the city. I followed them intently, fixing up my hair at the same time and pinning together my torn skirts. And all the time the killing of the wounded went on. Sometimes the revolver shots drowned the voices of Garthwaite and the officer, and they were compelled to repeat what they had been saying.

I lived through three days of the Chicago Commune, and the vastness of it and of the slaughter may be imagined when I say that in all that time I saw practically nothing outside the killing of the people of the abyss and the mid-air fighting between skyscrapers. I really saw nothing of the heroic work done by the comrades. I could hear the explosions of their mines and bombs, and see the smoke of their conflagrations, and that was all. The mid-air part of one great deed I saw, however, and that was the balloon attacks made by our comrades on the fortresses. That was on the second day. The three disloyal regiments had been destroyed in the fortresses to the last man. The fortresses were crowded with Mercenaries, the wind blew in the right direction, and up went our balloons from one of the office buildings in the city.

Now Biedenbach, after he left Glen Ellen, had invented a most powerful explosive—"expedite" he called it. This was the weapon the balloons used. They were only hot-air balloons, clumsily and hastily made, but they did the work. I saw it all from the top of an office building. The first balloon missed the fortresses completely and disappeared into the country; but we learned about it afterward. Burton and O'Sullivan were in it. As they were descending they swept across a railroad directly over a troop-train that was heading at full speed for Chicago. They dropped their whole supply of expedite upon the locomotive. The resulting wreck tied the line up for days. And the best of it was that, released from the weight of expedite, the balloon shot up into the air and did not come down for half a dozen miles, both heroes escaping unharmed.

The second balloon was a failure. Its flight was lame. It floated too low and was shot full of holes before it could reach the fortresses. Herford and Guinness were in it, and they were blown to pieces along with the field into which they fell. Biedenbach was in despair—we heard all about it afterward—and he went up alone in the third balloon. He, too, made a low flight, but he was in luck, for they failed seriously to puncture his balloon. I can see it now as I did then, from the lofty top of the building—that inflated bag drifting along the air, and that tiny speck of a man clinging on beneath. I could not see the fortress, but those on the roof with me said he was directly over it. I did not see the expedite fall when he cut it loose. But I did see the balloon suddenly leap up into the sky. An appreciable time after that the great column of the explosion towered in the air, and after that, in turn, I heard the roar of it. Biedenbach the gentle had destroyed a fortress. Two other balloons followed at the same time. One was blown to pieces in the air, the expedite exploding, and the shock of it disrupted the second balloon, which fell prettily into the remaining fortress. It couldn't have been better planned, though the two comrades in it sacrificed their lives.

But to return to the people of the abyss. My experiences were confined to them. They raged and slaughtered and destroyed all over the city proper, and were in turn destroyed; but never once did they succeed in reaching the city of the oligarchs over on the west side. The oligarchs had protected themselves well. No matter what destruction was wreaked in the heart of the city, they, and their womenkind and children, were to escape hurt. I am told that their children played in the parks during those terrible days and that their favorite game was an imitation of their elders stamping upon the proletariat.

But the Mercenaries found it no easy task to cope with the people of the abyss and at the same time fight with the comrades. Chicago was true to her traditions, and though a generation of revolutionists was wiped out, it took along with it pretty close to a generation of its enemies. Of course, the Iron Heel kept the figures secret, but, at a very conservative estimate, at least one hundred and thirty thousand Mercenaries were slain. But the comrades had no chance. Instead of the whole country being hand in hand in revolt, they were all alone, and the total strength of the Oligarchy could have been directed against them if necessary. As it was, hour after hour, day after day, in endless train-loads, by hundreds of thousands, the Mercenaries were hurled into Chicago.

And there were so many of the people of the abyss! Tiring of the slaughter, a great herding movement was begun by the soldiers, the intent of which was to drive the street mobs, like cattle, into Lake Michigan. It was at the beginning of this movement that Garthwaite and I had encountered the young officer. This herding movement was practically a failure, thanks to the splendid work of the comrades. Instead of the great host the Mercenaries had hoped to gather together, they succeeded in driving no more than forty thousand of the wretches into the lake. Time and again, when a mob of them was well in hand and being driven along the streets to the water, the comrades would create a diversion, and the mob would escape through the consequent hole torn in the encircling net.

Garthwaite and I saw an example of this shortly after meeting with the young officer. The mob of which we had been a part, and which had been put in retreat, was prevented from escaping to the south and east by strong bodies of troops. The troops we had fallen in with had held it back on the west. The only outlet was north, and north it went toward the lake, driven on from east and west and south by machine-gun fire and automatics. Whether it divined that it was being driven toward the lake, or whether it was merely a blind squirm of the monster, I do not know; but at any rate the mob took a cross street to the west, turned down the next street, and came back upon its track, heading south toward the great ghetto.

Garthwaite and I at that time were trying to make our way westward to get out of the territory of street-fighting, and we were caught right in the thick of it again. As we came to the corner we saw the howling mob bearing down upon us. Garthwaite seized my arm and we were just starting to run, when he dragged me back from in front of the wheels of half a dozen war automobiles, equipped with machine-guns, that were rushing for the spot. Behind them came the soldiers with their automatic rifles. By the time they took position, the mob was upon them, and it looked as though they would be overwhelmed before they could get into action.

Here and there a soldier was discharging his rifle, but this scattered fire had no effect in checking the mob. On it came, bellowing with brute rage. It seemed the machine-guns could not get started. The automobiles on which they were mounted blocked the street, compelling the soldiers to find positions in, between, and on the sidewalks. More and more soldiers were arriving, and in the jam we were unable to get away. Garthwaite held me by the arm, and we pressed close against the front of a building.

The mob was no more than twenty-five feet away when the machine-guns opened up; but before that flaming sheet of death nothing could live. The mob came on, but it could not advance. It piled up in a heap, a mound, a huge and growing wave of dead and dying. Those behind urged on, and the column, from gutter to gutter, telescoped upon itself. Wounded creatures, men and women, were vomited over the top of that awful wave and fell squirming down the face of it till they threshed about under the automobiles and against the legs of the soldiers. The latter bayoneted the struggling wretches, though one I saw who gained his feet and flew at a soldier's throat with his teeth. Together they went down, soldier and slave, into the welter.

The firing ceased. The work was done. The mob had been stopped in its wild attempt to break through. Orders were being given to clear the wheels of the war-machines. They could not advance over that wave of dead, and the idea was to run them down the cross street. The soldiers were dragging the bodies away from the wheels when it happened. We learned afterward how it happened. A block distant a hundred of our comrades had been holding a building. Across roofs and through buildings they made their way, till they found themselves looking down upon the close-packed soldiers. Then it was counter-massacre.

Without warning, a shower of bombs fell from the top of the building. The auto-mobiles were blown to fragments, along with many soldiers. We, with the survivors, swept back in mad retreat. Half a block down another building opened fire on us. As the soldiers had carpeted the street with dead slaves, so, in turn, did they themselves become carpet. Garthwaite and I bore charmed lives. As we had done before, so again we sought shelter in an entrance. But he was not to be caught napping this time. As the roar of the bombs died away, he began peering out.

"The mob's coming back!" he called to me. "We've got to get out of this!"

We fled, hand in hand, down the bloody pavement, slipping and sliding, and making for the corner. Down the cross street we could see a few soldiers still running. Nothing was happening to them. The way was clear. So we paused a moment and looked back. The mob came on slowly. It was busy arming itself with the rifles of the slain and killing the wounded. We saw the end of the young officer who had rescued us. He painfully lifted himself on his elbow and turned loose with his automatic pistol.

"There goes my chance of promotion," Garthwaite laughed, as a woman bore down on the wounded man, brandishing a butcher's cleaver. "Come on. It's the wrong direction, but we'll get out somehow."

And we fled eastward through the quiet streets, prepared at every cross street for anything to happen. To the south a monster conflagration was filling the sky, and we knew that the great ghetto was burning. At last I sank down on the sidewalk. I was exhausted and could go no farther. I was bruised and sore and aching in every limb; yet I could not escape smiling at Garthwaite, who was rolling a cigarette and saying:

"I know I'm making a mess of rescuing you, but I can't get head nor tail of the situation. It's all a mess. Every time we try to break out, something happens and we're turned back. We're only a couple of blocks now from where I got you out of that entrance. Friend and foe are all mixed up. It's chaos. You can't tell who is in those darned buildings. Try to find out, and you get a bomb on your head. Try to go peaceably on your way, and you run into a mob and are killed by machine-guns, or you run into the Mercenaries and are killed by your own comrades from a roof. And on the top of it all the mob comes along and kills you, too."

He shook his head dolefully, lighted his cigarette, and sat down beside me.

"And I'm that hungry," he added, "I could eat cobblestones."

The next moment he was on his feet again and out in the street prying up a cobblestone. He came back with it and assaulted the window of a store behind us.

"It's ground floor and no good," he explained as he helped me through the hole he had made; "but it's the best we can do. You get a nap and I'll reconnoitre. I'll finish this rescue all right, but I want time, time, lots of it — and something to eat."

It was a harness store we found ourselves in, and he fixed me up a couch of horse blankets in the private office well to the rear. To add to my wretchedness a splitting headache was coming on, and I was only too glad to close my eyes and try to sleep.

"I'll be back," were his parting words. "I don't hope to get an auto, but I'll surely bring some grub,* anyway."

And that was the last I saw of Garthwaite for three years. Instead of coming back, he was carried away to a hospital with a bullet through his lungs and another through the fleshy part of his neck.

*Food.

Martin Eden, Chapter 46

First published serially in the *Pacific Monthly,* September 1908–September 1909 ; reprinted from *Martin Eden* (New York: Macmillan, 1909).

No anthology of London's writings would be complete without a chapter from *Martin Eden,* his 1909 critique of the American Dream and meditation on the nightmare of success. It is probably his most perfectly crafted novel. Furthermore, no London anthology could be said to accurately reflect his life as a radical and a socialist without also including a sample from his writing on the subject of suicide, a deep and a lasting preoccupation, perhaps even an obsession. Of course, the last chapter of *Martin Eden* describes the suicide of the main character, an ex-sailor-turned-writer who has often been called London's surrogate, much as the novel itself has been seen as autobiographical or at least semi-autobiographical. No London novel has generated as much controversy as *Martin Eden;* in the last chapter, London renders Eden's suicide at sea so beautifully that suicide seems attractive—an aesthetic experience not to be missed. And at the end of the chapter, Eden seems to be in the midst of a psychedelic experience. Since London used hashish and felt that it enhanced his literary talents, it's possible that he wrote the section while on hashish, or at least with the experience of having used hashish to guide him as he wrote.

Initially, the novel appeared serially in the *Pacific Monthly,* and London made sure to end each chapter on a note of suspense that would keep readers on edge. From the start, he knew that his hero would commit suicide, though he did not know precisely how, and he kept the ending a carefully guarded secret from everyone, including his editor and publisher, who probably would have requested major changes had they known the grim ending. In his notes for the novel, which he initially entitled *God's Own Mad Lover*—a phrase that fit the author as well as his main character—London entertained different possibilities for his hero's suicide, pondering whether Eden would take poison, shoot himself, or drown at sea. He opted for drowning, possibly because he could draw on memories of his own attempted suicide at sea, and perhaps, too, because death at sea seemed appropriate for a sailor.

On Sunday, January 16, 1910, Charles R. Brown, pastor of the First Congregational Church in Oakland, gave a sermon entitled "London's latest book: Martin Eden." From the pulpit, he explained to his parishioners that Jack London and Martin Eden were one and the same, and that "Jack London does not believe in God." London sat in the audience, listening attentively; not surprisingly, he took issue with the sermon and wrote a public letter to defend the novel and to explain his own views.

"I wrote *Martin Eden,* not as an autobiography, nor as a parable of what dire end awaits an unbeliever in God, but as an indictment of that pleasant, wild-beast struggle of Individualism," he writes. Of his own hero, he notes, "He fought for entrance into the bourgeois circles where he expected to find refinement, culture, high-living and high-thinking. He won his way into those circles and was appalled by the colossal, unlovely mediocrity of the bourgeoisie." London concludes, "Being a consistent Individualist, being unaware of the collective human need, there remained nothing for which to live and fight. And so he died." Of course, London's emotional proximity to his individualistic hero undermined any detached, objective view he may have had of him. In the act of writing his novel, he crawled under Eden's skin, situating himself inside his character's tormented head. Reading the novel today, one has the impression that the creator and his character are as one, and that when Eden vanishes beneath the sea, London goes with him.

Indeed, to write *Martin Eden,* London drew on his experiences, emotions, and own morbid state of mind, and it's no wonder that, after years of denying any similarity between the author and his protagonist, he finally admitted in *John Barleycorn* (1913), "I was Martin Eden." Martin, a crude ex-sailor, appears at the start of the novel as a young writer, like London, on his way up in the world. In writing his portrait of the artist as a young man, London recalled his own climb out of obscurity and his dramatic appearance in the pages of American literature. At the same time, when he wrote *Martin Eden,* he created a kind of anti-self. Unlike London, Eden never becomes a socialist or a radical, and, by his own definition, he's a sworn enemy of socialists and socialism. He's London without London's identity as a class-conscious artist who has a sense of solidarity with the working class. By killing off this character, London may have exorcized the demon of suicide, at least temporarily, and prolonged his own life for another seven or so years.

"I am an individualist. I believe the race is to the swift, the battle to the strong," Eden insists in chapter 29, the pivotal political chapter in the novel, in which he argues bitterly with bourgeois representatives of society who see him as a danger and a threat to the established order of things. "I am an individualist," he tells them. "Individualism is the hereditary and eternal foe of socialism." Had London written a realistic novel about himself as an emerging writer, he would have made Eden a socialist. By 1907, London was no longer a young artist. He wrote *Martin Eden* during his tumultuous journey across the Pacific Ocean, aboard the *Snark* and during his stays in various ports of call, and he had already reached the nadir of his involvement in the cause of socialism. A wealthy, successful writer living the bourgeois lifestyle that he had condemned, he had largely withdrawn from active participation in the movement, and the novel reflects his state of mind at that moment.

Martin Eden is not the only character in the novel to commit suicide; Brissenden, a poet and a socialist and one of his closest friends, also takes his own life. Clearly, London had suicide on his mind when he wrote the book.

No aspect of London's life, of course, is more controversial and enigmatic than his death—except perhaps his enigmatic birth, out of wedlock, to a father whose identity he never knew for certain. Did Jack London commit suicide? Critics and biographers—and friends and family members—have debated the issue ever since London's death in 1916. Those who have argued that he did commit suicide have offered, in evidence, the last chapter of *Martin Eden.* Those who believe that he died of natural causes have argued that no correspondence or correlation exists between Martin Eden's end at sea and Jack London's death at home in Glen Ellen.

After all these years, the medical evidence may no longer be helpful to either side in the debate, though it's clear that London's alcoholism led to the failure of his kidneys, and that for months, if not years, he took morphine to alleviate his excruciating pain. That much is certain. But whether he deliberately or accidentally took an overdose, we will never know for sure. Too many doctors hovered over his corpse immediately after his death, and too many of them provided too many conflicting conclusions about the cause of death for any real clarity. London's manservant—the first person on the scene at London's deathbed—claimed he found a piece of paper on which London had calculated the amount of morphine necessary to take his life. Family members rejected the man's testimony, and if the paper ever existed, it has long since disappeared.

Charmian London, his widow, stood to inherit London's property, including the funds in his two hefty life insurance policies, so she clearly had a personal stake in the matter and may well have influenced the experts to say that her husband had died of natural causes, not by his own hand. Ironically, her account of her husband's life presents a compelling case that he did commit suicide, since it describes, in detail, his self-destructiveness, his suicidal state of mind, and his nervous breakdown in 1916. Jack refused to take care of his health, Charmian insists, and refused to stop drinking, though his doctors told him that alcohol would kill him. She even notes that his eating habits—his diet of half-cooked duck—"were nothing less than suicidal."

The facts of London's biography show that he attempted suicide and thought about it frequently. Moreover, a remarkable number of his characters commit suicide; one of his first stories, "One More Unfortunate" (1895), features a suicide by a musical genius and virtuoso violinist who takes his own life by drowning at sea—an incident inspired by London's own near death by drowning. In addition, London made notes for a whole series of stories about suicide. To him, suicide was never entirely an individual act; society, in the form of friends and lovers, often encouraged or aided and abetted the deed.

One of these stories was to be about the suicide of Eleanor Marx (1855–1898), Karl Marx's youngest daughter. Eleanor Marx was an author—of *The Factory Hell* (1885), among other books—and a feminist who took her own life by swallowing poison.

How often London thought about killing himself isn't clear, but his notes, letters, and fiction suggest that he was preoccupied with suicide. In an 1899 letter to Cloudesley Johns he writes about a "drunken attempt at suicide" when he was sixteen, "with the 'blues' heavy upon me." In a subsequent letter, he refers to a time in his life when it "seemed the clouds would never break" and when for "several weeks I meditated profoundly on the policy of shuffling off." In *John Barleycorn,* he writes at length about his attempted suicide at sea at the age of sixteen. There, he places much of the blame on his drinking, which put him, he explains, "in a drug-dream dragging me to death." On that occasion, he writes, suicide seemed "a splendid culmination, a perfect rounding off of my short but exciting career."

In *John Barleycorn,* London also describes an occasion when he had what he called a "desire to die," which doesn't seem to be the same as the desire to commit suicide. "Trying to die isn't like trying to commit suicide—it may actually be harder," the novelist Philip Roth has observed, "because what you are trying to do is what you least want to have happen."

In *John Barleycorn,* London describes, in vivid detail, his own longing for death. On that occasion—he provides no date—he thought that he might unconsciously shoot himself with his own revolver. "So obsessed was I with the desire to die, that I feared I might commit the act in my sleep, and I was compelled to give my revolver away to others who were to lose it for me when my subconscious hand might not find it," he writes. What saved him, he claims, was his belief in socialism and his faith in "the PEOPLE." "Love, socialism, The PEOPLE—healthy figments of man's mind—were the things that cured and saved me." By 1907, when he wrote *Martin Eden,* he had lost much of that faith, and in 1916, even more so, as evidenced by his resignation, eight months before his death, from the Socialist Party.

It seems possible, perhaps even likely, that on the last day of his life, London took so much morphine that he could no longer judge how much more he could safely take. One can't help but wonder, too, if on some level he thought, as he had thought earlier, that suicide would provide "a splendid culmination, a perfect rounding off of my short but exciting career."

If you aren't persuaded by any of these arguments, read the last, luscious chapter of *Martin Eden.* Here, London orchestrates the major themes of the novel beautifully—success and failure, strength and weakness, love and loss—and reintroduces, for one last time, many of the main characters—Martin's comrade Joe, and Lizzie, the working-class girl who loves him for who he is. All the details come together in this chapter. Fittingly, too, he mentions Nietzsche, whose work and whose life fascinated him, and he quotes a long passage from a poem by Swinburne, whose work he had long revered.

London captures perfectly Martin Eden's sense of existential dread: his feeling that he belongs nowhere and to no one. Alienated and alone in the universe, he makes his farewells, says goodbye to life. A stranger hands him "a bunch" of "socialist propaganda," but it has no appeal, and it cannot dissuade him from his path. He thinks about writing a suicide note and decides he doesn't have the time. One of his last thoughts before he submerges himself in the sea is that "there was no truth in anything, no truth in truth—no such thing as truth."

Read the chapter, and see if it doesn't convince you that London, the disillusioned socialist, took his own life. The text itself is compelling. As D. H. Lawrence (1885–1930) noted wisely in *Studies in Classic American Literature* (1923), "Never trust the artist. Trust the tale."

The last chapter of *Martin Eden* reads like London's own last will and testament. •

"Say, Joe," was his greeting to his old-time working-mate next morning, "there's a Frenchman out on Twenty-eighth Street. He's made a pot of money, and he's going back to France. It's a dandy, well-appointed, small steam laundry. There's a start for you if you want to settle down. Here, take this; buy some clothes with it and be at this man's office by ten o'clock. He looked up the laundry for me, and he'll take you out and show you around. If you like it, and think it is worth the price—twelve thousand—let me know and it is yours. Now run along. I'm busy. I'll see you later."

"Now look here, Mart," the other said slowly, with kindling anger, "I come here this mornin' to see you. Savve? I didn't come here to get no laundry. I come here for a talk for old friends' sake, and you shove a laundry at me. I tell you what you can do. You can take that laundry an' go to hell."

He was starting to fling out of the room when Martin caught him and whirled him around.

"Now look here, Joe," he said; "if you act that way, I'll punch your head. And for old friends' sake I'll punch it hard. Savve?—you will, will you?"

Joe had clinched and attempted to throw him, and he was twisting and writhing out of the advantage of the other's hold. They reeled about the room, locked in each other's arms, and came down with a crash across the splintered wreckage of a wicker chair. Joe was underneath, with arms spread out and held and with Martin's knee on his chest. He was panting and gasping for breath when Martin released him.

"Now we'll talk a moment," Martin said. "You can't get fresh with me. I want that laundry business finished first of all. Then you can come back and we'll talk for old sake's sake. I told you I was busy. Look at that."

A servant had just come in with the morning mail, a great mass of letters and magazines.

"How can I wade through that and talk with you? You go and fix up that laundry, and then we'll get together."

"All right," Joe admitted reluctantly. "I thought you was turnin' me down, but I guess I was mistaken. But you can't lick me, Mart, in a stand-up fight. I've got the reach on you."

"We'll put on the gloves sometime and see," Martin said with a smile.

"Sure; as soon as I get that laundry going." Joe extended his arm. "You see that reach? It'll make you go a few."

Martin heaved a sigh of relief when the door closed behind the laundryman. He was becoming anti-social. Daily he found it a severer strain to be decent with people. Their presence perturbed him, and the effort of conversation irritated him. They made him restless, and no sooner was he in contact with them than he was casting about for excuses to get rid of them.

He did not proceed to attack his mail, and for a half hour he lolled in his chair, doing nothing, while no more than vague, half-formed thoughts occasionally filtered through his intelligence, or rather, at wide intervals, themselves constituted the flickering of his intelligence.

He roused himself and began glancing through his mail. There were a dozen requests for autographs—he knew them at sight; there were professional begging letters; and there were letters from cranks, ranging from the man with a working model of perpetual motion, and the man who demonstrated that the surface of the earth was the inside of a hollow sphere, to the man seeking financial aid to purchase the Peninsula of Lower California for the purpose of communist colonization. There were letters from women seeking to know him, and over one such he smiled, for enclosed was her receipt for pew-rent, sent as evidence of her good faith and as proof of her respectability.

Editors and publishers contributed to the daily heap of letters, the former on their knees for his manuscripts, the latter on their knees for his books—his poor disdained manuscripts that had kept all he possessed in pawn for so many dreary months in order to find them in postage. There were unexpected checks for English serial rights and for advance payments on foreign translations. His English agent announced the sale of German translation rights in three of his books, and informed him that Swedish editions, from which he could expect nothing because Sweden was not a party to the Berne Convention, were already on the market. Then there was a nominal request for his permission for a Russian translation, that country being likewise outside the Berne Convention.

He turned to the huge bundle of clippings which had come in from his press bureau, and read about himself and his vogue, which had become a furore. All his creative output had been flung to the public in one magnificent sweep. That seemed to account for it. He had taken the public off its feet, the way Kipling had, that time when he lay near to death and all the mob, animated by a mob-mind thought, began suddenly to read him. Martin remembered how that same world-mob, having read him and acclaimed him and not understood him in the least, had, abruptly, a few months later, flung itself upon him and torn him to pieces. Martin grinned at the thought. Who was he that he should not be similarly treated in a few more months? Well, he would fool the mob. He would be away, in the South Seas, building his grass house, trading for pearls and copra, jumping reefs in frail outriggers, catching sharks and bonitas, hunting wild goats among the cliffs of the valley that lay next to the valley of Taiohae.

In the moment of that thought the desperateness of his situation dawned upon him. He saw, cleared eyed, that he was in the Valley of the Shadow. All the life that was in him was fading, fainting, making toward death. He realized how much he slept, and how much he desired to sleep. Of old, he had hated sleep. It had robbed him of precious moments of living. Four hours of sleep in the twenty-four had meant being robbed of four hours of life. How he had grudged sleep! Now it was life he grudged. Life was not good; its taste in his mouth was without tang, and bitter. This was his peril. Life that did not yearn toward life was in fair way toward ceasing. Some remote instinct for preservation stirred in him, and he knew he must get away. He glanced about the room, and the thought of packing was burdensome. Perhaps it would be better to leave that to the last. In the meantime he might be getting an outfit.

He put on his hat and went out, stopping in at a gun-store, where he spent the remainder of the morning buying automatic rifles, ammunition, and fishing tackle. Fashions changed in trading, and he knew he would have to wait till he reached Tahiti before ordering his trade-goods. They could come up from Australia, anyway. This solution was a source of pleasure. He had avoided doing something, and the doing of anything just now was unpleasant. He went back to the hotel gladly, with a feeling of satisfaction in that the comfortable Morris chair was waiting for him; and he groaned inwardly, on entering his room, at sight of Joe in the Morris chair.

Joe was delighted with the laundry. Everything was settled, and he would enter into possession next day. Martin lay on the bed, with closed eyes, while the other talked on. Martin's thoughts were far away—so far away that he was rarely aware that he was thinking. It was only by an effort that he occasionally responded. And yet this was Joe, whom he had always liked. But Joe was too keen with life. The boisterous impact of it on Martin's jaded mind was a hurt. It was an aching probe to his tired sensitiveness. When Joe reminded him that sometime in the future they were going to put on the gloves together, he could almost have screamed.

"Remember, Joe, you're to run the laundry according to those old rules you used to lay down at Shelly Hot Springs," he said. "No overworking. No working at night. And no children at the mangles. No children anywhere. And a fair wage."

Joe nodded and pulled out a note-book.

"Look at here. I was workin' out them rules before breakfast this A.M. What d'ye think of them?"

He read them aloud, and Martin approved, worrying at the same time as to when Joe would take himself off.

It was late afternoon when he awoke. Slowly the fact of life came back to him. He glanced about the room. Joe had evidently stolen away after he had dozed off. That was considerate of Joe, he thought. Then he closed his eyes and slept again.

In the days that followed Joe was too busy organizing and taking hold of the laundry to bother him much; and it was not until the day before sailing that the newspapers made the announcement that he had taken passage on the *Mariposa*. Once, when the instinct of preservation fluttered, he went to a doctor and underwent a searching physical examination. Nothing could be found the matter with him. His heart and lungs were pronounced magnificent. Every organ, so far as the doctor could know, was normal and was working normally.

"There is nothing the matter with you, Mr. Eden," he said, "positively nothing the matter with you. You are in the pink of condition. Candidly, I envy you your health. It is superb. Look at that chest. There, and in your stomach, lies the secret of your remarkable constitution. Physically, you are a man in a thousand—in ten thousand. Barring accidents, you should live to be a hundred."

And Martin knew that Lizzie's diagnosis had been correct. Physically he was all right. It was his "think-machine" that had gone wrong, and there was no cure for that except to get away to the South Seas. The trouble was that now, on the verge of departure, he had no desire to go. The South Seas charmed him no more than did bourgeois civilization. There was no zest in the thought of departure, while the act of departure appalled him as a weariness of the flesh. He would have felt better if he were already on board and gone.

The last day was a sore trial. Having read of his sailing in the morning papers, Bernard Higginbotham, Gertrude, and all the family came to say good-by, as did Hermann von Schmidt and Marian. Then there was business to be transacted, bills to be paid, and everlasting reporters to be endured. He said good-by to Lizzie Connolly, abruptly, at the entrance to night school, and hurried away. At the hotel he found Joe, too busy all day with the laundry to have come to him earlier. It was the last straw, but Martin gripped the arms of his chair and talked and listened for half an hour.

"You know, Joe," he said, "that you are not tied down to that laundry. There are no strings on it. You can sell it any time and blow the money. Any time you get sick of it and want to hit the road, just pull out. Do what will make you the happiest."

Joe shook his head.

"No more road in mine, thank you kindly. Hoboin's all right, exceptin' for one thing—the girls. I can't help it, but I'm a ladies' man. I can't get along without 'em, and you've got to get along without 'em when you're hoboin'. The times I've passed by houses where dances an' parties was goin' on, an' heard the women laugh, an' saw their white dresses and smiling faces through the windows—Gee! I tell you them moments was plain hell. I like dancin' an' picnics, an' walking in the moonlight, an' all the rest too well. Me for the laundry, and a good front, with big iron dollars clinkin' in my jeans. I seen a girl already, just yesterday, and, d'ye know, I'm feelin' already I'd just as soon marry her as not. I've ben whistlin' all day at the thought of it. She's a beaut, with the kindest eyes and softest voice you ever heard. Me for her, you can stack on that. Say, why don't you get married with all this money to burn? You could get the finest girl in the land."

Martin shook his head with a smile, but in his secret heart he was wondering why any man wanted to marry. It seemed an amazing and incomprehensible thing.

From the deck of the *Mariposa,* at the sailing hour, he saw Lizzie Connolly hiding on the skirts of the crowd on the wharf. Take her with you, came the thought. It is easy to be kind. She will be supremely happy. It was almost a temptation one moment, and the succeeding moment it became a terror. He was in a panic at the thought of it. His tired soul cried out in protest. He turned away from the rail with a groan, muttering, "Man, you are too sick, you are too sick."

He fled to his stateroom, where he lurked until the steamer was clear of the dock. In the dining saloon, at luncheon, he found himself in the place of honor, at the captain's right; and he was not long in discovering that he was the great man on board. But no more unsatisfactory great man ever sailed on a ship. He spent the afternoon in a deck-chair, with closed eyes, dozing brokenly most of the time, and in the evening went early to bed.

After the second day, recovered from seasickness, the full passenger list was in evidence, and the more he saw of the passengers the more he disliked them. Yet he knew that he did them injustice. They were good and kindly people, he forced himself to acknowledge, and in the moment of acknowledgment he qualified — good and kindly like all the bourgeoisie, with all the psychological cramp and intellectual futility of their kind. They bored him when they talked with him, their little superficial minds were so filled with emptiness; while the boisterous high spirits and the excessive energy of the younger people shocked him. They were never quiet, ceaselessly playing deck-quoits, tossing rings, promenading, or rushing to the rail with loud cries to watch the leaping porpoises and the first schools of flying fish.

He slept much. After breakfast he sought his deck-chair with a magazine he never finished. The printed pages tired him. He puzzled that men found so much to write about, and, puzzling, dozed in his chair. When the gong awoke him for luncheon, he was irritated that he must awaken. There was no satisfaction in being awake.

Once, he tried to arouse himself from his lethargy, and went forward into the forecastle with the sailors. But the breed of sailors seemed to have changed since the days he had lived in the forecastle. He could find no kinship with these stolid-faced, ox-minded bestial creatures. He was in despair. Up above nobody had wanted Martin Eden for his own sake, and he could not go back to those of his own class who had wanted him in the past. He did not want them. He could not stand them any more than he could stand the stupid first-cabin passengers and the riotous young people.

Life was to him like strong, white light that hurts the tired eyes of a sick person. During every conscious moment life blazed in a raw glare around him and upon him. It hurt. It hurt intolerably. It was the first time in his life that Martin had travelled first class. On ships at sea he had always been in the forecastle, the steerage, or in the black depths of the coal-hold, passing coal. In those days, climbing up the iron ladders from out the pit of stifling heat, he had often caught glimpses of the passengers, in cool white, doing nothing but enjoy themselves, under awnings spread to keep the sun and wind away from them, with subservient stewards taking care of their every want and whim, and it had seemed to him that the realm in which they moved and had their being was nothing else than paradise. Well, here he was, the great man on board, in the midmost centre of it, sitting at the captain's right hand, and yet vainly harking back to forecastle and stoke-hole in quest of the Paradise he had lost. He had found no new one, and now he could not find the old one.

He strove to stir himself and find something to interest him. He ventured the petty officers' mess, and was glad to get away. He talked with a quartermaster off duty, an intelligent man who promptly prodded him with the socialist propaganda and forced into his hands a bunch of leaflets and pamphlets. He listened to the man expounding the slave-morality, and as he listened, he thought languidly of his own Nietzsche philosophy. But what was it worth, after all? He remembered one of Nietzsche's mad utterances wherein that madman had doubted truth. And who was to say? Perhaps Nietzsche had been right. Perhaps there was no truth in anything, no truth in truth — no such thing as truth. But his mind wearied quickly, and he was content to go back to his chair and doze.

Miserable as he was on the steamer, a new misery came upon him. What when the steamer reached Tahiti? He would have to go ashore. He would have to order his trade-goods, to find a passage on a schooner to the Marquesas, to do a thousand and one things that were awful to contemplate. Whenever he steeled himself deliberately to think, he could see the desperate peril in which he stood. In all truth, he was in the Valley of the Shadow, and his danger lay in that he was not afraid. If he were only afraid, he would make toward life. Being unafraid, he was drifting deeper into the shadow. He found no delight in the old familiar things of life. The *Mariposa* was now in the northeast trades, and this wine of wind, surging against him, irritated him. He had his chair moved to escape the embrace of this lusty comrade of old days and nights.

The day the *Mariposa* entered the doldrums, Martin was more miserable than ever. He could no longer sleep. He was soaked with sleep, and perforce he must now stay awake and endure the white glare of life. He moved about restlessly. The air was sticky and humid, and the rain-squalls were unrefreshing. He ached with life. He walked around the deck until that hurt too much, then sat in his chair until he was compelled to walk again. He forced himself at last to finish the magazine, and from the steamer library he culled several volumes of poetry. But they could not hold him, and once more he took to walking.

He stayed late on deck, after dinner, but that did not help him, for when he went below, he could not sleep. This surcease from life had failed him. It was too much. He turned on the electric light and tried to read. One of the volumes was a Swinburne. He lay in bed, glancing through its pages, until suddenly he became aware that he was reading with interest. He finished the stanza, attempted to read on, then came back to it. He rested the book face downward on his breast and fell to thinking. That was it. The very thing. Strange that it had never come to him before. That was the meaning of it all; he had been drifting that way all the time, and now Swinburne showed him that it was the happy way out. He wanted rest, and here was rest awaiting him. He glanced at the open port-hole. Yes, it was large enough. For the first time in weeks he felt happy. At last he had discovered the cure of his ill. He picked up the book and read the stanza slowly aloud: —

> "'From too much love of living,
>   From hope and fear set free,
> We thank with brief thanksgiving
>   Whatever gods may be
> That no life lives forever;
> That dead men rise up never;
>   That even the weariest river
>   Winds somewhere safe to sea.'"

He looked again at the open port. Swinburne had furnished the key. Life was ill, or, rather, it had become ill — an unbearable thing. "That dead men rise up never!"

That line stirred him with a profound feeling of gratitude. It was the one beneficent thing in the universe. When life became an aching weariness, death was ready to soothe away to everlasting sleep. But what was he waiting for? It was time to go.

He arose and thrust his head out the port-hole, looking down into the milky wash. The *Mariposa* was deeply loaded, and, hanging by his hands, his feet would be in the water. He could slip in noiselessly. No one would hear. A smother of spray dashed up, wetting his face. It tasted salt on his lips, and the taste was good. He wondered if he ought to write a swan-song, but laughed the thought away. There was no time. He was too impatient to be gone.

Turning off the light in his room so that it might not betray him, he went out the port-hole feet first. His shoulders stuck, and he forced himself back so as to try it with one arm down by his side. A roll of the steamer aided him, and he was through, hanging by his hands. When his feet touched the sea, he let go. He was in a milky froth of water. The side of the *Mariposa* rushed past him like a dark wall, broken here and there by lighted ports. She was certainly making time. Almost before he knew it, he was astern, swimming gently on the foam-crackling surface.

A bonita struck at his white body, and he laughed aloud. It had taken a piece out, and the sting of it reminded him of why he was there. In the work to do he had forgotten the purpose of it. The lights of the *Mariposa* were growing dim in the distance, and there he was, swimming confidently, as though it were his intention to make for the nearest land a thousand miles or so away.

It was the automatic instinct to live. He ceased swimming, but the moment he felt the water rising above his mouth the hands struck out sharply with a lifting movement. The will to live, was his thought, and the thought was accompanied by a sneer. Well, he had will,—ay, will strong enough that with one last exertion it could destroy itself and cease to be.

He changed his position to a vertical one. He glanced up at the quiet stars, at the same time emptying his lungs of air. With swift, vigorous propulsion of hands and feet, he lifted his shoulders and half his chest out of water. This was to gain impetus for the descent. Then he let himself go and sank without movement, a white statue, into the sea. He breathed in the water deeply, deliberately, after the manner of a man taking an anaesthetic. When he strangled, quite involuntarily his arms and legs clawed the water and drove him up to the surface and into the clear sight of the stars.

The will to live, he thought disdainfully, vainly endeavoring not to breathe the air into his bursting lungs. Well, he would have to try a new way. He filled his lungs with air, filled them full. This supply would take him far down. He turned over and went down head first, swimming with all his strength and all his will. Deeper and deeper he went. His eyes were open, and he watched the ghostly, phosphorescent trails of the darting bonita. As he swam, he hoped that they would not strike at him, for it might snap the tension of his will. But they did not strike, and he found time to be grateful for this last kindness of life.

Down, down, he swam till his arms and legs grew tired and hardly moved. He knew that he was deep. The pressure on his ear-drums was a pain, and there was a buzzing in his head. His endurance was faltering, but he compelled his arms and legs to drive him deeper until his will snapped and the air drove from his lungs in a great explosive rush. The bubbles rubbed and bounded like tiny balloons against his cheeks and eyes as they took their upward flight. Then came pain and strangulation. This hurt was not death, was the thought that oscillated through his reeling consciousness. Death did not hurt. It was life, the pangs of life, this awful, suffocating feeling; it was the last blow life could deal him.

His willful hands and feet began to beat and churn about, spasmodically and feebly. But he had fooled them and the will to live that made them beat and churn. He was too deep down. They could never bring him to the surface. He seemed floating languidly in a sea of dreamy vision. Colors and radiances surrounded him and bathed him and pervaded him. What was that? It seemed a lighthouse; but it was inside his brain — a flashing, bright white light. It flashed swifter and swifter. There was a long rumble of sound, and it seemed to him that he was falling down a vast and interminable stairway. And somewhere at the bottom he fell into darkness. That much he knew. He had fallen into darkness. And at the instant he knew, he ceased to know.

If Japan Wakens China

First published in and reprinted from *Sunset,* December 1909.

The military defeat of Russia by the Japanese in the Russian-Japanese War alerted London to the military prowess of the Japanese and to the Japanese threat to American hegemony, and in 1904 he published a provocative essay in the *San Francisco Examiner* entitled "The Yellow Peril." He returned to the theme of the "yellow peril" in 1909 in "If Japan Wakens China," an essay in which he urges Americans to recognize the dangers posed by an alliance between the Japanese and the Chinese. Of course, such an alliance was unlikely. For centuries, Japan and China had been enemies, and in the twentieth century, they would continue to be enemies. Japan invaded China in the 1930s, and the Chinese fought fiercely to free their country from Japanese occupation. But London seems to have enjoyed conjuring up all kinds of fears. Indeed, fear acted as a catalyst for his imagination, and he could almost always be counted on to imagine the worst of all possible worlds. In his 1915 novel *The Scarlet Plague*, he creates a post-apocalyptic world in which humanity has been decimated by a global pandemic and lives in scattered tribes.

This essay begins on a note of compassion. London explains that the true artist has the ability "to get out of himself and into the soul of another man, thus enabling him to look at life out of that man's eyes and from that man's point of view—to be that man, in short." London did just that in many of his novels and stories. He transcended himself and put himself in the place of others unlike himself. He even looked out at the world through the eyes of a dog in *The Call of the Wild*. But for the most part, he could not see the world from the eyes of the Japanese or the Chinese. His ability to empathize did not extend to non-white races, though in "The Mexican," a late short story, he empathizes with the main character, a Mexican boxer and revolutionary.

Americans do not know the Japanese or the Chinese, London insists in "If Japan Wakens China." Moreover, if Americans believe that Asians think as Americans think, they are greatly mistaken. To argue his point, he turns to the life and writings of Lafcadio Hearn, a westerner who lived in Japan for much of his life and who concluded, after decades of observation and study, that he would never understand the "mysterious eyes of Asia, which had baffled him as they have baffled the men of the West from the days of Marco Polo to this our day." London allows that the Japanese soul may be superior to the western soul. He admires the Japanese ability to borrow and adapt western technology and industry. But he's also alarmed by the idea that a Japanese Napoleon might come to power and, with the backing of Chinese industry and labor, forge an empire. Then, American markets and American military prowess will be jeopardized, he insists. To prevent that day from arriving, he asks Americans to wake from their reverie.

Apparently no one in the movement, or outside it, confronted him directly about his racist ideas vis-à-vis the Japanese, though Emma Goldman might have. She certainly saw the Japanese differently than he. In 1907 in her magazine *Mother Earth,* she published the platform of the Social Revolutionary Party of Japanese in America, and she reached out to the Japanese anarchists she met on her speaking tours. Of course, London published his ideas about race outside radical magazines—in *Sunset* magazine, for example—and often in California, where racist ideas about the Japanese and the Chinese abounded in the early twentieth century.

The phrase "eyes of Asia" would provide a tentative title for London's last novel, which remained uncompleted at his death and was published under the title *Cherry* in 1999 in the *Jack London Journal.* •

When one man does not understand another man's mental processes, how can the one forecast the other's future actions? This is precisely the situation today between the white race and the Japanese. In spite of all our glib talk to the contrary, we know nothing (and less than nothing in so far as we think we know something), of the Japanese. It is a weakness of man to believe that all the rest of mankind is moulded in his own image, and it is a weakness of the white race to believe that the Japanese think as we think, are moved to action as we are moved and have points of view similar to our own.

Perhaps the one white man in the world best fitted by nature and opportunity to know the Japanese was Lafcadio Hearn. To begin with, he was an artist, and he possessed to an extreme degree the artist's sympathy. By this I mean that his sympathy was of that order that permits a man to get out of himself and into the soul of another man, thus enabling him to look at life out of that man's eyes and from that man's point of view — to be that man, in short.

Lafcadio Hearn went to Japan. He identified himself with the Japanese. To all intents and purposes he became a Japanese. A professor in a Japanese university, he took to himself a Japanese wife, lived in a Japanese household, and even renounced his own country and became a Japanese citizen. Being an artist, enthusiastically in touch with his subject, he proceeded to interpret the Japanese mind to the English-speaking world, turning out the most wonderful series of books on Japan ever written by an Occidental. The years passed, and ever he turned out more of his wonderful books, interpreting, explaining, elaborating, formulating, every big aspect and minute detail of the Japanese mind.

Just at the beginning of the Russo-Japanese war, full of years and wise with much experience, Lafcadio Hearn died. His last book was in the press, and it appeared shortly afterward. It was entitled "Japan: An Interpretation." In the foreward Lafcadio Hearn made a confession. He said that after all his years of intimate living with the Japanese, he was at last just on the verge of beginning to understand the Japanese. And he felt justified in this belief, by virtue of the fact that he had taken all those years to find out that he knew nothing of the Japanese. This was a hopeful sign. He had come farther than other white men, who still believed that they did know something, in greater or less degree, of the Japanese.

As for himself, after the many years of thinking, he knew, he frankly confessed, that the Japanese mind baffled him. He told of the Japanese schoolboys with whom he had been in daily contact—of how he had watched their minds unfold and expand as they grew into manhood. And then he sadly explained that now that they were men, Japanese men, out in the world of Japanese men, they were strangers to him. Oh, they greeted him, and shook hands with him and talked with him as of yore; but they were soul-strangers to him. He looked into their faces, but not into their souls. He saw their eyes, but no glimmering could he catch of what went on behind those eyes. Their mental processes were veiled to him. Why they did this or that or some other action was a puzzle to him. He found them actuated by motives he could not guess—motives generated in the labyrinths of their minds where he could not follow the process. Life appeared to them in perspective differently from the way it appeared to him. And he could get no inkling of that perspective. To him it was an inconceivable fourth dimension. And so he wrote that last sad foreward to the last sad book of his, gazing mournfully the while into the mysterious eyes of Asia, which had baffled him as they have baffled the men of the West from the days of Marco Polo to this our day.

The point that I have striven to make is that much of the reasoning of the white race about the Japanese is erroneous, because it is based on fancied knowledge of the stuff and fiber of the Japanese mind. An American lady of my acquaintance, after residing for months in Japan, in response to a query as to how she liked the Japanese, said: "They have no souls."

In this she was wrong. The Japanese are just as much possessed of soul as she and the rest of her race. And far be it from me to infer that the Japanese soul is in the smallest way inferior to the Western soul. It may be even superior. You see, we do not know the Japanese soul, and what its value may be in the scheme of things. And yet that American lady's remark but emphasizes the point. So different was the Japanese soul from hers, so unutterably alien, so absolutely without any kinship or means of communication, that to her there was no slightest sign of its existence.

Japan, in her remarkable evolution, has repeatedly surprised the world. Now the element of surprise can be present only when one is unfamiliar with the data that go to constitute the surprise. Had we really known the Japanese, we should not have been surprised. And as she has surprised us in the past, and only the other day, may she not surprise us tomorrow and in the days that are yet to be? And since she may surprise us in the future, and since ignorance is the meat and wine of surprise, who are we, and with what second sight are we invested, that we may calmly say: "Surprise is all very well, but there is not going to be any Yellow peril or Japanese peril"?

There are forty-five million Japanese in the world. There are over four hundred million Chinese. That is to say, if we add together the various branches of the white race, the English, the French, and the German, the Austrian, the Scandinavian and the white Russian, the Latins as well, the Americans, the Canadians, Australians and New Zealanders, the South Africans, the Anglo-Indians, and all the scattered remnants of us, we shall find that we are still outnumbered by the combined Japanese and Chinese.

We understand the Chinese mind no more than we do the Japanese. What if these two races, as homogenous as we, should embark on some vast race-adventure? There have been race adventures in the past. We English-speaking peoples are just now in the midst of our own great adventure. We are dreaming as all race-adventurers have dreamed. And who will dare to say that in the Japanese mind is not burning some colossal Napoleonic dream? And what if the dreams clash?

Japan is the one unique Asiatic race, in that alone among the races of Asia, she has been able to borrow from us and equip herself with all our material achievement. Our machinery of warfare, of commerce, and of industry she has made hers. And so well has she done it that we have been surprised. We did not think she had it in her. Next consider China. We of the West have tried, and tried vainly, to awaken her. We have failed to express our material achievements in terms comprehensible to the Chinese mind. We do not know the Chinese mind. But Japan does. She and China spring from the same primitive stock—their languages are rooted in the same primitive tongue; and their mental processes are the same. The Chinese mind may baffle us, but it cannot baffle the Japanese. And what if Japan awakens China—not to our dream, if you please, but to her dream, to Japan's dream? Japan, having taken from us all our material achievement, is alone able to transmute that material achievement in terms intelligible to the Chinese mind.

The Chinese and Japanese are thrifty and industrious. China possesses great natural resources of coal and iron—and coal and iron constitute the backbone of machine civilization. When four hundred and fifty million of the best workers in the world go into manufacturing, a new competitor, and a most ominous and formidable one, will enter the arena where the races struggle for the world-market. Here is the race-adventure—the first clashing of the Asiatic dream with ours. It is true, it is only an economic clash, but economic clashes always precede clashes at arms. And what then? Oh, only that will-o'-the-wisp, the Yellow peril. But to the Russian, Japan was only a will-o'-the-wisp until one day, with fire and steel, she smashed the great adventure of the Russian and punctured the bubble-dream he was dreaming. Of this be sure: If ever the day comes that our dreams clash with that of the Yellow and the Brown, and our particular bubble-dream is punctured, there will be one country at least unsurprised, and that country will be Russia. She was awakened from her dream. We still are dreaming.

Burning Daylight, Part II, Chapter 8

First published serially in the *New York Herald,* June–August 1910; reprinted from *Burning Daylight* (New York: Macmillan, 1910).

London returned repeatedly to the same basic themes in almost all his work. Time and again, he tackled the subject of the lone protagonist thrown into an unfamiliar, hostile environment, and how he or she survived and even thrived under adversity. Usually, the hero was London himself, thinly disguised, or a projection of the man, woman, or beast he might like to be, at least in his imagination and on the printed page. The adversarial environment might be the Arctic or the South Seas, a war or a revolution, the city or the country, the road or the prison, the brutal boxing ring, or the polite middle-class drawing room. London's variations on the theme were ingenious, and seemed endless. The battle went on and on.

Still, London liked to think that with each new book, he turned a new leaf, creating a work totally unlike any previous. Indeed, he seems to have been delighted to change direction, abruptly, in *Burning Daylight* (1910). In this novel, which he began to write in Ecuador and finished in California, he created his first capitalist hero. Elam Harnish, also known as "Burning Daylight" because of his boundless energy, is a Yukon gold miner who becomes a multimillionaire; he then turns into a reckless financier and a business tycoon in New York and the San Francisco Bay Area, finally settling in Sonoma County. Daylight is also London's first hero to embrace rural living. As a capitalist, he is the exception that proves the rule about capitalism as a rapacious economic system; indeed, all the other capitalists in the novel—especially the New Yorkers—are deceitful, corrupt, and hideous human beings. Daylight, by contrast, is a capitalist who learns to love and who tries his best to distribute his wealth to the poor. He's a liberated male who once regarded woman as "toy, harpy, wife and mother," but who comes to appreciate her as "comrade and playfellow and joyfellow." In creating Daylight, London seems to have reconciled his radical political ideology with his financial success. Elam Harnish is yet another incarnation of Jack London himself: London as husband, lover, rural landowner, and shrewd opportunist.

Like London, Daylight discovers the beauty of Sonoma County, retiring there with Dede Mason, his feisty, feminist secretary, who agrees to marry him only after a long, arduous courtship. Dede Mason brings out Daylight's feminine side, and the novel—largely sentimental and romantic—reads much like the popular women's fiction of the day. At its best, it's reminiscent of an Edith Wharton novel, only with Californians, not New Yorkers, in the major roles. (London admired Wharton's work and would have liked to write like her.) In the end, Daylight gets the girl of his dreams and still keeps his wealth, while Dede wins a husband and keeps her antimaterialist principles intact. This happy ending was guaranteed to please bourgeois readers, though anarchists such as Emma Goldman also praised its back-to-the-land theme.

In *Burning Daylight,* no major character commits suicide or murder, goes to jail, or falls on hard times. London does write about "the abyss," but this time it's "the abyss of sex." He explores human sexuality, and the scenes that describe Daylight and Dede on horseback are sensual and erotic.

London would soon read and praise D. H. Lawrence's controversial 1913 novel *Sons and Lovers.* In a telegram to Mitchell Kennerley, Lawrence's publisher, he wrote, generously, "No book like it. Splendid, sad, tremendous, true. It sweeps one off his feet with the powerful human impact of it. In it are the heart and hurt of life. All that is sordid. All that is noble, all blend together, in the flux of contradictoriness that is sweet warm frail palpitant human. Mail me all his other books and send bill." In *The Valley of the Moon* (1913), London would do his best to write a modern love story, à la D. H. Lawrence, that included an abortion by the novel's heroine—a daring theme in those days, and perhaps even in our own day.

Daylight—afraid at first to think about sex—turns into a sexually aware male animal; he also discovers poetry and music. In Sonoma County, he and Dede—like Adam and Eve in the garden—do not have to labor at anything, but "lent a hand to nature." Crops seem to grow on their own and to harvest themselves, as in a workers' paradise.

To create his main characters, London drew on himself and on Charmian Kittredge. Like London, Daylight worships "at the shrine of self," and then, like London, he discovers it's a hollow shrine. The scenes in which Daylight first explores Sonoma Mountain and the Valley of the Moon, on horseback, capture London's joy and elation in the midst of untrammeled nature. Daylight is an archetypal figure—an American Adam who is innocent, cheerful, and unspoiled. Sonoma County serves as his Eden; he wanders across a landscape absent of human beings, naming the plants, the trees, and the animals—the lilies, the oaks, the manzanita, the redwoods, the rabbits, the squirrels, and the deer. In a cultivated garden, he walks freely, picking and eating strawberries and peas to his heart's content. In a sense, he's the opposite of Martin Eden, who *falls* from paradise. Daylight wanders *into* a Garden of Eden.

In the Yukon—his inferno—Daylight witnesses the "vast devastation" of the environment in which every man works for himself and "the result was chaos." As a miner, he takes a part in that devastation. Now, in Sonoma County, he sees nature in a near-pristine state—"virgin wild," he calls it—and on his horseback journey across the landscape he also recognizes the possibility for his own personal redemption. Of course, as Professor Greg

Sarris, the Native American author of *Grand Avenue* (1994) and *Watermelon Nights* (1998) and a Sonoma County resident, has pointed out, the land wasn't "virgin wild." Native Americans had lived there for thousands of years and had created a rich and complex culture. In 1910, Sonoma County was still home to Native Americans, but Jack London does not acknowledge their presence or history in Sonoma County.

For London, as for the English romantic poets and the nineteenth-century American writers who celebrated "the virgin land" of the New World, nature was a force to be worshipped. Indeed, in *Burning Daylight*, the main character experiences a religious conversion in the woods. He feels a "holy calm" and has a sense that he is spiritually cleansed. He also realizes that birth and death, decay and rebirth are part of the cycle of nature. In naturalistic detail, Daylight describes the woods, the meadows, the valleys, and the flora and the fauna. He doesn't turn the flowers and the trees or the landscape itself into symbols. Like all good naturalists, he describes things as they are. The California lily that Daylight returns to again and again may make him think of purity and love, but it's first and foremost a lily. In this section from chapter 8, he looks back at San Francisco from the top of Sonoma Mountain and sees "smoke" and "haze"—the signs of the industrial world he has left behind. •

Daylight's coming to civilization had not improved him. True, he wore better clothes, had learned slightly better manners, and spoke better English. As a gambler and a man-trampler he had developed remarkable efficiency. Also, he had become used to a higher standard of living, and he had whetted his wits to razor sharpness in the fierce complicated struggle of fighting males. But he had hardened, and at the expense of his old time, whole-souled geniality. Of the essential refinements of civilization he knew nothing. He did not know they existed. He had become cynical, bitter, and brutal. Power had its effect on him that it had on all men. Suspicious of the big exploiters, despising the fools of the exploited herd, he had faith only in himself. This led to an undue and erroneous exaltation of his ego, while kindly considerations of others—nay, even simple respect—was destroyed, until naught was left for him but to worship at the shrine of self. . . . One week-end, feeling heavy and depressed and tired of the city and its ways, he obeyed the impulse of a whim that was later to play an important part in his life. The desire to get out of the city for a whiff of country air and for a change of scene was the cause. Yet, to himself, he made the excuse of going to Glen Ellen for the purpose of inspecting the brickyard with which Holdsworthy had gold-bricked him.

He spent the night in the little country hotel, and on Sunday morning, astride a saddle-horse rented from the Glen Ellen butcher, rode out of the village. The brickyard was close at hand on the flat beside the Sonoma Creek. The kilns were visible among the trees, when he glanced to the left and caught sight of a cluster of wooded knolls half a mile away, perched on the rolling slopes of Sonoma Mountain. The mountain, itself wooded, towered behind. The trees on the knolls seemed to beckon to him. The dry, early-summer air, shot through with sunshine, was wine to him. Unconsciously he drank it in in deep breaths. The prospect of the brickyard was uninviting. He was jaded with all things business, and the wooded knolls were calling to him. A horse was between his legs—a good horse, he decided; one that sent him back to the cayuses he had ridden during his eastern Oregon boyhood. He had been somewhat of a rider in those early days, and the champ of the bit and creak of saddle-leather sounded good to him now.

Resolving to have his fun first, and to look over the brickyard afterward, he rode on up the hill, prospecting for a way across country to get to the knolls. He left the country road at the first gate he came to and cantered through a hayfield. The grain was waist-high on either side of the wagon road, and he sniffed the warm aroma of it with delighted nostrils. Larks flew up before him, and from everywhere came mellow notes. From the appearance of the road it was patent that it had been used for hauling clay to the now idle brickyard. Salving his conscience with the idea that this was part of the inspection, he rode on to the clay-pit—a huge scar in a hillside. But he did not linger long, swinging off again to the left and leaving the road. Not a farm-house was in sight, and the change from the city crowding was essentially satisfying. He rode now through open woods, across little flower-scattered glades, till he came upon a spring. Flat on the ground, he drank deeply of the clear water, and, looking about him, felt with a shock the beauty of the world. It came to him like a discovery; he had never realized it before, he concluded, and also, he had forgotten much. One could not sit in at high finance and keep track of such things. As he drank in the air, the scene, and the distant song of larks, he felt like a poker-player rising from a night-long table and coming forth from the pent atmosphere to taste the freshness of the morn.

At the base of the knolls he encountered a tumble-down stake-and-rider fence. From the look of it he judged it must be forty years old at least—the work of some first pioneer who had taken up the land when the days of gold had ended. The woods were very thick here, yet fairly clear of underbrush, so that, while the blue sky was screened by the arched branches, he was able to ride beneath. He now found himself in a nook of several acres, where the oak and manzanita and madroño gave way to clusters of stately redwoods. Against the foot of a steep-sloped knoll he came upon a magnificent group of redwoods that seemed to have gathered about a tiny gurgling spring.

He halted his horse, for beside the spring uprose a wild California lily. It was a wonderful flower, growing there in the cathedral nave of lofty trees. At least eight feet in height, its stem rose straight and slender, green and bare, for two-thirds its length, and then burst into a shower of snow-white waxen bells. There were hundreds of these blossoms, all from the one stem, delicately poised and ethereally frail. Daylight had never seen anything like it. Slowly his gaze wandered from it to all that was about him. He took off his hat, with almost a vague religious feeling. This was different. No room for contempt and evil here. This was clean and fresh and beautiful—something he could respect. It was like a church. The atmosphere was one of holy calm. Here man felt the prompting of nobler things. Much of this and more was in Daylight's heart as he looked about him. But it was not a concept of the mind. He merely felt it without thinking about it at all.

On the steep incline above the spring grew tiny maiden-hair ferns, while higher up were larger ferns and brakes. Great, moss-covered trunks of fallen trees lay here and there, slowly sinking back and merging into the level of the forest mould. Beyond, in a slightly clearer space, wild grape and honeysuckle swung in green riot from gnarled old oak trees. A gray Douglas squirrel crept out on a branch and watched him. From somewhere came the distant knocking of a woodpecker. This sound did not disturb the hush and the awe of the place. Quiet woods' noises belonged here and made the solitude complete. The tiny bubbling ripple of the spring and the gray flash of tree-squirrel were as yardsticks with which to measure the silence and motionless repose.

"Might be a million miles from anywhere," Daylight whispered to himself.

But ever his gaze returned to the wonderful lily beside the bubbling spring.

He tethered the horse and wandered on foot among the knolls. Their tops were crowned with century-old spruce trees, and their sides clothed with oaks and madroños and native holly. But to the perfect redwoods belonged the small but deep cañon that threaded its way among the knolls. Here he found no passage out for his horse, and he returned to the lily beside the spring. On foot, tripping, stumbling, leading the animal, he forced his way up the hillside. And ever the ferns carpeted the way of his feet, ever the forest climbed with him and arched overhead, and ever the clean joy and sweetness stole in upon his senses.

On the crest he came through an amazing thicket of velvet-trunked young madroños, and emerged on an open hillside that led down into a tiny valley. The sunshine was at first dazzling in its brightness, and he paused and rested, for he was panting from the exertion. Not of old had he known shortness of breath such as this, and muscles that so easily tired at a stiff climb. A tiny stream ran down the tiny valley through a tiny meadow that was carpeted knee-high with grass and blue and white nemophila. The hillside was covered with Mariposa lilies and wild hyacinth, down through which his horse dropped slowly, with circumspect feet and reluctant gait.

Crossing the stream, Daylight followed a faint cattle-trail over a low, rocky hill and through a wine-wooded forest of manzanita, and emerged upon another tiny valley, down which filtered another spring-fed, meadow-bordered streamlet. A jack-rabbit bounded from a bush under his horse's nose, leaped the stream, and vanished up the opposite hill-side of scrub-oak. Daylight watched it admiringly as he rode on to the head of the meadow. Here he startled up a many-pronged buck, that seemed to soar across the meadow, and to soar over the stake-and-rider fence, and, still soaring, disappeared in a friendly copse beyond.

Daylight's delight was unbounded. It seemed to him that he had never been so happy. His old woods' training was aroused, and he was keenly interested in everything—in the moss on the trees and branches; in the bunches of mistletoe hanging in the oaks; in the nest of a wood-rat; in the water-cress growing in the sheltered eddies of the little stream; in the butterflies drifting through the rifted sunshine and shadow; in the blue jays that flashed in splashes of color across the forest aisles; in the tiny birds, like wrens, that hopped among the bushes and imitated certain minor quail-calls; and in the crimson-crested woodpecker that ceased its knocking and cocked its head on one side to survey him. Crossing the stream, he struck faint vestiges of a wood-road, used, evidently, a generation back, when the meadows had been cleared of oaks. He found a hawk's nest on the lightning-shattered tipmost top of a six-foot redwood. And to complete it all, his horse stumbled upon several large broods of half-grown quail, and the air was filled with the thrum of their flight. He halted and watched the young ones "petrifying" and disappearing on the ground before his eyes, and listening to the anxious calls of the old ones hidden in the thickets.

"It sure beats country places and bungalows at Menlo Park," he communed aloud; "and if ever I get the hankering for country life, it's me for this every time."

The old wood-road led him to a clearing, where a dozen acres of grapes grew on wine-red soil. A cow-path, more trees and thickets, and he dropped down a hillside to the southeast exposure. Here, poised above a big forested cañon, and looking out upon Sonoma Valley, was a small farm-house. With its barn and outhouses it snuggled into a nook in the hillside, which protected it from west and north. It was the erosion from this hillside, he judged, that had formed the little level stretch of vegetable garden. The soil was fat and black, and there was water in plenty, for he saw several faucets running wide open.

Forgotten was the brickyard. Nobody was at home, but Daylight dismounted and ranged the vegetable garden, eating strawberries and green peas, inspecting the old abode barn and the rusty plough and harrow, and rolling and smoking cigarettes while he watched the antics of several broods of young chickens and the mother hens. A foot-trail that led down the wall of the big cañon invited him, and he proceeded to follow it. A water-pipe, usually above ground, paralleled the trail, which he concluded led upstream to the bed of the creek. The wall of the cañon was several hundred feet from top to bottom, and so magnificent were the untouched trees that the place was plunged in perpetual shade. He measured with his eye spruces five and six feet in diameter and redwoods even larger. One such he passed, a twister that was at least ten or eleven feet through. The trail led straight to a small dam where was the intake for the pipe that watered the vegetable garden. Here, beside the stream, were alders and laurel trees, and he walked through fern-brakes higher than his head. Velvety moss was everywhere, out of which grew maiden-hair and gold-back ferns.

Save for the dam, it was a virgin wild. No axe had invaded, and the trees died only of old age and stress of winter storm. The huge trunks of those that had fallen lay moss-covered, slowly resolving back into the soil from which they sprang. Some had lain so long that they were quite gone, though their faint outlines, level with the mould, could still be seen. Others bridged the stream, and from beneath the bulk of one monster half a dozen younger trees, overthrown and crushed by the fall, growing out along the ground, still lived and prospered, their roots bathed by the stream, their upshooting branches catching the sunlight through the gap that had been made in the forest roof.

Back at the farm-house, Daylight mounted and rode on away from the ranch and into the wilder cañons and steeper steeps beyond. Nothing could satisfy his holiday spirit now but the ascent of Sonoma Mountain. And here on the crest, three hours afterward, he emerged, tired and sweaty, garments torn and face and hands scratched, but with sparkling eyes and an unwonted zestfulness of expression. He felt the illicit pleasure of a schoolboy playing truant. The big gambling table of San Francisco seemed very far away. But there was more than illicit pleasure in his mood. It was as though he were going through a sort of cleansing bath. No room here for all the sordidness, meanness and viciousness that filled the dirty pool of city existence. Without pondering in detail upon the matter at all, his sensations were of purification and uplift. Had he been asked to state how he felt, he would merely have said that he was having a good time; for he was unaware in his self-consciousness of the potent charm of nature that was percolating through his city-rotted body and brain—potent, in that he came of an abysmal past of wilderness dwellers, while he was himself coated with but the thinnest rind of crowded civilization.

There were no houses in the summit of Sonoma Mountain, and, all alone under the azure California sky, he reined in on the southern edge of the peak. He saw open pasture country, intersected with wooded cañons, descending to the south and west from his feet, crease on crease and roll on roll, from lower level to lower level, to the floor of Petaluma Valley, flat as a billiard-table, a cardboard affair, all patches and squares of geometrical regularity where the fat freeholds were farmed. Beyond, to the west, rose range on range of mountains cuddling purple mists of atmosphere in their valleys; and still beyond, over the last range of all, he saw the silver sheen of the Pacific. Swinging his horse, he surveyed the west and north, from Santa Rosa to Mount St. Helena, and on to the east, across Sonoma Valley, to the chaparral-covered range that shut off the view of Napa Valley. Here, part way up the eastern wall of Sonoma Valley, in range of a line intersecting the little village of Glen Ellen, he made out a scar on the hillside. His first thought was that it was the dump of a mine tunnel, but remembering that he was not in gold-bearing country, he dismissed the scar from his mind and continued the circle of his survey to the southeast, where, across the waters of San Pablo Bay, he could see, sharp and distant, the twin peaks of Mount Diablo. To the south was Mount Tamalpais, and yes, he was right, fifty miles away, where the draughty winds of the Pacific blew in the Golden Gate, the smoke of San Francisco made a low-lying haze against the sky . . .

War

First published in the *Nation* (London), July 29, 1911; reprinted from *The Night-Born* (New York: Century, 1913).

The protagonist in "War" bears no name; neither does his horse, or the war in which he dies. London does not describe the uniforms—whether they are blue or gray, for example—of the soldiers on either side of this unnamed war. All that he will say is that one side is the "alien invader"—for, as he knows, in every war there is always bound to be an invader and an alien. London wanted, in this story, to capture the archetypal truth of war, and the truth, for him, is that in war one kills—or is killed. Near the start of the story, the unnamed soldier on horseback, armed with a carbine, has a chance to kill an enemy soldier with an "unmistakable ginger beard," and he chooses, humanely, not to kill him. Of course, ironically that same soldier with the "unmistakable ginger beard" kills the protagonist at the end of the story. Moreover, the reader knows from the start that by the end of the story, the nameless soldier will be killed. London offers many clues; he had become a master of foreshadowing. The time of year is autumn. The apples on the trees are ripe, and the soldier picks them, as he, too, will literally be picked off. Dismounting from his horse, the soldier slides and stumbles "among the dead leaves," and, approaching an abandoned house, he sees two human bodies, their faces "shriveled and defaced." He has all the "careless grace of his youth"; inexperienced and untested, he does not know the ways of war. His rite of passage comes too late to make a difference for him.

London, long an aficionado of movies, used a distinctly cinematic style in "War." He knew how to present essential details so that the reader could visualize scenes, and, he knew, too, how to shift the camera's eye. Beginning with the first sentence, and all through the narrative, the author peers out at the world through the eyes of his protagonist; the reader sees what he sees: "the bunch of quail, exploding into flight," for example, and hears what he hears: "the boom of heavy guns from far to the west." The reader empathizes with the unnamed soldier, lonely and fearful, and understands his obsessive thought: "the crash into his body of a high-velocity bullet."

At the end, the reader looks back, through the soldier's eyes, and sees his enemies in the distance. At that moment, the story and the point of view change abruptly. Suddenly, the reader looks at the soldier through the eyes of his own enemies, as though through the crosshairs of the rifle itself. Then, from far off, and as though to distance our feelings, we see him fall, his body bouncing as it strikes the ground, the apples he has picked rolling about his dead body. London carefully crafted the story's last sentence, replete with irony: "They laughed at the unexpected eruption of apples, and clapped their hands in applause of the long shot by the man with the ginger beard."

As a writer, London had come a long way in the decade since his first short stories set in the Yukon. He had perfected his craft and mastered the genre; yet he had lost some of his original wildness, and so, perhaps, the unpredictability and messiness of life feels oddly missing from the pages of "War." •

He was a young man, not more than twenty-four or five, and he might have sat his horse with the careless grace of his youth had he not been so catlike and tense. His black eyes roved everywhere, catching the movements of twigs and branches where small birds hopped, questing ever onward through the changing vistas of trees and brush, and returning always to the clumps of undergrowth on either side. And as he watched, so did he listen, though he rode on in silence, save for the boom of heavy guns from far to the west. This had been sounding monotonously in his ears for hours, and only its cessation could have aroused his notice. For he had business closer to hand. Across his saddle-bow was balanced a carbine.

So tensely was he strung, that a bunch of quail, exploding into flight from under his horse's nose, startled him to such an extent that automatically, instantly, he had reined in and fetched the carbine halfway to his shoulder. He grinned sheepishly, recovered himself, and rode on. So tense was he, so bent upon the work he had to do, that the sweat stung his eyes unwiped, and unheeded rolled down his nose and spattered his saddle pommel. The band of his cavalryman's hat was fresh-stained with sweat. The roan horse under him was likewise wet. It was high noon of a breathless day of heat. Even the birds and squirrels did not dare the sun, but sheltered in shady hiding places among the trees.

Man and horse were littered with leaves and dusted with yellow pollen, for the open was ventured no more than was compulsory. They kept to the brush and trees, and invariably the man halted and peered out before crossing a dry glade or naked stretch of upland pasturage. He worked always to the north, though his way was devious, and it was from the north that he seemed most to apprehend that for which he was looking. He was no coward, but his courage was only that of the average civilized man, and he was looking to live, not die.

Up a small hillside he followed a cowpath through such dense scrub that he was forced to dismount and lead his horse. But when the path swung around to the west, he abandoned it and headed to the north again along the oak-covered top of the ridge.

The ridge ended in a steep descent—so steep that he zigzagged back and forth across the face of the slope, sliding and stumbling among the dead leaves and matted vines and keeping a watchful eye on the horse above that threatened to fall down upon him. The sweat ran from him, and the pollen-dust, settling pungently in mouth and nostrils, increased his thirst. Try as he would, nevertheless the descent was noisy, and frequently he stopped, panting in the dry heat and listening for any warning from beneath.

At the bottom he came out on a flat, so densely forested that he could not make out its extent. Here the character of the woods changed, and he was able to remount. Instead of the twisted hillside oaks, tall straight trees, big-trunked and prosperous, rose from the damp fat soil. Only here and there were thickets, easily avoided, while he encountered winding, park-like glades where the cattle had pastured in the days before war had run them off.

His progress was more rapid now, as he came down into the valley, and at the end of half an hour he halted at an ancient rail fence on the edge of a clearing. He did not like the openness of it, yet his path lay across to the fringe of trees that marked the banks of the stream. It was a mere quarter of a mile across that open, but the thought of venturing out in it was repugnant. A rifle, a score of them, a thousand, might lurk in that fringe by the stream.

Twice he essayed to start, and twice he paused. He was appalled by his own loneliness. The pulse of war that beat from the West suggested the companionship of battling thousands; here was naught but silence, and himself, and possible death-dealing bullets from a myriad ambushes. And yet his task was to find what he feared to find. He must on, and on, till somewhere, some time, he encountered another man, or other men, from the other side, scouting, as he was scouting, to make report, as he must make report, of having come in touch.

Changing his mind, he skirted inside the woods for a distance, and again peeped forth. This time, in the middle of the clearing, he saw a small farmhouse. There were no signs of life. No smoke curled from the chimney, not a barnyard fowl clucked and strutted. The kitchen door stood open, and he gazed so long and hard into the black aperture that it seemed almost that a farmer's wife must emerge at any moment.

He licked the pollen and dust from his dry lips, stiffened himself, mind and body, and rode out into the blazing sunshine. Nothing stirred. He went on past the house, and approached the wall of trees and bushes by the river's bank. One thought persisted maddeningly. It was of the crash into his body of a high-velocity bullet. It made him feel very fragile and defenseless, and he crouched lower in the saddle.

Tethering his horse in the edge of the wood, he continued a hundred yards on foot till he came to the stream. Twenty feet wide it was, without perceptible current, cool and inviting, and he was very thirsty. But he waited inside his screen of leafage, his eyes fixed on the screen on the opposite side. To make the wait endurable, he sat down, his carbine resting on his knees. The minutes passed, and slowly his tenseness relaxed. At last he decided there was no danger; but just as he prepared to part the bushes and bend down to the water, a movement among the opposite bushes caught his eye.

It might be a bird. But he waited. Again there was an agitation of the bushes, and then, so suddenly that it almost startled a cry from him, the bushes parted and a face peered out. It was a face covered with several weeks' growth of ginger-colored beard. The eyes were blue and wide apart, with laughter-wrinkles in the corners that showed despite the tired and anxious expression of the whole face.

All this he could see with microscopic clearness, for the distance was no more than twenty feet. And all this he saw in such brief time, that he saw it as he lifted his carbine to his shoulder. He glanced along the sights, and knew that he was gazing upon a man who was as good as dead. It was impossible to miss at such point blank range.

But he did not shoot. Slowly he lowered the carbine and watched. A hand, clutching a water-bottle, became visible and the ginger beard bent downward to fill the bottle. He could hear the gurgle of the water. Then arm and bottle and ginger beard disappeared behind the closing bushes. A long time he waited, when, with thirst unslaked, he crept back to his horse, rode slowly across the sun-washed clearing, and passed into the shelter of the woods beyond.

II

Another day, hot and breathless. A deserted farmhouse, large, with many outbuildings and an orchard, standing in a clearing. From the woods, on a roan horse, carbine across pommel, rode the young man with the quick black eyes. He breathed with relief as he gained the house. That a fight had taken place here earlier in the season was evident. Clips and empty cartridges, tarnished with verdigris, lay on the ground, which, while wet, had been torn up by the hoofs of horses. Hard by the kitchen garden were graves, tagged and numbered. From the oak tree by the kitchen door, in tattered, weatherbeaten garments, hung the bodies of two men. The faces, shriveled and defaced, bore no likeness to the faces of men. The roan horse snorted beneath them, and the rider caressed and soothed it and tied it farther away.

Entering the house, he found the interior a wreck. He trod on empty cartridges as he walked from room to room to reconnoiter from the windows. Men had camped and slept everywhere, and on the floor of one room he came upon stains unmistakable where the wounded had been laid down.

Again outside, he led the horse around behind the barn and invaded the orchard. A dozen trees were burdened with ripe apples. He filled his pockets, eating while he picked. Then a thought came to him, and he glanced at the sun, calculating the time of his return to camp. He pulled off his shirt, tying the sleeves and making a bag. This he proceeded to fill with apples.

As he was about to mount his horse, the animal suddenly pricked up its ears. The man, too, listened, and heard, faintly, the thud of hoofs on soft earth. He crept to the corner of the barn and peered out. A dozen mounted men, strung out loosely, approaching from the opposite side of the clearing, were only a matter of a hundred yards or so away. They rode on to the house. Some dismounted, while others remained in the saddle as an earnest that their stay would be short. They seemed to be holding a council, for he could hear them talking excitedly in the detested tongue of the alien invader. The time passed, but they seemed unable to reach a decision. He put the carbine away in its boot, mounted, and waited impatiently, balancing the shirt of apples on the pommel.

He heard footsteps approaching, and drove his spurs so fiercely into the roan as to force a surprised groan from the animal as it leaped forward. At the corner of the barn he saw the intruder, a mere boy of nineteen or twenty for all of his uniform, jump back to escape being run down. At the same moment the roan swerved and its rider caught a glimpse of the aroused men by the house. Some were springing from their horses, and he could see the rifles going to their shoulders. He passed the kitchen door and the dried corpses swinging in the shade, compelling his foes to run around the front of the house. A rifle cracked, and a second, but he was going fast, leaning forward, low in the saddle, one hand clutching the shirt of apples, the other guiding the horse.

The top bar of the fence was four feet high, but he knew his roan and leaped it at full career to the accompaniment of several scattered shots. Eight hundred yards straight away were the woods, and the roan was covering the distance with mighty strides. Every man was now firing. They were pumping their guns so rapidly that he no longer heard individual shots. A bullet went through his hat, but he was unaware, though he did know when another tore through the apples on the pommel. And he winced and ducked even lower when a third bullet, fired low, struck a stone between his horse's legs and ricochetted off through the air, buzzing and humming like some incredible insect.

The shots died down as the magazines were emptied, until, quickly, there was no more shooting. The young man was elated. Through that astonishing fusillade he had come unscathed. He glanced back. Yes, they had emptied their magazines. He could see several reloading. Others were running back behind the house for their horses. As he looked, two already mounted, came back into view around the corner, riding hard. And at the same moment, he saw the man with the unmistakable ginger beard kneel down on the ground, level his gun, and coolly take his time for the long shot.

The young man threw his spurs into the horse, crouched very low, and swerved in his flight in order to distract the other's aim. And still the shot did not come. With each jump of the horse, the woods sprang nearer. They were only two hundred yards away and still the shot was delayed.

And then he heard it, the last thing he was to hear, for he was dead ere he hit the ground in the long crashing fall from the saddle. And they, watching at the house, saw him fall, saw his body bounce when it struck the earth, and saw the burst of red-cheeked apples that rolled about him. They laughed at the unexpected eruption of apples, and clapped their hands in applause of the long shot by the man with the ginger beard.

Introduction to Alexander Berkman's
Prison Memoirs of an Anarchist

First published in *American Literature,* October 1989. Reprinted from the manuscript at the Huntington Library.

London wrote the introduction to Alexander Berkman's *Prison Memoirs of an Anarchist* in response to a request from Emma Goldman (1869–1940), but Berkman (1870–1936) did not include it his book, and it wasn't published until 1989. In 1911, Goldman wrote Jack London asking him to write an introduction to the memoir of Berkman, her lover and comrade. A Russian-born Jewish anarchist, Berkman unsuccessfully attempted to assassinate industrialist Henry Frick in his New York office in 1892, serving a fourteen-year prison term for the crime.

In 1910, Goldman's magazine *Mother Earth* favorably reviewed London's *Burning Daylight,* praising its depiction of the benefits of living close to the earth. In a letter to Jack she wrote that he was "the only revolutionary writer in America." Though she may have been merely flattering him, he certainly was the best-known radical author in 1911, if not the only one. And an introduction by Jack London might well have had a significant impact on the reception of Berkman's memoir. In 1906, London had written a glowing review of Upton Sinclair's novel *The Jungle,* helping it to become a bestseller. "It has truth and power," London wrote. "It has behind it in the United States over four hundred thousand men and woman who are striving to give it a wider hearing than any other book has been given in fifty years." Perhaps Goldman hoped London might also help Berkman's *Prison Memoirs of an Anarchist* sell well.

London, however, had strong reservations about anarchism. In 1901, shortly after the assassination of President William McKinley by Leon Czolgosz, a Detroit-born son of Polish immigrants, London had expressed his view that assassination was politically ineffective. "The president is dead," he wrote, as though shrugging his shoulders indifferently. "What of it? We have another president in his place, and so we will continue to have like presidents until society, economically ripe, compasses the inexorable change that is coming." Assassinations of presidents, senators, and millionaires would not change the world or accelerate the coming of socialism, he argued. As a socialist, he opposed assassinations and the use of violence; "we stand for all law," he wrote. Nonetheless, he expressed compassion for Czolgosz, and he could understand completely, he said, the "deeds of the reddest Reds," which, he believed, were "prompted by the highest motives."

Moreover, if anyone was truly violent, he insisted, it was the agents of the state—the police, judges, and hangmen who wanted to execute Czolgosz, along with all the other American anarchists and bomb throwers. "Who clamors for blood the loudest?" he asked rhetorically, "the poor devil of an anarchist, or the decent, law-abiding, law-upholding Americans who would subvert law and order that they might have their hands in his blood?" If he had to choose sides, he would choose the anarchists who wanted to abolish the law, not the law-abiding citizens—the slaves of "mob-emotion" who wanted to subvert the law and satisfy their "blood-lust" through executions. Jack felt sorry for Czolgosz, and, not surprisingly, he also felt sorry for Alexander Berkman, whom he met in New York in the winter of 1911 and with whom he argued "amicably," as Charmian put it in her diary. For London, the great "paradox" about the anarchists was that they were "so temperamentally opposed to violence that they are moved to deeds of violence in order to bring about, in the way they conceive it, the reign of love and cosmic brotherhood." It was a paradox that left him perplexed.

London's introductory essay has two distinct parts, the first of which mostly makes fun of Berkman as a bungling anarchist and would-be assassin who couldn't shoot straight; the second part is more sympathetic. The attempt to kill Frick struck London as "a silly thing." Berkman was far "too impractical," he writes, and, since he was "unable to kill another man at point blank range with a modern revolver," he would also likely be unable to "build another social order, establish a radically new & working relationship between the millions of common men & women."

In the second part of the essay, London sympathizes with Berkman, lauding his memoir for its depiction of the grim realities of prison life and its unswerving portrait of "the blind, brute cruelty of man to man." The essay that begins by dismissing Berkman's attempted assassination as a "silly thing" ends with resounding endorsement of the book. "This book is real; it is true; it is a great human document," London writes. "It reads like a report from some monstrous hell, rather than from a civilized prison-house of the twentieth-century." His praise sounds authentic, yet a comparison with his review of Upton Sinclair's *The Jungle* suggests that he felt much more impassioned about Sinclair's novel.

Still, London is often inspired in his essay on Berkman's book. He notes that it contains some of the most "sweetly terrible passages in the literature of revolution." Berkman's book also prompts London to conclude that too much reading, and too much thinking, might take radical intellectuals away from the practical realities of life—and thereby damage them. Moreover, London shows here how astute a "student of society" he could be. He notes that the violent anarchist, like Berkman, is a "social product" and that society is at fault for giving birth to him. The book resonates with "innate sweetness and kindliness and nobility," London writes, in what sounds like a comment he hoped might be used as a blurb.

Though Berkman's *Prison Memoirs of an Anarchist* did not sell well or alter the course of anarchism or revolution, it has at least survived. And, even though Berkman declined to include London's essay as the introduction to his book, he sent London a copy of *Prison Memoirs* when it was published. The inscription reads, "To my friend & brother Jack London with whom I often disagree, but whose ability and revolutionary spirit I admire." •

A socialist writing an introduction to the autobiography of an anarchist, may seem a bizarre thing; yet be it known that this socialist in the opposite intellectual camp from this anarchist writes this introduction out of love and comradeship as wide as the human world is wide. So wide love and comradeship, that bridges the abysses of human thought, is bound to seem absurd and lunatic, not merely to the stupid, average, political human, but to the stupid, average, conventional Christian. And since this is so, Nietzsche's classic contention still stands: *"There was only one Christian: he died on the cross."*

If my brother do a silly thing, a wrong thing, a thing repugnant to me and my concepts, is he any the less my brother? Alexander Berkman is my brother. My arms are about him in comradeship, despite the silliness of his act, as I chance to judge it. In face of the remoteness, and vastness and infinitely complicated social processes which have been at work in the evolution of society since the formation of the first human group, the attempted assassination of Henry C. Frick, to my mind, seems solemnly silly. Yet, with Alexander Berkman, this solemnity, this willingness to sacrifice his own life and all his dream for the ethical grandeur of his dream, for what he conceived to be the good of all his brothers in all the world, in a terroristic deed of microscopic unimportance, remains an incontestable human fact. It must be reckoned with, it might be understood by all of us if we are to understand the human world in which we live. And who will dare to say there was the slightest touch of sordidness, of self-seeking, of desire for personal aggrandizement and length of days and increase of physical comforts and sensual delights in the motive of Alexander Berkman when he invaded Henry Frick's office on assassination intent?

There is a vital worthwhileness in this book. We who desire to know all that is knowable of our sociality, must understand not merely the laws of gravitational & chemical reaction, the program of the Republican Party, or the motive behind the Boston Tea Party and John Brown's invasion of Harper's Ferry; we must understand, also, the strange spirit that moves strange men who are strangely provoked by the ridiculous social conditions of their time—which is our time. Of all paradoxes, is there one that will exceed the paradox of our anarchists—men & women who are so temperamentally opposed to violence that they are moved to deeds of violence in order to bring about, in the way they conceive it, the reign of love and cosmic brotherhood?

Perhaps it is right here that we catch the clue to their futility, put our hands on the pulse of their impractical inability to put an end to violence by the perpetuation of deeds of violence. For it must be granted that the anarchists do not know how to kill. A fatal inefficiency coupled with possession of the most marvelous devices for taking life, prevents them from succeeding more than very rarely in their sanguinary efforts for the regeneration of the world. The stupidest sailor or common laborer, with a practical mind, can vastly more successfully eliminate an undesirable fellow being than can the anarchist, despite their knowledge of the books and all their fine frenzy for human betterment.

"I am revolutionist first, man afterward," Berkman says of himself. Very true, and very well it was for Henry C. Frick that the man with a full revolver who opened fire on him at point-blank range was a revolutionist who had been too busy thinking about the world to learn the practical affairs of the world. The average farmer boy of our Western country, or the average delivery boy of the streets of New York, would have made a better job of it than did Berkman. But then, the average farmer boy and average delivery boy are *average* and do not want to kill anybody for the sake of the people. Some conventional politicians, down in Kentucky, only the other day determined to kill a man of the people by the name of Goebel [the governor of the state]. They shot him from so far away that never could be legally determined the identity of the one who pulled the trigger. But these men were average, practical men, possessing neither aversion to violence nor dream of the people. It is truly so that too much thought leads to inaction, or rather, to inability for action.

And yet, not entirely explained is the violent anarchist, reiterating his slogan of direct action. He remains a grim interrogation mark. He questions society in red. Likewise he is a social product. Society makes him, and the student of society must explain him. Hence, the value of this autobiography of Alexander Berkman, who takes us behind the scenes, opens his brain and his innermost heart-thoughts to us as he expounds the passion of his reasoning that propelled him forth in a wild attempt on the life of a steel king's lieutenant.

Nobody has understood this thing. The whole affair is replete with misunderstanding. Berkman, by his own confession, admits that he failed to understand the people. The people certainly failed to understand him. To the Homestead strikers he was an alien interloper from New York. Even the prisoners in jail failed to understand his deed. "You ain't no Pittsburgh man," the prisoner who had killed his business partner and was waiting trial, tells him. "What did you want to butt in for? It was none of your cheese." Jack Clifford, another murderer, sympathizes with Berkman. "Too bad you didn't kill him," says genial Jack Clifford. "Some business misunderstanding, eh?"

And I, for one, having read this autobiography, still fail to understand. That is, I glimpse Berkman's revolt clearly, but I cannot grasp the utility, or the rationality of his act. Yet much of understanding, glimmering and vague, may be gleaned from these pages, of the soul of the direct actionist, Alexander Berkman, which may enable us to understand somewhat the souls of other direct actionists.

And right here appears the value of this autobiography. It is a human document of anything but mean proportions. No one, unafraid of life & desiring to know life, can afford to miss this book. It is a chunk of life, torn out raw and bleeding. It sickens one with its filth, & degradation, and cruelty, with its relentless narration of the evil men do to men. It smells from the depths. Very well; then the depths are here. They are facts. We, who desire to be masters of life, must cope with these facts. No society in which we would live can be right in which these facts remain facts. We who would build the house beautiful for mankind must attend to the sanitation. We must smell all smells if we would remedy smells and make clean and pure the atmosphere of the house in which we live.

Berkman was very young, very naïve, when he went forth to do propaganda by deed. Also, he was hag-ridden by ideas and ideals & without contact with the real world. For instance, he came to blows with his dearest chum, the Artist, because, forsooth, the latter was so sybaritic as to spend twenty cents on a single meal, the first meal in two days. "We, the most intimate friends, actually came to blows. Nobody would have believed it. They had to call us the Twins . . . He had outraged my most sacred feelings. To spend twenty cents for a meal! It was not mere extravagance: it was positively a crime, incredible in a revolutionist. Even now—two years have passed—

yet a certain feeling of resentment remains with me. What right had a revolutionist to such self-indulgence? The movement needed aid; every cent was valuable. To spend twenty cents for a single meal! True, it was his first meal in two days, and we were economizing on rent by sleeping in parks . . . His defense was unspeakably aggravating: he had earned ten dollars that week—he had given seven into the pauper's treasury . . . I had no patience with such arguments. They merely proved his bourgeois predilections . . . One could exist on five cents a day. Twenty cents for a single meal! Incredible. It was robbery."

Surely it is not too much to say that there are few more sweetly terrible passages in the literature of revolution. Yet, so impractical was Berkman that he could not realize that a well nourished revolutionist was a more efficient revolutionist. Just as he failed in these simple, practical adjustments, so did he fail in his attempts on the life of Henry C. Frick and in the attempt on his own life in the police station. He was too much the fervid thinker, too little the practical man, to bring off a successful suicide. Stupid, ordinary folk achieve suicide everyday. It is so dreadfully simple a thing to do. Yet Berkman failed to do it. And so the inevitable query arises: how can a type of man, too impractical to be able to kill another man at point blank range with a modern revolver, too impractical to be able to kill himself with a successfully concealed capsule of modern poison—how can such a type of man be able to build another social order, establish a radically new & working relationship between the millions of common men & women?

Next to knowing the mind of an anarchist, perhaps the greatest value of this book lies in its bold matter-of-fact-narration of the unthinkable cruelty and lunatic management of our prisons. I, too, know our prisons and have worn the stripes and marched the lock-step, and I can vouch absolutely for the truth of the prison conditions described by Berkman. "Forty percent of the population is discovered in various stages of tuberculosis, and twenty percent insane," he says of his own prison. "The death rate from consumption is found to range between twenty-five and sixty percent." The convicts & the guards in all our prisons know this. The public only does not know—the huge, amorphous unthinking and uncaring public.

"New faces greet me in the cell-house. But many old friends are missing. Billy Ryan is dead from consumption; Pasquale and Ben have become insane; little Mat, the Duquene striker, has committed suicide. In sad remembrance I think of them, grown close & dear in the years of mutual suffering. Some of the old timers have survived, yet broken in spirit and health. Praying Andy is still on the range, his mind clouded, and lips silently moving in prayer. Old Aleck Millain, the oldest man in the prison in point of service, and the most popular lifer, has had his pardon refused by the Board. The police authorities are aware of his innocence."

So writes Berkman on his return to the cell-house after a prolonged burial in solitary, and there is no need to continue the excerpt. It reads like a report from some monstrous hell, rather than from a civilized prison-house of the twentieth-century. The blind, brute cruelty of man to man! The wild-animal management by our kind of the sick, of our kind! Here, in this stinging indictment of these mad and stupid conditions, is to be found much of the greatness of this book. It is a hard, warm, human challenge of our ability to apply to the affairs of society, the wisdom and the facts that are in all our books, hibernating on our countless library shelves. Yet, outside these same pages, from the inside, if you please, can be found nowhere more illuminating flashes of the innate sweetness and kindliness and nobility of human nature.

There is no apology in this book nor for this book. It is society that must apologize, that some day will apologize. This book is real; it is true; it is a great human document. There is no discounting. It has occurred. Its blood and sweat and bitter tears have occurred. Its cruelties and misunderstandings, and stupidities, and vilenesses, have been perpetuated. Its thoughts have been thought. No man, in the august commotion of the world *man* can question the nobility of these thoughts. They are incontestably a part of life. They exist. Here they are, stinging and flaming. We must know them if we are to know society of which we are a part and the whole of which is the sum of all of us.

PART IV

COSMIC VOYAGER

1913 – 1916

"on the Beach at Waikiki" 1915

John Barleycorn: Alcoholic Memoirs, Chapter 36

First published serially in the *Saturday Evening Post,* March–May 1913; reprinted from *John Barleycorn: Alcoholic Memoirs* (New York: Century, 1913).

London never wrote a complete autobiography, but in *John Barleycorn,* he describes a central aspect of his life: the stubborn alcoholism that plagued his physical and mental health. The consumption of alcohol touched on nearly every aspect of his life—personal relationships, political activity, and literary work. (London planned to write a companion volume, a confessional work about his sex life, but never followed through.)

In this 1913 memoir, London assigns alcohol the name "John Barleycorn," thus humanizing his ever-present companion. Alcohol gives rise to what London calls "the White Logic," an illogical logic that turns things inside out and upside down, deceiving him and tricking him. London explains that he began to drink alcohol as a boy and that he is still drinking, even while writing *John Barleycorn.*

In Chapter 36 of *John Barleycorn,* which comes near the end of the book, he writes, "I pour and sip my Scotch." London seems to have consumed alcohol both to mask and to escape from his intermittent bouts with depression. His alcoholism also added to that depression, and to his "long sickness," as he called it.

"I am oppressed by the cosmic sadness that has always been the heritage of man," he writes in *John Barleycorn.* "And I am sad because John Barleycorn is with me." London confesses that he has "everything to make me glad I am alive." He has "land, money, power, recognition from the world . . . a mate whom I love, children that are of my own fond flesh." Nothing makes him happy, however; he revels in his unhappiness and seems to enjoy—in a morbid way—thoughts about his own "disintegrating body which has been dying since I was born." London was only thirty-seven when *John Barleycorn* was published, but his body had already begun to fall apart, as he observed. His thumbs didn't work properly, the joints of his legs ached, his belly had lost its tautness, and he could no longer run swiftly. His youth was now only a memory. In the depths of his pessimism, he had come to entertain the idea that humanity was "a cosmic joke, a sport of chemistry" and that life itself was a "perpetual lie-telling process."

In *John Barleycorn,* London discusses his role in the socialist movement, but only in passing, and in a self-deprecating tone. He praises socialism for saving him from depression, and he defends his own role in the cause. But *John Barleycorn* isn't a defense of socialism. The "well-balanced radicals" of the day denounced him as "unsane" and "ultra-revolutionary," he writes, as though stung by their hurtful comments. London admits, too, that as a socialist he was "brutally careless of whose feelings I hurt"; self-mockingly, he says, "It is my fond belief that I accelerated the socialist development of the United States by at least five minutes."

London offers a gloomy, Poe-like portrait of himself in his "book-walled den, the mausoleum of the thoughts of men." In his mausoleum, "the White Logic" tells him to drink. He drinks, musing about the death-thoughts of the German romantic poet Heinrich Heine (1797–1856) and the philosophy of the ancient Chinese poet Chuang Tzu. It seems fitting that in his despair, London would find solace in Buddhism—"the annihilating bliss of Buddha's Nirvana," as he calls it—as well as in Taoism, which reminded him of the unimportance of the self, a hard lesson for him to learn.

At the end of *John Barleycorn*, London urges the prohibition of alcohol, though he also insists that he won't stop drinking. Not surprisingly, the prohibition movement made his memoir a bible for temperance, and it was widely read in the years immediately following his death. If Upon Sinclair's *The Jungle* helped to pass the Pure Food and Drug Act of 1906, *John Barleycorn* might be said to have led, in part, to the Volstead Act of 1919, which banned the manufacture, sale, and distribution of alcohol. •

Back to personal experiences and the effects in the past of John Barleycorn's White Logic on me. On my lovely ranch in the Valley of the Moon, brain-soaked with many months of alcohol, I am oppressed by the cosmic sadness that has always been the heritage of man. In vain do I ask myself why I should be sad. My nights are warm. My roof does not leak. I have food galore for all the caprices of appetite. Every creature comfort is mine. In my body are no aches nor pains. The good old flesh-machine is running smoothly on. Neither brain nor muscle is overworked. I have land, money, power, recognition from the world, a consciousness that I do my meed of good in serving others, a mate whom I love, children that are of my own fond flesh. I have done, and am doing, what a good citizen of the world should do. I have built houses, many houses, and tilled many a hundred acres. And as for trees, have I not planted a hundred thousand? Everywhere, from any window of my house, I can gaze forth upon these trees of my planting, standing valiantly erect and aspiring toward the sun.

My life has indeed fallen in pleasant places. Not a hundred men in a million have been so lucky as I. Yet, with all this vast good fortune, am I sad. And I am sad because John Barleycorn is with me. And John Barleycorn is with me because I was born in what future ages will call the dark ages before the ages of rational civilization. John Barleycorn is with me because in all the unwitting days of my youth John Barleycorn was accessible, calling to me and inviting me on every corner and on every street between the corners. The pseudo-civilization into which I was born permitted everywhere licensed shops for the sale of soul-poison. The system of life was so organized that I (and millions like me) was lured and drawn and driven to the poison shops.

Wander with me through one mood of the myriad moods of sadness into which one is plunged by John Barleycorn. I ride out over my beautiful ranch. Between my legs is a beautiful horse. The air is wine. The grapes on a score of rolling hills are red with autumn flame. Across Sonoma Mountain wisps of sea fog are stealing. The afternoon sun smoulders in the drowsy sky. I have everything to make me glad I am alive. I am filled with dreams and mysteries. I am all sun and air and sparkle. I am vitalized, organic. I move, I have the power of movement, I command movement of the live thing I bestride. I am possessed with the pomps of being, and know proud passions and inspirations. I have ten thousand august connotations. I am a king in the kingdom of sense, and trample the face of the uncomplaining dust. . . .

And yet, with jaundiced eye I gaze upon all the beauty and wonder about me, and with jaundiced brain consider the pitiful figure I cut in this world that endured so long without me and that will again endure without me. I remember the men who broke their hearts and their backs over this stubborn soil that now belongs to me. As if anything imperishable could belong to the perishable! These men passed. I, too, shall pass. These men toiled, and cleared, and planted, gazed with aching eyes, while they rested their labor-stiffened bodies, on these same sunrises and sunsets, at the autumn glory of the grape, and at the fog-wisps stealing across the mountain. And they are gone. And I know that I, too, shall some day, and soon, be gone.

Gone? I am going now. In my jaw are cunning artifices of the dentists which replace the parts of me already gone. Never again will I have the thumbs of my youth. Old fights and wrestlings have injured them irreparably. That punch on the head of a man whose very name is forgotten, settled this thumb finally and for ever. A slip-grip at catch-as-catch-can did for the other. My lean runner's stomach has passed into the limbo of memory. The joints of the legs that bear me up are not so adequate as they once were, when, in wild nights and days of toil and frolic, I strained and snapped and ruptured them. Never again can I swing dizzily aloft and trust all the proud quick that is I to a single rope-clutch in the driving blackness of a storm. Never again can I run with the sled-dogs along the endless miles of Arctic trail.

I am aware that within this disintegrating body which has been dying since I was born I carry a skeleton, that under the rind of flesh which is called my face is a bony, noseless death's head. All of which does not shudder me. To be afraid is to be healthy. Fear of death makes for life. But the curse of the White Logic is that it does not make one afraid. The world-sickness of the White Logic makes one grin jocosely into the face of the Noseless One and to sneer at all the phantasmagoria of living.

I look about me as I ride, and on every hand I see the merciless and infinite waste of natural selection. The White Logic insists upon opening the long-closed books, and by paragraph and chapter states the beauty and wonder I behold in terms of futility and dust. About me is murmur and hum, and I know it for the gnat-swarm of the living, piping for a little space its thin plaint of troubled air.

I return across the ranch. Twilight is on, and the hunting animals are out. I watch the piteous tragic play of life feeding on life. Here is no morality. Only in man is morality, and man created it—a code of action that makes toward living and that is of the lesser order of truth. Yet all this I knew before, in the weary days of my long sickness. These were the greater truths that I so successfully schooled myself to forget; the truths that were so serious that I refused to take them seriously, and played with gently, O so gently, as sleeping dogs at the back of consciousness which I did not care to waken. I did but stir them, and let them lie. I was too wise, too wicked wise, to wake them. But now White Logic willy-nilly wakes them for me, for White Logic, most valiant, is unafraid of all the monsters of the earthly dream.

"Let the doctors of all the schools condemn me," White Logic whispers as I ride along. "What of it? I am truth. You know it. You cannot combat me. They say I make for death. What of it? It is truth. Life lies in order to live. Life is a perpetual lie-telling process. Life is a mad dance in the domain of flux, wherein appearances in mighty tides ebb and flow, chained to the wheels of moons beyond our ken. Appearances are ghosts. Life is ghost land, where appearances change, transfuse, permeate each the other and all the others, that are, that are not, that always flicker, fade, and pass, only to come again as new appearances, as other appearances. You are such an appearance, composed of countless appearances out of the past. All an appearance can know is mirage. You know mirages of desire. These very mirages are the unthinkable and incalculable congeries of appearances that crowd in upon you and form you out of the past, and that sweep you on into dissemination into other unthinkable and incalculable congeries of appearances to people the ghost land of the future. Life is apparitional, and passes. You are an apparition. Through all the apparitions that preceded you and that compose the parts of you, you rose gibbering from the evolutionary mire, and gibbering you will pass on, interfusing, permeating the procession of apparitions that will succeed you."

And of course it is all unanswerable, and as I ride along through the evening shadows I sneer at that Great Fetish which Comte called the world. And I remember what another pessimist of sentiency has uttered: "Transient are all. They, being born, must die; and, being dead, are glad to be at rest."

But here through the dusk comes one who is not glad to be at rest. He is a workman on the ranch, an old man, an immigrant Italian. He takes his hat off to me in all servility, because, forsooth, I am to him a lord of life. I am food to him, and shelter, and existence. He has toiled like a beast all his days, and lived less comfortably than my horses in their deep-strawed stalls. He is labour-crippled. He shambles as he walks. One shoulder is twisted higher than the other. His hands are gnarled claws, repulsive, horrible. As an apparition he is a pretty miserable specimen. His brain is as stupid as his body is ugly.

"His brain is so stupid that he does not know he is an apparition," the White Logic chuckles to me. "He is sense-drunk. He is the slave of the dream of life. His brain is filled with superrational sanctions and obsessions. He believes in a transcendent over-world. He has listened to the vagaries of the prophets, who have blown for him the sumptuous bubble of Paradise. He feels inarticulate self-affinities, with self-conjured non-realities. He sees penumbral visions of himself titubating fantastically through days and nights of space and stars. Beyond the shadow of any doubt he is convinced that the universe was made for him, and that it is his destiny to live for ever in the immaterial and supersensuous realms he and his kind have builded of the stuff of semblance and deception.

"But you, who have opened the books and who share my awful confidence—you know him for what he is, brother to you and the dust, a cosmic joke, a sport of chemistry, a garmented beast that arose out of the ruck of screaming beastliness by virtue and accident of two opposable great toes. He is brother as well to the gorilla and the chimpanzee. He thumps his chest in anger, and roars and quivers with cataleptic ferocity. He knows monstrous, atavistic promptings, and he is composed of all manner of shreds of abysmal and forgotten instincts."

"Yet he dreams he is immortal," I argue feebly. "It is vastly wonderful for so stupid a clod to bestride the shoulders of time and ride the eternities."

"Pah!" is the retort. "Would you then shut the books and exchange places with this thing that is only an appetite and a desire, a marionette of the belly and the loins?"

"To be stupid is to be happy," I contend.

"Then your ideal of happiness is a jelly-like organism floating in a tideless, tepid, twilight sea, eh?"

—Oh, the victim cannot combat John Barleycorn!

"One step removed from the annihilating bliss of Buddha's Nirvana," the White Logic adds. "Oh, well, here's the house. Cheer up and take a drink. We know, we illuminated, you and I, all the folly and the farce."

And in my book-walled den, the mausoleum of the thoughts of men, I take my drink, and other drinks, and roust out the sleeping dogs from the recesses of my brain and hallo them on over the walls of prejudice and law and through all the cunning labyrinths of superstition and belief.

"Drink," says the White Logic. "The Greeks believed that the gods gave them wine so that they might forget the miserableness of existence. And remember what Heine said."

Well do I remember that flaming Jew's "With the last breath all is done: joy, love, sorrow, macaroni, the theatre, lime-trees, raspberry drops, the power of human relations, gossip, the barking of dogs, champagne."

"Your clear white light is sickness," I tell the White Logic. "You lie."

"By telling too strong a truth," he quips back.

"Alas, yes, so topsy-turvy is existence," I acknowledge sadly.

"Ah, well, Liu Ling was wiser than you," the White Logic girds. "You remember him?"

I nod my head—Liu Ling, a hard drinker, one of the group of bibulous poets who called themselves the Seven Sages of the Bamboo Grove and who lived in China many an ancient century ago.

"It was Liu Ling," prompts the White Logic, "who declared that to a drunken man the affairs of this world appear but as so much duckweed on a river. Very well. Have another Scotch, and let semblance and deception become duck-weed on a river."

And while I pour and sip my Scotch, I remember another Chinese philosopher, Chuang Tzu, who, four centuries before Christ, challenged this dreamland of the world, saying: "How then do I know but that the dead repent of having previously clung to life? Those who dream of the banquet, wake to lamentation and sorrow. Those who dream of lamentation and sorrow, wake to join the hunt. While they dream, they do not know that they dream. Some will even interpret the very dream they are dreaming; and only when they awake do they know it was a dream. . . . Fools think they are awake now, and flatter themselves they know if they are really princes or peasants. Confucius and you are both dreams; and I who say you are dreams—I am but a dream myself.

"Once upon a time, I, Chuang Tzu, dreamt I was a butterfly, fluttering hither

and thither, to all intents and purposes a butterfly. I was conscious only of following my fancies as a butterfly, and was unconscious of my individuality as a man.
Suddenly, I awaked, and there I lay, myself again. Now I do not know whether I was
then a man dreaming I was a butterfly, or whether I am now a butterfly dreaming I
am a man."

The Star Rover, Chapter 22

First published serially in the *Los Angeles Examiner American Sunday Monthly Magazine,*
February–October 1915; reprinted from *The Star Rover* (New York: Macmillan, 1915).

The Star Rover (1915) reads like the last imaginative work of an exhausted writer: a parting gift to himself and a farewell to the world. "This shall be my last writing," the narrator
proclaims. The penultimate novel that London would publish—*The Little Lady of the Big
House* would appear in 1916—*The Star Rover* rings with grandiose statements. "The greatest thing in life, in all lives, to me and to all men, has been woman, is woman." *The Star
Rover* brings together two of the author's lifelong, seemingly opposite, passions: radical
protest and what might be called radical acceptance. The novel celebrates defiance *and*
acquiescence. Though it doesn't reconcile these two opposing obsessions, it explores
them both.

Darrell Standing, the narrator and the main character of *The Star Rover,* tells his own
story as well as the life stories of the other people whose identities he assumes as he
awaits execution, a convicted murderer on death row. Though he's behind bars, often in a
straitjacket and in solitary confinement, too, he's a kind of space traveler with supernatural powers to become anyone he wants to become: a French aristocrat, an American pioneer, a Roman soldier at the time of the crucifixion of Christ, and a sailor marooned on an
isolated island. When he's not a Buddhist, or a follower of Christ, or Confucius, he's an
angry young man. He denounces the injustices he perceives at Folsom and San Quentin,
and he rails against his own incarceration.

To tell the prison story, which takes place in the present, London drew heavily on the
life of Edward Morrell, an ex-convict from San Quentin whom he met in 1913 and inter-
viewed extensively to obtain accurate details about incarceration. Darrell Standing—a
Berkeley professor who has murdered a colleague—is also a quietist, and he recognizes
that he need not be released from prison to explore the limitless possibilities of human
freedom. In fact, he's at liberty, in his own prison cell, to imagine anything and everything

and, in a way, protest has proved to be irrelevant and unnecessary for him. Indeed, if he can escape in his thoughts, then breaking out of Folsom seems pointless. Protesting seems irrelevant, too.

In *The Star Rover,* London adopts the kind of spiritualism he first heard from his mother, including the idea that human beings can travel outside their bodies and through time and space. Astral projection propels the plot forward, and Darrell Standing wills himself into the past, forcing his mind to obey his own thoughts. He's also the last of a long line of London's doomed, cerebral individualists, and, at times, he's a mirror image of his creator. Like London, Standing believes in the eternal flux of existence. Like London, he has more than one "me," as he proudly points out, and, like London, he explores the enigma of "the self." Standing makes good on the claim that London made in 1897, in a letter to Cloudesley Johns, that he had a dozen different astral selves.

As a writer, London had, of course, engaged in astral projection of a sort; he transported himself into the lives of his characters: Buck, White Fang, Martin Eden, Burning Daylight, Humphrey Van Weyden, and Wolf Larsen. He became a dog, a wolf, a wolf-man, a poet, a millionaire, and many other characters. Moreover, his best work often included a spiritual thread or a magical element, as in *The Call of the Wild,* where Buck enters an ethereal realm and becomes Ghost Dog, or in *Martin Eden,* where Martin, too, leaves the tangible world behind, entering a strange after-world on the frontier of another kind of consciousness.

From the start, London had also written works of fantasy and the supernatural in the mode of Edgar Allan Poe and Jules Verne—works about mad scientists, ghosts, and the reincarnation of souls, though he usually insisted he did not believe in the art of astrology, as practiced by his mother and father. Astral projection, occult divination, mind reading, and communication with the dead were so much nonsense, he claimed. In *The Star Rover,* however, he explicitly adopted his mother Flora's point of view as his own. Just before his death, occult divination seemed, at last, like a good idea, and, in the autographed copy of the book he gave his mother, he acknowledged her influence after a lifetime of pushing it aside.

The Star Rover provided London with the opportunity to look back at his own life, and at his philosophy of life, too, one last time. In his cell, Darrell Standing wonders whether, after his execution, he might wake up and find himself alive, and in another body, another life form. "I wonder. I wonder. . . . ," he murmurs, and there the novel ends, with the ellipsis, as though London means to suggest not only Standing's but also his own unfinished and incomplete thoughts. "I am eager to be gone, curious for the new places I shall see," Standing writes. London himself seems, in the tone and in the mood of the novel, no less eager to be gone, curious to find new, unexplored territories on the edge, and beyond, and it is there, on the brink of that unknown world, that the novel comes to an end. So, the novel is oddly optimistic, suggesting, as it does, reincarnation and rebirth and the constant flux of life. The man who began as a social and political revolutionary ended by believing in spiritual revolution. •

My time grows very short. All the manuscript I have written is safely smuggled out of the prison. There is a man I can trust who will see that it is published. No longer am I in Murderers' Row. I am writing these lines in the death cell, and the death watch is set on me. Night and day is this deathwatch on me, and its paradoxical function is to see that I do not die. I must be kept alive for the hanging, or else will the public be cheated, the law blackened, and a mark of demerit placed against the time-serving warden who runs this prison and one of whose duties is to see that his condemned ones are duly and properly hanged. Often I marvel at the strange way some men make their livings.

This shall be my last writing. Tomorrow morning the hour is set. The Governor has declined to pardon or reprieve, despite the fact that the Anti-Capital Punishment League has raised quite a stir in California. The reporters are gathered like so many buzzards. I have seen them all. They are queer young fellows, most of them, and most queer is it that they will thus earn bread and butter, cocktails and tobacco, room rent, and, if they are married, shoes and schoolbooks for their children, by witnessing the execution of Professor Darrell Standing, and by describing for the public how Professor Darrell Standing died at the end of a rope. Ah, well, they will be sicker than I at the end of the affair.

As I sit here and muse on it all, the footfalls of the deathwatch going up and down outside my cage, the man's suspicious eyes ever peering in on me, almost I weary of eternal recurrence. I have lived so many lives. I weary of the endless struggle and pain and catastrophe that come to those who sit in the high places, tread the shining ways, and wander among the stars.

Almost I hope, when next I reinhabit form, that it shall be that of a peaceful farmer. There is my dream-farm. I should like to engage just for one whole life in that. Oh, my dream-farm! My alfalfa meadows, my efficient Jersey cattle, my upland pastures, my brush-covered slopes melting into tilled fields, while ever higher up the slopes my Angora goats eat away brush to tillage!

There is a basin there, a natural basin high up the slopes, with a generous watershed on three sides. I should like to throw a dam across the fourth side, which is surprisingly narrow. At a paltry price of labor I could impound twenty million gallons of water. For, see: one great drawback to farming in California is our long dry summer. This prevents the growing of cover crops, and the sensitive soil, naked, a mere surface dust-mulch, has its humus burned out of it by the sun. Now with that dam I could grow three crops a year, observing due rotation, and be able to turn under a wealth of green manure. . . .

I have just endured a visit from the warden. I say "endured" advisedly. He is quite different from the Warden of San Quentin. He was very nervous, and perforce I had to entertain him. This is his first hanging. He told me so. And I, with a clumsy attempt at wit, did not reassure him when I explained that it was also my first hanging. He was unable to laugh. He has a girl in high school, and his boy is a freshman at Stanford. He has no income outside his salary, his wife is an invalid, and he is worried in that he has been rejected by the life insurance doctors as an undesirable risk. Really, the man told me almost all his troubles. Had I not diplomatically terminated the interview he would still be here telling me the remainder of them.

My last two years in San Quentin were very gloomy and depressing. Ed Morrell, by one of the wildest freaks of chance, was taken out of solitary and made head trusty of the whole prison. This was Al Hutchins' old job, and it carried a graft of three thousand dollars a year. To my misfortune, Jake Oppenheimer, who had rotted in solitary for so many years, turned sour on the world, on everything. For eight months he refused to talk even to me.

In prison, news will travel. Give it time and it will reach dungeon and solitary cell. It reached me, at last, that Cecil Winwood, the poet-forger, the snitcher, the coward, and the stool, was returned for a fresh forgery. It will be remembered that it was this Cecil Winwood who concocted the fairy story that I had changed the plant of the nonexistent dynamite and who was responsible for the five years I had then spent in solitary.

I decided to kill Cecil Winwood. You see, Morrell was gone, and Oppenheimer, until the outbreak that finished him, had remained in silence. Solitary had grown monotonous for me. I had to do something. So I remembered back to the time when I was Adam Strang and patiently nursed revenge for forty years. What he had done I could do if once I locked my hands on Cecil Winwood's throat.

It cannot be expected of me to divulge how I came into possession of the four needles. They were small cambric needles. Emaciated as my body was, I had to saw four bars, each in two places, in order to make an aperture through which I could squirm. I did it. I used up one needle to each bar. This meant two cuts to a bar, and it took a month to a cut. Thus I should have been eight months in cutting my way out.

Unfortunately, I broke my last needle on the last bar, and I had to wait three months before I could get another needle. But I got it, and I got out.

I regret greatly I did not get Cecil Winwood. I had calculated well on everything save one thing. The certain chance to find Winwood would be in the dining room at dinner hour. So I waited until Pie-Face Jones, the sleepy guard, should be on shift at the noon hour. At that time I was the only inmate of solitary, so that Pie-Face Jones was quickly snoring. I removed my bars, squeezed out, stole past him along the ward, opened the door and was free . . . to a portion of the inside of the prison.

And here was the one thing I had not calculated on — myself. I had been five years in solitary. I was hideously weak. I weighed eighty-seven pounds. I was half-blind. And I was immediately stricken with agoraphobia. I was affrighted by spaciousness. Five years in narrow walls had unfitted me for the enormous declivity of the stairway, for the vastitude of the prison yard.

The descent of that stairway I consider the most heroic exploit I ever accomplished. The yard was deserted. The blinding sun blazed down on it. Thrice I essayed to cross it. But my senses reeled and I shrank back to the wall for protection. Again, summoning all my courage, I attempted it. But my poor blear eyes, like a bat's, startled me at my shadow on the flagstones. I attempted to avoid my own shadow, tripped, fell over it, and like a drowning man struggling for shore crawled back on hands and knees to the wall.

I leaned against the wall and cried. It was the first time in many years that I had cried. I remember noting, even in my extremity, the warmth of the tears on my cheeks and the salt taste when they reached my lips. Then I had a chill, and for a time shook as with an ague. Abandoning the openness of the yard as too impossible a feat for one in my condition, still shaking with the chill, crouching close to the protecting wall, my hands touching it, I started to skirt the yard.

Then it was, somewhere along, that the guard Thurston espied me. I saw him, distorted by my bleared eyes, a huge, well-fed monster, rushing upon me with incredible speed out of the remote distance. Possibly, at that moment, he was twenty feet away. He weighed one hundred and seventy pounds. The struggle between us can be easily imagined, but somewhere in that brief struggle it was claimed that I struck him on the nose with my fist to such purpose as to make that organ bleed.

At any rate, being a lifer, and the penalty in California for battery by a lifer being death, I was so found guilty by a jury which could not ignore the asseverations of the guard Thurston and the rest of the prison hangdogs that testified, and I was so sentenced by a judge who could not ignore the law as spread plainly on the statute book.

I was well pummeled by Thurston, and all the way back up that prodigious stair-way I was roundly kicked, punched, and cuffed by the horde of trusties and guards who got in one another's way in their zeal to assist him. Heavens, if his nose did bleed the probability is that some of his own kind were guilty of causing it in the confusion of the scuffle. I shouldn't care if I were responsible for it myself, save that it is so piti-ful a thing for which to hang a man . . .

I have just had a talk with the man on shift of my death watch. A little less than a year ago, Jake Oppenheimer occupied this same death cell on the road to the gallows which I will tread tomorrow. This man was one of the death watch on Jake. He is an old soldier. He chews tobacco constantly, and untidily, for his gray beard and mus-tache are stained yellow. He is a widower, with fourteen living children, all married, and is the grandfather of thirty-one living grandchildren, and the great-grandfather of four younglings, all girls. It was like pulling teeth to extract such information. He is a queer old codger, of a low order of intelligence. That is why, I fancy, he has lived so long and fathered so numerous a progeny. His mind must have crystallized thirty years ago. His ideas are none of them later than that vintage. He rarely says more than yes and no to me. It is not because he is surly. He has no ideas to utter. I don't know, when I live again, but what one incarnation such as his would be a nice vegetative exis-tence in which to rest up ere I go star-roving again. . . .

But to go back. I must take a line in which to tell, after I was hustled and bustled, kicked and punched, up that terrible stairway by Thurston and the rest of the prison dogs, of the infinite relief of my narrow cell when I found myself back in solitary. It was all so safe, so secure. I felt like a lost child returned home again. I loved those very walls that I had so hated for five years. All that kept the vastness of space, like a monster, from pouncing upon me were those good stout walls of mine, close to hand on every side. Agoraphobia is a terrible affliction. I have had little opportunity to experience it, but from that little I can only conclude that hanging is a far easier matter. . . .

I have just had a hearty laugh. The prison doctor, a likable chap, has just been in to have a yarn with me, incidentally to proffer me his good offices in the matter of dope. Of course I declined his proposition to "shoot me" so full of morphine through the night that tomorrow I would not know, when I marched to the gallows, whether I was "coming or going."

But the laugh. It was just like Jake Oppenheimer. I can see the lean keenness of the man as he strung the reporters with his deliberate bull which they thought involun-tary. It seems, his last morning, breakfast finished, encased in the shirt without a collar, that the reporters, assembled for his last word in his cell, asked him for his views on capital punishment.

— Who says we have more than the slightest veneer of civilization coated over our raw savagery when a group of living men can ask such a question of a man about to die and whom they are to see die?

But Jake was ever game. "Gentlemen," he said, "I hope to live to see the day when capital punishment is abolished." I have lived many lives through the long ages. Man, the individual, has made no moral progress in the past ten thousand years. I affirm this absolutely. The difference between an unbroken colt and the patient draft horse is purely a difference of training. Training is the only moral difference between the man of today and the man of ten thousand years ago. Under his thin skin of morality which he has had polished onto him, he is the same savage that he was ten thousand years ago. Morality is a social fund, and accretion through the painful ages. The new-born child will become a savage unless it is trained, polished, by the abstract morality that has been so long accumulating.

"Thou shalt not kill" — piffle! They are going to kill me tomorrow morning. "Thou shalt not kill" — piffle! In the shipyards of all civilized countries they are laying today the keels of dreadnaughts and of superdreadnaughts. Dear friends I who am about to die, salute you with — "Piffle!"

I ask you, what finer morality is preached today than was preached by Christ, by Buddha, by Socrates and Plato, by Confucius and whoever was the author of the "Mahabharata"? Good Lord, fifty thousand years ago, in our totem families, our women were cleaner, our family and group relations more rigidly right.

I must say that the morality we practiced in those old days was a finer morality than is practiced today. Don't dismiss this thought hastily. Think of our child labor, of our police graft and our political corruption, of our food adulteration and of our slavery of the daughters of the poor. When I was a Son of the Mountain and a Son of the Bull, prostitution had no meaning. We were clean, I tell you. We did not dream of such depths of depravity. Yea, so are all the lesser animals of today clean. It required man, with his imagination, aided by his mastery of matter, to invent the deadly sins. The lesser animals, the other animals, are incapable of sin.

I read hastily back through the many lives of many times and many places. I have never known cruelty more terrible, nor so terrible as the cruelty of our prison system of today. I have told you what I have endured in the jacket and in solitary in the first decade of this twentieth century after Christ. In the old days we punished drastically and killed quickly. We did it because we so desired, because of whim, if you so please.

But we were not hypocrites. We did not call upon press and pulpit and university to sanction us in our willfulness of savagery. What we wanted to do we went and did, on our legs upstanding, and we faced all reproof and censure on our legs upstanding, and did not hide behind the skirts of classical economists and bourgeois philosophers, nor behind the skirts of subsidized preachers, professors, and editors.

Why, goodness me, a hundred years ago, fifty years ago, five years ago, in these United States, assault and battery was not a civil capital crime. But this year, the year of Our Lord 1913, in the State of California, they hanged Jake Oppenheimer for such an offense, and tomorrow, for the civil capital crime of punching a man on the nose they are going to take me out and hang me. Query: Doesn't it require a long time for the ape and the tiger to die when such statutes are spread on the statute book of California in the nineteen-hundred-and-thirteenth year after Christ? Lord, Lord, they only crucified Christ. They have done far worse to Jake Oppenheimer and me. . . .

As Ed Morrell once rapped to me with his knuckles: "The worst possible use you can put a man to is to hang him." No, I have little respect for capital punishment. Not only is it a dirty game, degrading to the hangdogs who personally perpetrate it for a wage, but it is degrading to the commonwealth that tolerates it, votes for it, and pays the taxes for its maintenance. Capital punishment is so silly, so stupid, so horribly unscientific. "To be hanged by the neck until dead" is society's quaint phraseology. . . .

Morning is come—my last morning. I slept like a babe throughout the night. I slept so peacefully that once the death watch got a fright. He thought I had suffocated myself in my blankets. The poor man's alarm was pitiful. His bread and butter was at stake. Had it truly been so, it would have meant a black mark against him, perhaps discharge—and the outlook for an unemployed man is bitter just at present. They tell me that Europe began liquidating two years ago, and that now the United States has begun. That means either a business crisis or a quiet panic and that the armies of the unemployed will be large next winter, the bread-lines long. . . .

I have had my breakfast. It seemed a silly thing to do, but I ate it heartily. The warden came with a quart of whiskey. I presented it to Murderers' Row with my compliments. The warden, poor man, is afraid, if I be not drunk, that I shall make a mess of the function and cast reflection on his management. . . .

They have put on me the shirt without a collar. . . .

It seems I am a very important man this day. Quite a lot of people are suddenly interested in me. . . .

The doctor has just gone. He has taken my pulse. I asked him to. It is normal. . . .

I write these random thoughts and, a sheet at a time, they start on their secret way out beyond the walls. . . .

I am the calmest man in the prison. I am like a child about to start on a journey. I am eager to be gone, curious for the new places I shall see. This fear of the lesser death is ridiculous to one who has gone into the dark so often and lived again. . . .

The warden with a quart of champagne. I have dispatched it down Murderers' Row. Queer, isn't it, that I am so considered this last day. It must be that these men who are to kill me are themselves afraid of death. To quote Jake Oppenheimer: I, who am about to die, must seem to them something "God-awful." . . .

Ed Morrell has just sent word in to me. They tell me he has paced up and down all night outside the prison wall. Being an ex-convict, they have red-taped him out of seeing me to say goodbye. Savages? I don't know. Possibly just children. I'll wager most of them will be afraid to be alone in the dark tonight after stretching my neck.

But Ed Morrell's message: "My hand is in yours, old pal. I know you'll swing off game." . . .

The reporters have just left. I'll see them next, and last time, from the scaffold, ere the hangman hides my face in the black cap. They will be looking curiously sick. Queer young fellows. Some show that they have been drinking. Two or three look sick with foreknowledge of what they have to witness. It seems easier to be hanged than to look on. . . .

My last lines. It seems I am delaying the procession. My cell is quite crowded with officials and dignitaries. They are all nervous. They want it over. Without a doubt, some of them have dinner engagements. I am really offending them by writing these few words. The priest has again preferred his request to be with me to the end. The poor man—why should I deny him that solace? I have consented, and he now appears quite cheerful. Such small things make some men happy! I could stop and laugh for a hearty five minutes, if they were not in such a hurry.

Here I close. I can only repeat myself. There is no death. Life is spirit, and spirit cannot die. Only the flesh dies and passes, ever a-crawl with the chemic ferment that informs it, ever plastic, ever crystallizing, only to melt into the flux and to crystallize into fresh and diverse forms that are ephemeral and that melt back into the flux. Spirit alone endures and continues to build upon itself through successive and endless incarnations as it works upward toward the light. What shall I be when I live again? I wonder. I wonder. . . .

Letter of Resignation from the Socialist Party

First published, in an edited version, as a broadside in 1916 under the title "The Resignation of Jack London"; reprinted from the *Overland Monthly,* May 1917.

London never wrote the socialist autobiography he wanted and planned to write, and he never explained, as he had promised, why he ceased to be an active socialist. He did, however, write a short letter of resignation from the Socialist Party, on March 7, 1916—eight months before his death—in which he criticized the party for swinging to the right and becoming too conservative.

In his March 7, 1916, letter, London writes that he wanted a party emphasizing the "class struggle"—a party with "fire and fight." In fact, as he knew, the Socialist Party, as well as the socialist movement at large, had lost much of its revolutionary fervor. As early as 1911, Eugene Victor Debs had warned that the cause might well be "permeated and corrupted with the spirit of bourgeois reform," and, with the outbreak of World War I, his prediction seemed to come true. Socialists who had sworn never to go to war against their comrades in other countries suddenly became patriotic and nationalistic, as German workers and French workers slaughtered one another on battlefields across Europe. Debs was shocked by this outcome.

London himself had proclaimed, in "Revolution" in 1905, "The French socialist workingmen and the German socialist workingmen forget Alsace and Lorraine, and, when war threatens, pass resolutions declaring that as workingmen and comrades they have no quarrel with each other." Less than a decade later, however, the cry of "international solidarity" had fallen largely by the wayside, and London, like many British and American socialists, became pro-war and virulently anti-German. "I believe intensely in the pro-ally side of the war," he wrote on August 28, 1916, three month before his death.

Anyone who had been paying attention to his work ought not to have been surprised by his resignation from the Socialist Party. Granted, on February 4, 1911, he wrote an open letter "to the Comrades of the Mexican Revolution" in which he noted that American socialists "are with you heart and soul in your efforts to overthrow slavery and autocracy in Mexico." Even here, though, his tone was at times light and mocking, especially when he called himself "a chicken thief and a revolutionist" and noted that other "chicken thieves, outlaws, and undesirable citizens" also supported the Mexican revolution. In keeping with his fiery personality, however, he did not go quietly into the folds of conservatism. On February 7, 1913, he insisted that he believed "in direct action and syndicalism"—suggesting that he'd aligned himself with the Industrial Workers of the World (IWW). He also observed sadly that the American socialist movement seemed "doomed to become the bulwark of conservatism." On April 18, 1913, he claimed that he was "too revolutionary" for the "socialist movement in the United States," and, in an interview with the *Western Comrade,* he boasted, "I still believe the Socialists should strive to eliminate the capitalist class and wipe away the private ownership of mines, mills, factories, railroads and other social needs."

In the same interview, however, he lashed out at what he called "the ghetto socialists of the East." Of course, London could claim—as much as he liked—to be a genuine revolutionary on the far left of the political spectrum. But his radical activity had ceased, and his books had become increasingly apolitical and even critical of the cause. Not surprisingly, socialists expressed disappointment that he had abandoned them and that he now lived a bourgeois lifestyle and wrote romantic, bourgeois novels like *The Little Lady of the Big House*.

"We don't know Glen Ellen, and we do know Jack London," the Socialist Party observed in an article published in the *New York Call* on March 27, 1916. "The name of the place does sound rather too idyllic to harmonize with the author of *The Sea Wolf* and *The Call of the Wild*." Even in his apostate phase, his former comrades recognized him as one of their own, and in his letter of resignation he still called them "Dear Comrades" and signed off, "Yours for the Revolution." Moreover, at the very end, he continued to think of "superior" and "inferior" classes and races, unable to transcend the basic concepts that fettered his thinking. •

Honolulu
March 7, 1916

Dear Comrades:

I am resigning from the Socialist Party, because of its lack of fire and fight, and its loss of emphasis on the class struggle.

I was originally a member of the old, revolutionary, up-on-its-hind-legs, fighting, Socialist Labor Party. Since then, and to the present time, I have been a fighting ember of the Socialist Party. My fighting record in the Cause is not, even at this late date, already entirely forgotten. Trained in the class struggle, as taught and practiced by the Socialist Labor Party, my own highest judgment concurring, I believed that the working class, by fighting, by never fusing, by never making terms with the enemy, could emancipate itself. Since the whole trend of Socialism in the United States during recent years has been one of peaceableness and compromise, I find that my mind refuses sanction of my remaining a party member. Hence my resignation.

Please include my comrade wife, Charmian K. London's, resignation with mine.

My final word is that liberty, freedom, and independence, are royal things that cannot be permitted to, nor thrust upon, races or classes. If races and classes cannot rise up and by their own strength of brain and brawn wrest from the world, liberty, freedom, and independence, they never in time can come to these royal possessions . . . and if such royal things are kindly presented to them by superior individuals, on silver platters, they will know not what to do with them, and fail to make use of them, and will be what they have always been in the past . . . inferior races and inferior classes.

Yours for the Revolution,
Jack London

Of Man of the Future

First published in *Komsomol Pravda,* September 20, 1959, in Russian; reprinted from *Jack London and the Klondike,* by Franklin Walker (San Marino: The Huntington Library, reprint 1972, originally published 1966).

London always wanted to be a poet, and in the 1890s he wrote dozens of poems, many of them never published during his lifetime. Of course, he went on to write poetic prose, as readers of *The Call of the Wild* and many of his other major works know. In the short, powerful poem "Of Man of the Future," London looks into the future and sees both the possibility for galactic war and the majestic prospects for peaceful travel to distant planets. Even as his life came down to its last moments, his mind reverberated with war and revolution. Brief though it may be, "Of Man of the Future" shows London's cosmic consciousness, which crops up in many of his books and which made him far more than a writer of realistic fiction. A fabulist, a romantic, and a dreamer, he never hesitated to imagine the unimaginable, think the unthinkable, break new ground, and venture into distant spaces— even into outer space. •

Of man of the future! Who is able to describe him?
Perhaps he breaks our globe into fragments
In a time of warlike games.
Perhaps he hurls death through the firmament.
Man of the future! He is able to aim at the stars,
To harness the comets,
And to travel in space among the planets.

BIBLIOGRAPHY

During his lifetime, Jack London fought as fiercely to control the copyright on his work as he fought for everything else in his life, from success and socialism to a sense of selfhood. After his death, his books appeared in all sorts of editions, and in dozens of languages, with his literary estate exercising relatively little control. Now, nearly a century later, all of his published work is in the public domain, which no doubt would rankle him. Moreover, there is no definitive edition that encompasses all of his work, though during his lifetime he aimed to collect and publish as much of his writing as he could, including the essays and articles that appeared in newspapers and magazines. Had he lived to a ripe old age, he surely would have anthologized everything that he wrote—his poetry along with his short stories and novels—and copyrighted it. During his lifetime he collected his work on war and revolution in two volumes, *War of the Classes* (1905) and *Revolution and Other Essays* (1910). Some of the work he did after 1910 appeared in *The Human Drift,* which was published in 1917, the year after his death.

This bibliography does not list all of London's work, but rather the books and articles that I found most useful and that might appeal to readers who want to deepen their understanding and appreciation of London. The three-volume collection of London's letters provides a behind-the-scenes look at the author from 1896 to 1916. *No Mentor but Myself* contains London's writings about writing, the literary marketplace, and many of the authors of his day—from Gorky to Kipling, Frank Norris to Upton Sinclair. It shows that he had a coherent aesthetic and suggests that he was less than honest when he boasted to his publisher in 1900, "I have had no literary help or advice of any kind."

No definitive biography of London exists, but there are many books that provide insightful observations and comments about him, both by his contemporaries and by scholars and critics from the 1920s to the present day. A number of women have written with clarity and insight about London: his second wife, Charmian, his older daughter, Joan, and his editor, Ninetta Eames. Rose Wilder Lane psychoanalyzed him in her seven-part "Life and Jack London," published in 1917–1918, and Anna Strunsky composed a brilliant 1917 obituary for *The Masses.* Those women have been joined by a host of others: Georgia Loring Bamford, Joan Hedrick, Carolyn Johnston, Jeanne Campbell Reesman, Jacqueline Tavernier-Courbin, and Clarice Stasz. London was also the subject of commentary by Jorge Luis Borges, H. L. Mencken, Leon Trotsky, George Orwell, Anatole France, and Jack Kerouac—as well as other esteemed writers and thinkers. To appreciate the full spectrum of the many—and often contradictory—aspects of self that Jack London presented to the world, it is necessary to sample a wide range of observations about him. The work about London can often be as exciting to read as London's own work. For several Web sites that offer work by London, google "Dan Wichlan." Two publications—the *Jack London Newsletter,* edited by Hensley Woodbridge, and the *Jack London Journal,* edited by James Williams—provide a wealth of information about the author, his life and work. To uncover lost and forgotten work by London, I was helped greatly by Hensley C. Woodbridge, John London, and George Tweney, *Jack London: A Bibliography,* published by the Talisman Press in 1966.

Selected Works by Jack London

BOOKS

The People of the Abyss. New York: Macmillan, 1903.
War of the Classes. New York: Macmillan, 1905.
The Road. New York: Macmillan, 1907.
The Iron Heel. New York: Macmillan, 1908.
Martin Eden. New York: Macmillan, 1909.
Burning Daylight. New York: Macmillan, 1910.
Revolution and Other Essays. New York: Macmillan, 1910.
The Cruise of the Snark. New York: Macmillan, 1911.
When God Laughs and Other Stories. New York: Macmillan, 1911.
John Barleycorn: Alcoholic Memoirs. New York: Century, 1913.
The Valley of the Moon. New York: Macmillan, 1913.
The Night-Born. New York: Century, 1913.
The Mutiny of the Elsinore. New York: Macmillan, 1914.
The Scarlet Plague. New York: Macmillan, 1915.
The Star Rover. New York: Macmillan, 1915.
The Human Drift. New York: Macmillan, 1917.

ANTHOLOGIES OF LONDON'S WORK

London's Essays of Revolt. Edited by Leonard D. Abbott. New York: Vanguard Press, 1926.

Jack London: American Rebel—A Collection of His Social Writings with an Extensive Study of the Man and His Times. Edited by Philip S. Foner. New York: Citadel Press, 1947.

The Bodley Head Jack London. Edited, with an introduction, by Arthur Calder-Marshall. Vol. 2. London: The Bodley Head, 1964.

Jack London on the Road: The Tramp Diary and Other Hobo Writings. Edited by Richard Etulain. Logan: Utah State University, 1979.

No Mentor but Myself: A Collection of Articles, Essays, Reviews, and Letters by Jack London on Writing and Writers. Edited by Dale L. Walker. Port Washington: Kennikat, 1979.

Revolution: Stories and Essays. Edited, with an introduction, by Robert Barltrop. London: Journeyman, 1979.

Novels and Social Writings. Edited, with notes and chronology, by Donald Pizer. New York: Library of America, 1982.

Novels and Stories. Edited, with notes and chronology, by Donald Pizer. New York: Library of America, 1982.

The Letters of Jack London. Edited by Earle Labor, Robert C. Leitz III, and I. Milo Shepard. 3 vols. Stanford: Stanford University Press, 1988.

The Portable Jack London. Edited by Earle Labor. New York: Viking, 1994.

Northland Stories. Edited, with an introduction and notes, by Jonathan Auerbach. New York: Penguin, 1997.

Jack London's Golden State: Selected California Writings. Edited by Gerald Haslam. Berkeley: Heyday, 1999.

ESSAYS AND ARTICLES

"Washoe Indians Resolve to Be White Men." *San Francisco Examiner,* June 16, 1901.

"The March of Kelly's Army: The Story of an Extraordinary Migration." *Cosmopolitan,* Oct. 1907.

"Novelist Explains the Hop Riots." *San Francisco Bulletin,* Dec. 12, 1913.

Secondary Sources

BOOKS

Bamford, Georgia Loring. *The Mystery of Jack London.* Oakland: Piedmont Press, 1931.

Boylan, James. *Revolutionary Lives: Anna Strunsky and William English Walling.* Amherst: University of Massachusetts Press, 1998.

Bykov, Vil. *In the Steps of Jack London.* Translated by Julia Istomina and Charles Hoffmeister. Edited by Susan M. Nuernberg and Earle Labor. http://www.jacklondons.net/writings/Bykov/titlePageCredit.html.

Franklin, H. Bruce. *The Victim as Criminal and Artist: Literature from the American Prison.* New York: Oxford University Press, 1978.

Hedrick, Joan D. *Solitary Comrade: Jack London and His Work.* Chapel Hill: University of North Carolina Press, 1982.

Irvine, Alexander. *Jack London at Yale.* Westwood: Connecticut State Socialist Party, 1906.

Johns, Cloudesley. *Who the Hell "Is" Cloudesley Johns?* Unpublished manuscript, Huntington Library.

Johnston, Carolyn. *Jack London—An American Radical?* Westport: Greenwood, 1984.

Kingman, Russ. *A Pictorial Life of Jack London.* New York: Crown, 1979.

Labor, Earle, and Jeanne Campbell Reesman. *Jack London,* rev. ed. New York: Twayne, 1994.

London, Charmian. *The Book of Jack London.* 2 vols. New York: Century, 1921.

London, Joan. *Jack London and His Time.* New York: Doubleday, 1939.

Noel, Joseph. *Footloose in Arcadia: A Personal Record of Jack London, George Sterling, Ambrose Bierce.* New York: Carrick and Evans, 1940.

Sinclair, Andrew. *Jack: A Biography of Jack London.* New York: Harper and Row, 1977.

Starr, Kevin. *Californians and the American Dream.* New York: Oxford, 1973.

Stasz, Clarice. *American Dreamers: Charmian and Jack London.* New York: St. Martin's Press, 1988.

Stone, Irving. *Sailor on Horseback: The Biography of Jack London.* Cambridge: Houghton Mifflin, 1938.

Tavernier-Courbin, Jacqueline, ed. *Critical Essays on Jack London.* Boston: G. K. Hall, 1983.

Walker, Franklin. *Jack London and the Klondike.* San Marino: The Huntington Library, rpt. 1972, originally pub. 1966.

Watson, Charles N., Jr. *The Novels of Jack London: A Reappraisal.* Madison: University of Wisconsin, 1983.

ARTICLES

Atherton, Frank Irving. "Jack London in Boyhood Adventures." *Jack London Journal,* no. 4, 1997.

Bland, Henry Meade. "Jack London." *Overland Monthly,* May 1904.

"A Discarded Wife." *San Francisco Chronicle,* June 4, 1875.

Eames, Ninetta. "Jack London." *Overland Monthly,* May 1900.

Franklin, H. Bruce. Introduction to *The Iron Heel.* Westport: Lawrence Hill, 1981.

"Jack London the Socialist: A Character Study: Why the Author of *The Call of the Wild* Became a Convert and Propagandist." *New York Times,* Jan. 28, 1906.

James, George Wharton. "Jack London: Cub of the Slums, Hero of Adventure, Literary
    Master and Social Philosopher." *National Magazine.* Part 1, Dec. 1912; Part 2, Jan. 1913.
Lane, Rose Wilder. "Life and Jack London." Seven-part series. *Sunset,* Oct. 1917 – Apr. 1918.
London, Joan. "The London Divorce." *American Book Collector,* Nov. 1966.
———. "W. H. Chaney: A Reappraisal." *American Book Collector,* Nov. 1966.
Orwell, George. "Introduction to *Love of Life and Other Stories,* by Jack London." In *The
    Collected Essays, Journalism and Letters of George Orwell, 1945 – 1950.* Edited by Ian
    Angus and Sonia Orwell. New York: Penguin, 1980.
Sinclair, Andrew. "The Man Who Invented Himself." *American Heritage Magazine,* Aug.
    1977.
Sinclair, Upton. "About Jack London." *The Masses,* Nov. – Dec. 1917.
Strunsky, Anna. "The God of His Fathers — Jack London." *Impressions,* Oct. 1901.
Walling, Anna Strunsky. "Memoirs of Jack London." *The Masses,* July 1917.
Waters, Hal. "Anna Strunsky and Jack London." *American Book Collector,* Nov. 1966.

WEB SITES

The Jack London Online Collection. http://london.sonoma.edu.
Jack London State Historic Park. http://www.parks.sonoma.net/JLPark.html.
The World of Jack London. www.Jacklondons.net.

ACKNOWLEDGMENTS

I want to thank Doris Lessing and Tillie Olsen for encouraging me to work on Jack London, while so many other individuals thought that he and his work were a waste of my time. I have been fortunate to live in Jack London country: a short distance from his birthplace in San Francisco; an hour from Oakland, where he spent much of his youth and adulthood; and in the heart of Sonoma County, his country home in the last years of his life. I have benefited from conversations about London with I. Milo Shepard, a descendant of Jack's stepsister, Eliza Shepard, and with Lou Leal, the lead docent at the Jack London State Historic Park. E. Breck Parkman, with the California State Parks Department, generously made available the photo archive of London in the town of Sonoma. Joseph Lawrence at the Jack London Research Center, housed at the Benzinger Winery, fished out and copied material I thought was lost forever.

When I began to conduct research about London, Professor Earle Labor—who has devoted his life to London's work—offered advice and encouragement. "Welcome to the wolf pack," he said. For years, he answered all the questions I sent him in Louisiana by e-mail. I conducted research at the Huntington Library in San Remo, California, where the librarians gave assistance every step of the way. Sue Hodson found material I thought irretrievable and offered guidance in my search for little-known London manuscripts. The Huntington has kindly granted permission to publish London's essay "The Salt of the Earth" and his introduction to Alexander Berkman's memoir. Claude Zachary at the Doheny Memorial Library at the University of Southern California made available the London material there. Dayle Reilly and Deb Swan at the Jean and Charles Schulz Information Center at Sonoma State University aided this book from the beginning all the way through, and unearthed first editions in the Waring Jones Room. Richard Geiger, of the library at the *San Francisco Chronicle,* gave me the opportunity to roam through his files. As always Jack Ritchie has been ready and willing to track down articles and books.

London and his work have, of course, been studied for decades, and so my own work is indebted to scholars who proceeded me. Clarice Stasz, my colleague at Sonoma State University and the author of two books about London, read my earliest essays about London, pointed me in the right directions, and urged me to follow a road of caution and balance, not always as easy as it might seem. At Sonoma State University, I have discussed London over the years with several colleagues, including Robert Coleman-Senghor and Sarah Baker. I have learned a lot about London by talking to their students in California studies about his work and his life. Chip McAuley proved to be an astute reader and critic of the manuscript. Professor H. Bruce Franklin at Rutgers and Paul Buhle at Brown University recognized the importance of London's radicalism and provided useful suggestions. Professor Eric Foner also made insightful comments about the Socialist Party and the tradition of radical American literature. Victor Wallis published my essay "Jack London: Burning Man" in *Socialism and Democracy,* where I first set forth ideas about London's radicalism. At *The Nation,* Adam Shatz published my essay about London and Kerouac—"Kings of the Road." My conversations about London, especially on the subject of *Martin Eden,* with Paul Berman were also illuminating. At the University of California Press, my editor Naomi Schneider gave the initial go-ahead for this book and saw it though publication. Valerie Witt assisted with all sorts of details, in a painless way. Marilyn Schwartz was the able project editor and Sue Carter the vigilant, understanding copy editor. I also want to thank my uncle, H. Quitkin, for introducing me to *The Iron Heel,* the first London book I read.

J. R.

FOR CLASSROOM DISCUSSION

I have written this book, of course, in the hope that Jack London's work will be more widely read than it is today, and that more of his work will be read — not only *The Call of the Wild* and *The Sea-Wolf*. I imagine that this anthology will be used in American literature and American history courses and that it will also be used in courses in which the topics and themes include class, race, gender, art and autobiography, and politics and the novel, as well as war and revolution.

To facilitate discussion, debate, and dialogue about Jack London and his work, I have prepared these twenty-five questions. I think that they can help students, teachers, and readers of literature who want to understand and explore his life and times, and the extraordinary body of novels, memoirs, stories, essays, and travel books that he produced in just twenty years. For those who want to read more of London himself, and more about him, the bibliography provides the titles and authors of books I have found useful in preparing this volume.

I suggest that students read London's work first and then use these questions as a way to delve further, plummet deeper, and as a springboard for discussion in classroom and reading groups. I think that these questions also suggest topics for writing assignments.

Jack London: Questions for Discussion Groups and for Classrooms

1. If Jack London were alive today, what would his politics be? For what causes would he advocate?

2. London died in 1916, at the age of forty. If he had lived, say, another forty years, in what ways might he have evolved as a writer?

3. Why is it that Jack London's career as a radical and as a socialist has been largely ignored, buried, and neglected in the United States?

4. The literary critic Alfred Kazin once said that Jack London's greatest book was his own life. How accurate and insightful do you think that comment is?

5. Do you see Jack London as mainly a late-nineteenth-century writer, or an early twentieth-century writer? Or does he span both centuries and look both backward and forward?

6. In what literary tradition would you place Jack London? Does he belong with Herman Melville and Mark Twain, or Rudyard Kipling and Joseph Conrad?

7. Why do you think that London believed that he had to have a dozen or so different selves in order to express his personality?

8. How much do you think that London's birth, out-of-wedlock, explains his personality and his character?

9. Do London's views about nonwhites make you feel less positive about him as a writer and as a person?

10. Would you describe London as a "racist"? If so, why do you think he deserves that label? If not, why not?

11. If you could ask Jack London one question about himself, what would you ask?

12. Which books by London do you feel are his best books?

13. Though socialism and the Socialist Party were once powerful in the United States, they have largely lost their influence. Does London's socialism have a message for Americans today, in the twenty-first century?

14. London was a radical in almost everything he did and wrote. He called himself an "extremist." Was his extremism counterproductive, or was there something useful about his adoption of extreme positions?

15. In *The Iron Heel* (1908), London predicted the coming of a dictatorship to the United States. How prophetic do you think he was as a writer? What predictions did he make about the future that have come to pass?

16. London was praised, in 1929, in *The New Masses,* as the only "proletarian" writer in the United States. How do you view him as the author of books, stories, articles, and essays about workers and working-class life? Is he a class-conscious writer?

17. London tended to see women as either goddesses or whores. Anna Strunsky, one of his closest friends, wrote that he believed women were biologically inferior to men. Do you see evidence of this in his fiction?

18. London wrote about the Yukon, the South Pacific, England, and, indeed, about the whole world. He may have been the first really global American writer. Does that make him a father of contemporary writers?

19. London turned to spirituality near the end of his life. Do you think that means that he recognized that a spiritual revolution was more important than the kind of political and economic revolution that he espoused in his youth?

20. Do you think that Jack London committed suicide? What evidence would you offer in support of your position?

INDEX

DESIGNER: SANDY DROOKER
TEXT: 10.25/14 ADOBE GARAMOND
DISPLAY: AKZIDENZ GROTESK
COMPOSITOR: BOOKMATTERS, BERKELEY
INDEXER: RUTH ELWELL
PRINTER AND BINDER: MAPLE-VAIL BOOK MANUFACTURING GROUP